THAD SAVES THE GALAXY
An Epic Space Adventure

A novel by C. T. Fleck

chandra

Table of Contents

ACKNOWLEDGEMENTS

I'd like to thank my parents for always being supportive and allowing me to be true to myself. My brother, Nathon, for being one of my best friends for the entirety of my life. My grandparents for always seeing the best in me. My old dog for keeping me company as I write by taking naps in my lap. Rest in peace Thor the Thunder God. A big thanks to all my friends who helped me relax during the process. Finally, much appreciation to Chandra Press for believing in one weirdo's dream of becoming an author.

FOREWORD

Space is both endless and constantly expanding. It's a contradictory statement, but that's what existence is. Everyone on this planet is both unimportant and vital at the same time. Anyone can make a difference, even if you're not important and no one knows your name. My name is Thaddeus Kingsley. Fancy name, I know, but I'm far from it.

Now I have a question for you. Have you ever pondered if there is life outside of our own little world? Considering the sheer immensity of the universe and factoring in the Drake Equation, other life must exist. Yes, I am aware of the Rare Earth Theory, but it just doesn't make sense to me. Regarding the enormity of the universe, can anything really be rare? Getting off topic again. The bottom line is that, statistically, we are not alone. There is a possibility of thousands or even millions of races of intelligent life in our own little galaxy. Races that are so much more advanced than the talking apes on this planet, and unintelligent races as well (but this isn't about them).

I know we keep hearing things about aliens. Like people saying that they've gotten abducted only to have bizarre things shoved up their sphincters. Which is an odd thing for an alien to do, if you think about it. In addition, there are those oh so lovely tabloid magazines. They inevitably have titles like, "Alien Found in Woods," or "Man

Sleeps with Alien," or even, "Alien Woman Gives Birth to Alien Human Hybrid Baby in Underground Base in Toledo." Well, you can never trust those things. Trust me, I know. There's nothing in Toledo. Toledo is completely void of anything even remotely interesting.

This story isn't about tabloids, Toledo, or non-consensual sphincter exploration, though. The story does have exploding heads, dirty words, weed, and descriptions of extraterrestrial genitals, so there is that to look forward to.

Now, I don't know about you, but I always looked towards the sky wondering if a faraway race was looking at the star we call Sol (our sun) and considering what could be around that dot in the night sky. It is possible some race already knows that humans exist but just never really gave a damn about us because of how primitive we appear.

Seriously, we are just apes that use our manmade construct of diversity to fuel our own narcissism. Racism, homophobia, sexism, nationalism; it's all just fodder to raise our own opinions of ourselves. I'm this race. They are that race. I must be better. I'm this sexual orientation. They are that one. I must be better. I have this between my legs. They have something different down there. I must be better. I'm from here. They're from there. I must be better. People just love feeling so damn superior. That's why ancient man used to believe we were the center of the universe and why some people feel like they are the center of the universe today.

If I was part of an alien race, intelligent enough to develop faster than light speed travel, I would stay the hell away from us too. Honestly, I already want to stay away from us but, unfortunately, I'm stuck on this rock (or at least I thought I was). I came across aliens, anal probe free (I feel a little insulted by that). Some of them seemed reasonably friendly. Others, however, were just a bunch of pricks. This is how it all went down.

CHAPTER 1

The sun peeks through the blinds of my bedroom windows. I get out of bed and check the clock. Why the hell did I wake up at seven in the morning on a Saturday? Why does morning have to exist? Oh well, bitching does nothing productive. I get up and head to the bathroom. Time to get ready for the day. I shower in my ordinary shower. I dress in my ordinary clothes. I brush my ordinary teeth.

At least I don't have to go to work today. My job is one of the most loathed occupations in existence. Probably should have tried harder in school so I wouldn't be stuck in a shitty fast food job. I can't tell you the place I work for, you know, lawsuit reasons. I will say this, though: I'm not lovin' it.

It probably would have also helped if I was smarter. Now don't get me wrong, I'm not a complete idiot. I'm not a flat-earther. I'm not one of those people that blame everything on video games. I'm not one of those people who blame Obama for the 9/11 terror attacks. With all those factors accounted for, I could be a lot higher on the intelligence scale. But, basically, I am just stupendously average.

Another day in paradise, I guess. Leaving my apartment for my first smoke of the day, I look at the early morning rays blasting down on the hard, concrete sidewalks of my town. I know that I should quit smoking. I know it's unhealthy. I know that it's expensive, but I just can't bring myself to do it. The nicotine makes me happy and disappointed at the same time. Which is probably how my parents feel about me.

The people around me are hurrying off to their jobs or their duties as my useless ass is just sitting around getting fat and taking up precious space. Seems to be my greatest talent, taking up space. A close number two is probably the getting fat thing.

The smoke fills my lungs as my eyes scour the hick town that is my home. This is my life. The smoke pours out of my nose as I exhale. Looking up at the bright sunshine sort of makes me feel out of place. The rays seem happy as does all sunshine for some reason. Yet, I feel drab. It's almost as if the entire world is a little happy that I'm miserable. Stupid bastard world.

At least I have my own world. My world always seems to look so much better masked by a thick layer of carcinogenic smoke. The smoke obscures a little of the sunshine. Almost as if my body is in a haze. My sense of peace comes back to me as I welcome the foreign cancerous substance into my body. If bodies are temples than mine is one of those that love burning incense. But, instead of incense it's cigarettes.

It's a shame, though. As my thoughts drift off into nothingness, my cigarette burns down. With puff after puff, my personal time comes closer to an end. I hit it for the last time before the butt is reached by the burning tip. The remains get put out in my ash tray and I walk back into my solitary apartment shutting the door behind me and blocking out all that happy sunshine. Stupid sunshine. Stupid world. Stupid life.

Another ordinary day in my boring existence. When is something exciting going to happen around here? It's always the same thing. I really need change. There has got to be more to the world than this. Drugs are fun, but even that gets boring after a while. In the past, I have made efforts to change things up. Some of them were realistic goals. Others were a stretch. Part of me just wants to accomplish something that would make me as good of a person as my mom thinks I am. I wish that life would just change.

The dull routine of life gets everyone down now and again, me included. Oh well, that's life, I guess. Long, boring, and essentially meaningless when you get down to the truth. Sounding like a nihilist right now.

The day is spent drinking my booze and smoking my cigs. There are also large amounts of reefer going into my lungs. Everyone has their vices, though. In my case, it's multiple vices. Hooray for vices.

Night has fallen faster than I can focus on it. That's how it always goes. The days spent off work always go by in a flash. While, the days when one is at work drag on for eons.

Taking a glance out of my window, the sky takes my attention for a moment. Stars glimmer, and I realize it's time for another smoke. I leave my apartment and go into the cool night air. Fire from the lighter catches the tip of my cancer stick so that I may start welcoming the smoke into my body. I love my private time. It's so peaceful. It's so quiet.

"Help me! Somebody, help!" comes a woman's voice from seemingly nowhere.

Well, so much for my quiet time. I make my way over to where I heard the scream. Nothing could have prepared me for what I see: six rednecks chanting nonsense. The chanting is incomprehensible, or it may be because thick southern accents make what they're saying even harder to grasp. This is odd considering I live in rural New York. The accents do sound a little fake, though. Almost like these people are just wannabe rednecks.

Then my eyes see the source of the scream. A young woman cowering against a wall. The stereotypical ginger. She has the red hair, the freckles, and the pale skin. Now could be the time to make a soulless redhead joke, but that's just in poor taste. I wanted something different but not this. I should have been more specific with my wish. I guess that this is still an opportunity to do the right thing and make my mom proud.

"What the hell is going on here?" I question as I stand between the girl and the impromptu angry mob. "You kind folks want to explain why you are cornering a young woman?"

The biggest one, who I am assuming is the leader of the posse, steps forward. His large beer belly protruding from his flannel vest.

The shirt is about two sizes too small for him. It's like he wanted to show off the muscles that he doesn't have. Now, it is never right to body shame someone, but when someone is an asshole, you tend to feel less guilty about it. A tattoo of a burning confederate flag adorns the wide flabby canvas that is his arm. The words "The South Will Rise Again" were written above it. The meaning of the tattoo is lost on me, though. If he thinks the South will rise again, then why is he burning what is now viewed as the symbol for the confederacy? The large man speaks in a booming voice which is laced with his faux southern dialect.

"This here is an alien. I watched her change into a disguise myself," he slurred.

It's obvious this guy has had one too many whiskey shots today. Not to mention that he reeks of a brewery mixed with a slight hint of chewing tobacco. It's very aromatic.

"Alien? Look, I know rednecks hate foreigners, but this is kind of extreme. Don't you think?" I reply confusedly as I stumbled into what is my version of a fighting stance. Did I mention that I don't know how to fight?

Shit might get ugly. I knew I should have taken karate classes or something. Then I could just go kung-fu on their asses. Who am I kidding? My laziness makes any attempt to improve myself completely futile.

"No, you god damn Liberal. Like an alien. You know, coming from outer space and whatnot." Captain Inbred drunkenly slurred. "And I ain't lettin no E.T. probe me. I ain't gay. I don't roll like that."

My mouth momentarily hangs agape. I just stare at the man in shock trying to comprehend the amount of stupidity that has just entered my ears. What the hell is wrong with this man? If I had to make a guess, I would say that inbreeding is somehow involved.

"Okay first off, there is nothing wrong with gay people. Homosexuality is a very natural thing. Second, why would an alien capable of traveling an immense amount of light years care what's in your ass? And third an alien, really?"

"Hey, you socialist," he said while getting in my face. There are few things in this world worse than alcohol breath. "I seen it. There I was, just minding my own business, telling this girl that she would look much prettier sitting on my face."

He seems so charming. The man continues his ramblings.

"She was not interested. I'm guessing cuz she is one of those queer sexuals."

Yes, because what woman wouldn't fall for this guy's wit? I think I may already be smitten. My zoned-out look does nothing to deter him, so he keeps talking.

"But as you know, women exist only to bang men. They never do their job, though. Hell, it has been years since I've been with a woman like God intended. They owe it to men sleep with us. That's why the bible says the gays is wrong."

My lord. Why would I care about that? Plus, I didn't think to judge that he was one of those weirdos that feel entitled to sex (although it makes sense now that I think about it). He probably blames things like feminism and common decency. It also might help if he took a shower. He just keeps going on with his story.

"Then, she turned into a giant bug. I gathered my friends and we started chasing her. Trust me, I seen it with my own two eyes."

He finishes off the last sentence by pointing at both of his eyeballs. Seems to be an irrelevant gesture considering everyone knows what eyes are.

"So, in your drunken haze, you think a woman is an alien, so your immediate reaction is 'let's kick her ass!'?" I ask, genuinely trying to follow this guy's logic.

"We is gonna show her what happens when you mess with Earth."

"How very Christian of you. Hey, that person is different, so let's murder her because Jesus would want us to." I reply while rolling my own eyes.

"Don't mock my faith, you socialistic snowflake!" He shouts at me.

"Yeah okay then. Hey, I have a question. How many shots did you have today?"

"What's that have to do with anything?"

"You're drunk. Go home and sleep it off, big guy." I reply as I look at the five other hillbillies here.

They all seem sober, enough, so I turn my attention to them.

"And you guys, what the hell are you doing? I know that the whole mob mentality thing is infectious, but you guys were ready to attack a young woman because a drunkard says she's an alien? What the hell were you thinking?"

This seems to have quelled their rage. Some look down in shame at what they could have done. So, I continue.

"Now, you guys go home, and will someone make sure the big guy here gets home safe? Don't want him drinking and driving."

I look back at the rotund man just in time to see a fist coming at my face. Now, I may have accomplished any number of things from the time that I noticed the fist until it reached my face. Counting to one is something that I could have started. Coming up with a reason why I'm more qualified to lead the country than President Landon is another. Reconsidering some of the life choices that I've made is yet another. I had no time to block or dodge the blow however, as I feel his hand collide with my left eye, the absolute force of it knocking me on my ass. A stinging feeling shoots across my face. That's going to hurt tomorrow. Hell, it hurts right now.

"Dammit Bubba," one of the spectators says. "You can't go around hitting people again. Remember what the judge said after the last time."

He then grabs him and holds him back from striking again. Of course, they call him Bubba. Can you get anymore hillbilly than that? Maybe if someone gave him a banjo and he was masturbating to the likeness of Robert E. Lee. Oh, please sweet, non-existent god, don't let anyone give him a banjo or a picture of Lee. Not sure which one of those would be worse.

The rednecks start to walk away, two of them needing to drag the leader out of there as he was yelling, "She's an alien! You all will see!"

Hmm, he may be an alright guy when sober, key word: may. I don't know him personally. As a drunk, however, that guy is a lunatic. I stand up and instantaneously grab at my eye. Shit, that hurts. And the butt pain from landing on the hard ground coursing through both of my cheeks doesn't help.

My attention turns back to the girl. I see she is still curled up in a little ball, cowering against the wall. As I get closer to her, my nostrils are filled with the delightful scent of cookie dough. She smells delicious.

I bend down and put a hand on her shoulder hoping to comfort her. This has the opposite effect. The action nearly makes her jump out of her skin and causes another fist to collide with my left eye. Why is it my left eye again? Why can't life just throw a little variety my way and have the next one come for my right eye? Change is good, dammit.

"Ow, god dammit!" I yell as I clutch my eye.

"Oh shit." I hear her exclaim. "I'm so sorry. It was a reflex. Are you okay?"

"Hey, it's fine. If it makes you feel any better, you have a much better right hook than the hillbilly."

She stops trembling and gazes up at me. I see her eyes for the first time, and I'm shocked to see that they are orange, and I mean entirely orange. It must be colored contacts. Who am I to judge? If this girl wants her eyes all orange, that's her business. I have no right to tell others what they can do with their bodies.

"Thank you," she replies quietly.

"Hey no problem. You know, if I wasn't feeling generous, I would have laid his ass out." I say trying to hide the fact that I'm a wussy with false bravado. "Are you okay?"

"Yes. I didn't know what happened. Suddenly, they just started chasing me. Shouting obscenities at me as well."

"Yeah well, welcome to New Haven, the town filled with assholes···and me. I'm not an asshole, though. I am delightful. I haven't seen you here before. You must be new."

"I don't know how to..." she started, but she is interrupted by a loud static sound.

Suddenly, her entire body seems fuzzy like it's just simply data. Before I know it, the sweet, pretty girl in front of me is replaced with a green creature. It has two large orange orbs as eyes. No nose or ears. Two antennae were atop her head where her hair used to be, giving her a bug-like appearance, except that her antennae curled behind her head and down to her lower back. Her boobs seem to have disappeared. Probably because her species doesn't breast feed their young. Not one hundred percent on that, but it seems like a safe assumption.

But just as quickly as it appeared, it was gone. Replaced again with the young girl. I see her eyes go large with fear and anticipation as she was waiting for my reaction. Finally, I muster up a response. The only one I could possibly think of for what I just witnessed.

"Well, that's something you don't see every day."

She looks at me confused like she was expecting some grander reaction. Some negative response to her glitch thingy. Really anything except an overstating of the obvious. Little does she know, one of my top talents is stating the obvious. Wait a minute, that means that I have three talents. Woo, I'm a triple threat.

"What?" she asks perplexedly.

"I wasn't lying. It's not every day you see a staticky alien. Well, I mean, you might see it every day, but I sure as hell don't. "

"Why aren't you freaking out like that other member of your race?"

"I knew aliens existed. I mean, come on, a vast number of galaxies and solar systems but this rock is the only one that is special enough to have life on it? That would just be stupid. Looking at it in either a religious or scientific way, it would just be stupid. I am a little shocked to see one here, though. Especially considering how many light years the nearest planet with the right conditions for life would be but, hey, it is what it is."

She just stares at me, confused. That brings up a question however that I need to voice.

"How do you speak the same language as me?"

"What?"

"Well, I highly doubt an alien race would speak fluent English. Hell, I don't even speak fluent English."

"This necklace," she says as she points to her choker, "allows me to understand and speak the language of any being I am talking to."

"How does that work?" I question.

"Well, you see the device picks up on waves emitted from the..."

And that is all I heard until she lost me with her science mumbo jumbo. I really should have paid more attention during science classes in school. I highly doubt, however, that knowing what fusion and fission are would help me understand what the hell this lady is saying. My zoned-out stare must have lasted longer than I originally anticipated because I hear her now elevated voice.

"Hey, are you okay? You were staring off into nothingness for my entire explanation?"

"Yes," I lie. "That just allows me to better absorb info."

I nailed that lie.

She looks at me skeptically as if considering my response and then finally just seems to shrug it off. I decide to take a crack at guessing the basic gist of what she probably said.

"Your necklace acts as a sci-fi trope that is pretty much just a cop out to help explain one of the biggest issues of dealing with different alien species that originated from a different evolutionary tree."

She appears to pretty much ignore my comment. She knows that I'm right. She can't deny it.

Then my ears pick up the staticky sound again and my eyes see the fuzz. I know her disguise is going to go on the fritz again. At least, we are the only ones out here. At times like this I really wish my brain would be better at remembering the tried and true Murphy's Law. What can go wrong will go wrong.

Due to said Murphy's Law, it is at this time that I notice a young couple walking towards us. My first thought being, 'oh shit, it may turn into another angry mob.' So, without thinking, I remove my sweatshirt and throw it over her, making sure the hood covers her head. As soon as the hoodie is settled, her disguise is gone. I must have reflexes like a god damn ninja. The couple passes without a second thought. My attention goes back to her and I notice her disguise is still gone.

"Why did you?" she asks not really finishing the question, but common sense and basic thought can fill in the blank.

"I don't want to cause anymore panic. Plus, you've done nothing wrong, that I know of, so you don't deserve what will happen if they find out you're an alien."

"What would happen?" she asks clearly terrified.

"I···honestly don't know but judging by Bubba's reaction, it probably wouldn't be too good. Some religious nut-jobs might even start claiming you're a demon or the Antichrist here to usher in the second coming of Satan or whatever the hell they think is going to happen. Maybe, the government will come to do a vivisection on you to try and figure out how all of your organs do the whole organ thing?"

Seeing her now horrified expression, I decide to try and steer the conversation on a different route.

"Now why hasn't your little disguise thingy kicked back on yet?"

"I don't know. It appears to have malfunctioned, and I don't feel comfortable being exposed like this. What if those large humans come back?" She replies while examining her ring.

"Hey, I have an idea that can't possibly come back on me. Why don't you just come to my apartment and hide out till you get your do-hickey fixed?"

"You would hide an alien in your home? But why?"

"This is the most exciting thing to happen in a long time. Not sure if you know this but this town is terrible and dull. Don't ask me to think about my actions. Now onward to adventure."

"I thought we were going to your home?"

"Just follow me." I say as I lead her to my shitty little dwelling. "By the way my name is Thaddeus, but people usually just call me Thad."

"You can call me Zinkatianalynn Delcheroseantia."

"Alright... I'm just gonna call you Zinka."

"Why would you do that?"

"It's a nickname."

"What is a nickname?"

"It's a name someone else gives you."

"Why would you give me a name when I already have one?"

"Cause it's... Well, it's just what humans do."

"Alright then Thad. I will give you a nickname as well."

"Well," I start, "technically Thad is a nickname."

"I will give you one of my own nicknames. You shall be known as Little Balls."

"Wait, what? Why?"

"Cause your eyeballs are half the size of mine."

"I don't think that would be the best nickname."

"It is too late, Little Balls. I have already dubbed you as such," she says with an almost mischievous smile on her face.

Part of me thinks she knows the joke there. How would she know the joke there? Does she know that balls are slang for male genitalia?

"Ugh fine." I surrender as we make our way to my tiny little apartment.

Now, usually I'm skeptical of people coming in to my place, but an alien can't possibly have any grasp on how humans live. She won't know that I'm severely lower class. I open and then close the door to my apartment after we both step inside. She removes the hood and takes a calculating look around. I see her taking in every detail of the diminutive space. She turns towards me to ask a question.

"Do all humans live in such a cramped environment? This place seems so small. You can't really get any work done."

Great, even an alien knows my place sucks. God damn my wallet for being empty.

"Well, people live in different size accommodations." I simply reply.

"Oh, I see. You are just lacking the monetary credits needed for a bigger place."

Stupid, smart alien woman knowing I'm broke. She continues.

"Judging by your living conditions on my planet, you would probably be a mindless service drone."

"Well here, I work in the fast-food industry, so I guess it's the same thing. Well except my employer is just another corporation that puts profits ahead of their human employees' wellbeing just so it can shove a disgusting burger down people's throats." But she probably doesn't care about any of this.

"Now let's begin our amazing adventure!"

"Why are you yelling?" She asks, holding her antennae to shield them.

"To build excitement for our adventure!"

"I will never understand humans. Now I require quiet so that I can concentrate on seeing what's wrong with my disguise ring."

"Okay. Then let's get ready for quiet!" I hoarsely whisper as I sit down and wait for her to finish fixing her thingy.

She simply rolls her eyes and removes her ring. She opens a side panel and starts examining the bit of alien tech. I have no idea what I'm looking at, but there are lots of blinking lights in there. It reminds me of what a drug induced rave party would look like if it had a sci-fi theme. If I ever attended one of those. Which I did not.

CHAPTER 2

Hours seem to pass with us making no progress. Impatience is wearing down my resolve. I need to do something, anything. My leg starts tapping with restlessness. What the hell is taking so long?

"Shit!" she yells.

I wasn't aware she was knowledgeable about English swear words. She continues.

"It's destroyed, and I need to return to my pod to repair it. Now what am I gonna do? I doubt I could make it to my ship without a human seeing me."

She puts her face in her hands and lets out a frustrated sigh. Seems to be having a rough time of it. That doesn't seem right. Adventures are supposed to be fun. A random thought pops into my head.

"Hey, I have a question." I comment.

"What is it?" She questions, still exasperated from the ordeal.

"Why are you here?"

"My race banished me from my own planet because...well because I'm a defect."

"A defect?"

"Yeah, my mind doesn't work properly, and they didn't want me tarnishing the great race of the Aldinians," she admits sadly.

"They banished you cause your mind doesn't work properly?"

"Yeah. What does your planet do to defects?"

"Well, we made the last one president of the United States," I smirk.

"You mean there is no banishment here?"

"Not to my knowledge. At least not for the sole reason of being odd. Hell, everyone on this planet is a weirdo."

"You are a strange race indeed."

"I know, right, but humans aren't robots. None of our brains work the same. Hell, your race's brains probably don't work the same either. Brains are very complex organs. Weird that everything we are is that soft mushy thing in our skull. Why did you pick this planet when you were banished, though? With the whole global warming thing, this planet is essentially dying. You came to a dying world."

"I crash landed on your moon. I kept trying to build a resistance against Derask's empire. He did not take too kindly to that and decided that banishment wasn't enough. So, he tried to execute me. I escaped, but he is following me. I may have inadvertently caused an interplanetary war simply by crashing here. Derask will see your planet as trying to stand in the way of his galactic conquest, for he will see you as harboring an escaped convict."

"Alright, so let me get this straight. You are an escaped convict, and an evil alien prick is following you and trying to destroy you. The bastard will also likely destroy the Earth."

"Yes, that is right," she confirms grimly.

"Do you know what that means?"

"No. What?"

"We are going on an adventure!!!" I yell as I stand up in excitement.

She holds her antennae in pain. I'm assuming that is how she hears. Makes sense that different planets and different species develop in different ways. She finally opens her mouth to address the situation.

"So now let me get this straight," she breaks it down. "You are gonna help an alien you have never met before not only escape her own execution but also save your own planet by taking down an evil space empire bent on galactic control?"

"Well when you put it like that, it just sounds silly and irrational. That is in fact the basic idea, though. Why?"

"Do you know how insane that sounds?" She's incredulous.

"Well, you know what they say. Insanity is just sanity with extra sanity."

"That really doesn't make any sense. We could die."

"That won't happen." I front like I'm braver than I actually am.

"If we are going to save the world, then we are gonna need to fix my disguise. It has a blocker on it to make it harder for Derask to track me. I keep all my tech repair supplies in my ship. Follow me." She says as she pulls up the hood. "I keep my ship in a cave out in the forest."

So, I get up and follow her out of my apartment. We make our way out to the forest as she makes a point to keep her face hidden. Don't want any stray passerby to notice the extraterrestrial lady. The streets seem entirely barren.

The night sky, yet again, draws my attention up towards it. I always love staring at the stars. It makes me forget my problems even if it's only for a moment.

I find myself looking up for too long, though. Not watching where I'm walking, my foot catches on an exposed tree root. The sudden jolt breaks my thoughts and my faces crashes to the ground.

Then I hear a laughing sound and as I look up, I see it's coming from Zinka. She is trying to be polite and hold it back, but she can't do it.

She continues to chuckle as she holds out her hand, and I take it to help myself up.

"That is not very funny," I say struggling to hold back the big smile on my face.

"You're an idiot."

"Yes, but I'm a delightful idiot."

We continue our epic journey as we make it to the path of the woods at the edge of town. Epic may be a bit of an over-dramatization. A better word might be slow. We continue our slow journey. That doesn't sound as exciting, though. Would arduous work here? I have no idea.

"We have to continue down this path for a little way," Zinka comments.

The path winds through the trees, sort of like a drunk pretending to be sober. I never realized how terrifying these woods were at night. It's like something out of a horror movie. Except for the fact that I have an alien companion. There is also the fact that I am on a mission to save an alien and my planet. Okay, so I guess this is nothing like a horror movie. It's more akin to a sci-fi flick. I need a smoke.

I reach in my pocket and pull out my cigarettes and light one. I take a long drag and notice Zinka is looking at me curiously. It reminds me of the tilted head thing that dogs do when they are confused.

"What is that thing you are putting in your mouth?"

"This? It's a cigarette."

"What is it for? I have seen several humans with those. Is it necessary for a human's life?"

"No, not really. It gives the brain a chemical called nicotine which just makes people feel happy."

"So, these cigarettes are a good thing?"

"No, not really." She looks confused, so I continue. "They cause a lot of health risks and are pretty much killing me slowly. Me smoking these is essentially one of the stupidest things that I've ever done. You may not know this, but that is saying a lot."

"Then why do you do it?"

"The world is such a chaotic tragedy – and, apparently, the universe is, too. It doesn't really make sense to want to live forever. Only a masochist or a sadomasochist would want that. I am neither of those things."

"That's a morbid outlook on things. Don't you think?"

"I prefer to call it a realist view on things. Not everything is all puppies and rainbows and free internet porn."

"You are an odd creature."

"What do you mean?"

"Well, you go from odd and silly to morbid and deep in a matter of seconds. It's like you can't focus on just one emotion at a time." She seems mildly confused.

"I told you, I'm one of a kind."

"I feel like there is more to it than that and I will find out what it is sooner or later. But we are here now," She motions to a cave.

She then crawls in. I simply shrug and follow. What fun is an adventure if you think about what you do? There is no down side that I could possibly think of that would lead me to think that this was a bad idea. After what seemed like forever, we get to what appears to be a giant metal sphere. Reasoning dictates that this ought to be her spaceship. It looks odd. So of course, I have to voice my thoughts on the odd spherical vehicle.

"It looks like a metal testicle."

She immediately stops in her tracks and gives me a blank, confused stare. I think she may be confused at what a testicle is. Human biology lesson time. Knowledge is power.

"Do you not know what a testicle is? Well, you see in the male anatomy they have these..."

"No!!! No, I know what a testicle is. I don't know everything that you beings say, or why you do some of the things you do, but I am fully aware of the genitals of your species. Your species mating habits and genitals are vastly different then our own. It is common Aldinian protocol to learn the nature of native beings."

It is evident that this conversation leaves her feeling discombobulated. Eyes avoiding direct contact. Skin gaining slightly darker pigmentation. All the signs of embarrassment. Curiosity gets the better of me.

"How does your species do it?"

"The genitalia are in the same location. The female's ovarian womb goes all the way up towards our lungs. The males have a long penis. It could extend up to three feet. When cut off it could regenerate. Plus, it is prehensile. They evolved that way for similar reasons as your native duck species have adapted. Essentially it was an evolutionary tug of war for rape and not wanting to be raped."

"What does prehensile mean? This is bullshit. I've been speaking English for so much longer. How do you know words that I don't?"

"Prehensile essentially means they can move it and grab things with it."

"They can grab shit with their dick? That is··· kind of cool. I wish I could grab things with my dick. Wait, why do you know about our genitals?"

"It is protocol to know about mating habits of local inhabitants of whatever planet we are on." She looks literally anywhere but at me as she speaks. "Sex is a primary function of most organic beings."

"So, you watched porn?"

"It is protocol like I said."

"That is exactly why I watch it too. Wink wink."

"Can we please just stop talking about... this subject?" She says motioning frantically with her hands. "I must get to work repairing my disguise before I get--"

"Did you enjoy the porn?"

"Aggghhhhh. Enough with the porn." She shuts me down, annoyed.

"Should I take that as a yes?"

"Enough, Little Balls." She threatens with a scowl that means business.

"Alright, alright. No more porn talk."

"Thank you," she murmurs, returning to her ring thing.

I look around her crude headquarters. There is nothing much in here except her ship and a few gadgets thrown about haphazardly. I take a glimpse inside and the thing is just big enough for one or maybe two people. It might be possible to squeeze three in there. It depends on their sizes.

"I have a question," I interrupt.

"Of course, you do," She sighs, looking up from her work. "What is it, Little Balls?"

"How does this thing fly? Like, I don't see any rockets or anything. I don't understand how it goes. Is it powered by magic and love? Is it the power of friendship?"

"What? No, you see its propulsion mechanism works by using the gravitational forces of nearby celestial···"

And again, my focus is gone. I really wish I was smarter. Then again, a smart man would probably not be in the situation I am now. That would be boring. So, I guess the moral is that it's better to be stupid and fun than smart and boring. That doesn't sound like a very good moral. A better one will come up eventually. At least, I hope one does. Then again why does everything need a moral? Can't some things just simply happen? Especially considering morality is entirely subjective. Though, society does tend to influence morals as it slowly progresses⋯

"HEY!! You were staring off again," she interrupts. "I really don't think that helps you understand information any better."

"Yes, it does. That's how it works. I'm not lying. You're lying," I blurt without taking a breath.

Though tooting my horn isn't my thing, I am somehow the greatest liar that has ever lied with lies. Suck it, Nixon. You saggy cheeked bastard.

She just looks at me weird until she gives a little chuckle.

"If you say so, Little Balls. If you say so."

She goes back to work fixing her ring. This adventure is progressing excessively slowly. I thought that by this point, I would have already saved the galaxy and been back home taking a nap. Maybe eating a sandwich. Possibly both at the same time. If only I had the technology to do that. Get on it, scientists. I demand something to feed me while I'm napping.

"There, it's finished." Her smile is triumphant.

She stands and slips the ring back on. She hits a button on the side, and in a flash, the ginger lady is standing in front of me again.

"Okay," her voice is hopeful. "I finally feel safe to walk around in public."

"So, what's the plan on taking down an evil space empire?" I ask, like the smug jerk I can be sometimes (yeah, I admit it).

"I... I have no idea." She says as she looks down dejectedly. "I honestly don't think we can do it. I believe the saying on your planet is 'we are up the crack without a paddle.'"

"Creek."

"What?"

"The saying is up the creek without a paddle." I correct gently, so she'll know for next time. "I have an idea, though."

"What's your idea?" She clearly isn't expecting much.

"Let's just wing it."

"Humans have wings?" She questions with a look of bewilderment on her face.

"No. It's a saying. It means we will just make it up as we go along."

"You don't think things through, do you? Do you have any idea how dangerous and stupid that is? No, we need a plan." Her face clouds over as she clearly begins to think of something.

I mumble a nearly inaudible "Piss off, that's a good plan," and walk to the other side of the cave to think.

"I heard that, Little Balls" she smirks.

I'm starting to think she knows the innuendo and is just messing with me. She comes up to me to speak.

"I need to get some sleep. I will see you tomorrow, Little Balls. That is if you're serious about helping me."

"Where are you going to sleep? This cave isn't exactly a five-star hotel." I reply, looking around the minuscule cavern.

"I'm going to sleep in my pod. It's a bit cramped, but I will be fine."

"You could always just come crash on my couch. It isn't much, but it's probably better than that little pod thingy."

"You would invite some strange alien to spend the night at your home? I may not know much of your culture, but from what I gathered, your people seem to be obsessed with thinking aliens want to explore your rectums. Who's to say that I may not try to probe you? Maybe I was lying when I said I wouldn't. Maybe the real end game here is me wanting to shove something up your anus."

"Hey, just promise you'll be gentle." I chuckle, and so does she. "Besides what fun is an adventure if you try and think through everything that you do? Just like my unhinged uncle always said: never let the possibility of anal probes deter you from a space adventure."

"Your uncle said those exact words?" Disbelief clearly furrows her brow.

"Close enough. He was a little off. It seems relevant in this instance. Now what would be the point of thinking this through?"

"Well, it would probably be safer and would definitely go a lot smoother."

"Exactly, it would be boring," I reinterpret.

"Okay. If you're sure, then I will stay. It would actually be nice to be able to stretch my legs out and sleep."

So, we exit the cave and make our way back to my shithole. The walk is entirely silent. It seems like she has something on her mind. I don't want to interrupt that. Maybe she is considering something of massive importance. It could be the looming fight and arduous journey that we are facing.

We make it to my place quickly. I open the door and let her inside. Before I cross the threshold myself, I take one last look at the night sky. I wanted different and I got it. My mind can't help but wonder what exciting events will take place tomorrow. The only thing that I know for sure is that regardless of what happens, my life will never be the same. With that last thought, I walk in my home and close the door. Effectively sealing out the world around me.

CHAPTER 3

Ugh, why is it so bright? Oh, the sun is rising. Guess I should open my eyes. I open them as I get up out of bed. The sun is invading my room through the window. I make a point to glare at the sunshine.

My drowsy state reminds me: I've got to go make a pot of coffee. Leaving the bedroom and stretching my tired body, a familiar scent fills my nose. It is at this point that the form of the green female sleeping on my couch and wearing my hoodie appears in my peripheral. It stops me in my tracks. Oh yeah, the alien adventure that's going on. My mind really needs to improve its short-term memory. Also needs to improve its long-term memory. It just needs to improve, in general.

Well, can't save the world without a pot of coffee. I head into the kitchen and start brewing a pot, and the aroma fills the apartment. My patience starts to wear thin as the waiting slowly becomes excruciating. Finally, the last drop falls from the top of the old coffee maker and lands in the glass carafe. I could have easily put my mug underneath it and could have already been drinking it, but for some unknown reason that annoys me. Everyone has their little pet peeve.

"What are you drinking?" I hear a tired voice coming from the doorway.

I look over and see Zinka walking lazily to the kitchen table. She takes a seat. Clearly still drowsy. No matter what species you are, waking up is terrible. This is a very important scientific discovery. Where is my Nobel Prize?

"This? It's coffee." I reply. "So, you know what my dick looks like, but you don't know what coffee is? I'm pretty sure that you just enjoyed the porn too much."

"Shut up, Little Balls. Now what does this coffee do?"

"It adds caffeine to the body and gives you a little pep," I clarify.

"May I try some?"

"Sure." I grab a mug and pour her a cup of it. "This may wake you up."

She takes the cup and stares at it almost calculatingly. She brings it up to her mouth and takes a big drink. Probably, a bigger drink than a person should have of a hot beverage. It hurts my mouth just to watch it.

"So how do you like it?" I ask tentatively, watching her reactions.

I see she hasn't swallowed. Her eyes go real big, and it appears she is going to explode. This is going to be a short experience if my alien friend explodes this early.

"Hey, are you o--" I'm suddenly interrupted as the hot liquid spews from her mouth all over me.

"Ah! Burning flesh!" I shout as I feel it burning my skin, quickly wiping off the offending liquid.

"That was absolutely horrid!" she looks clearly disgusted. "Why the hell do you drink that?"

"I guess it's an acquired taste." I continue to wipe the remainder of the hot drink off me.

"I apologize for spitting that abhorrent drink on you, but you kind of had it coming since you're the one who gave it to me. Why would you think it was okay to give me that crap? Why would you think it's okay to drink that?"

"It's alright. Sometimes life will just spit hot liquid on your dick." I reply as I take a seat at the table. "Since you didn't like my plan of winging it, did you think of a plan yet? If not, we could always just make it up as we go along. That could be fun."

"We are not winging it and yes, I do have one, but it won't be easy," Zinka's face is serious, and she's clearly given it a lot of consideration.

"Nothing in life is. So, what's this plan?"

"I was trying to put together a resistance, but I only managed to get the military backing of a low level Demerian officer. He should be waiting on Demer with news of his meeting with the council. Unfortunately, planet Demer is a small planet, and their population is only about five million. So, it is safe to say that their military core isn't quite the most threatening in the universe. However, it is better than nothing. We must get more planets behind us, though. We have to make them see what a menace the Aldinian Emperor is."

"Do you have any planets in mind?" I question.

"Just two: the Gorons and the Nebulites. Neither has large populations, but if we can unite all three, then we could have a decently sized army."

"All of those are weird names for species but aren't we on a time frame? Isn't the Emperor coming now? Do we really have time to do all of this?"

"The Emperor's ship, The Colossus, is a large and powerful vessel but it is extremely slow. They will not be here for a while. So, we have time, but we still don't have any to spare. I need to repair my ship so that we can meet with my contact on Demer."

"How long till you get your ship fixed?"

"It shouldn't take too much longer," she considers. "We should probably head out now to fix it."

She stands up and turns on her disguise. The bug lady is replaced with the ginger lady from before.

"Thank you for cloaking me from those humans last night. Here is your apparel back."

"Nah, just keep it. You don't know when your glitchy thing will screw up again. It'll be perfect camouflage."

"Thanks. That's actually a pretty good idea," she admits with a soft smile.

She then throws the old sweatshirt back on as we get ready to leave. She simply follows me outside. We make our way back to her cave. A slight breeze blows. Technically, I'm supposed to go to work today, but I think that this is an excellent excuse. Suddenly a thought pops in my mind.

"Why would these three races help us anyway?"

"Emperor Derask has made enemies with most of these races. For the Demerians, it took the form of a mass genocide. You see, the Demerians are battle ready warriors who had an extensive military. One hundred years ago, the Emperor feared that they were too advanced in methods of warfare and grew threatened. He had his scientists create a horrible virus that would attack the ovaries of the females on Demer. It murdered all the females on that planet and half the males. Since the average lifespan of a Demerian is two hundred of your earth years, over eighty percent of the population has passed."

"That's horrible," I can't believe what I'm hearing. She continues.

"As for the Gorons, they were the direct result of the slave trade Derask has established. The Gorons are large strong creatures, but their minds are simple. Derask took control of the planet a while back. He sends ships there regularly. The Gorons' leader, Chancellor Yer Te Sung, is a spineless coward. He fears fighting would lead to the end of his species. So, he lets them take some of the young Gorons for slaves, hoping to bring about peace. Safe to say, the Goron race is not happy with the Empire."

I say nothing to this. This Emperor Derask seems like a real prick, though. I assume she takes my silence as a suitable answer because she continues.

"The Nebulites are the only ones who haven't had a run-in with the Empire yet."

"Then why would they help us?" I can't wrap my head around it.

"They know of the atrocities that Derask has committed across the galaxy and understand that he needs to be stopped. If not, it will only be a matter of time before the Empire comes down on them. They, however, will still need a little bit of convincing. They are self-centered beings by nature and don't resort to violence easily."

"Well, thanks for the lesson, and you really think we can get all these races on our side to take down space Hitler?"

"I'm not going to lie, getting the entire planet of each will be hard, but we need them. We need a military to help stop the menace. I'll try to figure out other races that may help us. As for your race, I feel like the earthlings should not know of the threat, though. Your species has neither training in space conflict, nor do they have the resources to contribute. Them knowing would simply incite a panic."

"Well, I do agree with that. Hell, most of us still believe in a magic sky man." As I say that, I notice we are at her base.

I enter the cavern behind her and follow her to the opening where her ship is kept. She opens a back panel and starts messing with shit. What she's doing is beyond me, so I do what anyone would do in this situation: I start poking around alien equipment that I have no idea what it does or how to work it.

Most of the stuff, though flashy and shiny, still seems boring. That is, until my eyes catch sight of something that looks like a gun, only much more futuristic. I can see no down side whatsoever to playing with alien weaponry. The weight of the gun fills my hand as a very important question fills my mind. Am I crazy? I can't play with an alien gun. I can't have fun with it till I know how to turn off the safety mechanism thingy.

"Hey Zinka."

"What is it?" she replies, not looking up from the spaceship.

"How do I turn off the safety on this gun? I want to play with it."

"How do you do wha...." her voice trails off as she sees what's in my hand.

I didn't even know she could move so fast, as it literally seems like she teleports right in front of me. Before anything about what happened could cross my thoughts, she yanks the gun out of my grip. I could tell she was livid by the look in her wide, orange eyes. Apparently, sometime since she's been working here, she'd turned off her disguise. Her eyes stare daggers at me. Lots and lots of angry daggers going directly into my soul. Scary, angry aliens are scary.

"Are you insane or just stupid?" she hissed.

Yep, she is mad.

"Hmmm, yes." I respond with a shrug.

"Do you have any idea the damage you could have done by messing around with a weapon that you have no clue how to work?

You have no idea how much you could have hurt yourself. You idiot."

She is good at telling people off in English.

"Aw, that's so sweet." I reply with a chuckle.

"What do you mean?"

"You care about me." I finish the sentence off with a laugh.

Her cheeks suddenly go a darker shade green. Wait is that her form of a blush? She's embarrassed. I should use this to my benefit.

"Are you blushing?"

"Shut up, Little Balls." She drops her threatening stance and goes back to work on the ship.

I honestly wasn't sure if that was going to work. I am good. Silence takes hold of the cave.

"Dammit!" I heard her shout from the end of the pod.

"What is it?" I'm afraid to move, after that last incident, so I stay put and watch for her reaction.

"Well, the ship is airworthy, but the navigation system is completely shot. Plus, with the navigational system in this pod being linked to my master ship, that means we can't use it. We won't have any navigation for the trip. I'll have to go to Demer solely based on memory."

"So, what's the problem?" I'm confused.

"In space travel, if you're off by the smallest degree, you will miss it entirely."

"But you have been there before?"

"Yeah why?" she can't tell where I'm going with this runaway train of thought.

"So, let's go for it!"

The shouting causes her to grip her antennae temporarily before she replies. I've gotta tone it down with the outbursts. Don't really want to cause her any pain.

"But what if I miscalculate and we end up in hostile territory or something? Not all planets are full of friendly faces," she's clearly concerned.

"Don't think too much about it. It's an adventure, remember? Never think about your actions."

"You've said that about half a dozen times since we've met. Yet again, that seems horribly dangerous."

"You will be fine. I can kick anyone's ass," my false bravado is back.

"Like you did with that large human from last night?" She pokes my black eye. That action causes me to let out the manliest whimper that you will ever hear. "Aww, poor baby. Does that hurt?"

"Hey, that redneck is just lucky I was feeling nice." I double down on the bravado, like an idiot.

She simply laughs before turning serious and asking, "Are you sure we can do it?"

"I am always sure of everything I do." My practiced nonchalance falls flat. "But how are we both going to fit in your pod?"

"It will be a tight fit, but we only have to get to the moon. I landed my actual ship there, and just flew my pod down here, so I could be less conspicuous. Don't worry, though. It will take us less than a minute to get to your moon," her voice was reassuring as she explained.

I simply nodded in response. Less than a minute to get to the moon from Earth. My primitive species seemed to take ages to get there. There is still a debate on whether we went when we said we did because people are stupid.

We really are nothing but dumb apes too busy fighting amongst ourselves over imaginary lines and whose deity is more loving. My money is on Thor. He has a hammer and is part of a beloved superhero franchise⋯

"Little Balls, are you okay?" Her voice breaks me out of my thoughts.

"Yeah, just thinking. Hey, I have a question. Do your people believe in a god?"

"What is a god?" she asks confusedly.

"You know a magical deity that people credit with creating the universe and the creatures in it. You know, like a religion." I struggle to clarify.

"Our race? No, but I have encountered different races with different belief systems. Why do you ask?"

"I guess I was just wondering if other races made up stories to explain things that they don't understand."

"You don't believe in a deity?" she seems genuinely curious.

"Well no. No, I don't. Look, I know there is a chance that I'm wrong. I know that there are wonderful people out there that do believe in a deity, but the loud minority always ruin everything. They damage the reputation of otherwise good or innocent movements. Every social, political or religious school of thought has that loud hate-filled minority screaming their heads off about nonsense."

She looks at me confused for a bit. Probably because I went on a bit of a tangent.

"Hey Zinka, if something bad happens to me, I want you to do me a favor."

"You can't talk like that, Thad."

"Just hear me out. If I'm out there, on my death bed, I want you to do something for me. Think of it as a predetermined last request," I say in a flat, serious tone.

"What is it?" She asks, waiting for my favor.

"Well, I figure it might be a good thing to cover all of my bases. I was just wondering if you would pray for me. Haven't exactly been a saint in my life. It might be a good idea to have someone on my soul's side when the time comes."

"I think your soul will be fine, but I'll pray to all of the gods that I know," she replies with a smile.

She turns around and grabs items that are sitting in her pod. She then proceeds to thrust them in my hands. Noticing my confused facial expression, she decides to fill me in, or as the kids call it, 'Give me the 411'. I was never good with young people lingo. The sad thing is that I'm only 25. Damn kids and their music.

"If you go into space, you will need a few provisions. I have a neck translator just like mine that you can use. You'll need to talk to several different alien species out there. I also have a space suit. I did the research, and ours is far superior to your earthling ones. It is lighter and more mobile. It also has faux gravity boots, so you can walk instead of hopping around like a jackass. Now put them on, we should get going soon."

I comply and throw on the necklace and the suit. It fits like a glove.

A bit tight in certain areas, though. Extremely snug around my gentleman bits. I look over and see her patting the spot beside her in the pod.

"Here, you will also need this," she hands me a small tube-like thing.

"What is this?" I question, looking at the odd device.

"It is an air filtration device. It will regulate the oxygen level to make it more comfortable for you to breathe. Not all planets have the same oxygen level as Earth. It also helps stave off foreign bacteria. It will help kill any dangerous pathogens that your body may not be used to fighting."

"Okay? What do I do with it?"

"Shove it in your main respiratory orifice," her answer is matter-of-fact.

"Put it in my what now?"

"Shove an end of that tube up each nostril. It will clip in place."

I, yet again, comply with the odd command that the alien lady gives me. She has been in space. I, unsurprisingly, have never been in space. I applied to NASA but apparently being able to flip a hunk of over processed cow carcass isn't an applicable skill for space travel. Never understood why.

Now I get to be crammed in a small pod with an alien. I look at the ground I'm standing on one last time. I'll be back, Earth. I don't know when, but I'll be back. I promise. I then look back up at Zinka, who is busy typing things in and pushing random buttons. I see the hoodie I gave her sitting neatly in the back.

"Hold up," I call as I jump into the pod. "We need to make a stop first."

"Are you insane?" She gives me a pointed look. "This isn't like one of your earth vehicles. I can't just use it to run your errands."

"Ah, don't worry. No one will see. Just fly down that dirt road for a mile until you see a small store and park there." I say as I point her in the direction to go.

"We can't just--"

I cut her off, though.

"Come on. There are certain provisions I need that you did not supply me with. Just trust me."

"Fine, but if we get captured and murdered, I will kill you," I believe every word she says as she drives the craft low to the ground.

The ship maintains only a two-foot lift off the ground. Weaving through the trees for fear of going down the main path, we finally get to the store. She sets the ship to hover and hesitantly disembarks. She then proceeds to cautiously follow me inside. God damn, she's paranoid. We make it to the counter and are greeted by the friendly and extremely high face of a young black man with astonishingly long dread locks.

"Hey, Thad!" The man calls in excitement. "How you been, man?"

His focus then turns towards Zinka, and his smile grows.

"Aww, does someone have a girlfriend?" He questions in a sing song voice.

"No, Danny, this is my friend Zinka. I came in to ask a little favor from you." I reply.

"Sure, what do you need?"

"I am going on a little trip, and I was wondering if you could lend me some weed and cigarettes. A few cartons of cigs and several pounds of the devil's lettuce."

Without even a moment's hesitation, Danny answers with a smile.

"No problem. You know I've got you when you need me. Where you going, though? You've never asked for this much of an advance before."

Danny deserves an explanation. I've never been able to lie to him. He is way too trusting and kind. He's been my best friend for half a decade now. He deserves the truth.

"Well, my friend here is actually an alien, and I may have to go into space for a bit. There is a jerk. He is trying to kill her. Also, since she is here, he may try to destroy the planet."

I look over to Zinka and she is just staring at me in shock. Danny breaks the silence.

"Huh, he sounds mean." He replies as he begins to shove my items into a duffel bag. "Best of luck with the whole saving the world. I know you can do it."

Zinka then shifts her bewildered stare towards Danny. He seems unfazed by this.

"That's your reaction?" She questions, incredulous. "Why do you humans have such mixed reactions to me?"

Danny replies, "Look, I've had this gas station for years now. This isn't the strangest thing that I've heard."

"What was the strangest?" I ask curiously.

"Did you know that there are beauty pageants for children? One lady came in with her kid dressed like··· well, dressed like how a kid shouldn't be dressed. That's just stupid."

He goes back to putting the provisions into the bag. He is putting in more than I asked.

I look over at Zinka, and she is just looking around the small store in a curious fashion. She seems to just accept that my friends are weird.

"Why is there a refueling station out here in the woods? It doesn't seem too profitable."

I answer for Danny. "Danny won the lottery a few years back. He bought this place, so he can sell weed to people. He wants everyone to have access to pot that isn't laced with anything. He hates hard drugs."

Danny finally finishes throwing the things in the bag. I'm set for a while now. He hands the bag to me and gives me his signature goofy smile.

"Here you go, man." He smiles a big smile that says it all. "After you save the world, come back and we can have a party."

"Will do. Thanks again for this. You know I'm good for it. Later man."

Zinka and I leave the store. Her face is still confused, but she'll get it worked out.

"That was an odd interaction, Little Balls."

"Really? From my perspective, that was the most normal event of the past day."

She shakes her head and gives a little chuckle but remains silent, otherwise. We both climb into the pod.

"Blast off, Zinka," I command in my best sci-fi voice.

She looks at me with an unimpressed expression. "Use your

manners, Little Balls."

"Please blast off."

"There you go. That wasn't so hard, was it?"

"No, ma'am," I reply sarcastically.

She hits a few buttons, and without a word, we shoot towards the moon. The force pushes me back into my seat. I wonder if outer space is a nice place to visit.

CHAPTER 4

Before I know it, we are already docking with her ship on the moon. Damn, that really was quick. We exit her pod and I can't help but ogle at my surroundings. I take off my helmet when I see that she does. I can only think of two words to sum up the awe-inspiring alien tech that I am witnessing: "Holy fuuuu…" I trail off as my mind boggles at the sight.

"I'm guessing that is a good thing?" Zinka questions.

"Are you kidding? Look at all this. I have no idea what any of it does, but it definitely looks bad ass."

"Well, I'm glad you like it. I will show you to your cabin, so you can put your provisions away. Then I will take you to the cockpit, so we can begin our voyage to Demer."

I simply nod and stare. I follow her through the ship's corridors. We stop at a door, and she opens it ushering me inside.

"This is your quarters. You can leave your stuff here. Hurry up so we can get going."

Yet again, I just nod and stare. I set my stuff down then follow her down to the cockpit.

"Let me just punch in the coordinates for where I remember Demer being. I will still have to watch it to make sure my calculations are correct, but the autopilot should do most of the work." She says as she walks over to the controls and presses a whole bunch of buttons and twists a knob or two.

"There that should do it. Now we have some time to relax. I'm thinking maybe I should use this time to actually show you how to use an Aldinian weapon."

"Look," I interject. "You have no idea how awesome shooting shit with alien weaponry sounds, but I have to do something first. Priorities, you understand."

"Alright. What do you have to do?"

"I'm going to be the first human to smoke weed in space." I say as I pull out my pipe.

"Are you sure? Not sure how it will affect me."

"Just think of this as an experiment. My hypothesis is that an alien can smoke weed. Now I have to test it. That's the scientific process. Now, come on. Let's pop your weed cherry." I say as I begin to pack the bowl.

"Pop my what? That sounds like an inappropriate treatment of fruit!" Jeez, I thought I yelled loud.

"Relax, it's just an expression. Now would you like to?" I ask holding the filled bowl up to her.

"Sure. I guess there is no harm in it. What do I do?"

"Here I'll show you." I hold it up, so she could see clearly. "With your left hand hold the pipe. Make sure your thumb is covering that hole which is called the choker. Put the other end in your mouth and light it." I light the weed in the bowl then I release the choker as I inhale. "Make sure you move your thumb as you inhale and hold it for as long as you can."

I breathe out the remaining smoke and then pass it to her. She hits it like a pro. Ah, they grow up so fast. My heart is bursting with pride, right now. It may be that I am incredibly unhealthy, and that is just a sign of cardiac issues.

"Hey, I have a question." I break the silence between puffs. "How far can we go in this ship?"

"What do you mean?" She replies.

"Well are we able to go across the universe? Or is there only so far we can get?" I question as I pass the bowl back to her.

"If you're asking if we can go to other galaxies then the answer is no." She says taking a hit. "We can only stay within the confines of this galaxy. The one you humans call the Milky Way."

"Why is that?" I say taking the pipe back and smoking it.

"Well, why do you humans call this galaxy the Milky Way?"

"I'll answer yours if you answer mine."

"Fine. In between galaxies there is essentially just a massive vacuum of nothingness. There is the occasional runaway planet or space debris that escaped its gravitational pull, for one reason or another, but not much else. At least that is what is believed. We call this the void. For some reason, the void messes up the multi-core drive in the ship and causes ships to stall. No one has ever survived the trip. Occasionally, a ship will drift back from the void, but all of the crew have disappeared."

"Hmmm, I guess there is still stuff in space that remains unknown."

"Okay, I answered yours. Now you answer mine. Why do you people call this galaxy the Milky Way?" She asks.

"We named it after milk." I state simply.

She just stares at me. She continues to stare at me. I'm not lying it was named after milk.

"Come again?" She finally questions.

"We saw it and we named it after milk. I don't know what you're not understanding about it. I thought I was rather clear."

"Why?"

"Because people in ancient times named all kinds of shit after weird shit." I reply. "It's just how it is. Well, how it was."

She seems to accept this answer as she just shrugs it off. It was either her acceptance or her no longer caring. Either way, the conversation is done. Which is a good thing, because I should not be held accountable for what the early people did. I did not exist at that time.

Soon, between the two of us, we kill the bowl. I am not sure if she is really feeling anything, but damn I feel great. My eyes turn towards her and I notice that she doesn't look so good. She looks a little green. Well, greener. Super green? Don't really know how to explain it.

"Hey Zinka?" I ask. "Are you feeling all right?"

No later did the question leave my mouth when she looks at me. Her mouth opens like it wants to form words but that is not what comes out. What comes out is a thick greenish liquid, which looks like vomit but has the scent of dog shit wrapped in rotten sushi. The vomit hits my suit with a wet, disgusting 'plooosh' sound. Well, I guess her and pot don't mix. My hypothesis is proven wrong. That's a shame.

"I am so sorry, Little Balls. It just did not sit well. I guess my body just couldn't handle it inside of me." She looks down apologetically before she looks back up at me and gives me a glare. "Why do you keep giving me gross things? What the hell, Little Balls?"

Ignoring every instinct in me telling me to make a "that's what she said" joke regarding the whole 'inside of me' thing, I try to comfort her.

"Hey, it's okay. At least we know now that you and pot don't mix. At this point, I'm becoming slowly accustomed to you spitting things on me. I need to get cleaned up. Where can I go to do that?"

"Every cabin has its own personal wash and there are also fresh uniforms in the closet. Just throw your used uniform down the chute. It will be taken care of."

Her face still appears to be discolored. A little guilt inducing seeing what the pot, that I gave her, has done to her.

"Alright, I'll be back." I head down to the cabin and grab fresh clothes.

I then make my way to the bathroom or whatever she called it. The shower didn't spout water but instead some scented pink goo. It felt all tingly. Now I would never admit this out loud, but I rather enjoyed the tingling feeling. It felt like being surrounded by tons of tickling fingers. That is a terrible metaphor. It sounds more a horror show like than something enjoyable. I get dressed and make my way back to the bridge. I see her looking at the screen of flashing lights and shiny things. She appears to have gotten it out of her system. Mostly because it went all over my clothes.

"By my calculations, Little Balls, we are still on course to Demer." She sighs, standing up and stretching. "I am going to my quarters to relax. Do not, I repeat, do not break anything. Understand."

"Aye, aye, captain," I give her a mock salute.

Judging by her facial expression and her rolling eyes, she is not impressed.

"I mean it." She reiterates. "This is very important. Do not make me put you on a leash."

She then makes her way out of the chamber towards her room. Now one question remains. What the hell am I going to do to entertain myself?

I never claim to be a smart man or even a talented man, but if there is one thing I'm good at, it's finding shit that could be fun as hell. So, I'm not all that surprised that when I begin wandering through the ship, I stumble upon something awesome.

I find the armory/shooting range. So many shiny, shiny weapons. Weapons that I will have to figure out how to use myself, considering someone decided to go to sleep on me. Oh well, what's the worst that can happen? You know besides the stuff that involves me accidentally killing myself or something. Those don't count. Other than that, though, I'm sure it's a perfectly safe thing to try and do with absolutely no supervision at all. I gaze at the wonder of the tools in front of me. My hand dives into my pocket and grabs a cig. I light the death stick, and a smile spreads across my face. I'm going to have a good time with this.

I grab the first gun I see. I examine it closely and see a button. I press it and wait. Nothing happens. So, with my brilliant deducing skills, I conclude that that was the safety. Only one way to test my hypothesis. I raise the weapon and aim at the target. My finger gently squeezes the trigger. I'm being as careful as I possibly can with a dangerous tool that I have no idea how to use.

Then suddenly, I find myself flying and into the wall. That was one hell of a kick.

'THUD'

My back hits the wall behind me and my head snaps back at the sudden stop. As my head contacts the wall, my vision fades to black and I find myself succumbing to unconsciousness.

"Wak....uck........ttle balls."

I hear a voice, but it keeps fading in and out.

The scent of cookies assaults my nostrils. Is someone baking? I hope so. Some fresh baked cookies would be amazing right now.

"You......pid.......fuc...."

Damn it. Focus on the voice. Focus harder.

"I........if you're dead I'll bring you back to life just to kill you again."

Hey, it's Zinka. Come on, wake up. I finally muster up the strength to open my eyes. The bright florescent lighting assaults my viewing globes. My eyes start to adjust to the room.

"Zinka what the hell happ--"

That was all I could get out before I felt a firm slap across my face. The force of the slap causes my face to recoil. Pain hurts.

"Are you stupid?" She berates me. "You could have gotten yourself killed. That gun is supposed to be mounted before you fire because of the kick. Are you trying to die?"

"Woah, I was just curious, there is no need to injure me further." I say rubbing my sore cheek.

"I swear you're like a damn child. Do I have to watch you constantly, so you don't maim yourself?"

"Well... adult supervision would be helpful." I shrug.

"Ugh. One of these days, your stupidity will get you killed. When that happens, don't come crying to me. Now, stand up; there doesn't appear to be anything broken." She helps me to my feet.

"That's what you say, but your yelling broke my feelings."

She rolls her eyes before replying.

"You're fine, you big baby. Here now, let me show you how to use these so that your dumb ass doesn't get yourself killed."

She spends the next few hours teaching me how to shoot things. It is amazing. The guns are very advanced. It's apparent that I'm not very good. At least not yet. By the end of our session, I've only hit the target five times out of about a hundred. In all fairness, I haven't even shot an Earth gun. Five shots seems impressive, given the circumstance. If that was a real fight, those five shots would have been kill shots. Sometimes, you need stay positive.

My inner confidence and reassurance are interrupted by a loud growling sound. Hmmmm, it appears I need nourishment. I was so worried about my smokes and weed that I forgot all about other requirements like food. I could really go for a peanut butter and jelly sandwich. She seems to have read my mind or, at the very least, heard my stomach as she answers my unasked question.

"Don't worry. The food we have on the ship should be safe for your consumption, but you may not like the taste considering your natural eating habits. It will also keep your body hydrated since we do not have any water on the ship."

"You never know. Maybe I will find your odd extraterrestrial cuisine simply delightful."

I follow her to the mess hall, and as I walk in, I notice it is entirely spotless like the entire ship. Why is this place so clean? Who cleans it up? Is it a robot? Is it part of some robot maid union so that all its robot needs are met?

My thoughts are interrupted as Zinka sets a plate down with some weird looking blue goop on it. Looking at it, it only brought one thing to mind: Oh my god, I'm eating liquefied Cookie Monster. Yet still I ate it, and it was horrible. The Cookie Monster is not delicious. I'd kill for a PB&J.

The entire time I am eating the blue goo, my face must be making odd, contorted expressions by the weird and concerned facial expression Zinka keeps giving me. Still, I power through the final bites, and although it tastes like shit stuffed with shit then cooked with shit after being marinated in shit for roughly twenty-four shitty hours, it does fill me up at least. It will keep me from dying, and that is what is important. Zinka grabs my plate and throws it into a large machine that is on the wall. She stands up and leaves. Not knowing what else to do, I stand and follow her.

We enter the control room. She goes to the controls and pushes more buttons and knobs. She doesn't seem panicky, so I assume all is going according to plan. If she was acting erratic, then would be the time to panic.

A loud sound is coming from the ship. Sounds like you would imagine an ambulance sounding like if it were being destroyed by a fire truck and then lit on fire.

"What is that noise?" I ask as the annoying sound assaults my ear drums.

My hands shoot up to try and protect my ears. This doesn't seem to accomplish much, though. The sound is still easily heard. It is only slightly muffled now. Now it sounds like hundreds of ambulances going off at the same time.

"It's an incoming transmission." She presses more buttons, causing a screen to be lowered from the ceiling. "I'm patching it through."

Suddenly, I see a smirking face on the screen. Clearly this dude is the same race as Zinka. His eyes are bright pink, and his antennae are shorter. Other than that, it's clear they both belong to the same species. I am about to inquire about who it is when she breathes a single word: "Derask." Her voice is a near whisper.

"Hello defect," he cackles, staring at Zinka, but then his attention turns towards me. "I see you got yourself a pet. I sure hope it's house trained." With that he lets out a maniacal laugh.

Why do all villains laugh the same? It must be a job requirement. Maybe it's covered in Villainy 101. But I just can't let that insult slide, so I step forward and say the first thing that comes to mind.

"Oh yeah, well...your mother is of scandalous repute!"

He simply fakes a yawn and speaks again. Clearly, he is not impressed by my witty retort and he is going out of his way to show that he doesn't care. Doesn't really make sense if you think about it. Can't really try when it comes to not caring. That's just redundant.

"Yes, although this little chat has been very invigorating, I simply should insist we move this along. I have things to do. If you will just keep your eyes on the monitor, I'll show you what I mean."

The camera then zooms to a planet outside his cockpits window. It seems to be a mostly blue planet. It looks like water with some land thrown into the mix. Seems like a nice place. Maybe, I could take a vacation there one day. Wait a minute. Oh shit, I know that place.

"Holy shit. That's Earth." I whisper. Though, he still seemed to hear it because the grin seemed to grow at my reaction.

"Yes, Earth as you call it, is right outside The Colossus," He grins like a psychopath.

"But how?!" Zinka interrupts. "Your ship is powerful, but it's not that fast. You shouldn't have arrived for weeks."

Apparently, he found this humorous as he started to cackle again.

"My Dear, I've long since made upgrades to it. I have simply been toying with you. I could've killed you anytime I wanted, but this is just too much fun for our game to be over. Now, I'm not stupid. I know that you two are long gone, but this planet still needs to pay for its crimes against the empire. Now to help me with the honors, I have someone from your own planet to help me. I believe you know him."

He steps aside to reveal a very familiar face. Beady eyes sit upon on a wrinkled, worn out face. Grey hair cut into what can only be described as the stereotypical politician style. Rolls upon rolls of chins extend down his bloated features.

"Jesus Christ," I breathe out. "President Landon? What the hell are you doing helping Derask?"

"President Landon here," the hideous troll replies. "Always glad to meet a voter."

"I didn't vote for you."

"Why not? All the issues that matter to you matter to me. I agree with all of your political views."

"You don't know my political views."

"Doesn't matter, whatever you believe, I believe. Please vote for me."

"You're already president."

"True but re-election is in only three and a half years. Have to start running now."

"Dammit Landon, enough of this nonsense!" Derask says as he turns around and pushes a button.

I'm frozen in shock. What the hell is he going to do? My mouth feels dry and when I try to find words to shout at the maniac, I find my brain unable to form a syllable. I simply stand there, mouth agape, knowing that I can't stop what this asshat is doing. My mind races trying to figure out a way out of this. A way to stop him from doing what he's trying to do, but nothing comes.

I hear it before any other sense picks it up. It's a loud buzzing noise. It gives me horrible images of what's going to happen, but I hope against hope that I'm wrong. Unfortunately, I'm not. Shortly after the buzzing noise starts, a bright blue beam leaves his ship heading directly towards Earth. The beam appears to be going in slow motion as my heart skips several beats. My brain fills with thoughts of all the people I care about on that rock, who are just living their ordinary lives. The beam connects and shatters my home like a piñata. The blast causes chunks to fly off into all directions. I fall to my knees, too stunned to do anything. Hunks of where my home used to be float absently by in space.

More images fill my head. My father working in his garage, trying to get that old '57 Chevy running. My mom telling every person she meets how proud she is of me, even though I am a complete and total failure. My baby sister lying in her crib. She won't even get the chance to see her first birthday.

I'm broken from my thoughts by that goddamn laugh again. The laugh ricochets around the inside of my skull, echoing to the point that every single laugh feels like it hits me a million times over. Laughing like this whole thing is just one big jape. Like everything is just a joke to this monster.

"Aww··· too bad," he crows, with false sympathy oozing from every syllable. "And I heard it was such a nice place too."

I stand up almost as if in a trance and make my way closer to the screen, my mind completely unaware of what it will do or what I'm even doing. Purely on instinct, my body gets right up to the screen. I turn my focus on Derask.

"I will kill you," I intone flatly and emotionlessly. "Kill you like the cliche asshole that you are."

With that, I stand staring at the black screen before me. A hand lands on my shoulder and Zinka gives me a look of concern and sympathy. I brush the hand off in an apathetic fashion.

"I'm going to go to my room for a while," I walk out of the room. "I just need some time alone. Need some time to think"

I walk down the corridor to my room. The shiny metal reflecting the fluorescent light from the ceiling. It is damn near blinding, and this just makes me hate it. Where the hell does it get off? Why is it so bright? The light seems contradictory to the mood. It's just like the sun. Damn light always seeming so happy. My zombified body enters my cabin, and the door shuts when I enter. The door seals away the rest of the galaxy and in this room, it is only me in my own personal universe.

I sit in my bed and light a cig. I ash it in random scrap that I found around the ship. Leave it to the man that always has to inhale things into his lungs to have rigged up ashtrays in every room. My cigarette burns as my thoughts somehow manage to get even darker. Darker and darker thoughts transpire, and the smoke begins to cloud and swirl around me.

"All those goddamn people," I marvel aloud as I take another drag.

Though it is still, I'm assuming, morning, I feel as though I am already beat. I take one more hit of my cig before I put it out in the ashtray and lay down for a nap.

CHAPTER 5

I open my eyes and my parents' house surrounds me. I look down and see my little sister laying in my arms. She looks up at me, smiling her toothless smile. A smile graces my own face in return, but something seems off. No one else is around. They aren't upstairs. They aren't in the basement. They aren't in the garage. I move over to the window to look outside, still holding my sister. I push the curtain open, and the sight requires every ounce of self-control to stop from vomiting.

Outside is nothing but charred, decomposing, and mutilated corpses. Several corpses are impaled upon various tree branches. Everyone of their faces is stuck in an expression of either fear or pain. Houses and cars are burning in every direction. The stench of death fills my unprepared nostrils, causing me to gag in response. I retreat from the window, not wanting to see anymore.

My ears perk up as I hear what sounds like Lilly crying upstairs. She can't be. She was just in my arms. I look down and see that I am holding nothing but air. My mind, being unable to make sense of it, goes completely blank.

My confusion paralyzes me until the crying assaults my ears again. I jolt from my shocked state and run up the stairs as fast as my legs will carry me. I push open her bedroom door and see her in her crib.

She is laying down and I no longer hear the cries. My brain wills my legs to carry me, so I can make my way over to her bedside. When I get to her, I cannot fight my gag reflex this time as I turn and vomit all over the floor.

My sister is in her crib, but her skin is burnt and, in some spots, even melted off. Her eyes are caught in an eternal snapshot of fear. I try to get my composure back when I hear movement in her crib. I look, and I am absolutely horrified by the sight. Her dead lifeless head starts turning towards me as I just stare.

She then unleashes a horrible cry, like a banshee, nearly splitting my eardrums. I fall to my knees as I clutch my hands over my ears. Religion was never big in my life, but I begin to pray to anyone that can hear me. The screaming stops, and there is nothing but silence.

My eyes open, and I see that I am alone in a never-ending black abyss. Just floating there. Nothing around me. No way of knowing up from down, or if those things even exist here.

"Don't change the baby," a woman's voice tears me from my sorrow.

"M-mom?"

"I will always be proud of you. You will never be a failure."

"Mom! Where are you? Mom!" I screamed, nearly going hoarse. I looked around but could only see the abyss before me. "Mom please. Please come back."

I finish off with sobs from a heavy heart. My eyes snap open, and I see the metal walls and ceiling of my room. Damn that was one hell of a nightmare. Hand groping for my cigs, I finally grab them. Pressing one against my lips, I light it and take a large inhale.

A knock at the door catches my attention.

"Who is it?" I call, out of habit, even though I am on a spaceship with literally only one other living being. God, I'm dense sometimes.

"It's Zinka," I hear her muffled voice through the door.

On the plus side, at least she decided not to call me out on my temporary stupidity.

"Can I come in?" her voice is soft and careful.

"Sure," I sit up in my bed and light up another cigarette.

She steps in cautiously, almost as if she is approaching a baby deer and doesn't want to scare it off. She takes a seat next to me on the bed and puts a comforting hand on my shoulder. The smell of cookies overwhelms the smell of my cigarette.

"How are you holding up? I know that's a generic question, but I really don't know how else to start this conversation." Each one of her words laced with sincere concern.

"I'll....I'll be okay. Well as okay as I could possibly be, I guess." I answer while taking a long drag off my cigarette. "Don't get me wrong, I'm still going to kill that son of a bitch in the most brutal way I can think of, but my family would want me to be happy. I highly doubt I'll ever be entirely okay, though."

I look down at the ground and just stare there for what feels like an eternity until Zinka's voice yet again pulls me from my reverie.

"Look, I know nothing I can do can bring back your family, friends, or planet, but we can still save some of your race."

I stare at her completely confused, so she continues.

"Earth isn't the first planet Derask has destroyed, and every time he does destroy one, at least in the past, he takes enough of the species to be able to reproduce and, essentially, makes them mate so he can sell off the offspring for a high price."

"What is wrong that sick twisted freak?!" I shout. "Seriously, who sells a baby?"

"He is an asshole, but I was able to hack into the ship where they house these individuals. The ship is simply referred to as Prison AA54. I was able to gain information that, like the other planets he destroyed in the past, he took two random humans from Earth before destroying it. If you're up for it, we could rescue them and all the other prisoners on that ship."

"You would really be willing to risk breaking into a space psycho's prison and saving what's left of my race? Why?"

She stands up and smiles.

"It's an adventure, remember? Don't think about your actions. Besides, this ship could use a crew. So, you up for it?"

"Zinka?" I ask.

"Yeah."

"Get ready for an adventure!!!" I shout striking the best heroic pose I have yet to strike.

CHAPTER 6

"We are coming up to Prison AA54," Zinka slows on approach to the outside of the ship. "We need to proceed the rest of the way in the escape pod."

"Okay, so what's the plan?" I feel like I should know what's going on.

"We need to enter the docking port. Derask is extremely confident. He doesn't think that anyone would dare to defy him. Therefore, he only has two armed guards to take care of the prisoners. All we have to do is take them out and then we are home free." Zinka explains.

"How are we going to get them out of there though if we just have the escape pod?"

"This device," she says, holding up an odd-looking device thingy, "is a teleporter. It will transport them directly to the ship. Then, you and me just take the pod back here."

"Alrighty, it sounds simple enough," I shrug.

"See, this is what happens when you plan things ahead of time, Little Balls," Zinka just grins at my annoyed look. "Do you see how smooth this is going?"

We make our way into the docking port undetected. I still have no idea how we manage to do that. Zinka is one sneaky little alien.

As we quietly land the pod, the docking bay door closes. We exit the ship and remove our hood helmet things. The ship appears to be massive on the inside. What look to be red LED lights line the walls and the floor. The lights give everything a reddish glow and the whole thing just screams space prison. Everything is so goddamn eerie. Doesn't help that everything around us is quiet.

"You remember how to use this?" Zinka says while holding up a gun.

"Whoa, there. Just take it easy. I don't want to kill these guys," I say while backing away from the gun.

"This army destroyed your planet and killed your family. They are despicable beings and evil beings. Why wouldn't you want to take revenge?" she wonders with genuine confusion in her voice.

"These two didn't push the button to destroy it. That is all on Space Dictator Guy."

"You really aren't meant for war, are you?"

"I'm a pacifist. I can't help it," I wink, shrugging my shoulders. "I may be a tad bit of a hippie."

"No idea what a hippie is, Little Balls. Fine, we will set them to stun. It will paralyze them for about twelve hours." She then toggles a switch on both guns and hands me one. "Do you think you will be able to pull the trigger on Derask?"

"Without hesitation," I confirm as the nightmare of my family comes back to mind.

"Okay, as long as it's understood that we have to kill him to stop all of this." She then starts to walk. "Follow me, I believe I hear the two guards down this corridor."

I follow close behind her.

"I still don't know why he would only have two guards," I state, confused by the odd turn of events.

"Derask's ego is massive. He believes no one would dare defy him," she replies like it was the most obvious thing in the world.

We continue walking, when she stops me and points down a corridor. This hallway is just like all the others. It gives off the same red and creepy glow. I look down and see the two guards with their backs turned towards us. Why does everything seem terrifying with a red undertone? We both raise our guns up and pull the triggers.

"Pew pew," and with that, both guards fall unconscious to the floor.

I look over and I see her staring at me.

"What?" I ask, as I start feeling very self-conscious.

"Did... did you just make a 'pew pew' noise?" She finally asks.

"That's the sound a gun makes."

"These are silent. They don't make any noise," she states.

"What fun is a gun that doesn't make the pew noise?"

"A stealth one. It doesn't need a noise."

"Boo stealth. No pew noise equals no fun. Stealth is for losers."

"What is actually wrong with you? It's a waste of breath to do the pew noise."

"It's a waste of breath for you to argue about the pew noise," I respond with a smug face.

"It's only to stop you from doing it in the future."

"I'm still going to do it."

"Whatever," she finally relents. "According to my data, there are only five prisoners aboard this vessel. There are two humans, two Voltans, and one Litethite."

"Why is there only one Light Bright?"

"Litethites asexually reproduce. They have no gender."

"Damn. What would be a proper pronoun then? Would it be he or she or it or what? I wouldn't want to offend." I ask genuinely curious.

"They have an all for one and one for all mentality. So, refer to the Litethite as they or them. You know, just make it plural."

"Alright then, lead the way," I say as we come around another corner.

Navigating the odd hallway of the prison seems like it would be difficult. Zinka expertly traverses them though. I guess she has a map. Either that or she has an amazing sense of direction.

"The first prisoners are over here," Zinka says as she opens a door revealing two aliens.

They each have four legs and four arms. They are purple in color and have, what looks like feathers growing from the top of their heads.

Their bottom halves seem rather insect-like. Their eyes, however, are very similar to the Aldinian eyes. Their noses are long and pointed. Ears don't exist, though. At least I don't notice any. I am no expert on alien anatomy. Not even an expert on human anatomy. These beings appear to be the result of an insect and bird orgy. Why does everything up here fill me with horrid images?

"Hello. I am Zinka and this is Little Balls," she introduces us, still using my nickname. "We are here to rescue you. Follow us."

The larger of the two comes forward and speaks.

"Hello, I am Leonidas," he politely responds. "And this is Stuan."

The other simply nods her greeting and doesn't say a word.

"Great, we are all acquainted, now we need to keep going," I cut the conversation abruptly as I leave the room toward the next cell.

Zinka gets there first. I should really start working out. Don't know why I was in such a rush. Zinka is the one who knows where to go. She opens the next cell to reveal another green alien. This one however is excessively skinny. Its arms dangle all the way to the floor and its knuckles drag. Its eyes resemble that of a spider, meaning there are eight of those sons of a bitches. It has no mouth or any other facial features. Its initial reaction is to sprint to the corner and cower from the sudden surprise visit. Zinka approaches the strange being.

"Don't worry," she reassures in a very calming voice. "We are here to get you out of here. We won't hurt you."

The being takes a long, calculating look at the four creatures that just burst into his cell. He seems to physically relax.

"Hello, we are Litethite." It speaks, well more like grumbles, from its throat, considering it still doesn't have a mouth. It stands up straight, giving us a full view of its five-and-a-half-foot tall frame.

"Hello, Litethite." I say. "I am Little Balls, this is Zinka, and over there are two beings I just met. You can learn their names later. We still have two more prisoners to rescue, so let's move."

Zinka, again, is the first one out of the cell, with me close behind. All I can think of is the chance to see two more humans. I don't want to be the last one in existence with Landon. That is a lonely, lonely life. No one wants to be alone with that guy. We get to the next cell.

"My data shows that they are kept in here," Zinka says as she opens the door.

The sight that greets me is one I did not expect. Though it's not like me being in space today was entirely planned either. The person standing before is one that I know very well.

"Holy shit." I say at last. "Danny?"

"Oh, hey man," he replies. "Haven't seen you in ages. Apparently, I'm on a space journey too. Mine is a bit weird, though. I think the aliens are into some really kinky stuff. They keep pointing guns at me and motioning to me to have sex with that girl." He says as he motions to a girl strapped to the table.

Zinka is currently working on untying the woman.

"Wait," I replied. "They picked you, so you could reproduce offspring?"

At that I just could not stop laughing.

"What is so funny?" Zinka asks as she continues to untie the girl.

"Because," I answer, "Danny is gay."

"I know, man," Danny chimed in. "I tried telling them that, but they kept pointing guns at me and I'm like whoa. Then they motioned me to have sex with this girl and I'm like whoa. Then they are like we need your offspring and I'm like whoa. Like I said, weird space trip."

I look over and see that Zinka finally got the girl off the table. She's a young woman, maybe a little older than me and Danny, with darker skin than him too. Her body is thin and covered with tattoos. Her hair is cut in a weird mohawk style. She kind of looks like the poster child for the afro punk movement. I also notice her right eye is a lazy eye and is looking off to one side.

"Hello. I'm Zinka. Little Balls. Leonidas. Stuan. Litethite" Zinka points to each individual as she says their names.

Why am I still Little Balls?

"Pangaea," she says as she stands up.

"Pangaea?" I question. "That's a weird name."

She glares me. I think she might be considering killing me. I had a good run. Well maybe not good, but I did have some sort of run. Good is subjective anyway. Bottom line is that I existed for a certain amount of time. That is something to be proud of, I guess.

"Alright time to get out of here," Zinka leads the way back to the pod.

Finally, we come down the corridor where we left the two guards unconscious. Suddenly, I see a blur run past me. It's Pangaea, and she is running right for the guards. I wonder what she is going to do. Before I even have time to think about it, she jumps up and stomps the one guard's throat. Her foot lands with a terrible crunch. She then grabs his gun and shoots the other one five times in the head. After the fifth shot, the guard's head was practically non-existent. The first one killed him. The other four were literally overkill.

All of us have stopped what we were doing to gawk at the sight. She then turns towards us. Apparently, I was the most offensive in my gawking, because she got right in my face.

"Don't you dare stand there and judge me!!" she screams right in my face. Then her voice takes an almost sad and distant tone. "You have no idea what those two bastards did to me."

With that, she just keeps walking, as we all head to the ship. That was unusual. I'll figure that out later. We keep walking till we get back to the pod. Zinka runs ahead and aims the transporter at the five rescued... let's just call them people. She's fires and, in an instant, all five of them are gone. Humans really are behind on the whole technology thing. I am going to go ahead and just blame the dark ages for that. Damn you dark ages for your scientific chastising and overly religious bullshit.

I guess I'm standing there ogling too long, as I feel her grab my collar and throw me into the pod. My shoulder hits the side of the ship. I'm just going to go out on a limb and assume she is in a very big hurry.

"Hurry up, Little Balls. We need to get back to the ship," she is clearly anxious.

"Why in such a rush?" I question.

"If your friend, Danny, is anything like you, there may not be a ship to return to if we do not hurry."

"You know Zinka," I reply, "I would probably be offended··· you know, if that wasn't the truth."

She launches the pod and we make our way back to the ship. The only thought that crosses my mind is: I'm not the last human. Look, I know I should be happy we got the other three passengers out, and, don't get me wrong, I am. However, you have no idea how soothing it is knowing you're not the last person alive, except for President Landon.

There may only be four of us, but now I know that if something happens to me, humanity will continue. I guess I was lost in thought because the next thing I know, we are pulling into the docking port. Wow, I have been spacy lately.

We see all five of them standing in the docking port looking slightly confused. Well, all except for Danny. He is just smiling, happy to be off that ship. Zinka steps forward and addresses them.

"Look," she gets their attention. "We are forming a resistance. You five are free to join this ship if you wish. If you do not, we will drop you off at the nearest friendly planet. We will not force you to join our fight. However, part of me knows that every one of you has as much reason to have a vendetta against Derask as me and Little Balls. If you choose to join us, then there are a few simple rules. Number 1, I am your captain. I am in charge. Number 2, this is Little Balls. He is my second in command. Now, if any of you wish to leave this fight, this is the time to say so." She finishes off quickly scanning the crowd.

No one is backing down. Well, this is an improvement. Instead of two against the empire, now we have seven. I may not be a magical math wizard, but seven is larger than two. This is progressing nicely. It is Litethite who breaks my thoughts this time.

"Excuse us, Captain Zinka," they start. "We are highly trained in biology and medicinal remedies for an extensive number of races. If this ship does not currently have medical staff, then we will gladly volunteer for the occupation."

"Well, we do need a doctor for when Little Balls inevitably hurts himself," she replies. "Sure, you have the job, Litethite. Come on, I'll show you to the med bay and to all of your cabins."

Maybe I should have followed Zinka on the tour, considering I have no idea where any of them are currently at. Why is this ship so big? Oh well, I guess I'll just wander aimlessly until I find someone. Just how I deal with life. Wandering aimlessly through life like the winners do.

CHAPTER 7

I make my way down a random corridor, till I come to a door with writing that I can't understand. Seems like some gibberish scribbled on the wall by a toddler. I'll go in here. The door opens, and I notice that it is full of strange objects. It kind of looks like the anal probe stuff you see in comics and whatnot.

"Hello Sir, Little Balls. What do we owe this pleasure to?" Litethite inquires as I turn towards them.

"Hey Litethite. I just thought this was a good time to go around and meet the crew. So, how are you holding up? The med bay has all the equipment you need? Hope so, because to be honest, I have no idea what the hell any of this stuff is."

My hand grabs an odd device. The machinery looks like it is specifically designed to go up a rectum. What appears to be a drill is on the very tip of it. Two-pointed metal extensions are protruding from the sides of it. I'm going to have nightmares from this device.

"We are good." They say, looking rather nervous. "But I do suggest that you put that down. That is an advanced cauterizing laser. It can burn at up to 500 degrees Celsius."

He then takes the device from my hands and sets it gingerly on the table. On the plus side, that is not going anywhere near my butt.

"Oh, phew. I thought that was an anal probe," I say with relief clear in my voice.

It is a little insulting that I have been in space for how long and have not been probed yet. Not saying I want it, but dammit I'm pretty. Pretty enough to be probed.

"We are sorry, Sir, but we have no knowledge of what an anal probe is. Is that some sort of device that needs to be directly inserted into the anal cavity?"

"Uh...forget it, Litethite. It's nothing," I stammer. "I'm going to go meet with the rest of the crew now. So, I'll see you later." I say leaving the med bay.

"Have a good time, Sir Little Balls. We will see you later," he replies before the door shuts.

Damn Zinka and her nickname. I really hope that meeting the rest of the crew goes a lot smoother than that did. My reflection in the shiny metal sidings is my only company as I repeatedly knock on random doors. The answer at each door is the same old silence. God damn, this ship is massive. Finally, I get an answer at one of them. Unfortunately, it isn't exactly the warmest of welcomes.

"Go the fuck away!" I hear Pangaea shout from the other side of the door.

"Come on, Pangaea. It's just me. I'm going around chatting with the crew. Trying to get to know the people on this ship," I prod.

Suddenly, the door slides open, and I am face to face with a very angry woman.

"What, you want to be friends? Well, I don't need any. I am on this ship for the sole purpose of watching that son of a bitch, Derask, writhe in pain and agony before he dies. I don't need, nor do I want, any god damn friends." She says as she turns back around.

She did not shut the door when she went back into her room. Now I may be wrong, but I think that's an invitation inside. As soon as I step past the threshold, however, I realize that I am horrible at reading social cues. She spins around, with anger flashing in her eyes.

"Get out of here, you jack ass," she yells as she grabs the closest thing to her.

I have no time to notice what it is as she hurls the object at my skull. I dodge the projectile and sprint out of the room.

The door slams shut behind me. Hmm, well that was an interesting time, I guess. I decide I'll just check on her later and continue down the hallway. Maybe later, she will be more welcoming of a conversation. Either that or she will just throw more things at me. Hell, she may even kill me. I'll find out when it happens.

Yet again, I'm just knocking on random doors. Door after door yields no result until I finally get another answer. Zinka really has them spread out. The door opens revealing Stuan. She gives no verbal greeting, but she does smile at me. It's a tiny and reserved smile, but a smile nonetheless. She seems friendly enough.

"Hey Stuan, I'm just going around checking on the crew. So, are you doing good over here?"

She simply nods and waves before she shuts the door again. She shuts it carefully as if not wanting to shut it in my face. I'm left staring at a blank metal door. She isn't exactly much of a talker. Well, I met three of the crew so far and every single one of them was awkward.

Ah well, only two more to talk to. I knock on the next door over and was surprised someone answered. Before this, Zinka had all of them spread out more. I look up to see Leonidas with a huge grin on his face.

"Well hey there, Little Balls. I already thanked Zinka for the rescue, but I have not had the pleasure of thanking you yet. So, on behalf of everyone, I'd like to thank you."

"Not a problem, man. I was just going around checking on the crew. Do you happen to know what is up with Stuan? I was just over there, and she seemed friendly, but she didn't say a single word."

His smile instantly vanished and was replaced with a look of pure sadness and empathy.

"You see, Little Balls, I heard about your planet, and don't get me wrong, you have my utmost sympathy but, on our planet, Derask was a little more personal. Stuan was a single mother. Before he took her, she had to watch him skin her own children alive."

"Jesus Christ," I breathe out not really knowing what to say to that.

"I saw it with my own eyes. Stuan and I have been friends for longer than you can imagine. On that ship, they did everything they could to try and make me bond with her. In our culture bonding is looked at as the most sacred act two beings can perform."

"What did they do to you?"

"You can see for yourself," he says as he turns around and lifts his shirt, showing me his back.

I could barely hold back from vomiting as I gaze at the wounds. Flesh had been literally skinned off in some places and those appear to be the least severe wounds. The worst of them seem like chunks of flesh had been removed so that you can clearly see muscle tissue. A shoulder blade is even visible.

"You really care about her, don't you?" I ask.

"Yes, that is why I requested to bunk in the room next to her, so I can keep an eye on my friend," he says quietly as he puts his shirt back on and turns around.

"No, I mean you care about her as more than a friend. You love her, don't you?" He simply sighs and looks down before responding.

"I don't want to do anything about it. I don't want ours to be a relationship solely based on circumstance."

"Well, all relationships are, in a sense, a matter of circumstance, but it's your call, man. I know you will know what to do when the time comes," I offer.

He looks up and smiles, "Thank you, Little Balls."

"No sweat, but if you ever need advice, just come to me. I'm here for you. Now I've got to go; there is still one more crew member to talk to. I'll see you later," I say as I leave, and hear the door shut.

Now where is Danny at? I've missed that crazy, stoned son of a bitch. I continue knocking on random doors till I hear a yell coming from the other side.

"Who is it?" I hear Danny shouting from inside.

"It's me, Danny."

The door opens revealing a smiling Danny. "Hey, dude. How's it going?"

"Good man. I was wondering if you wanted to get stoned and just chill out for a bit." I pull out some of the weed that I had in my pocket and my pipe.

"Yeah, come on in. Let's get high in space. Although, since the Earth was in space before it exploded, we always got high in space."

"So, you heard about Earth, huh?"

"Yeah. They brought in a video screen when we were in the prison, so I could watch," he replies as his face drops slightly.

He brightens up quickly, though. "Enough about that. Come on. Let's smoke up."

I enter Danny's room and the door shuts behind me. When I saw the Earth destroyed, I never thought that I'd be able to do this again. Words can't describe how ecstatic I am that this man is alive. Friends are nice.

CHAPTER 8

"So, think about it, man." Danny continues his high epiphany. "What if we are just characters in a book following a predetermined plot line. We essentially have the illusion of free will, but all of our actions are already written in stone, man."

"I wasn't prepared for an existential crisis when I started smoking, Danny."

"Well, it could be worse, man. We could be in one of those fan-fictions," he suggests, somehow keeping a straight face.

"Dude, to be a fan-fiction, we would need fans."

"Yeah, you're right. A fan-fiction without fans would just be fiction. Holy shit dude, we are fiction."

"Yet again, existential crisis. If this was a fan-fiction, someone would be having us make out right now," I reply with a slight chuckle.

"Dude, you're a beautiful person, but that would be gross. It'd be like making out with my brother," he says with disgust on his face.

"I know, right? The internet doesn't care, though. "

"I guess there is no more internet," Danny says in a slightly saddened tone before brightening up. "At least no more political propaganda posts."

"Speaking of politics, President Landon is also alive. He is working with Derask," I tell him.

"Seriously, man? There are four people left and he has to be one of them?"

"I know, man, I know. I find it best to not focus too much on it. New topic though, so Pangaea is kind of... something. I went to talk with her, and she threw something at me. Do you happen to know what that's about?"

"Well, I was up there on that ship with her. I had a lot of time to talk with her. She is a sweet girl but fought back hard. They beat her almost to death. And they constantly tormented her, called her names like 'freak' and 'weirdo', kept her locked up, deprived her from sleeping, starved her, basically tortured her. It was terrible. She cried to herself when she was alone, but never broke down in front of them."

"God damn, dude," I don't have much else to add.

I guess she had a damn good reason for killing those two.

"That shit pissed me off, man. I broke out of my neck harness and nearly beat them to death. No one deserves to be treated like that."

"What happened next, man?" I ask as I pull out a cigarette and light up.

"Well, that got me a good beating, but they did leave her alone. Plus, they also forgot to hook my harness back up. So, I got to roam free. I was trying to figure out a way to release her, but then you guys showed up."

"Those bastards deserved what she did to them."

"Yeah so just do me a favor man. I know Pangaea can be a bit... abrasive but just be patient with her. She will come around. She's a sweetheart."

"Alright, I'll be patient," I reply.

A silence comes over us. The silence gets to me. I can't deal with long silences. So, I try and break it.

"Well I uh--" A sudden jolt sends me crashing against the wall.

"What was that?" Danny questions in a stupor.

"I have no idea."

"Well we aren't dead, so it can't be that bad, right? That's a win."

"Take the wins when you can, Danny."

'Attention crew,' Zinka's voice echoes over the loudspeaker. 'our multi-core drive is damaged. I am preparing for an emergency landing on the nearby planet of Chrysoth. All crew please meet at the Docking Port One. Thank you.'

"Well, looks like we get to visit our first alien world," I'm genuinely ecstatic at the idea.

"Yeah, and we get to visit while we are high," Danny says equally enthused, but he is that way about most things.

We stand and make our way to the main hall, where Zinka and everyone else are waiting for us. Zinka doesn't look happy about the predicament.

"I just got off the comm with the technician," Zinka starts. "It will take time for them to repair the multi-core drive. It looks like we get a little shore leave before we even get started."

"Woo, unearned vacation and other worldly partying!" Danny pumps his fist, excited.

Every single eye turns to Danny.

"What?" He questions. "Sometimes you just have to enjoy life regardless of what happens."

"Good advice, Danny," Pangaea says, slightly sarcastic.

Though her tone was sarcastic, a slight smile appears on her face. It seems Danny did earn her trust. Maybe she and I will be friends one day.

"Can we please just focus?" Zinka interjects. "This is planet Chrysoth. It is a neutral planet and is very open and tolerant of other cultures. So, I don't see any reason why you can't go out and explore but leave your comms on. Is that understood?"

"Roger that, captain," Danny salutes.

"Look, captain," Pangaea says, "I'm just going to stay on the ship. There are too many people out there, and I want to make sure this 'technician' isn't up to any shit." With that Pangaea goes back to her room without another word.

"I am also unsure of the inhabitants of this planet. I will continue my research in the med-bay," Litethite comments.

"Oh, come on Lite, it's a party!" Danny enthusiastically shouts.

"I am unsure of what the appeal is to go out and party, Mr. Danny, but I assure you I will be quite content in the med-bay."

The rest of the crew leaves the docking port to check out the alien planet. Zinka walks up to talk to what I assume is the technician. The aliens on this planet are odd in appearance. Then again, I probably seem abnormal to these people. Their eyes and mouth resemble that of humans. The only difference in the mouth is that they don't have any visible teeth. They also don't have noses or ears. The males have a sort of lion's mane around their face while the females grow hair just in the center of their heads. The hair goes down the center all the to their lower back. Their bodies are similar except they have two extra arms and their knees are bent in the other direction. They use their lower set of arms to aid them in walking, but when not in motion, they stand bipedal.

I take a moment to look at the surroundings. Strange flora dots the landscape. Large plants with spinning, pink flowers surround the outskirts of the landing pad. Smaller plants are scattered around the big ones. They are miniscule by comparison and resemble tiny gray torture spikes. The spikes give a hostile appearance to this world. Lakes of red liquid can be seen in the distance. I'm going to stay away from those. It might kill me. Everything around is strangely familiar and simultaneously foreign.

Odd little creatures hop around which look like a mixture of kangaroos and bullfrogs. The most peculiar thing is that they are eating each other. Well, cannibalism is a thing in the animal kingdom back on Earth. I notice a small insect land on the back of one of the kangaroo frogs. A mouth opens on the stomach of the bug, and it swallows the other creature.

"So," I say turning to the rest of the crew, "what sort of shenanigans does everyone want to get into?"

"Me and Stuan are going to that festival over there," Leonidas says, pointing to a group of buildings and tents that are radiating peculiar lights and sounds. "Apparently today is a global holiday."

"A holiday for what?" Danny wonders.

"I have no idea, but that doesn't mean that I can't enjoy the festival," he smiles.

"Great," I reply. "Hey Danny, you want to smoke another bowl and wander aimlessly around an alien world?"

"That is never a question that you have to ask. Let's do it."

Leo and Stuan make their way off to what I am now going to call The Extraterrestrial Carnival Extravaganza. I notice Zinka making her way back over to us with that look that says she has some very important warning that neither Danny nor I will listen to.

"Alright, listen," Zinka states in a commanding tone. "I need you two idiots to behave yourselves. You're on an alien world, and I expect you to show these people and their culture respect. Is that understood?"

"Calm down, captain lady," Danny speaks up. "We are so respectful. We are the most respectful respecting people that ever respected."

"You guys are just going to smoke pot, aren't you?" She asks raising her eyebrow at us.

"Well yeah, what else would we do?" He asks as though there's literally no other thought in his head.

"Maybe something productive," she deadpans, disapproving.

"Hey," I interject. "Weed is a very productive past time."

"How is it productive, again?" She questions, raising another eyebrow.

"It makes us happy." Danny replies.

"And nothing is more productive than our happiness," I finish.

"Whatever," she gives up, "just don't do anything stupid. I need to go take care of something. You two assholes be good and play nice with the locals."

Zinka turns to depart, leaving Danny and I completely unsupervised. Danny pulls out his pipe and starts to pack it.

"We're going to have a great time here, man," Danny says as he finishes packing his bowl. He then starts to push the pipe towards me. "I think you should have the honor of being the first to smoke up on a new world."

"You sure, man?"

"Yeah, you are way more into space and aliens than I am. I figure this is a much more enlightening experience for you than me."

"Thanks, man. This means a lot to me," I say as I take the bowl and start to light up.

I can feel the smoke fill up my lungs as I perform the standard puff, puff, pass routine. I can slowly start to feel the weed effect my mind, bringing in a blissful fog to my stressful thoughts. The foreign substance starts to chase away the inner demons. The time passes, and the bowl is finished.

The weed making my brain relax gives me a moment to take a more in-depth look at the surroundings of my current location. The trees, or what I assume are trees, are tall. There are no branches or really anything. They pretty much are just sticks in the mud. Though their bright purple color is a bit weird. Well, I am not a hundred percent sure whether they are purple, or if this pot is laced with something. Usually, Danny is good about not getting the laced shit. He hates hard drugs and believes they give weed a bad name. That makes the first option so much more likely.

I look down and see that we are still on the landing pad. We are still surrounded by the spinning flowers, but all the animals are gone. Maybe the weed caused them to scatter. It seems plausible, since it isn't a natural substance here.

"Hey, man," Danny interrupts my zoning out. "Want to go wander around town and gawk at random things?"

"Yeah, why not?" I reply.

Danny and I start making our way down the street, staring at the random buildings lining the roads. The architecture is hard to explain. Buildings tilt in odd directions. Most of them appear very fragile, like the slightest breeze would bring them down. The small furry frog kangaroos dash around at our feet.

"I···can···see···your···fuuuuuuuuuuuuttttttttuuuuuurrrrrrreeeeeee!" A loud voice interrupts my thoughts.

"What the hell?" I can't catch myself before exclaiming aloud.

"I···know···all···and···foretell···all···nothing···escapes···my···vision s!"

We trace the yelling to an odd local. The man is dressed in odd clothing. Why the hell does everything on this planet seem odd? I guess that is what happens on an alien world.

"Hello···outsiders!" The strange man yells while I'm right in front of him.

"Dude, why are you yelling?" Danny questions.

"I···knew···you···would···ask···that···fuuuuuttttuuuurrrrrreeeeee!"

"Right," I reply. "Now what do you want, man?"

"Of···course···I···could···see···your···fuuuuuuuuuuuutttttttttttttuuuuuurr rrreeee!"

"Uh, that's not what I asked," I'm confused.

"Come···and···touch···me···and···I'll···tell···you···your···fuuuuuuttttt tttuuuuuurrrrreeee!"

"Am... am I going to get molested?" I question.

"Only···if···you···want···me···toooooooo!" The strange man yells.

"Hmmm," Danny pitches in. "Maybe... I'll let you know later. Now what was that about seeing the future?"

"I···can···see···eeevvvveeerrryyyyything!" The old man screams as he motions to the entrance of an ancient, decayed home.

Danny and I simply exchange a glance and a shrug before following the odd stranger into his house. Now, the inside of this home isn't exactly nice or pretty or pleasant smelling. The inside is almost as bizarre as the outside.

"Now," the old man finally appears to find his inside voice. "Come have a seat and I shall tell you all that you can know."

The old man then takes a seat. It is a little disturbing watching a man whose legs bend the opposite direction sitting down. I'm not sure if that makes me an intolerant racist or not. I mean, at the very least, I should feel ignorant.

I look around as I manage to sit on the oddly shaped piece of furniture. There are candles burning along the walls. Unfortunately, the candles do not, in fact, smell nice in any way shape or form. Pretty sure they make everything smell worse. I'm not sure how that happens. To each their own though.

"Let me grab your appendage so I can see the visions before me."

"Yeah." I interject. "I am pretty sure that I'm going to get molested."

He replies defensively. "No, no sir, your gripping appendage."

"I'm not gripping my appendage."

"Dude," Danny leans in. "I think he means your arm."

"Right, right," I say.

My arm extends up towards the stranger and he grips it with his spider-like fingers. The pupils of his eyes draw back into his head and his body starts to convulse rapidly. The grip he has on my arm begins to tighten to the point of pain. Eons seem to pass before his eyes snap open and he stutters his vision.

"Y-you have a dark future ahead of you." He takes a breath before continuing. "People you hold close to you will die. I foresee a plethora of betrayal coming your way. Finally, your compassion will be the downfall of all."

"Well, that's just depressing." I try to comprehend the information given.

"Dude," Danny interrupts. "I wouldn't worry too much about it."

"Do you think he's wrong?"

"I have no idea, but we don't actually know what he meant."

"I could answer all of your questions," the old man offers to clarify.

Me and Danny glance at him before turning back to our conversation.

"What could he mean then?" I ask as Danny and I stand up and start walking to the exit of the building.

"Hey," the future dude yells after us, "the reading wasn't free."

Danny and I leave the broken-down old house and walk into the twilight of outside. The strange smells of the foreign planet fill my nostrils. Oddly enough, it is a delightful change of pace from the inside of the hovel. We begin walking through town.

"Well maybe the whole people dying thing actually means that people are dying to... party. You know, after we win," Danny tries to look at the bright side as we continue down the street.

"That seems highly unlikely."

The carnival lights shine as we get closer to the fair.

"And maybe the whole plethora of betrayal thing is actually just some kinky sex position."

"So, you think an interstellar orgy is what the old dude meant?" I question.

The smell of alien food fills my nostrils, and it smells quite good.

"Yeah man, why not? Plethora of betrayal definitely sounds like one of those Kama Sutra things." Danny replies. "And that shtick of that compassion will be your downfall, he never said whose downfall that was."

"Yeah he did. He said it would be the downfall of all."

"Maybe he got it wrong. You never know. Or maybe his vision got interrupted. Maybe he meant it would be the downfall of all villains."

"That makes sense, I guess." I think for a moment. "Wait, what about that whole dark future thing?"

"Maybe you forgot to pay the electric bill."

CHAPTER 9

We reach the carnival, and my ear drums are assaulted by strange alien music. The music is happy, though. It seems like really upbeat music to dance to.

The strange sights around me catch my attention. I see strange games and rides surrounding me. My eyes catch sight of a strange-looking game. I don't know what the hell it is or what you do in it, but that has never stopped me before. I turn to Danny.

"Hey man, let's go play that game."

"What is it?" He questions.

"I have no idea, but let's go. How hard can it be?"

Danny and I make our way over to the crudely made stand. The being at the stand greets us with a strange accent.

"Heellllo," the strange creature drawls. "You gentlemen want to play a game? It's real simple, even for outsiders like you."

I speak up. "Well, what do you do in it? Like, how do you win?"

The stand-owner speaks up, "Well, it's simple. All you do is take the blatnort and try to throw it in the caper hole. If you get it in the wingle crevice, you automatically lose though. If you somehow make the ball sit on the hoovian pedestal, however, then you get to pick one of our upper-class prizes."

"Hmmmm," I hum. "So, I do what with the what?"

Danny answers, "Throw the ball and either aim for the hole or land it on the pedestal. Avoid that crack. You lose if your ball falls in the crack."

"Alright, so... just throw the ball and hope for the best," I say as I take the ball from the odd stand-owner.

My focus falls on the ball and then I put my focus back on the pedestal thingy, the crack thingy, and the hole thingy. You know what, screw it. The ball sails through the air. It arches upwards and goes towards the board. The ball finally touches down and somehow it magically stays on the pedestal thingy. That seems like it goes against physics. Round balls are supposed to roll, not just stop. Take that, Einstein.

"Wait," I say. "That means I win, right?"

The stand owner just stares at the board in shock. He was not expecting me to do it. I showed him. At least I think I did. He finally manages to speak.

"Well, it looks like the outsider got lucky. Just go ahead and pick a prize from this wall over here," he gestures towards the wall on the side.

There are odd prizes adorning the wall. Everything looks so strange and yet, somehow, still so boring. Most of them appear to be shiny or flashy trinkets.

Finally, my eyes land on an odd snow globe. It isn't the globe itself that fascinates me, though. It's what's inside. In the globe is, well, a globe or more precise my globe. Hovering inside of it is a smaller replica of the Earth. My home.

"I'll take that," I say as I point to the snow globe.

"Sure thing, stranger," the owner saunters over and grabs the knick-knack for me.

When he places the globe in my hand, I can't look away from it. This is my home. This is my planet. It isn't an exact replica, but it is still close. Danny's voice breaks me from my thoughts.

"Holy shit, man. That looks like Earth."

"Yeah," I reply. "Yeah, I know it does, man. I know."

"Well, now you always have something to remember it," he says.

Danny and I walk away, and I place the globe in my pocket. We stroll down the roads of the fair. Along the way, we look at the foreign sights around us, but nothing really catches our attention. That is, until Danny's hand bashes me in the chest.

"Oooof. What the hell, Danny?" I question.

"Look over there, dude," he says as he points.

I follow his finger and see Stuan and Leonidas sitting on a bench. Stuan appears to be sleeping with her head resting on Leonidas' shoulder. It looks absolutely adorable. Ah, to be young and in love and⋯ an alien.

"Come on," Danny says quietly. "We probably shouldn't disturb them."

Danny starts walking away, and I follow. I give one last look at the cute E.T. lovey-dovey shit.

"Hey, man!" Danny yells three inches away from my ear. "Let's go on that thing."

I see him pointing and follow his finger to a weird looking ride. All I see is a giant metal ball. Everything in space is metallic and spherical. There is absolutely no one in line and the ride operator looks thrilled to be there. His face is the same as every ride operator that I have ever seen on Earth. An expression made up of boredom with a pinch self-loathing.

"I don't know," I'm skeptical. "What does that thing even do?"

"Well, that's part of the fun. We don't know, but we can have fun finding out."

"Ugh, fine," I concede.

Danny jumps up and down like a child at Christmas. He then drags me to the ride.

"You two want to ride?" The operator questions in a monotone.

"Yeah, we do. Come on Thad, let's go, let's go, let's go." Danny says as he pulls me into the strange metallic sphere.

There is nothing inside the sphere. There are no seats or safety bars or anything to hold on to. The metal sphere has soft padding inside of it. This gives me some comfort. The comfort is momentary at best, though.

"So...." I say looking around the sphere. "What happens n--"

A loud noise interrupts me and a strong force pushes me flat against the floor. This does not feel safe. I can feel the sphere ascending towards the sky as my body remains pinned to the floor.

"What the hell?!" I yell to no one in particular.

The force pushes and keeps me on the ground. I look over to Danny and see the largest smile spread across his face. I am pretty sure I am going to die, and Danny will die with a smile on his face. The sphere slows down as it stops going up. Then it starts to fall. I go from being pinned to the floor to being pinned to the roof. This is it. I'm going to die. My space adventure is over, and it just started. Good bye, cruel universe. I feel my body then crash to the padding on the ground miraculously unscathed.

"Get me out of here!" my shrill voice screams as I bust open the door.

"Damn," the ride operator mocks, "It's just the rocket simulator. Calm down, you big baby."

"Simulator?" I question. "You have got to be kidding me."

"Woo!" Danny yells as he leaves the sphere.

"Dude, did you know that was just a simulation?" I ask.

"Of course. Didn't you?"

My response is an annoyed stare.

"What the hell was that?" I ask.

He replies, "I think that may be the communicator that Zinka gave me. But now the question is, how do I answer this thing?"

"Hmmm, I don't know. Just start hitting buttons. It can't be that hard, right?" I reply.

Danny starts pressing random buttons on the odd circular device until Zinka's face pops up on the screen.

"Danny, Little Balls." Zinka addresses us. "You need to get back to the ship, right now."

"Zinka?" I question. "What happened?"

"No time to explain," Zinka says in a rush. "Just get here now. Everyone else is on their way."

With that, she cuts the call. Danny and I give each other a quick look before we both bolt for the ship. We move our way through the crowd, trying to get back. I have no idea what's going on, but if Zinka is that worried, then it can't be good. We make our way up the entrance ramp to the ship and the door closes right behind us. As soon as it closes, the craft begins to rise.

Danny and I run to the cockpit, where Zinka is trying to furiously pilot the ship out of the atmosphere. She is all concentration, and her hands move swiftly around the control panel.

"Zinka?" I ask. "What happened?"

"Well, it's Pangaea," she replies without removing her eyes from the controls.

Upon hearing this, Danny jumps in. "What's wrong with Pangaea?" He asks.

"Nothing is wrong with her, but something is wrong with the technician."

"Oh god," Danny says. "What did he do?"

"Well, she was watching the technician fix the core. After he finished fixing the core, he then decided to, well, get a little handsy with all four of his hands."

"She put him in the morgue?" Danny asks.

"No, she just broke three of his arms and one leg," she answers. "Then he started screaming and dragging his body out of the ship. Luckily, he finished fixing it before this little⋯ transgression occurred."

"See," Danny says instantly brightening up. "She's getting better. She could have throat stomped him. We all know she can do it."

"Yeah, but we need to get out of their space zone," Zinka says. "They won't go past it, but we cannot go back there now."

"I hope you don't blame her for that," Danny says with concern.

"No," Zinka replies. "Hell, I would have done the same thing. That doesn't change the fact that we have to leave, though."

"I'm going to talk with Pangaea to make sure she's okay."

Danny leaves the cockpit, forgetting that we are still technically in danger. I guess we are actually in danger. To be perfectly honest, I don't feel threatened by them in the slightest. Something about them just makes them not very frightening.

"And we are out," Zinka says as she types in the coordinates and stands up.

"So, we're safe then?" I ask.

"We should be for now. I don't know for how long, though. We do still have to deal with Derask."

"Alright, you do that; I'm going to take a nap," I yawn. "I feel tired and this whole lack of Earth's rotation is really screwing with my internal clock."

"You sleep a lot; have a good nap."

I leave the cockpit and head to my cabin. The only thing that can be heard is the soft taps of my footsteps. Everything else seems silent. That feels odd, considering we were in danger moments ago.

That was an interesting shore leave, to say the least. The door to my cabin opens and I'm greeted with the bright fluorescent lighting. I light a cig and sit on my bed, breathing in the smoke before I lay down. My head is filled with random thoughts. I think about when Leo and Stuan will hook-up. Now that's not a perverted thought mind you. I'm just curious. I think about why everyone tries to molest Pangaea. It's not like she's ugly by any means but it just seems like she always gets that sort of attention. Lastly, I wonder why the hell Derask saved President Landon. That dude is an idiot. Any other person would have been more competent. A potato would have been more competent.

I extinguish the butt of my cigarette in the ashtray and lay my head down. My eyes close and darkness greets me. All thoughts evaporate from my mind.

CHAPTER 10

The world around me is, well, Earth. I don't see fire or anything. Just normal, boring Earth. People are walking around like any other day. Was all that crap just a dream? Don't understand what's happening here.

There is a woman walking a stroller. There is a kid flying a kite. There is a dog taking a shit. Isn't it all just wonderful? I look around and see that I'm standing in the yard of my parents' house. How did that happen? Was I drunk again? Wouldn't be the first time I drunk-walked to my parents' place. At least this time, I'm wearing pants.

"Honey," My mom's voice calls from the house. "Come in dear. Your date will be here soon. You have to get ready."

God, I missed my mom. Wait, date? I don't go on dates. I spend my weekends playing video games and getting fat.

"Okay mom. I···I'm coming," I say, still confused by everything.

Going into the house, the familiar sights bring a smile to my face. All confusion aside, this is an amazing feeling. It's my home. Life is good again. As soon as I enter the house, I am enveloped in a big hug by my mom. I return the embrace happily.

"Come on honey," she says as she releases me, "Your date will be here any second now. So, go get ready. You don't want to make the poor dear wait, now do you?"

"Uh⋯yeah mom. I'll, uh, I'll go do that now."

I make my way up the all too familiar stairs towards my old room. The house seems quiet. I don't hear my dad or my sister. They may be out. I'm sure it's nothing to worry about.

With nice clothes on, the sound of the doorbell ringing catches my attention.

"Thaddeus," My mom calls. "Your date is here."

"I'm coming, mom."

Descending the stairs, my mind wanders to one thing. How the hell did I get a date? Women don't like me. They find my appearance unappealing and my personality too nerdy. I come around the corner and see my mom in the living room. The person sitting next to her was someone that I wasn't expecting.

"Holy shit, Zinka?" I question.

My mom scolds, "Thad, language."

"Uh, sorry mom. Uhm, hey Zinka. You look very⋯nice."

That wasn't a lie. She did look pretty good. Which is odd, considering she is an alien. Do I think a space bug lady is sexy? What the hell is wrong with me? I'm going to blame internet porn for making her appealing to me. Dammit porn.

Zinka runs over to me and puckers her lips. She is doing the whole fish face thing. Is⋯is she going to kiss me? She stops and begins to speak though.

"Wakey, Wakey," a voice is calling in my ear.

It comes from her mouth, but it is not her voice. It sounds like Danny.

"Eggs and Bacey."

What the hell is a bacey?

A loud shout causes me to immediately sit up.

"What? What happened?" I come to staring up into Danny's smiling face.

He replies, "Zinka says that we are now at Demer and we have to go to the docking port."

"Stupid internet porn," I mumble.

"Uh⋯what?" Danny questions.

"Oh⋯uh, never mind. Let's go, man."

I stand up sluggishly and follow Danny out of my room towards the docking port. The dream keeps playing on repeat in my thoughts. What the hell did that mean? Am⋯ am I attracted to a space bug? I'll figure that out later. We reach the room and see the rest of the crew sitting there waiting for us. We are always the last ones.

"Alright," Zinka addresses the crew. "We need to go in a small group to avoid any interstellar conflict. Little Balls, Danny, you two are with me on the surface. Leonidas, you are in charge while we are away. Now back to you two," she turns her attention to me and Danny. "You guys better be on your best behavior. I'm taking a big chance bringing you two, so you better not make me regret it. Understood?"

"Aye aye, captain," I say with another mock salute.

Yet again, my reward is an eye roll. One day her eyes are going to roll right out of her head or at least that is what my mother always told me.

We follow Zinka outside, and we are greeted with an alien race that could only be described as space Cthulhu. They look badass, like something out of a Lovecraftian horror story.

"Now we are meeting my contact at a pub up ahead. Do both of you have your communication necklace on?" Zinka questions as we keep moving.

"Yes, ma'am space lady," Danny replies.

"Yup, it's on," I confirm.

"Good, the Demerians don't have these so you will need them to communicate."

We walk through a city street that looks empty when you consider the immense size of the buildings. I guess they have all that extra space because over half of their population were wiped out by Derask. We are going to make damn sure that that son of a bitch pays for what he did, but there may be a line forming on who gets to pull the trigger.

I take a moment to survey the rest of my surroundings. Nothing out of the ordinary. There's green plant life and a bluish tint to the sky. The only thing off about it is the double moons.

We approach a building with strange writing on it and follow Zinka inside. Bars on other planets are just like the ones on Earth. They are

filled with sad souls just trying to drown out their sorrows. We follow
Zinka to a back table where a much larger space Cthulhu is sitting.
God damn this dude is ripped.

"Hello Tik," Zinka greets as the large Cthulhu stands up to
welcome us.

The being is easily eight feet tall.

"Hey Zinkatianalynn." His massive arms envelop her in a hug.

"These are two humans who joined the rebellion," Zinka motions
towards us. "This is Danny and Little Balls."

Seriously, why am I still Little Balls?

She continues. "How did the meeting with the council go?"

"I have bad news," Tik intones. "The council will not give military
backing. They feel it will be a suicide mission. They think our
resources will be better used continuing the work on the faux womb."

"Faux womb?" I interrupt.

"Since the genocide, we have been working on a way to reproduce
without females. We need to continue our species. We are trying to
breed artificial eggs with our own DNA in a large-scale incubator."

"Don't they see that if Derask isn't stopped, even if they do
manage to save their population, he will just come back and do it all
over again?" Zinka laments.

Well, it sounds like we will get no support from the Demerians. Oh
well, we've still got hope. I gaze around the bar as Zinka and Tik
continue talking. They seem entirely enthralled in their conversation.
Then something catches my eye: alien alcohol. I nudge Danny and we
sneak away from Zinka.

"Hey man, you want to go try some alien booze?" I ask.

"Yay, getting drunk," he replies as we make our way over to the
bar.

We get to the bar and I come to a profound realization: "Wait
Danny, we don't have any currency. We are entirely broke and for
once, I have an excuse besides my job being terrible."

"Hey, not a problem," the bartender cuts into our conversation.
"It's pretty clear you two are visitors. The first one is on the house,"
he says as he pushes two fluorescent green drinks towards us.

"Hey thanks, man," I say as I pick up my drink and hand Danny his.

However, before we could even get a sip, Danny and I each get a very hard slap to the back of the skull. Before we know what's happening, two green hands take away our drinks.

"What do you idiots think you're doing?!" Zinka gives us a death stare that would terrify even the heartless bastards known as televangelists. She explains, "This stuff is acidic towards humans. Drink it and you will die a horrible, painful death, you morons."

"Jesus," I whine, "I think I have a migraine from all of the shouting."

"Then stop being an idiot and don't do things that will kill you.".

"You are a very angry space lady," Danny murmurs.

"Idiots," she walks away.

Tik just watches the scene play out, before he finally busts out laughing. "Ah, to be young again." He's still chuckling as he follows Zinka out of the bar.

Danny and I just stare at each other and shrug before we follow them. Apparently, they are going to talk to the Demerian Council.

We come upon a giant building. Holy shit, it's a god damn mansion. This council has got to be filthy rich. Tik approaches the guards at the entrance.

"We request a meeting with the council. It is of the utmost importance," Tik explains to an extremely heavily armed guard. The dude looks like a walking armory.

"Is this about your revolution again, Tik?" the guard asks in a clearly exasperated tone.

"Yes, you fool. We need to convince the council that Derask needs taken care of, once and for all."

"Fine, but don't come crying to me when they shoot you down again," the guard shrugs as he turns to lead us to the council.

"We will take our chances," Tik seems to have hope they'll succeed this time.

As we navigate our way through the maze of corridors, I can't help but gawk at the art decorating the hallways, and the lavish amount of gold.

He then leads us to this ridiculously over-sized door. Why is the door so big? Why do I keep asking myself these questions? I think I may be going insane. Damn, too bad I can't get therapy anymore.

Somewhere during my self-monologue, the guard has opened the door, so we follow him inside. I see three beings sitting in floating chairs and wearing elaborate decorative robes. Everything is very fancy here.

"What do you want now, Tik?" the center floaty man asks in a deep voice.

"Your Honors," Tik takes a knee and bows his head. "We must give aid to the rebellion. Derask must be stopped."

"With all due respect, Tik," left floaty man says with a snooty tone, "We have to focus on the continuation of our species. If we get involved in this rebellion, then our species will surely perish."

"Well, with all due respect, Councilor Shab," Tik counters, "Did you happen to forget what that bastard did to our race? Did you forget all the innocents who died by his hand?"

"That's enough, Tik!" Right floaty man's voice cuts him off. "We need to have our priorities in order. Our top priority is to perfect the faux womb. Now if you will kindly exit my court and never step foot in--"

Unexpectedly, a section of the windows behind them bursts. The shock-wave causes the middle floating man to fall on the floor. I look up to see a robed individual standing in the middle of the other two council members. The large door behind me shatters as armed guards flood into the meeting room.

"Freeze!" shouts the guard who let us in.

The guard has his laser pointed at the cloaked figure, who doesn't even seem to care. The cloaked man throws what looks like a weird computer screen on the floor. We all get distracted momentarily by the strange device and wonder what kind of weapon it is.

The assassin pulls two guns out of his sleeve and points one at each of the councilmen. Before anyone has time to react, the man pulls the triggers and splatters the two council members' heads on the adjacent walls. Purple blood drips down the gold paint. The guards move quickly, running to protect the last Council member while simultaneously firing a barrage of blasts from their weapons.

Oddly enough, the assassin seems to dance away from the blasts. He contorts his body in the strangest of ways, as if it were entirely malleable. He then swirls his way out the window and vanishes from sight. The guards help the surviving councilman up and check him for injuries, as I pick up the strange device that we all forgot about in the chaos.

"What the hell is this thing?" I ask as I hand the strange device to Zinka.

"It's a message pad," she hits the button on the strange device.

"Hello, children. I do hope you enjoyed the show," Derask's voice oozes from the message pad.

I tear it out of Zinka's hand as I bring my face an inch away from the screen. "Fuck off, you sadistic prick," I shout at the inanimate piece of tech in my grasp, but he just continues.

"Now, I'm guessing at this point your little pet has decided to scream obscenities at the screen. Don't bother, primitive. This is a prerecorded message," he laughs that same grating laugh. "And before you say anything, no, the guards did not save the councilor's life. I told her to keep one alive."

The assassin is a she?

"I hope you enjoyed the company of Elisar, though she is quieter than most Tauranians are. I believe you humans call them the Grays. I digress. I bet you are wondering why I instructed Elisar to spare a counselor."

Well yes, I am, you prick. On a side note, I guess Grays do exist. Maybe there is some merit to the whole abduction thing.

"Well it's quite simple, actually. You see, if one Demerian Council member is left alive, then it will be easier to incite them to join your pathetic cause. Why would I do this, you may ask?"

Why do villains always go on long monologues about their evil plan? Why do they always have long convoluted plans? Stories would be so much shorter if they just did what they wanted to do.

"Well, long story short, it makes it much more enjoyable to me. I could have destroyed Earth with Zinkatianalynn still on it. I could have stopped your little rescue mission on Prison AA54. I could have destroyed Demer in a heartbeat, before you even got there. But that would end our little game, and this is just way too much fun for me to give up now. So, I decided to help you on Demer. Oh, there is no need to thank me." Derask finishes as the screen goes to static.

"Now what's the plan?" I ask.

"We do as he wishes," the Councilor decrees.

"Sir," Tik interjects, "Do you really want to play Derask's game?"

"If he wants a war, we will give him one." The Councilor continues, "I'd rather die on my feet than live on my knees, cowering before that monster."

"Thank you, Councilor Tronce," Zinka bows. "We appreciate your support."

"I was hoping that he would leave us alone long enough so we could perfect the womb, but if this is how my race will go extinct, then so be it. The fleet will be assembled and awaiting your command when you need them."

"We will first head to Goro and Nebul to try and gain their support. I will give the word when we are ready for the final assault," Zinka lays out her plan. "We will make him regret letting us live."

She proceeds to the exit, with me, Danny, and Tik in tow.

"Tik, what are you doing?" She asks as she turns towards the man.

"I'm joining you. I'd go crazy waiting to join the action. Plus, you and your friends seem like an interesting bunch."

"As long as you behave," she warns him. "I already have two children to babysit." She motions towards me and Danny. "I definitely do not need another one."

"Hey!" Danny protests. "I'll have you know that I am a grown ass man. Now let's get back to the ship. I need a snack and maybe a nap."

We make our way back to the ship, where Zinka introduces Tik to the rest of the crew. So now we have eight on this ship, plus a small militia from Demer to help us stop Derask. Our chances just keep getting better and better. In no time, we will be able to kill him, maybe.

I decide that I like Danny's idea of a nap, and head to my cabin. Literally just woke up from a nap before we landed on Demer, but I'm tired dammit. I sit in my bed and light a cig before I go to sleep. With puff after puff, I can't help but think what a controversial topic aliens were on Earth and here I am, in space with four alien species, trying to save what's left of the universe. Well, galaxy, considering I can't get to the rest of the universe.

For the first time, the full weight of the situation hits me. If we fail, then all planets will meet the same fate as Earth. I can't let that happen. I promise you, mom, that I will do what I can to help everyone I possibly can. With one last puff, the cigarette dies.

I lay my head down. My eyelids close, and all around me fades to black.

CHAPTER 11

I look around and see nothing. Just blackness, as far as my eyes can see. Does it count as seeing? I mean, no light means no sight. So, I guess lack of seeing would be a better description.

Suddenly, laughing assaults my ears. It's coming from all around me, like it is echoing off the vast nothingness surrounding me. It's that damn cliched laugh again.

"Poor little lost monkey," the bodiless voice croons. "I will make your kind extinct! All you are doing is prolonging the inevitable."

The voice laughs and laughs and laughs, like my torment is the funniest thing ever. The laugh invades my eardrums, and I can feel it bouncing off the insides of my skull. It then fills my sight with horrid images.

I can see my dad caught in a massive explosion. Only the vision was in slow motion, so I had to watch him suffer. I watch his skin peel off, exposing muscle tissue. Then the tissue starts to tear away with the force of the blast. I can hear his pain-filled screams.

The vision then changes to that of my mom being crushed by flying debris. Yet again, the vision is in slow motion. I watch as my mother is crushed between two objects. I can hear and see each bone snap and break, some ripping through the skin with a sickening tearing sound.

The next vision is the worst. I see my little baby sister laying in her crib. It lights aflame. I can hear her little pain filled cries as I can do nothing but watch her flesh melt. I can't take the god damn visions anymore.

I fill up my lungs and let out all my anguish in one guttural scream.

My eyes snap open, and I see Zinka almost bust the door down with a gun raised and ready to fire. I control the shaking as I hug my knees to my chest. I feel wetness streaking down my cheeks. I just sit there and cry as the horrid visions stay burned into my skull. I feel arms wrap around me and pull me close.

"Shhhhh, it's okay Little Balls. It's okay."

I feel a gentle stroking on my back. The scent of cookie dough, which has now become a security blanket, washes over my senses. I try with everything in my power to hold it back, but nothing I do seems to work. Everything just makes it worse. I let all my frustration, sadness, and loss release from my eyes till nothing but quiet sobs come out. As my sorrow temporarily ebbs, I feel a sense of calm come over me. I unfold my knees from my chest and look at the concern in Zinka's face.

"Thank you, it was just a nightmare. I'm fine now," I say once I get my breath back.

"It's no problem. Are you going to be okay?" She is clearly still worried about me.

"I'll live."

I reach on the table for my pack of cigs and light one up. I take a sharp inhale hoping it will calm my nerves.

"Was it about your family?" She asks, still rubbing soothing circles on my back.

"Yeah, it... it was horribly realistic. Everyone I cared about was dying and there was nothing I could do to stop it. I... I failed them. I failed everyone."

"There was nothing you could do for them, but you can still do so much for so many living things in the galaxy. They need you and so does this crew. Your family would be proud."

I take a moment to think about what she said, and she does have a point. There is still so much I can do. I could help prevent anyone else from suffering the same fate as me. Wallowing in my despair won't do any good. Zinka's voice breaks me out of my thoughts.

"What were they like? Your family, I mean. What type of people were they?" She asks. I let out a chuckle just thinking about it.

"Well, my Dad, he was one hell of a man. He taught me that you should never take life too seriously. By the end of it, we all wind up in the same place. He taught me a person's worth isn't the size of their checkbook or the size of their house. A person's worth is only measured by how he treats others. Not to mention he was the toughest person you could ever meet. I remember this one time he came in from working in the garage. He had cut off his finger. He showed my mom and she started freaking out. Asking 'oh my god what happened? what happened?' and my dad looks her right in the eyes and says with a chuckle in his voice, 'Well, you always said I wasn't handy.' She was not impressed." I finished with a chuckle as I recounted the tale. "Not to mention the tough bastard beat cancer when the doctors only gave him weeks to live."

"So that explains where you got your carefree attitude and stubbornness from." She says with a slight smile in her voice.

"And my mom," I continue. "My mom was always so damn proud of me. No matter what I did she would always tell people how she is proud of the man I became. Even when I felt like a total failure. She was always the one I went to when I was feeling down. She always knew what to say or what to do to make me smile again. Not going to lie, I was always a bit of a mama's boy. I remember when we first found out my dad had cancer. That was the first time I ever saw her cry. Seeing her like that made me angrier than I ever was before that. I tried to fight the doctor that told us because I was six and didn't understand. I didn't know what cancer was, but I assumed it was the doctor's fault that my dad had it and my mom was crying."

"And that explains your ego and hero complex," she says smiling at my story.

"And finally, there's my baby sister Lilly," my voice takes a sadder tone. "I have no idea what type of person she would've grown up to be. She was only five months old. She loved me though. Every time I visited my parents, she would reach for me and would always let out this little sob when I put her down. She liked to pull my hair and play peek-a-boo. She was so innocent."

A hand falls on my shoulder, and I look up to a very determined look on Zinka's face.

"Don't worry," she reassures. "We will find Derask. We will kill him. We will stop him from tearing apart any more families. He will suffer. Now come on, I have a surprise for you." She stands up and motions for me to follow.

I shrug and stand up. I follow her out of my room and down a corridor. She leads me to a door with strange writing on it. I really need to learn how to read that. She punches a few buttons on a keypad next to it. The door slides open with the typical swoosh sound you'd expect a secret door to make. I look in and see stairs. I did not know the ship had another floor.

"Come on up here." She grabs the sleeve of my shirt and drags me up the damn stairs.

We get to a small hallway with only two doors, one on each side. She pulls me to the one on the right and opens the door. When my eyes catch the sight inside, they go wide, and my mouth seems to have forgotten how to make words.

Now, there was nothing special about the room itself. It only had a small table and a couple chairs, but that's not what caught my eye. The walls of this room were entirely made of windows that could look out into the vastness of space. I can see planets and stars. I can see gas clouds and asteroid belts. I can see the universe in its actual glory without being masked by the atmosphere of the Earth.

"Up here is my private space," Zinka says. "The room on the other side is my room and this," she motions towards the window, "is where I come to clear my head. I know that nothing I can do can alleviate your pain or loss, but I know how much you liked to look at the sky down on Earth and so," she hands me a piece of paper with strange symbols on it, "you can come here whenever you like."

"What's this?" I examine the piece of paper.

"That's the code for the keypad downstairs. Like I said, whenever you need to clear your head or take away the stress, maybe this will help."

I look down at the paper, then back up into the immensity of space.

"Thank you, Zinka," I say. "And not just for this. Thank you for what you did in my room and thank you from stopping me from doing stupid shit."

"Someone has to make sure you don't maim yourself," she smiles at me.

Why does my brain go stupid every time she does that?

"Just stay here for as long as you like. I need to double check the coordinates I have set for Goro."

She takes her leave, and I'm left with my thoughts and the view. I look out at all the stars, letting my mind wander. Slowly the stress and anxiety melt away. The horrid vision of my nightmare seems to temporarily recede. My mind is at ease. I look out and see a star in the distance that I can't seem to look away from. It's large and round. Its surface burns with a bright orange glow just like... Zinka's eyes. God dammit, I think I have a weird crush on an alien woman.

I guess there are only two options now that I know of. Option one, I grow some balls and tell her how I feel, which will possibly lead to rejection, heartbreak, and ridicule. Option two, I do nothing and simply take this secret with me to the grave. Option two seems to be the best choice.

A strong odor enters my nose. The foul stench assaults my senses. Sniffing around the room, I finally pinpoint the source of the stink. Turns out that it's me. A shower is extremely necessary. After taking one last look out the massive window, I exit the room and head towards my own cabin. A pink tingly shower may be just the thing to clear my head. The door to my room opens revealing the mostly empty space. My clothes are thrown to the floor as I enter the wash room. I make sure to empty my bladder first. Don't know why my bladder didn't need to be emptied before this.

After turning on the shower, the faucet spits out the pink goop. I step inside of it and let the tingles wash all over me. The strange liquid washes away my thoughts as it massages my skin.

"Hey, buddy. Can you pass the shampoo?" A voice behind me asks.

I let out a scream that isn't exactly manly.

My body spins around and my hands snap down to cover my junk. I see the smiling face of a naked Danny staring back at me. When the hell did he get here? He doesn't seem to care about being nude in a shower with me. I care though. I am very self-conscious about my body.

"Danny, what the hell are you doing in my bath tub?"

"Well I was taking a nap, but someone turned on the shower, so I figured it was time to wake up."

"You were napping in my bathtub? Why?"

"It's more comfortable than mine," he replies as though it's perfectly normal to sleep in a bathtub.

"Okay. Why are you naked?" I ask the stoned man.

"Because it's a bathtub. Who wears clothes in a bathtub? Need someone to wash your back?" He smiles and holds up a brush.

"No thanks," I reply. "Well, if you would be so kind could you give me some privacy? I kind of like to shower alone."

Danny shrugs his shoulders before he exits the shower and leaves my room. Yup, he is still naked. He is just going to walk down the hall··· naked. I wonder if anyone will see him?

"What the hell?" I hear Zinka's voice shout. "Where are your clothes?"

"In my room," he replies breezily.

"Why aren't they on your body?"

"Because if they were, then they wouldn't be in my room."

"Go put on your clothes, Danny," Zinka deadpans.

"Aye, aye, captain."

I can't refrain from shaking my head. The goo continues to run over my body. I finish cleaning myself and leave. I pick up my old uniform and throw it down the provided chute. After getting dressed, my mind is cleared of all the thoughts from the nightmare. My stomach growls after a new uniform adorns my body.

Huh, damn. I need a bite to eat. I leave the room and head towards the mess hall. My brain is not really focused on where I'm going until I run into a body. The body is smaller than me, so it fell but I remain standing. I look down to see a very angry Pangaea staring up at me with pure abhorrence in her eyes.

"Oops, sorry. Here, let me help you," I extend a hand towards her to help her up, but she swats it away and stands up.

"I don't need your help," she spits out as she turns to walk away.

"Everyone needs help sometimes," I say with a shrug.

I really need to learn to watch what I say. She spins around on her heels and glares at me.

"I don't need your help, or anyone's help. Do you understand that? Only the weak need help."

"And we are all weak sometimes, so my point still stands."

Seriously, mouth, stop saying words.

"No, you are weak sometimes. Face it: you couldn't save the Earth, you couldn't save the ones you care about, so what makes you think you can save the rest of the galaxy?"

"Are you talking to me or that wall over there?" I take a cowardly cheap shot at her lazy eye.

Insert foot in mouth. As soon as that sentence leaves my mouth, I regret it. It seriously looks like she's fighting back tears. She has been through more than I can imagine. I am mocking a person's appearance. I am no better than President Landon. Though her comment stung, I should have been more understanding. Why am I such a dick? My parents taught me better. Sorry mom.

"Look," I start. "I didn't mean that, I'm just..."

"Fuck off, you jerk." She grabs something and throws it at my head.

Yet again, I barely dodge it and rush down the hall, away from the incensed female. Seriously, where the hell is she getting the stuff to throw at me? I look back mid-run and see that she isn't chasing me. She is just sitting on the floor with her back against the wall and her head buried in her knees. I get a flashback of moments ago, of me in the same position. Zinka was there to help me. I look and see nobody is around. Nobody to help her out except me. Dammit.

Well, it looks like this is how I'm going to die. I make my way back over to her. Be brave dammit. Be brave dammit. Be brave dammit. I repeat this mantra in my head, trying to build up my confidence. It's not working. I am now standing over her. She hasn't even noticed I'm here. From this close, I can hear her low saddened sobs. I kneel next to her and put my hand on her shoulder. She jumps to her feet, the sudden motion causing me to fall on my ass. I feel as though I have spent a good portion of this adventure on my ass.

"What do you want?" She glares daggers at me.

"Well, a couple things," I say as I stand up. "First off, I wanted to see if you're okay. Second off, I wanted to apologize for being a jackass. Or would that be better the other way around? Whichever one seems more appropriate, I guess."

"Yes, I'm fine. I'm wonderful. I'm fucking peachy. There, happy? Now leave me alone." Pangaea begins to walk away, but before she can leave, my hand grabs her by the shoulder.

This may have been a mistake. She turns towards me and bats my hand away from her. She grabs an object that hangs from the wall. I'm going to get another thing thrown at me. At this point, my mind is telling me to leave. The fight or flight response is telling me to get the hell out of here as I see her raise her arm to launch the projectile at me. My feet remain planted firmly. Fuck you, fight or flight. I am in charge.

The item leaves her hand and flies towards me, but something is off. It smashes a good foot and a half away from my head. She never wanted to hurt me, just to scare me away. I look at her face and see her eyes go wide as she figures out that I figured it out. My eyes see her tough exterior start to crack again. She can't hold back very long. She turns to walk away, but I grab her again and turn her to face me. I stare straight into her eyes.

"Please Pangaea, just tell me what's wrong."

"Do you want to know what's wrong?" She rhetorically questions. "I'll tell you what's wrong!"

She gets right in my face. Well, as in my face as someone who is seven inches shorter than me can get.

"Tell me, you jackass, what do you remember from Earth? What is your best memory?"

"Well," I'm thinking as I talk, "probably when my little sister was born. She was so cute and chubby. It is scientifically proven that fat babies are cuter. That is just science."

"Now what is your worst memory?" She says as somehow her 5'4" stature seems much larger.

"Well, I got my ass kicked a lot in high school, so --."

"Aww, poor baby," she mocks. "Do you want to know what I remember from Earth?"

Answer carefully, Thaddeus. "Uhhhh, sure."

"Not a god damn thing!" She shouts. "Not a fucking thing. The first memory I have is of waking up on that table. Hell, I don't even know my own name. Danny gave me the name Pangaea cause it's the first one he could think of. Well, not the first. Originally, he wanted to call me Taco."

Yup, that's Danny.

She starts to pace around in front me. She is clearly distressed. Context clues.

"So, you don't remember anything?"

"No, I was just lying to you because it was fun. Of course I don't, you god damn stoner. I remember things about Earth like the history and what things are, but none of the things that involve me. It's like I don't exist. Hell, it's like I'm not even human. Maybe I'm not. I don't know."

"Well, if you want, I could help you figure out who you are after we deal with this whole space Hitler thing."

"Great." More sarcasm. "And you would do this out of the kindness of your heart? What would you get out of it?"

I think carefully before I reply, which means I don't think at all. Thinking gets in the way of action.

"For that warm fuzzy feeling of doing good?"

She raises an eyebrow at me and looks me up and down. I'm guessing, it's to see if any of my body language gives off a liar vibe. Either that, or to find the best place to punch me. It's about 50/50 right now. The best place to punch me would be either in the throat or genitals. I don't want her to do either, but that is my analysis.

"Why?"

"Why, what?" I ask.

"You would help me?" She asks after the momentary awkward silence of us just looking at each other. Well, her looking at me and me looking everywhere but her to avoid the awkwardness of it all.

"Of course."

"But why?"

"'Cause everyone needs a little help sometimes. Now, to show you I am sincere, I have a little present for you." I rummage through my uniform's pockets. "I know I have it here somewhere," I mumble to myself.

She stares at me skeptically. My hand continues to fiddle in my pockets to try and find what I'm looking for. I feel my hand touch the round object. I pull it out and hold it in the palm of my hand.

Her eyebrow raises as she looks at the thingy that came from the carnival. She takes a few moments to stare at it, trying to calculate what to make of it.

"What's that?" She questions as she pokes the snow globe.

"Well, I have no idea what it actually is, but it looks a lot like Earth. I won it at the carnival. The reason I picked it is because of how close it looks to Earth. Just a little reminder to me of where I came from."

"Holy shit. It does look like Earth."

"Yeah, yeah it does," I say as I still gaze at the object.

I look up to see her staring at it with a melancholy expression. My eyes go from the trinket to her face. I repeat this over and over again. She hasn't removed her eyes from the snow globe. I make a snap decision, which seems like a great idea.

My free hand gently grabs her wrist. I turn her hand palm up and place the tiny thingy there before simultaneously removing my grip on the sphere and her wrist. She gawks at the sphere then looks up at me, waiting for some explanation. I hate explaining things. Explaining things is hard.

"Wh⋯why?"

"Because." I reply before pausing to carefully think of a response. This is a very delicate situation. "Look, I wanted this to remember my home by, but I will always have my memories. Maybe having something that resembles the Earth will help you. If not, then just look at this as a personal promise from me. It's my promise that I will help you. You can go ahead and keep that and when, keyword when, we get your memory back, you can give it back to me."

I suddenly feel two arms surround me in an unexpected embrace. My mind doesn't know what to do here. Hugs are awkward. Do I hug back? When is an appropriate time to let go? Do I pat her back? Do I do the rub her back in comforting circles? Is that awkward? I never thought this would happen. My arms hesitantly go back around her in a friendly, if not awkward, hug.

"Thank you," she whispers just loud enough for me to hear before she releases.

"Anytime," I reply.

The hallway is engulfed in a pleasant silence. A question pops into my mind.

"Why did Danny call you Pancreas? I mean, it's not usually a name. I know that much."

"It's Pangaea, not Pancreas."

"Polygon?" I question.

"Are we really doing this? No. Sound it out with me. Pan···"

"Pan." I mimic.

"Gee."

"Gee."

"Ah."

"Ah."

"Very good. Now say it all together. Pan-gee-ah. Pangaea."

"Pantie Party."

She raises an eyebrow at me. "You're just messing with me. Aren't you?"

"Yup. Now what is Pangaea?"

"You don't know what Pangaea is? Open a book for fuck's sake. It is the prehistoric supercontinent," she answers like I'm a total dumbass.

"Supercontinent?"

"Large land mass containing several continents. As to why he called me that, I have no idea how his thought process works. Like I said, at first, he wanted to call me Taco. I was not okay with that, but surprisingly I was okay with being called a supercontinent. Now that I think about it, it kind of sounds like he's calling me fat."

"I don't think anyone understands Danny's thought process. He is··· well, he is one of a kind."

"He really is. Hey, I need to go but I'll see you around... Little Balls." She says the last part with a grin and a laugh as she walks away.

I may as well accept the Little Balls thing. I make my way to the mess hall and, as I'm entering it, I see a very high Danny hanging out with Tik who... wait is he high?

The mess hall door shuts behind me, causing me to jump. "Hey guys, what's up?" I regain my composure from my jump scare.

"Science, man. Science is up," Danny replies as he looks up from the table.

"What are you talking about?"

"Well you see, while you took a nap, Zinka told me about her smoking weed with you and how it made her sick." Danny continued, "So, I decided to do science to see which species could and could not smoke pot. Voltans is a no. They get sick. Litethite, well they have no mouth. But Demerians, Demerians can smoke the hell out of pot."

He then motions towards Tik who I'm guessing is delighted. The Demerian appears to be smiling. Which is a little unnerving when a man with tentacles does it. His solid black eyes seem glossy. The entire mess hall smells of weed.

"Why am I so happy!" Tik jumps up and yells, scaring the shit out of me.

"Dude, you are supposed to be happy; that's the point, man," Danny says with a placid smile.

"I love you guys!" Tik yells.

He grips both me and Danny in a bone crushing hug before I even know what the hell is happening. The dude's muscles clench me and press me against his man boobs. My lungs are having a hard time getting air. They kind of need air.

"Aww, we love you too, big guy," Danny seems oblivious to the fact that the life is being squeezed out of us.

"Yes, we love you too. Now would you please let me breathe?" I gasp out.

"I'm sorry," he says as he releases his death grip. "I'm just so happy right..." He trails off as he stares at Danny for what seems like forever before he suddenly shouts out. "Your hair looks like my face!"

I just kind of stare back and forth between them, till I realize he has a point. Danny's dreadlocks do look like the tentacles on Tik's face. Tik is a lot more observant than I am when I'm baked. Hell, he is more observant than I am when I'm sober.

"How many bowls did you guys smoke?" I am a little afraid of the answer.

"Yes." Danny replies.

"No Danny. Give me a number."

"One billion."

"I doubt you smoked one billion bowls."

"Well, I rounded up."

"Rounded up? Rounded up from what?"

"Five."

I stare at Danny like a dog would stare with a tilted head. Danny continues. "Moral is, it's not enough, man. We were just getting ready to smoke up another. You want to join?" Danny asks while holding his pipe up to me.

"Sure, why not." I take the pipe and light up.

We spend the next half hour killing the bowl and talking about subjects that I will never remember. I look over and see Tik laughing and hugging Danny. That dude is a very touchy-feely stoner. Danny just takes it all in stride. That is how Danny handles everything in his life.

"Dude," I finally realize, "I just remembered why I came in here. I wanted some food."

"You got to get the purple goo, man," Danny speaks up. "It's delicious."

"I'm pretty sure it all tastes the same," I say back.

"No man, the purple is better."

"What does it taste like?"

"It tastes like purple, man."

"Purple isn't a flavor, Danny."

"It isn't a flavor. It is the flavor," he replies with a goofy grin plastered on his face.

"Whatever, man." I grab some of the purple goo and eat it.

It doesn't taste very purple, but maybe I'm just not high enough to taste a color. I wonder if Danny knows what being sober is like. I will admit that it tastes a little better than the blue, but that's not much of an accomplishment. The bitter taste of the food lingers on my tongue longer than I would like.

"Attention, crew," Zinka's voice cuts in over the loud speaker. "Would all crew members report to the simulation room next to the armory for flight training."

The speaker cuts out.

"Flight training?" I ask out loud.

"Yeah, Zinka wishes to train us on the Aldinian fighter pods," Tik answers.

Not only do I get to shoot amazing weapons on this adventure, I get to learn how to fly a space ship? Danny and Tik follow me as we leave the mess hall. Though I don't know where the simulation room is, I do know where the armory is. We enter a doorway and there are about twenty machines hooked up with Zinka standing in the middle of them. All the machines are flashing bright colors and making an unusually loud bumblebee noise. When everyone is present in the room, Zinka begins talking.

"Hello, we are going to start training for the flight mechanisms. You will have to fly in battle. This training exercise is for everyone, so even Litethite will have to learn. Please sit in a machine and it will hook you up automatically." She sits in her own machine to demonstrate.

I look around and notice everyone else picking machines. As soon as they sit down, the machine places an odd helmet over their heads. This is badass. It's like some VR video game back on Earth. This is going to be a fun time. I pick my own machine and sit down. The helmet is placed over my head, blocking out my vision so all I see is black. So much black.

The screen changes to static before being replaced by a view of the inside of an alien craft's cockpit. The various buttons and dials are flashing before my eyes. Looking out the cockpit, I'm greeted by a massive number of stars. No idea what any of the controls do, but still, most epic video game ever!

CHAPTER 12

I hear Zinka's voice interrupt my moment of Zen.

"This is a flight simulator. The controls are standard. The control bar will turn it. Push it forward to dive. Pull back to pull up. The acceleration is on right side of the bar. To decelerate, press the trigger on the left. The button on the right fires lasers. The button on the left fires galactic missiles, but you only get five of those, so use them wisely."

"Uh···what?" I question.

"We do not feel comfortable with this," I heard Litethite say over the intercom.

"It's alright, Litethite," Zinka reassures. "This is only a simulation. No harm will come to any of us. This is just a practice to get you prepared for the real thing."

"I love all of you!" I hear Tik yell.

He is clearly still high.

"Tik, why are you yelling? Is something...." Zinka trails off as she realizes. "Dammit, Danny. Did you give Tik weed?"

"It was for the sake of science!" I hear him yell back in retaliation.

"Smoking a plant is not science, Danny." She is clearly perturbed by the recent developments.

"Don't try and discredit my scientific achievements," Danny says defensively. "This work has Nobel Prize written all over it."

"Great, now I have to babysit three of you children." Zinka sighs.

"Don't worry," I hear Pangaea say. "I'll help you keep the three idiots in check."

"May we get back to our concern?" Litethite interjects. "Even if this is just a simulation, the adrenalin and shock could do harm to our physical bodies. We are afraid that this could be fatal towards our body. We do not want our species to end."

"Calm down, Litethite. It'll be okay. I promise," Zinka is clearly trying to remain calm and collected in spite of her current frustrations.

"I am so happy!" Tik's loud voice cut in.

"May we please continue with this training?" Leonidas politely intones. "I wish to learn this skill."

"Yes," Zinka seems glad someone is on board with the training. "Now, I will begin the simulation. We will be thrown into a dog fight. If your ship is destroyed, your simulation will end. Please bear in mind, this is a simulation and no harm will come to you, but the simulation will stimulate the neurons of your brain. This will put you under the impression that it is real."

"It's stimulating what in my brain?!" I shout.

"Quit being a bitch, Little Balls."

Litethite speaks. "That does not help with our concerns. Why does it need to make us feel like it is real?"

"It will simulate the stress of an actual space fight, to see how you react under pressure," Zinka replies. "Now is everyone ready?"

There was a collective chorus of, "Yes."

"Alright." Zinka says. "Beginning simulation now."

With that, the view of empty space changed to a view of a massive amount of alien ships. Hmmm, this may be a tad harder than a normal video game.

"Alright," Zinka says, breaking me from my thoughts. "Engage enemies now."

With that last sentence, we all piloted our ships forward. Litethite hesitates for a bit, but even he joins the rush. I find myself flying around dodging blasts and shooting down enemy ships. The light from lasers blasting is all around. I'm forced to maintain constant control of the ship. There are so many enemy ships that if I lose focus, for even a moment, I'll smash into one. I can't decide which is more fun, shooting the guns or flying this ship. I feel like I am better at flying. I'm a little more accurate with the lasers of the simulated ship.

After fifteen minutes of this the brain helmet thing does what Zinka said it would do earlier. It makes me forget it's just a simulation. I genuinely fear for my life.

"We have enemies on our tail. Requesting assistance," I hear Litethite plead.

I see that he has a massive number of enemies on his ass. I pull down to help and shoot three of them down before the rest pull away to avoid my barrage of blasts. The remaining ships fork off in opposite directions, probably to try and get someone else from behind.

"We appreciate your assistance," Litethite thanks me.

"I'm hit," I hear Leonidas say, "I'm going down."

"Hang in there, Leo!" I hear Danny say.

"Can't hold on. Going down."

"LEONIDAS!" I hear a female voice cry out.

Wait was that Stuan? I watch as Leonidas crashes towards a nearby star until he is entirely cut off. With Leo down, we now have only seven left to fight against the endless number of enemies.

I see Litethite flying below me with another trail of enemies behind them. They make a beeline towards Tik. What the hell is he doing? Litethite flies past Tik, but the following ships weren't so lucky. Tik didn't even have time to scream as the collision causes both him and the enemy ships to explode.

"Litethite!" I shout over the intercom as I dodge another blast aiming to kill me. "What did you do that for?"

"We have no idea what you are talking about. We were just trying to avoid the enemies. We sincerely mourn the loss of Tik," They said.

Something about Litethite just doesn't seem right, but I'll let it go for now. The thought of dying replaces my anger. A blast hits me in the back of my ship causing my cruiser to rattle and shake.

"I will kill all of you," I hear the female voice say.

I am still positive that is Stuan's voice. I look over and see her going ape shit on the simulation drones. Hell, hath no fury like a woman scorned, apparently. Unfortunately, she can't keep it up. She sacrifices all maneuvering for a straight up offensive assault.

I look on in horror as a rogue blast punctures the cockpit causing her ship to explode. We are now down three, and although we have destroyed many of their forces, we barely put a dent in their numbers. This is an intense simulation. Suddenly, an explosion behind me draws me from my thoughts. I look back and see Pangaea.

"Hey, Little Balls," she says. "You might want to get your head out of your ass and get in the game, you dumb shit. I'm not always going to be here to pull your ass out of the fire."

"Oh yes you will. I'm one of your three favorite humans."

"There are only four humans left, you moron, and being better than Landon isn't really an accomplishment."

"So, you admit I'm right."

"Whatever, Little Balls." I see her fly off to chase down a drone.

"I'm hit, man," I hear Danny say. "I think I'm going to exfoliate."

I think he means explode. "Danny? Where are you? I'll come help you out, man."

"Naw, don't worry ab--" His intercom cuts out.

The bastards shot down my best friend. My anger boils as the closest thing to a brother that I've ever had goes down in flames. The rage causes me to go aggressive like Stuan did, except for the fact that I'm still focused on avoiding drones coming from behind. I make an honest attempt at it, at least. Unfortunately, like Stuan, my anger gets me in trouble as a blast hit me from the side. I look back and see that my ship is a tiny bit destroyed. If I'm going down, I'm taking down as many of them as I can. I see a large gathering chasing Pangaea.

"Hold on, Pangaea." I say over the intercom. "My ship is hit, so I'm going straight rogue on them."

"What the hell?" She shouts. That is the last thing I hear before my ship contacts theirs.

I see a flash and then my simulation ends. Tik and Danny are still in the room when my vision comes back. Both Voltans are gone. No idea where they wandered off to.

"Where are Leo and Stuan?" I ask.

"Stuan ran off as soon as she was out of the simulation." Tik says as he is clearly sobering up. "Leonidas went chasing after her to see if she is okay."

"So, I guess we should just wait for them to get out of the simulation?" Danny asks gesturing to the three that are still hooked up to the machines.

"I guess." I say as I shrug my shoulders not really knowing what else to do.

"You guys want to smoke another bowl?" Danny asks as he holds up his pipe.

"I'm in." Tik says way too quickly.

"Sure, why not." I reply.

Just as we start lighting up, we hear a shout from Pangaea. Guess she got eliminated.

"God damn motherfucker!" Her simulation must have ended sourly.

"What happened?" Danny asks.

"That little weasel Litethite got me killed to save his own ass."

She stomps around. She is very open about her aggression.

"Wanna smoke a bowl with us?" Danny offers. "It might make you feel better." He holds up the bowl towards the seething girl.

"Sure, why not." She takes the pipe and lights it up.

We split the bowl between the four of us and soon find it dead as we are sitting in the simulation room waiting for the last two to get out. They appear to be a lot better at it than me.

"You know," I speak up. "I'm not really sure if I trust Litethite. I mean after what he did to Tik and apparently Pangaea, too. I'm not sure he can be trusted."

"On Demer we have a saying," Tik shares. "Face your friends to watch their back and face your enemies so that you can watch your own."

"That is some awesome wisdom, dude," Danny grins.

"Well," Tik clarifies, "It was kind of invented to sell people a beverage. So really not that wise but still seems to apply to this situation."

"Still seems to work, man," Danny replies.

"Hey Danny," Pangaea interrupts. "I've got a question: when was the last time you weren't high?"

"I'm sober when I'm sleeping, my dear," Danny replies with his trademark goofy grin.

"I don't know why I was expecting differently," she laughs.

"I really love all of you!" Tik says as he opens his arms to give us a group hug.

I can avoid it, but Pangaea isn't knowledgeable enough about the situation to know what to expect, and Danny just doesn't care. So, I sit back and watch her try to escape the death grip until he finally lets go of them.

"Jesus Christ, big guy," Pangaea gasps. "Easy with the hugs before you kill us and end this rebellion before it can even start."

"I'm sorry," Tik shrugs. "I'm just so happy!" Tik shouts at the top of his lungs.

I'm starting to get used to his high outbursts, at least.

"Of course, you three are getting high," I hear Zinka sigh. "At least Pangaea is here to make sure you idiots don't hurt yourselves."

I turn around and see Zinka standing there staring down at us with a smirk on her face.

"We are out," Litethite exits the machine. "We shall return to the medical bay now."

They then walk out of the room and down the corridor. I still don't trust that guy, but Tik's words of stoned wisdom ring in my head. I decide to let it go but keep an eye on him.

"Well, I'm proud of all of you," Zinka says. "You all did well for your first time."

"Why were we training with those ships? Do we have those on board? Cause I would love to take it out for a real flight." I'm getting excited at the idea of flying a real ship.

"You are still not ready for that yet. Don't worry. You will get better with practice," she reassures. "I need to go to the control room and check the coordinates. We should be close to Goro by now."

Zinka leaves us four stoners to our own devices. This can only end well. There is no single moment in history where four stoned individuals have done any harm.

"Hey man, I got an idea," Danny stands up excitedly. "Let's go back into the simulation."

"Why?" Pangaea questions.

"Imagine how much more fun it could be if we are all baked as we do it," Danny says as if it is the most obvious thing ever.

"I'm in!" Tik shouts.

"Why not?" I shrug.

"I'm not so sure about that. Plus, you were high when you did it the last time," Pangaea says skeptically.

"Oh, come on Pangaea," Danny pleads. "Think of this as a bonding exercise."

"Do you even know how to set that thing up?" She asks.

"Well," Danny is making it up as he goes along, "I think one of us needs to sit in the master one at the center of the room. Then you probably just have to hit a few buttons and ta-da: an epic space battle."

"Fine, but I'm the one to sit in the master chair," she takes the lead. "I don't need any of you idiots destroying Zinka's machine."

"Do you know how to use it?" I ask.

"No, but I'd trust me doing it more than one of you morons."

"Woo, I am so pumped!" Tik yells. "Bonding exercise!"

Tik runs towards one of the machines as we make our way to the other machines. Pangaea heads toward the main one in the center to get everything started.

I know I've thought this before and in every instance been proved wrong, but there is no way this could come back on me. Famous last words. I sit myself down in the machine as the helmet lowers itself on my head. My vision goes to static before turning into an image of the night sky.

"Everyone ready?" Pangaea asks over the intercom.

"Yes!" Tik yells.

"Let's have some fun!" Danny exclaims.

"I'm ready for anything."

"Initiating simulated flight now," Pangaea says, sounding an awful lot like Zinka.

To say I am prepared would be a lie. Instead of the endless amount of fighter drones we had before, we now have what appears to be double the amount, as well as a large ship that looks like a small planet.

"What is that?" I ask, not believing my own eyes.

"Um, oops," Pangaea murmurs.

"What did you do Pangaea?" Danny inquires.

"Well, I may have thought it would be better if I set the difficulty up to a higher setting."

"What setting did you put it on?" I ask.

"I only set it to two and it goes up to ten," she says defensively.

"This is a two?" I can't believe it.

"Well, my ex was a two," Danny comments clearly out of his shocked demeanor, "but he was a ten in bed."

"What does that have to do with anything." She's clearly annoyed with Danny's inability to remain serious.

"I don't know," he shrugs. "I just thought we were making conversation."

"Let's do this!" Tik yells as he guns it straight into the enemy fleet.

"Dammit Tik, no. We need a plan," Pangaea yells, flying after him.

"Well, let's go blow shit up." Danny excitedly goes next.

I shrug and follow. Now, to say it was a short fight would be an understatement. As soon as we got within range, a large blast came from the massive ship and annihilated us all with one single shot. All our simulations ended at the same time and we exited our machines.

"Well, that was a confidence killer," Danny grimaces.

"I think we need to train at that more before we actually try it in real life," Pangaea says as she stretches.

"Why don't you seem bummed about that shit? We were seriously at preschool level and got our asses handed to us," Danny seems surprised.

"Well, considering none of us have flown one of those prior to the simulation, I didn't really expect us to be good at it," she says, logically.

"Well, someone is optimistic," I say.

"I wouldn't call it optimistic," she admits. "It's more or less me being stubborn."

"Let's do it again!" Tik yells.

"Easy, man. We'll practice again tomorrow." I tell them, "I'm going to go check and see how much longer till Goro."

I head towards the cockpit. My mind wanders as I traverse the halls of the massive ship. I sure as hell hope that the Gorons and Nebulites decide to help. The simulation made me realize just how fucked we are. We need all the help we can get. I will do everything I can to stop Derask, though. The cockpit opens and Zinka is typing away at the computer.

"Hey, how much longer till we get to Goro?" I ask.

"Shouldn't be much longer," she answers without looking up from her screen. "It's going to be difficult to convince the Chancellor. I'm not sure if we can reason with a man like him. He is a spineless coward, who only thinks of his own self interests."

"Sooooooo, he's a jerk."

The ship cruises through the vast reaches of space, moving along silently, even though I don't understand how it moves through space or does any of the things that it can do. No point in hurting my brain trying to figure out how things work. If they work, that is all that really matters.

"I see planet Goro up ahead," she points out.

I look up and see a mostly brown planet with three moons revolving around it. That is one weird looking planet. I guess it's time we try to beg for assistance from these people.

"I need to send a message through, so I can get clearance to land," Zinka says more to herself than to anyone. I see her press some buttons on the screen. "This is Captain Zinka requesting clearance for the ship —"

Now before she can say a name, I see a great opportunity here that I cannot pass up.

"Gravity Bong." I say into the speaker before she can say whatever the ship's name really is.

"What the hell is a Gravity Bong?" Zinka questions while glaring at me in annoyance.

"Fun, Zinka. A gravity bong is fun."

"That doesn't answer my question." She shoots back.

"Alright, alright." I relent. "A gravity bong is something you use to smoke weed. Personally, I always preferred a pipe. A soda can also works; if you're in a pinch."

"Ugh." Zinka groans in exasperation. "You and your stupid plant."

"This is outpost 537B1" I heard the voice from the speaker reply. Clearance denied, Gravity Bong. What's a bong?"

And cue another death glare from Zinka when the dude says the name. I, however, am way too preoccupied laughing my ass off. My ass may be kicked, later but it will be worth it.

I turn towards her. "How don't they know what a bong is?"

"Not every word translates, Little Balls." She deadpans, obviously still peeved at me.

Zinka turns back towards the man on the screen. "Reason for denial."

"The Chancellor will explain that. Patching in a video call from his office now."

A face suddenly appears on the video monitor. I see a rounded head with what appears to be some type of hard scaly structure on top. I also see a crown of spikes protruding from around the scaly scalp. Two beady little eyes are staring daggers at us.

"Hello Chancellor," Zinka bites out between her grit teeth.

CHAPTER 13

"What are you doing here, Zinka? We want nothing to do with your galactic war. I refuse to let my race be exterminated because of you." The Chancellor's voice drips with pure loathing.

"You're a god damn coward, Te Sung. We are here to help your people. Something that you know nothing about," she shoots back.

"How dare you?" He pounds his large meaty hands against his desk. "I am doing this for my people."

"No, you are doing it for your own selfish reasons. You don't care about your people. The only thing you're worried about it saving your own ass."

"My people are still alive, aren't they?"

"What about all the mothers that lost their kids?" Zinka points out, "The lovers who got separated? The children who will never know their parents?"

"The needs of the many outweigh the needs of the few," he replies coolly.

"We are here to see how many of your people agree with you," Zinka boldly states. "I have a feeling that most don't feel the same way you do."

"They are like children," the Chancellor dismisses her. "They don't know what is best for them. It is my job to keep their best interests at heart. Even if they don't realize it."

"It's sad when a man would rather live on his knees then fight on his feet," I paraphrase what the councilor said on Demer.

Suddenly, the screen splits, and I can see the cold smile of Emperor Derask. "Sorry to interrupt," he says to all of us, clearly not sorry in the least. "But I grow tired of this conversation."

"Derask?" Te Sung seems surprised. "What are you doing here? I gave you your quota of slaves for this month."

There is a slave quota? I'm pretty sure if there is an afterlife, then both of these assholes have a reserved spot in hell. I notice a robed figure and President Landon standing behind him. That figure is much too large to be Elisar. Dammit, he has more minions.

"Yes, you did, but I grow tired of you, Te Sung, and I see that the monkey just noticed my other little friend. It's not just Elisar by my side. She is with me, but I also have this gentleman behind me, and another that you will meet soon enough. Oh, and I guess Landon, as well."

"Why do I gots to wear this dress. I ain'ts no queer-o-sexual," the robed figure speaks up.

I barely see Derask facepalm, as I realize who that voice belongs to.

"Oh my God, Bubba?" I stutter out every syllable, confused.

"Hey, it's the socialist," Bubba removes his hood, recognizing me from before.

"Bubba, what the actual shit? You're working with the man who is the sole reason why there are only like five humans left in the universe?"

"The Earth was a sinful place full of heathens, and gays, and those transsexuals who always trick me into thinking they have lady parts." Bubba tries to justify himself. "That was a blessing."

"Why you stupid, inbred, mother fuc--"

"Can we get back to the matter at hand?" The Chancellor interrupts. "Derask, why are you here?"

Part of me knew what was coming next. I didn't want to believe it, though.

"Check my monitor, Chancellor." Derask moves to the side, and I see the massive laser pointing to the other side of the planet.

"You son of a bitch!" I shout at the screen. "Haven't you done enough?"

He simply grins. A smile that nearly stretches all the way across his hideous face.

"Too late, monkey. Pawn, push the button." He clearly means Bubba.

"Yes, Sir," Bubba replies dumbly as he presses the button.

The laser fires, but we don't have to watch the monitor, as the planet shatters right in front of us. The screen that had Te Sung on it went immediately to static but that doesn't stop the horrid pain filled screams we hear coming from the other end for a few torturous seconds. His line then goes entirely dead. Planet Goro was obliterated right in front of our eyes. I get horrible flashbacks of my home, destroyed just like Goro. I personally just witnessed a mass genocide again. I am broken out of my thoughts by that laugh. The same one that was in my nightmare. The same one that cackled after Earth was gone. The same one that kills a piece of my humanity every time I hear it.

"Let me guess: you think you're a god, don't you? You think that you can just do whatever you want?" I can't seem to control my outburst.

"My dear monkey," he replies with a sneer, "I am the only god."

"You are the same villain from nearly every story on Earth. Just another typical prick with a god complex who feels that they have the right to kill whoever they want, even if they are your allies. If those stories have taught me anything, it's that you are going to die like a little bitch."

I cut the screen, but not before I get a good look at the sneer he's giving me. I think I may have struck a nerve, and God damn does it feel fantastic. I look back and see all the crew, except Stuan, standing in the cockpit. I guess the sound of the explosion caused all members to be at attention. I look back at the remains of Goro then back at the crew.

"Don't worry," I address them. "He'll get what he has coming."

I make my way out of the cockpit, still deep in thought. I walk down the hollow metal corridors towards my cabin. I feel a hand on my shoulder, and my body stops me before I can think about it.

"Hey, you okay?" I hear Zinka's voice.

"Yeah, just had some flashbacks is all," I come back to myself. "Visions of my family again."

"All of this will be over soon enough." She promises, "We will destroy the bastard and prevent him from doing anything like this ever again. Then, maybe we will go out for ice cream."

"Is there still ice cream?"

"Please. You think you're the only race that froze a mammal's milk and artificially sweetened it?"

"Fair enough... I just hope it's not too late."

"It won't be. Look, you can never save everybody. The most we can do is build the resistance and start an assault to take him down. Until we do that, he will be responsible for countless more deaths, but you can't hold yourself personally responsible for each one of them."

"Then why do I feel like I should? "

"That's just the way it is, Little Balls. The evil and corrupt go through life without a care or regret, while the good are cursed to endure the burden of not only their own guilt but that of others too."

"Then why does anyone want to be a superhero? Why do I feel guilty when Derask can do whatever he wants and not give a fuck? I'm starting to question why anyone wants to be a hero."

"Sometimes it's not a choice. Even when it seems like we chose the path we did, we only ever had one direction we could go. Sure, there are still choices, but sometimes one of those paths is the only direction, while the rest conflict with our personalities or energies. It's at those moments when we could be given a thousand different choices or as many re-dos as possible and we would still do the exact same thing."

"That reminds me of a saying. The definition of insanity is doing the exact same thing and expecting different results. If that's the case, then what is it called when you do the exact same thing and knowing it's going to be the exact same results?"

"I don't know. Maybe being fun?"

At this I can't help but let out a loud chuckle. "Thanks, I needed that."

"No problem. Just remember, the hero always wins," she wisely points out.

"Excuse me, Little Balls," Leonidas calls out to me as he comes walking down the hall. "May I ask you a favor?"

"Sure thing."

"I'm going to go set course for Nebul. Don't destroy anything. And just remember space ice cream," Zinka says as she leaves.

"What do you need, man?" I turn my attention to Leonidas.

"Stuan will not open her door. She has not come out since the simulation, and I am starting to grow rather concerned for her."

"You want me to go and see if I can talk with her?" I ask.

"I would greatly appreciate that, sir."

"No problem. I'll go see if I can get her to open her door. I'll let you know, okay?"

"Thank you. I just don't know what to do."

"I'll see what I can do." I wave to Leonidas and head down to Stuan's cabin.

I wonder what is wrong with her. I know for a fact that she spoke in the simulation, and I know she went on an all-out 'roid rage whenever Leonidas went down, but that wasn't real. It was just a video game. Although it did feel real after a bit. Why would she still be upset over it, though? I realize I am in front of her room.

"Stuan." I knock on the door. "It's me, Little Balls. Open up. I need to talk."

Still no answer. Hmmm, what can be done to get her to come out?

"Stuan," I say in a more stern and commanding voice. "As second in command on this vessel, I'm ordering you to open this door now."

A few seconds go by as I start to think that I accomplished nothing, but then the door starts to slide open. Holy shit, it worked. The sight of a very teary-eyed Voltan standing in front of me breaks me from my thoughts.

"May I come in?" I ask in a much softer tone.

She nods, and I make my way into her room. The door closes behind us. I have a seat on her guest chair, and she joins me in the other chair a second later. All she does is look at the ground.

"So, can you please tell me what's wrong?" I am worried about my crew member.

She remains silent, still staring at the ground.

"Come on," I urge. "I know you can talk. I heard you in the simulation. Please, I just want to help."

The seconds turn to minutes as she remains silent. Part of me is beginning to wonder whether this was a good idea. Can't really do anything to make her talk. This is all just me winging it. As the idea of leaving knocks around in my skull, I hear a faint voice speak in a low hoarse whisper.

"Leonidas."

"What about Leonidas?" I ask quietly.

"When I saw him go down, something just snapped."

"Well, it was a very realistic simulation," I try to sound encouraging.

"No. It's not just that. Look, I know it was all fake. I know that he didn't really die, but still seeing it filled my head with horrid images. Images of my life without him. I realized that it was horrible. I need him here."

"You care about him a lot, don't you?" I ask.

"Yes. I have known him most of my life. I never met anyone like him. He is always caring, always polite. He doesn't have a hurtful bone in his body. Plus," she takes a breath before continuing. "I know about what he went through on the prison. No matter how hard he tried to hide his back from me when they returned him to the cell, I saw it. The marks and scars, the missing flesh and exposed muscle tissue, I saw all of it. He was willing to do that for me."

"You love him, don't you?" I ask, already knowing the answer.

She turns a different shade of purple and doesn't answer my question. So, I continue. "Look, you should probably tell him how you feel. Leo is all gaga over you too. Between you and me, I think this ship could use a happy ending, for once."

"But how... how would I do that?" She seems genuinely terrified.

"Just go up to him and tell him."

"Why does it never seem that easy?"

"Because people tend to overthink these types of things," I answer. "Our minds come up with a whole bunch of scenarios that will never happen, but it is still enough to scare the shit out of ourselves."

"I am not a people, though. I am of a different species."

"I refer to all sentient beings as people. If one has an advanced enough brain, then they will overthink things."

"I... I will think about it," she says in a low voice.

"No, don't think about it. Just do it. Now I'm going to go to the mess hall. You need to go find Leo and let him know and that is an order." I give her a mock salute.

"Yes, sir." She laughs and gives me a salute back.

Part of me wonders if I will ever follow my own advice on this situation. We exit her room and go in different directions. It is time to go get me some food. As I walk into the dining hall, I notice Leonidas sitting there. Well, I guess Stuan will wander this way eventually.

"Hello, Little Balls," he greets, ever polite. "Did you happen to have a talk with Stuan?"

"Yeah, I did, man, but I'll let her explain everything to you. Don't worry. Everything is fine," I add at the end when I see his worried expression.

I head over to the cabinet and grab some blue goo. I'm getting sick of eating goo.

"I can't help but be worried," Leonidas admits to me as I sit down with my food.

"I know, man. I know but you've just got to relax. Trust me. Everything is alright."

Just as I finished that sentence, the door opens, revealing Stuan. Well, let's see how this turns out.

"Oh, Stuan," Leo says as he rushes up to meet her. "Are you okay? Is everything alright? Do you need any--"

"Shhhh," Stuan interrupts. "I have something I need to tell you, Leonidas."

"Did you just talk?" He asks with a mixture of happiness and confusion.

"Yes, and I'm about to tell you something very important. Leonidas, I... I wish for you to be my bond-mate Leonidas. I need you.

I... I love you."

Leo seems a little, I don't know, saddened by this news. What the hell? This is supposed to be a happy thing.

"Stuan," he says in a saddened tone. "I can't. I... just can't."

Well, this could have gone a hell of a lot better.

"What? But..." She can't even finish the sentence as it dies on her lips.

"Stuan, I do not feel right about taking advantage of the situation. It would not be right for you to bond with me simply because we are the last two Voltans. You deserve better than to have to bond simply based on circumstance."

"Leonidas." She cuts him short.

"Yes?"

"Stop being an idiot." At this he seems confused, so she continues. "Of course, I love you based on circumstance. Because of the circumstances, you have grown to be caring. Because of the circumstances, you have become my best friend. Because of the circumstances, you turned into the amazing person you are. I feel that most love comes from circumstance. It's not a choice and it never is. Whether there are two Voltans or two trillion Voltans, I still love you, and I still want you to be my bond."

They then put their foreheads together and put their hands on the sides of the other's head. I guess that is like their equivalent of kissing. I honestly don't know but it seems like a good thing. Yay, happy times. I sneak out of the mess hall, because, let's face it: I should have cut out earlier.

I look down the hall and see that both Pangaea and Zinka are coming towards the mess hall.

I decide to step in here.

"Look, Leo and Stuan are just talking in there."

"Stuan is talking?" Zinka asks.

"Yes, I think they're confessing their love to each other."

"Aw."

"Gross."

Zinka and Pangaea reply respectively.

Zinka just grumbles under her breath and walks off.

Danny and I follow her down the halls. She storms off, and we lose track of her. We continue our walk and head towards the bridge. Danny is walking quietly beside me. My thoughts drift off to much darker things as I continue my trek.

'You can't save everyone.' I can hear Zinka say in my head.

'You can't save everyone.' It just won't leave my head.

'You can't save everyone.'

Each time, doing more to anger me than the initial soothing effect it had.

'You can't save everyone.'

The last one stops me dead in my tracks, as visions of my family flood my skull again. I may not be able to save everyone, but I'm sure as hell going to try.

CHAPTER 14

We arrive at the bridge, and I see Zinka at the main controls. Tik is off to the side of the room, pressing some buttons on a thing. I really should start trying to figure out what the hell these things do.

"Hey Tik," I address the large alien. "You seem kind of sober at the moment."

"Hello, Little Balls," he turns around to greet me. "Yes, I'm sober.... for now."

"Yup, now I have another idiot to babysit," I hear Zinka say from the side.

"At least we make it entertaining." I chime in.

Tik goes back to pressing different buttons and knobby things on his screen.

Pangaea enters the room. She sits quietly next to Tik and begins to watch some monitors. Everyone is just lost in their own thoughts.

"Excuse me, companions," I hear Leonidas say as he comes through the door. Everyone's attention turns to him. "I wish to make a proposal to you, since you are the closest friends that Stuan and I have. I wish to invite all of you to our bonding ceremony."

"What's a bonding ceremony?" I ask.

"The bonding ceremony is a ceremony in which the two involved invite their closest friends and families for the metaphorical binding of two beings."

"So," Pangaea pipes up, "it's like a wedding for your race."

"I have no idea what a wedding is Madame Pangaea, but I will take your word for it that they are similar. We would like to have the ceremony on the ship, if Captain Zinka approves?"

Everyone turns to wait for her response.

"We have had enough tragedy. We need a little bit of joy on this ship. We will have the ceremony," Zinka replies with a smile.

"Well," I jump in. "Looks like we are going to have a Voltan wedding on the ship. Now how do we do that?"

"It is a rather simple ceremony. We exchange an oath in front of our friends, and then partake in the symbolic mind melding exercise."

"Well, that sounds good," I say. "I'm in."

"Aw man, I always cry at weddings," Danny pipes up. "But I'm in."

"I will be there," Tik says.

"Why the hell not," Pangaea manages a small smile.

"I'll be delighted to attend," Zinka agrees.

"That is great news," Leo replies with a smile. "We are planning to have the ceremony tomorrow morning. Stuan is inviting Litethite now. The ceremony will be held in the mess hall, as that place now has special meaning to us."

Leo then leaves the room to do whatever it is that Voltans do before their wedding ceremony. Things really do have a way of changing rapidly.

"Does Litethite really need to be invited?" Pangaea asks in vexation.

"I know you don't like them Pangaea," Zinka says. "But you are going to have to let it go for now. We are doing this for Leo and Stuan. Not to mention, I feel like this little ceremony will be the perfect morale booster."

She momentarily pauses for thought before sighing loudly and rolling her eyes all the way back. "Fine, but I still hate the prick. Now if you don't mind, I'm going to have a little talk with the bride-to-be."

"What for?" Danny asks.

"If she is going to get married, we are definitely making this a bigger deal. I'm going to see if she wants to incorporate some human marital elements into it. It's going to be a party, plus we are gonna have a little bachelorette party, and guess what? You're invited Zinka!" Pangaea says as she leaves the room whilst literally dragging Zinka out with her.

Bachelorette parties have strippers, don't they? They can have the best of luck trying to find some strippers all the way out here. Unless they are going to get Litethite to do it. That is a disturbing image. This does give me a brilliant idea.

"Hey, you guys thinking what I'm thinking?" I ask Danny and Tik.

"That depends," Danny replies. "What are you thinking?"

"Bachelor party."

"Oh, no that's not what I was thinking, but I like your idea better."

"What were you thinking?"

"Uh, not important. Bachelor party time!"

"What is this 'bachelor party?'" Tik asks.

"Essentially, we take the soon to be groom and get him wasted to celebrate him getting a partner." I reply. "Now do we have any mind-altering substance that Voltans, Demerians, and Humans can all take without getting sick?"

"Well, I do have these," Tik pulls out a cube of what looks like fudge.

"What is it?" Danny asks, curious of the new drug.

"This is called Paxinax. It is a non-addictive hallucinogen."

"Non-addictive? I'm in." Danny replies without a second thought.

"Are you sure it's not harmful to people or Voltans?" I ask.

"I guarantee that it is not harmful. I was saving it for a special occasion. This seems like the ideal time to use it."

"Well, alright. What the hell. Let's go get the groom to be and get baked."

We make our way down the corridor and pound on Leonidas' door. It slides open, revealing a slightly confused Leo staring back at us.

"Sir Little Balls, I am most confused," he states when he fully emerges from his room. "Miss Zinka and Miss Pangaea came over and took Stuan. They were saying something about a bachelorette party."

"It's an Earth custom and speaking of that, it's also an Earth custom to have a bachelor party for the groom." I grab him by the arm and make my way to the simulation room. "So, we are going to get you nice and high for your last night or day or whatever as being a single man."

"We are not smoking that 'pot' that Sir Danny gave me earlier, are we?" He asks, skeptically. "I cannot partake of that substance."

"Don't worry, man," Danny assures. "We are gonna do something from Tik's stash. He says it's fine for all of us take. I trust Tik."

"It's called Paxinax," Tik says.

"I never heard of this substance before. Are you sure it is not harmful?"

"Trust me," Tik responds. "It is entirely safe. You have my word."

With that, we make it into the simulation room. We figured this would be the ideal spot for drug use exploits. Why did we figure that? I honestly don't remember but it seemed like a valid option whenever it was brought up. Tik removes the Paxinax from his pocket and starts breaking off chunks of it.

"We each just need to eat a little square," Tik says as he hands each of us a cube of it.

"Alright, who wants to be first?" I ask looking around.

"Wait, we were going to decide who went first?" I hear Danny ask.

I look towards him and notice his square is already gone. Well, that settles that, I guess. I notice both Tik and Leo are eating their pieces, so I just shrug and start biting mine. Before I know it, we've each finished our squares and wait for the stuff to kick in.

"I don't feel anything yet, man. Are you sure this is gonna work?" Danny questions.

"Yes, just trust me. It takes a short while for it to kick in but when it does you all are in for a trip," Tik replies coolly.

"I don't know. I know drugs and I don't think these things are gonna........" Danny trails off, staring at the wall.

"Danny, man? Are you okay?" I ask.

There is several more seconds of silence before he finds his voice and speaks. "I can see the face of God......and she is beautiful!" Danny exclaims with excitement.

"Whoa, are we all going to see God?" I ask.

"Each high is different," Tik replies before suddenly jerking into a standing position and running circles around the room. "I'm going back in time." He then stops and changes directions while yelling. "Now I'm going forward in time."

This just keeps continuing. I look over and see Leo sitting perfectly still.

"How are you doing, Leo?" I ask as the chaos unfolds around us.

"Shhhh, I'm a plant."

"You're a plant?"

"Not just a plant, I'm the best god damn plant around."

"The best, huh?"

"Yes, just check out my petals and gaze at my photosynthesis."

"Leo, you can't gaze at photosynthesis."

"Your face is way too out of focus for your opinion to matter."

My vision starts to fade, as odd visions swim in front of my eyes. They start off as formless blurs, but slowly start to take shape. The vision in front of me becomes horrifying and traumatic.

I see my mom, her body broken and torn. She starts hobbling towards me. I see my dad, his flesh missing, exposing muscle tissue and bones. He slowly starts sliding his feet over to me. I see my baby sister, her body singed and covered in horrid blisters and burnt flesh. She starts crawling towards me. I am too horrified to move or even will a sound to come out of my mouth. The three grotesque figures start to get even closer to me.

My mind goes numb as the specters are within reach of me. I see all their hands reaching towards me. I swear I can even feel the heat from their freshly burnt corpses. This is all my fault. I couldn't save them, and they loathe me for it. They know I should have tried harder. They know I should have done something, anything, to prevent their cursed fate. I deserve this. I deserve whatever hell they have planned for me.

Before the specters can touch me, the vision takes a hard-left turn. The ghoulish figures evaporate and are replaced with a less scary but much more confusing apparition. The haunting visions, which were once nightmares, are now an anthropomorphic platypus. It appears as if it was drawn in a Japanese anime style. It starts to sing.

"Oh, I'm a platypus.

The coolest you ever saw.

Don't make fun of a platypus.

The males have poison claws."

I love this singing anime abomination. It continues.

"My ass looks like a beaver.

My mouth looks like a duck.

If you hate it, I don't care.

I don't give a fuck."

I love this song. He sings another verse.

"For reasons, I lay eggs.

People like to mock.

If you are one of them.

Then you can suck my cock."

Please be a fourth verse. As if god heard my prayers, he goes on.

"So, look at my glory.

Look at my pose.

If you hate me, then, oh well.

Cause I get all the hoes."

Before I could even register a response, the vision fades into black. My consciousness slips away, and I leave this world for the realm of sleep.

My first semi-waking thought is: why is my bed so hard? I look underneath me and see that I am laying on top of Tik. That was one hell of a drug. I look to the left and right to see that Danny and Leo are also in on this cuddle party. Meh, I'm comfortable with my sexuality.

I wake them up, because we need to get ready for the wedding. We are going to get them hitched. We make our way to the mess hall and stand in awe at all the decorations strung up. The girls put themselves to work. We hear the door open and see the girls and Litethite enter.

"Alright, so here is what we've decided to do," Pangaea steps forward. "They are going to exchange vows and do the symbolic mind merge, as is Voltan tradition. Then we are going to have the couple share their first dance, and the bride is going to throw out a bouquet as is Earth custom."

"Speaking of the bride, where is she?" Danny asks.

"She is going to walk down the aisle. She liked the idea when Pangaea told her. So, everyone, stand in position," Zinka says as she and Pangaea begin to place all of us in designated spots. We all follow their orders. It seems best to just go with the flow on this one.

"Alright, start the music." Pangaea pushes a button, and the wedding song comes over the loud speakers.

I'm not even going to ask where she got the song. Suddenly, the door opens, and Stuan walks in, dressed in a fancy dress. Yet again, not going to question where that dress came from. My attention goes to Leo, and I see that his jaw is close to hitting the ground. She makes it to her spot and grabs Leo's hands.

"Why are weddings so beautiful?" I hear Danny sob as he cries and clutches onto Tik.

Tik pats his back in a comforting manner.

Leonidas starts to say his vows first. "Stuan, I Leonidas, vow to love you till the end of days. I acknowledge you as my eternal bond-mate. I would face the entire galaxy and universe to protect you from any harm. My life, I swear to you. My heart, I give to you. Every part of my being belongs to you and you alone."

Stuan stares deeply into his eyes and begins her vows, "Leonidas, I Stuan, vow to--"

Her vows are interrupted by a buzzing noise and a bright flash. When the flash clears, all I can see is Stuan's headless corpse laying on the floor. My shock prevents my movement. I finally get enough sense to move and I notice the room and everyone in it is covered in what once was Stuan.

I look up and see Litethite still holding the smoking laser. We all just stare, too shocked to move or react. Nothing could have prepared us for this situation. Leonidas is the first to react, crossing the room in a blur, he grips them by the throat and slams them against the wall.

Leo grips their neck tighter, preventing even a whimper from being allowed to come out of Litethite's throat. Leo grabs Litethite's arm and rips it from its socket. I can hear all the tendons being pulled apart. I can see the pain on their face, but the death grip on their neck still prevents any sound from coming out. He proceeds to the next limb, and then the next. He pulls each one off slower than he did the previous one. Finally, when the last limb is removed, I can see their agony filled squirms start to slow down and die as they do. Their body stops moving. Their life leaves their eyes. Litethite is dead, and when Leo knows that too, he drops the corpse which lands with a loud thud.

An endless moment of motionless silence follows. It is only Leo's sobs that break the deafening quiet. They start as small whimpers and slowly escalate into the cries of a hysterical man holding the limp, lifeless body of his one and only. Zinka springs to his side and brings him into a soothing embrace. She hugs him until the sobs begin to calm; when they do, she looks over to Pangaea.

"Pangaea, can you take Leo to his room and stay with him? I need to make.... preparations," Zinka says while helping up the mourning Voltan.

"Of course," Pangaea gently takes hold of the weeping widower's arm. "Come on. Let's go to your room. You need plenty of rest."

Pangaea leads him out of the room and the door closes behind them. The faint sound of sobs can still be heard.

"Little Balls, Danny, I need you two to help me get Stuan ready for her funeral," Zinka commands. "Tik, I need you to dispose of the trash."

"Yes ma'am," Tik understands he has the task of getting rid of Litethite's body.

"You two, help me wrap her in this blanket," Zinka says turning her attention back to us.

We slowly pick up her body and set it gingerly on the blanket. Zinka then proceeds to wrap the corpse with the blanket.

"Captain Zinka," Tik interrupts. "You might want to come and look at this."

We all turn to look at Tik and see a very familiar looking device. That son of bitch. We go to Tik, who is still holding the message pad, and press play. The device buzzes to life and I see a familiar face pop up on the screen. The ugly face of a true monster.

"Hello, children," Derask says with a smirk. "I told you that you would meet my other pawn soon enough. It's amazing what you can get someone to do. All it takes is a promise: something that they desire. For your little friend Litethite, I promised him a new planet for his race. Everyone has a price. But I digress, if you are watching this, then that means that they are dead. Sometimes a king must sacrifice a pawn to win the game. See you around."

With that, the message ends and I am filled with a renewed hatred for the prick. Also, how the hell does that dude know what chess is?

"We will have the service for Stuan in one hour. Tik, you can just throw that in the garbage compactor?" Zinka orders.

"Yes captain," Tik gathers the rest of the limbs and throws them in the chute for garbage.

"Everyone, meet in Docking Bay One in an hour, and we will have a proper service for Stuan. Dismissed," Zinka says, and we all salute and take our leave.

Everyone makes a solemn walk back to their own rooms. I guess we're all just occupied by our thoughts. My mind torments me with its own dark constructs. It took a death of a crew mate for me to realize that we aren't all going to make it. I guess in my naivety, I thought that we were the good guys and that nothing bad could happen to us. This just solidifies the fact that not everyone gets a happy ending. In a way, no story has a happy ending. Everyone's story ends the same anyway. It ends with death. The stories may be different up to that point, but it will end with death.

I get to my room and light up a cig. A large inhale fills my lungs and my eyes stare up at the ceiling. I don't know what I'm looking for, but I'm staring at it expecting it to reveal to me the secrets of all of life's biggest questions. Maybe it can reveal the future. Maybe it will tell me exactly what to do to end this. Unfortunately, it just stares back at me with stoic silence.

CHAPTER 15

I pass the hour in my room chain smoking, and before I know it, it's time to attend Stuan's funeral. I head down the metallic corridors to the docking bay. The corridors, which when I first saw them seemed to radiate an awe-inspiring feeling in me, now just seem like a cold, metallic coffin.

The docking bay doors open, and the entire crew is gathered around, wearing somber expressions. They are standing beside a metal tube. One that contains the remains of a friend.

"It is customary that when a crew member passes, we hold a special ceremony." Zinka addresses the beings in the room. "It is tradition that we launch the fallen's body into the nearest star. We do this as the greatest possible honor that can be bestowed upon an individual. Their atoms will be returned to the source from whence they came. Does anyone have any parting words for our fallen comrade?"

Leonidas makes his way up to the casket as we all wait with bated breath. This is when the reality truly sinks in. It's easy whenever you hear about death over the television or the radio to just ignore it and continue with your day-to-day life. To witness the one closest to the victim try to give their eulogy, however, abolishes all trace of anonymity from it. Every victim is someone's daughter or son, mother or father, or lover.

"Dear friends," Leo starts out. "I really don't know what to say. Nothing can prepare someone for this situation. You would think I'd be able tell stories of her until my last breath but I... I am left speechless. Nothing I can say can do justice to her legacy. Every story, every anecdote just, I don't know, pales in comparison to who she truly was."

He fights back a sob before continuing.

"Life is a fragile thing. One moment you are enjoying it to the fullest. The next you are a corpse. The only solace I can take from this situation is that hopefully, my situation will act as a lesson to everyone here. Never take anything for granted. Never be afraid of failure. Never let moments slip through your fingers like I did. Thank you."

I look around at the rest of the crew. I see Danny crying on Tik's shoulder, while the latter is trying his damnedest to put on a brave face. I see Pangaea clenching her fists. I could tell her anger is boiling. It would be a lot more intimidating if it weren't for the tears streaming down her cheeks. I then notice Zinka standing with her hands folded, head bowed, and eyes closed. She then looks up and walks towards the casket. Her hand hovers over a button. "May you forever live among the stars, Stuan," she says as she pushes the button and fires the coffin into the nearest star.

There is a heavy silence as we all watch the monitor and watch our friend go towards the star which, according to Zinka, the locals of this system have named Pelagross. The name roughly translates to God. We watch Pelagross welcome Stuan with open arms. In my head, I make a promise: we will take Derask down for you, your children, and all others who have been tormented by his plague.

"Everyone dismissed," Zinka says, and we all wander back to some semblance of our routines.

This entire ordeal seems to have taken the wind right out of my sails. I am worn out beyond belief and need the sweet embrace of unconsciousness. I lay down in my bed and it swallows me. Not like a warm, loving embrace, though. It feels more like it is simply caving in and crushing me in a claustrophobic tomb.

I dread the thought of my inner demons coming back in my dreams. I feel fear as sleep completely takes me away from this world.

I look around and I am standing on a desolate land. There are no signs of life. There are no plants. There are no animals. There is just me standing on dirt, but even that seems strange. Upon closer examination of the dirt, my mind is still having a hard time as it tries to figure out what is odd about this place.

A state of shock overtakes me, as faces start to form out of the ground beneath my feet. There are five distinctive individuals emerging from the dirt right before my very eyes. I see Zinka, Pangaea, Tik, Danny, and Leonidas all standing before me. The temporary happiness fades as each one of them starts to decay and rot before my very eyes. I can do nothing but gawk as their flesh tears and melts. I'm left with five horrid skeletons of what used to be my friends. All of whom seem to be staring at me with pure hatred.

"You can't save us," Tik croaks.

"Yes, I can. I'll do anything to save you and everybody else," I'm defensive.

"Like you saved Stuan?" Leo questions accusingly.

"I didn't know. I... I would have done anything if I could have."

"All you did was stare," Danny says.

"No, I would have--"

"You would have done nothing," Pangaea interrupts.

"You will let us all die," Zinka snaps. "Just like you let your family die."

I can't bear it anymore as I clutch my ears and fall to my knees. I try so damn hard to try and block out the voices, but everything just makes it louder. My eyes shut tight, hoping that it will all go away if I ignore them. Hoping that it will all be okay. Hoping that I may retain what little bit of my sanity remains.

CHAPTER 16

My eyes snap open. I really need to stop having those nightmares. God only knows the last time that I had a good night's rest.

"Attention Crew," Zinka's voice sounds over the intercom. "We have arrived at planet Nebul. Please report to Docking Bay One for assignments."

The intercom goes dead. I blearily stand up and stretch my sore muscles. Hopefully this trip is a lot more productive than the visit to Goro. The docking bay doors open. The rest of the crew has already gathered. It appears that we are all worn out by recent events.

"For this trip," Zinka starts, "I am only taking Pangaea in the landing party. The rest of you remain on the ship. Little Balls, you are in charge."

"Oh, come on," I interject. "Why can't I go too? I want to see all the planets that I can."

"Males are treated as second class citizens in this society."

"That's stupid. Why would someone be treated different simply because of what gender they are?"

"I don't know. It doesn't make sense, but it is what it is."

"I'll have you and Pangaea to protect me. I just want to see as much of the Universe as I can. You know I love space," I reply.

"Okay, fine," Zinka relents. "But you will keep quiet and you will do exactly as I say. Is that understood?"

"Aye aye, captain," I salute.

I am rewarded with yet another eye roll.

"Tik, you are in charge. Crew dismissed."

Pangaea, Zinka, and I get ready to depart on the strange alien planet. "Now remember, Little Balls," Zinka reminds. "You will be quiet and not speak until spoken to. I really hate to do that, but it is the only way to ensure that you make it off this planet in one piece."

"I'm an adult. I don't need a babysitter," I'm already proving her point.

"Yes, you do," Pangaea backs her up. "You need one. Danny needs one. Now, thanks to Danny's 'science', Tik also needs one."

"You're no fun, Pangaea. I thought we were friends."

"I tolerate you, Little Balls. That is why I need to keep your dumb ass from getting killed."

Something seems off about this world we've just set foot on. I can't put my finger on it, though. There are still buildings. They appear to be made of glass. There is still a walkway. It appears to be made of cement. That's when it hit me. There is no nature here. There are a few trees randomly placed. Everything else seems to be man-made. Upon closer inspection, even the trees are fake. I see gathering drains. I'm assuming to collect some type of rain.

"Hey Zinka?" I question, breaking her rule already.

"What is it, Little Balls."

"Why is there no actual nature on this planet?"

"In their quest to advance technologically, they exploited the planet until it could no longer sustain life. The only reason they still exist is because they can gather food from other planets. They also have a reserve of water which is filtered and stored underneath the planet."

"Then what is the deal with those gutters?"

"Those are not gutters. They are filters for the air on this planet."

I take all this in as I look at the inhabitants of the planet. Imagine snake people with arms and legs. Looking around, I mostly see females. The few males appear to be attached to the women. The men walk with a meek demeanor. They seem nervous. It's as though they don't feel safe in their own society.

"We need to head to the palace up ahead and talk to the Queen," Zinka motions to the gigantic building up ahead. We make our way up to the giant gate of the palace, and a guard steps in front of us.

"What business do you have with the queen?" The guard barks at us as she points a sharp spear at us. I step forward to answer.

"Well, we mmmmph." I am cut off as I feel Zinka's hand clamp tightly over my mouth.

"We have important galactic news, and we need council with the queen to discuss the threat to all sentient beings across the universe."

The guard stares at us analytically and pauses to give me a particularly nasty looking glare.

"I will call the Queen to see if she is accepting visitors at the moment."

The guard goes into her guard shack. I guess that is where the phone thingy is. I look over and see Zinka giving me a glare. Why is everyone glaring at me? Seriously, everyone needs to stop being so mean to me.

"What did I tell you before we left?" She asks sharply while glaring at me.

"Uh something like.... wait it was it that I should.... Okay, I give up."

"You. Need. To. Shut. Up." She says as she pokes my chest with each word she utters. There may be a bruise there now.

"Okay, fine," I say while rubbing my sore chest.

"The Queen has granted you a meeting," The guard says as she comes back out of her shack. "Do not touch anything, and remember," she pauses to look pointedly at me, "Keep your pet on a leash."

She spits out the last sentence as if even addressing me in a sentence was like poison. I'm not a pet, dammit. We make our way through the gate and up to the large mansion. We are greeted by yet another guard who is pointing her pointy thing at us. Well, to be perfectly clear it seems more directed at me.

"Stop right there," the guard yells.

"The other guard gave us permission," Pangaea says, garnering the attention of the pointy stick to her face. "And I swear to whatever God you believe in, that if you don't get that out of my face, I'm going to take it and shove it right up your ass."

"Oh, you can go in," the guard replies before looking at me. "But your pet needs to stay outside."

"Pet?" Pangaea asks bluntly.

"Attention!" A commanding voice cuts Pangaea short. "Stand down. These three have been given permission to see the Queen." The mystery woman then turns towards us. "If you will kindly follow me."

She walks through the doors and we follow. I glance at the guard one more time and see her giving me that glare. I really wish she would stop that. As the door closes, our escort begins to talk while we navigate the corridors.

"I really am sorry about that. Males aren't treated as equals on this planet. My mom and sister wish to keep it that way, but I want to change that if I can. My name is Halissy, by the way."

"No problem, Halissy," Zinka speaks up. "I'm Zinka, and this is Little Balls and Pangaea. Don't your mom and sister want equality?"

"Not in this lifetime. It's a power struggle. They are in charge and they really don't want to change that. Here we are."

Halissy opens the double doors, and we are greeted with a giant throne. Next to the throne, there are two smaller ones on each side. To the queen's left is, I'm guessing, Halissy's sister. On the other side is an empty chair, which is probably Halissy's chair.

"Queen Polt. I have brought the visitors that wish to have a council with you." Halissy says as she walks to the other chair and sits down.

"Your highness. My name is Zinka, and these are my cohorts, Little Balls and Pangaea. We request aide from the Nebulite military," Zinka steps forward. "The universe faces a great threat from Derask."

"So?" The queen is indifferent.

"So? So, if something isn't done soon, trillions of living creatures are going to die."

"What concern is it of mine if Derask wants to wipe out a few inferior species? That is survival of the fittest."

"How long do you think it will take before he turns his attention to

Nebul? He will keep building his army until he has enough soldiers to pose a threat to you, and everyone else in the galaxy," Zinka pleads.

"If he makes it here, we will destroy him. Until then, getting into your little squabble is none of our concern."

"Wow, you're an idiot, aren't you?" Pangaea blurts.

"How dare you?! No one comes talks to me like that."

"Then it was long overdue. "

"Your majesty," Zinka interjects. "Please, we need your help to stop this. If we don't, then Derask will destroy countless more planets. We can't put this off for long."

"If these races can't defend themselves, that is their problem." Queen Polt replies smugly. "My answer is no."

"But mother, surely--" Halissy starts.

"Surely nothing. We are not instigating a war that we have no place in. Halissy, see the visitors out."

"Yes mother," Halissy stands and leads us out the door.

"I wish to join you in the fight. May I come with you?"

"You want to be a member of the crew?" Zinka asks, incredulous.

"If that will help, yes. I wouldn't be able to sleep at night knowing what a criminal is ravaging the universe and I've done nothing to stop him."

"What do you think, Little Balls?"

"I don't see why not."

"I have extensive medical experience. If your ship doesn't have a doctor, I will gladly take that role," Halissy offers.

"Just don't go crazy like our last one did," Pangaea snarks.

"Before we go, I have one request," I say, and it elicits everyone's attention.

"What is it?" Halissy questions.

"I need real food in my stomach. Do you have anything on this planet that won't kill me if I eat it."

"We have food here that is agreeable to most types of digestive tracts. What type do you have?"

"The kind that... digests... things?" I reply, not really understanding my own body.

"The human digestive tract resembles that of an Aldinian

wildoworm," Zinka helpfully offers.

"Yes, we have food that should be safe for you to consume," Halissy answers.

"Can we take a lunch break real quick, Zinka?" I ask.

"I don't know. I'm not sure if that would be such a good idea."

"Oh, come on. We could get the rest of the crew and have a... what do you call it? Oh yeah, bonding exercise."

"Fine," she replies as she takes out a small device. "This is Zinka calling The-"

"Gravity Bong." I cut in making sure that becomes the name of the ship.

Zinka's death glare is the immediate response that I receive.

"Gravity Bong?" Danny's voice cuts in over the device. "Is that what the ship's name is?"

"Danny," Zinka glosses past it to the topic at hand. "We are going to have a little shore leave for crew bonding. We are going to eat. Halissy assures me there is food you are able to ingest."

"Do they have purple goo?"

"They might but I want you, Tik, and Leonidas to meet us right outside of the ship."

"Aye aye, bossy lady." Danny cuts off the connection and Zinka goes back to giving me a glare.

"My ship is not named Gravity Bong, Little Balls."

"Then why do people keep saying it?" I question.

"People don't keep saying it. You keep saying it."

"I am a people, though."

"Shut up." She turns on her heel and walks back to the ship with me, Pangaea and Halissy in tow.

We get to the ship and see Danny standing on Tik's shoulders and painting something on the side of the ship. I have no idea where he got the paint from, but with Danny, it is better not to ask.

"There you guys are," Danny says as he finishes up and gets off Tik. "So, what's for eats?"

"What were you two idiots painting on the side of my ship?" Zinka questions accusingly.

"Well, since we didn't even know this ship had a name, we decided that to avoid further confusion we would paint the name on the side of your ship. It is in English letters since those are the only letters that I know," Danny explains.

"Oh my god!" Zinka exclaims. "You didn't?"

"We did. No need to thank us."

Zinka runs to the side of the ship and gawks up at it. I decide, against my better judgment, to join her. There on the side of the ship in bright red paint are the words: Gravity Bong. Now, a smart man would see this as an opportune time to get out of there. I, however, am not a very smart man.

"You're going to slap my head, aren't you?" I ask.

"Oh yeah, Little Balls. I am going to hit you. I just need time to fully process my anger."

"About how long will that take exactly? Are we talking about a minute or a year or a decade or a century or a-?"

That is all I got out till a firm hand met the back of my skull.

"Where is Leo at, Tik?" Pangaea asks.

"He needs some time to himself. I'm sure you understand."

"Yeah, he has been through a lot," I reply. "Should we cancel it? I mean, it very well can't be a crew bonding if not all of the crew is there."

"Well, I asked him that," Tik responds. "But he said it is fine, and he wishes to be alone."

"Alright," I reply. "We will bring him a dish, though. I really don't like leaving him alone when he is like this."

"I don't either, but he seems set on his solitude," Tik stands firm.

"Alright, Halissy," Zinka leads. "Where is this fine Nebulite cuisine?"

"There is a restaurant not far from here. We can walk."

"How are we going to pay for it if we have no money?" Danny asks.

"I stole a lot of credits from the Aldinian Treasury," Zinka winks. "Trust me. We're good."

"I keep liking you more and more Zinka," Pangaea crosses to walk beside Zinka. "Let's go get some food."

We follow Halissy down the path, until she stops in front of a massive but ugly building. I think the architect may have been blind when he designed it. Also, the construction crew was blind when they built it. Let's not forget the blind painters who decided to make it the ugliest brown that you will ever see. We walk through the door behind Halissy. I take the time to look around at all the Nebulites around me.

The women are dressed in intricate decorative robes. Shiny rocks adorn these robes, causing them to sparkle in the light. The men, however, are dressed in skimpy outfits. Most of them aren't even eating, just sitting there waiting to be told what to do. I notice my party is leaving without me, so I hurry to their side. We are going to a private room. I guess that is one of the perks of being the queen's daughter. As we take our seats, the waiter begins to speak.

"And what would the party like to eat?" The waitress' voice is haughty.

"The three Humans will have the Brotast. The Aldinian will have the Hertzil. The Demerian will have a Fettish Groon. And I'll take the Perror Fish," Halissy orders.

"As you wish, Madame." The waitress did not open her eyes once. That takes skill.

"I have no idea what any of that stuff is," I say, still trying to figure out how to spell the first meal.

"It is safe for you to eat. I assure you," Halissy reaffirms.

"You play with weaponry you don't know how to use, go head long into an interstellar conflict, and try to drink acidic alcohol, but you are worried about a little bit of food killing you?" Zinka questions.

"That is a very good point."

I sit and listen to the music filling the room as I wait for my meal. It is sounds weird and I don't really know what to make of it. To me, it's just like a bunch of random beeps like someone hitting buttons on a microwave. Hell, to each their own I suppose.

The table begins to talk amongst themselves. It becomes impossible to focus on what is being said around me as my stomach begins to growl loudly. The thought of actual food excites me far more than anything else that is going on around me.

Danny's voice raises above all the others. "Halissy, can I ask you a question?"

"Yes. What is it?"

"Why are all the dudes here dressed like prostitutes? Well, most of them at least."

"Males on this planet are objectified. Their value is determined by their appearance."

"That's stupid." Danny states the obvious.

"Yes, but yet so familiar⋯" Before I space out even more, I see the waiter approaching with our food.

"Here are your meals. Please do enjoy and let me know if you need anything else," she says while still not opening her eyes.

I look at the food in front of me. It kind of looks like meatloaf. I like meatloaf, so I dig my fork in and pull off a piece. It. Is. Delicious.

"God damn this is good. What is it?" I ask.

"Well," Halissy begins, "It is the flesh of a Brot with its genitals diced up and mixed in. It is then wrapped in the tubing of its own digestive tract."

I look over and see that Pangaea is sickened by the description and decides to stop eating. Danny is way too high to even listen to Halissy, let alone to give two fucks about it. I, on the other hand, am just going to pretend she said it's made of rainbows and just a pinch of love. I need solid food, dammit.

"Hey, what on the menu can a Voltan eat?" I ask as I finish my meal.

"They could probably eat the Ranco," Halissy supposes.

"Alright. Hey waitress? Can I get a Ranco to go, please?"

"Certainly. I will tell the chefs and it will be ready shortly."

With that the waitress leaves.

"Getting something for Leonidas?" Pangaea asks.

"Yeah, the dude deserves to have a good meal too. I'm just hoping he is doing alright on the ship by himself."

"May I ask what is wrong with your friend? I don't think you ever told me." Halissy wonders.

"Our last doctor killed his bond-mate at his own wedding," Pangaea explains. "So, if you don't shoot any of us, then you are already better than the last doctor we had. Trust me when I say this though. If you try to hurt anyone on this ship, I will kill you."

Pangaea's comment seemed to have scared Halissy a bit, as her eyes go wide.

"Leo took care of him though," I hear Danny say through a mouthful of food.

"Yeah, he literally ripped him limb from limb," I add. "It was really messy."

The rest go back to their food. It is a little surprising that the talk of removing limbs hasn't banished anyone's appetite. Before long the waitress comes back to our table with a box.

"Here is your Ranco to go. Please have a good day." She leaves the table again.

I still have not once seen that lady's eyes. I got a very good view up her nostrils though. With enough focus, I may have been able to see her brain. I look around the table and notice everyone else is still eating.

"I'll meet you guys back at the ship. I'm going to take Leo's food to him while it's still hot," I say as I stand up and grab the food box.

"Do you want someone to go with you to keep you out of trouble?" Zinka questions.

"How much trouble could I possibly get into on that short of a walk?"

Her response is simply a raised eyebrow. She doesn't have eyebrows, but she raised the muscle where her eyebrow would be. So, I guess I'll say she raised her eye muscle at me.

"Come on, Zinka," I say. "I don't need supervision all the time."

Yet again, her response is a raised eye muscle.

"I'll be fine, Zinka."

"Fine," she relents. "But don't touch anything or talk to anyone. Understand?"

"I'm not a child, Zinka."

And another raised eye muscle.

I let out an indignant huff and proceed to the door. On my way, I can't help but notice that as I am walking, every single eye is on me. What type of so-called advanced society thinks it's a normal thing to treat someone different based on their gender? Oh wait, ours does, or I guess did is more appropriate. No wonder it seemed familiar. I get to the ship, enter the hull, and walk down the corridors towards Leo's room. I hope he likes...whatever the hell Halissy called this thing.

I reach his door and knock. I wait for what seems like forever. I'm not a very patient person. How long have I been waiting? I check my watch and see that it has been a whole twenty seconds. That's enough waiting. Maybe he's sleeping. I'll just leave his whatever–it's–called on the bedside table. I open the door and notice that the lights are out. My eyes can't make out a damn thing. My hand goes up to grope around for a light switch.

My hand contacts it and I flip the switch. When light fills the room, I see Leo sitting with his back against the wall and a small gash on his head.

"Oh fuck. Leo what happ--"

A sharp pain to the back of my skull cuts off my sentence, and I feel myself slipping into unconsciousness. The black envelops all my senses and the world is dark.

CHAPTER 17

I hear movement. I slowly start to open my eyes to figure out where the hell I am and why the hell can't I move my limbs. The first thing that I notice is that Leo is bound to the wall parallel to me. He seems to be trying to break his shackles free. Wait shackles. I look up at my wrists and notice the metal cuffs around them. Well, I either got kidnapped or I blacked out and forgot that I was at a bondage orgy. Either way, I am not okay with this. Or am I?

"Leo, man, what happened?"

"I don't know, but I don't think it's good."

"You could lie to me to make me feel better."

"I can try... this is just a really weird hallucination, courtesy of Danny's drugs?" He seems to wonder if the lie he's spinning is effective as he tells it.

"Oh, come on man. That lie... is not that bad. I mean, I could buy it at least."

We hear the door open, and it interrupts our conversation. A short, robed figure enters. It is the same figure that we ran into in the Demerian Council chamber.

"Elisar?" I ask aloud, though I know damn well the answer. "We are going to die, aren't we?"

She pulls down her hood and the sight that greets me is the same overdone caricature that humans call the grays.

"If it was up to me, then no," she replies in an indifferent tone.

"You know, you could always just not kill us. I mean that would be better for us." I pray to all the nonexistent deities that she can be reasoned with.

"Everyone has their price," she responds before going to the other end of the room.

"Whatever Derask promised you, he isn't going to give it to you," Leo pipes up from the other side of the room. "Just look at Litethite."

"I know, but I still have to attempt to obtain my promised reward, and hope that he comes through." She looks to the ground and quietly finishes with, "Hope's all I have left."

She pulls out a needle: a large needle, to be exact. I really don't like needles. She sees me staring at it and decides to enlighten me.

"This needle is filled with a serum that will knock you out. You won't feel a thing when I... when I do what I have to."

She moves to Leo first.

"No, you can't do this!" He tries to move away from the needle.

You can only go so far when you are chained to the wall, though. She injects the strange substance into his body. His struggles start to slow. His body starts to go limp. Before he can even utter a word, he is unconsciousness once again. I watch her come towards me with the needle.

"If you were going to kill us, then what is up with the needle? Why not just kill us on our ship? Why any of this?"

"I'm supposed to make it appear to the others that they can save you. To answer your question about the needle, I really don't wish to cause you any pain if it can be avoided."

"Look," I try to plead. "Whatever Derask said to you or promised you, it's not worth it."

"You are obviously not a parent."

"Wait, what?"

"Nothing, but if it is any consolation, you will haunt my nightmares for the rest of my days. They all do."

"No!" I shout as I struggle against my binds.

Luck would appear to be on my side as I am somehow able to pull the cuffs from the wall. Might have been a loose bolt, or maybe I am just really strong. The latter helps my self-esteem, so I'm going to go with that one. My flailing body falls down on the hard ground. I stand up and move just quickly enough to avoid the needle. I see this as an opportunity and reach for it. I'm able to knock it out of her hands. As soon as the container full of... whatever the hell is in there shatters, a gun is pointed right at my head.

"Now hold on," I say raising my hands. "I know shooting me may seem like a good idea, but you'll see that it is actually a horrible idea. If for no other reason then I won't enjoy it."

"You have to die. I'm···I'm sorry."

She doesn't pull the trigger, though. I have no idea what's going on in her head, but I can only assume that she is trying to talk herself into it. Knowing that it's only a matter of time before she works up the courage, I scour my surroundings.

I see a random hunk of metal on the ground. It may be my only hope. I grab the scrap as fast as I can and then throw it is hard as I can at her head. I watch it fly, getting closer and closer. Then I watch as it sails a good bit wide of her face and hits the ground behind her. I am not very athletic. She points the gun back at my head. I am getting very tired of having weapons pointed at me.

"Now hold up," I say as I roll on my back and scoot backwards. "I... I really like being alive. I think it's neat. One of my favorite things to do is to exist. It's up there right after cigarettes, weed, and booze. So how about we both go our separate ways so that we can each continue, you know, existing?"

"I'm so sorry."

Yet again though, I catch a lucky break as a steel bar cracks against the side of her cranium knocking her to the floor unconscious.

"Well, looky there, it's a damsel in distress." I look up and see a smirking Pangaea.

"Pangaea!" I can't contain my excitement and jump up to wrap her in a hug.

My actions are interrupted by a hard slap behind the back of my skull.

"No," she shuts me down. "None of that. Now come on, we should get you and Leo out of here. This ship is set to blow."

"It has a self-destruct button?"

"What? No. I just beat the fuck out of all the electrical shit on my way to this room. What would be the purpose of any ship to have a self-destruct button?"

"That is... a very good question."

Pangaea then jumps over to Leo and begins to free his limbs. I help her, so we can get out of here. This would be easier if he didn't have those extra legs.

She says, "Get ready to catch him."

"Okay, I'm on it." I stand up and put my arms out waiting for him.

No sooner said than Leo comes free from the wall. I watch him fall past my outstretched arms and hit the ground. He fell a different direction than I was expecting. This earns me a death glare from Pangaea.

"What?" I ask as I put my hands up in defense.

"You really couldn't even do that one thing?"

"Shut up. It's an honest mistake."

Her response is simply a raised eyebrow.

"It was," I try to plead my case.

"Whatever, just help me lift him up, so we can get the hell out of here."

We hoist him up, throwing his arms over each of our shoulders and begin dragging his limp body to... however Pangaea got here.

"How did you get here anyway?" I ask.

"Well, I came back to the ship shortly after you did. I was done with that disgusting meal after she told us what it was. When I came back, I saw that cloaked figure drag you and Leo out of the ship. Honestly it's surprising that she was able to lift you two fat asses."

"Hey, don't be mean," I'm slightly offended.

"Oh, relax you big baby. After that, I jumped into Zinka's pod and followed her ship out here."

"How do you know how to pilot Zinka's pod?"

"What? Oh, I just sorta guessed. Besides, she didn't go too far. I guess she just wanted to get far enough away so we wouldn't know where you guys went off to."

"You were able figure out how to fly a spaceship?" I ask.

"Sometimes Little Balls, it's better to be lucky than good."

"That's fair enough, I guess."

We make our way to the escape pod carrying the still unconscious Leo. The walls of the ship are entirely smashed. Electrical wires are sparking and somehow the water in the sink is on fire. How this is possible is concerning.

"Come on," Pangaea demands. "The pod is just on the other side of this door."

We cross the threshold and I see the all too familiar pod sitting there. That lovely, glorious, testicle-shaped ship sitting there, ready to take us away from this place. Pangaea hits a hidden button on the side and the canopy opens to welcome us. We lift Leo into the craft and hop in.

"Time to get away," Pangaea says, hitting a button on the panel.

When the canopy is closed, she hits another button, opening the side panel of the ship.

"Punch it, Pangaea," I demand as she guns it out of Elisar's craft.

"I know what to do, dipshit."

"I know you know, but I also know that giving demands makes me feel important."

"Little Balls?"

"Yes, bestest buddy?"

"Shut up," she says calmly. Eerily calm.

"Aye, aye, scary lady. Shutting up now." I finish with the zipping the lip motion.

My reward is a roll of the eyes. So many people giving me eye gestures around here. If it's not the eye roll then it's a glare or a raised eye brow.

The seemingly endless expanse of space catches my attention, as the nearby star burns brightly. My mind loses itself in the endless possibilities of the universe. I look over and notice Elisar's ship erupting in explosions. No sound enters the pod, but the sight itself is unnerving, to say the least. My mind goes back to the stars around me before a slight gleam on the dash breaks my thoughts. I look down and notice an odd yet familiar device sitting there.

"Oh shit," is the only response I can muster.

"What is it, Little....oh shit." She notices the device in my hands.

I hesitantly press play and see the screen come to life. A familiar face appears on the screen. "Hey, valuable voter," Landon says. "I'm glad that I have the chance to talk. What can I do to earn you vote today?"

"Landon!" Derask shouts off screen. "Give me that, right now."

The image blurs briefly before it settles down. Derask stands, staring at me.

"We have been over this. Stop trying to get people to vote for you. You will have power over a planet when this is all settled," Derask says.

"I'll appeal to everyone there. I will be the most beloved leader ever."

"You just can't get good minions nowadays," Derask moans to himself before turning his attention to the screen. "Hello, little monkey. I hope you don't mind, but I had Elisar slip this in your pod before she abducted you. It always pays to be one step ahead." He pauses his self-monologue to smirk at the camera.

This smirk seems to be lasting an awkwardly long time. I'm not aware if there is a special social etiquette for the appropriate length of time that a smirk should last, but I'm pretty sure this surpassed it. He finally breaks the silence.

"Now before you ask, Elisar did make it out safely but a little banged up in the head thanks to your angry friend there."

"She had it coming, jackass," Pangaea defends.

"I'm not arguing that, just keep your beast on a leash, monkey boy. Now back to the matter at hand. This device isn't the only thing that I had Elisar plant in your ship, but you will see the other surprise in 5...4...3...2...and 1."

We all look around waiting for something to happen. Well not everyone. Leo is still sleeping like a big purple cockroach-type baby thing.

"Uh, nothing happened," I say.

"Dammit Bubba, you were supposed to hit the button!" Derask

yells off screen.

"Well, which button am I supposed to press? There's like a dozen here."

"There is one button on the pedestal and then there is a lever. Just hit the button."

"Alright, alright jeez."

"Good bye, kiddies," Derask taunts as he cuts the screen to black.

The ship violently jerks to one side and back. The entirety of it seems to be rattling with immense force. If it weren't for the fact that we were squashed so tightly in the small craft, we would surely be thrown haphazardly about.

"Oh shit!" I hear Pangaea shout from beside me.

"No, no. Oh, shit is bad. Don't do bad."

"Well, do you want the hard truth or a comforting lie?"

"Can I have both? The truth first, then a lie to make me feel better," I reply.

"Okay. The truth is our controls are locked and it is bringing us down towards planet Nebul."

"Okay," I mull over what she said. "Now tell me a comforting lie to make me feel better so I don't die terrified."

"Well, the planet is just pulling us in for a nice, loving embrace."

"Aw, that sounds sweet."

"Engaging the safety harnesses," Pangaea says. "I'm going to do what I can to slow our descent."

I see the safety bars drop from the ceiling, but this presents a certain problem. There are three people in this pod and two safety bars. Now I may not be an intelligent man or some kind of math wizard, but I know for a fact this isn't going to work. The sight of Pangaea trying to pull back on a bar momentarily takes my focus. She has her safety device attached, and part of me knows that she hasn't even noticed the math problem.

After five seconds of serious thought, the decision is clear. I lock the bar over Leo and manage to squeeze my left arm and shoulder in the harness. This should turn out fine, maybe.

"The ground's coming up fast. Prepare for impact," Pangaea says through clenched teeth.

The view from the canopy clearly shows the ground getting closer and closer. Pangaea has done a phenomenal job in slowing us down. Unfortunately, I am still under the impression that this is going to hurt like hell.

"Ungh, get ready, Little Balls," she continues her strain.

I wonder if there's air conditioning in hell. Before my self-monologue can focus on anything else, I see that the planet has us in an embrace. The force of the impact sends me flying out of the seat. I feel an intense pain shoot up my left side. However, the pain is short lived as the front of the pod meets my cranium for a little rendezvous. A very, very painful rendezvous. My world goes dark as the last thought to cross my mind is: I didn't expect to die like this. I guess I'm coming, God. You better prepare your genitals for a meeting with my foot. The world goes dark.

CHAPTER 18

A dark void surrounds me. It feels like the nightmares I keep having, but this time seems different. I can see a bright light in the distance. It seems to be coming towards me or I'm going towards it. Spatial awareness is extremely hard when you have no landmarks to check.

The light makes a sudden stop in front of me and explodes even brighter. My hands shoot up to shield my retinas from damage. When it dims, I look and see the image of a beautiful woman.

"What the hell?" I question.

She gives a warm, comforting smile before she replies.

"Hello there. I've been expecting you."

"You have? Why? Where am I? Who are you?"

"You are in a dark void. I thought that was obvious. As to who I am, that is for you to decide," she says.

"What?"

"Well, one possibility is that I'm God. Another possibility is I'm Satan. Could be that I'm the grim reaper. Or I'm just a hallucination. Who's to say?"

"Wait, does that mean I'm dead?"

"Maybe."

Silence overtakes us. I'm too busy trying in vain to make out anything about my surroundings. She is just floating there patiently. A gentle smile is still adorning her face.

"So, God···person···thing, how about that uh···baseball team?" I awkwardly question when the silence becomes too much for me to handle.

She stares at me with confusion in her eyes. Her mouth, however, has remained unaltered.

"I don't like baseball," she finally replies. "I find it too boring."

"Yeah, me neither. I'm just terrible with the whole small talk thing."

"You are face to face with the being that is possibly the creator of the entire universe. Do you have anything that you wish to ask of me?"

I ponder this question. What do you ask the being that supposedly knows all? What are the most important questions that human kind has that plague our minds? Oh, I've got it.

"Why is the sky blue?"

"Because it looked ugly in green."

"What is the point of the pope?" I ask.

"Someone has to wear the funny hat."

"Why do ghosts wear clothes?"

"Modesty."

"Hmmm," I hum. "What is the purpose of life."

"To die."

"Well, that's morbid," I state.

"Don't blame me. That's just the way it is. Not everything can be all happy all the time. Your cells will eventually deteriorate. That's just a fact. Nothing lasts forever. Just look at the bright side: the fact that you have life at all is a gift."

I take a moment to look around the world where I find myself. It's still just a dark void. Nothing here but me and the maybe-God-lady. Her aura is still shining bright. She is still just floating there, smiling at me.

"I've got another question," I say.

"Go ahead, child."

"Why do terrible people exist? You plagued this world with Nazis, murderers, and televangelists. Why would you do that?"

"Hey, don't lay that on me. I gave you people free will. It's not my fault you all screwed it up."

"Wake up, Thaddeus," I hear a voice call through the dark void.

It sounds like Zinka. Shit, she used my real name. Does this mean I'm in trouble?

"I need you here with me, with the crew. Please just wake up," she continues.

Well from the sound of her voice, she doesn't sound mad. In truth, she sounds a little sad.

"Wake the hell up and that's an order," she says, trying to take the commanding tone that she does.

"It will be okay," I hear Halissy comfort. "All his vitals are normal, and his cloned limb is responding well to the neurological sensors."

Well that's good. It is nice to know that I have normal vitals. Wait a minute, did she just say cloned limb? God dammit Thad, wake up. The God or Satan lady slowly starts to vanish. My eyes slowly start to open, which, in hindsight, was a little bit of a rushed decision. The bright fluorescent lighting blinds me as it invades my eyeballs. Out of pure instinct, my hands come up to cover my sensitive little light receptors.

My right hand feels normal, but something is off with my left hand. I can feel my left arm slightly, but it doesn't seem to reach my face.

Before I can dwell on this thought, though, my body is enveloped in a hug. My nostrils also pick up the strong scent of cookies.

"I'm so happy you're okay," Zinka sounds relieved.

"How are Leo and Pangaea?" I ask.

"They are both okay. The safety bars saved them, but of course your dumb ass just had to play hero. Now the second you get better, you can be damn sure that I'm going to give you a firm hit to the back of the skull."

I look down at my body and see the strangest sight that I have ever witnessed. My left arm looked normal except for the fact that it was the size of a toothpick.

"I've got another question now. Why the hell do I have a tiny arm?" I question as I examine my new appendage.

The minuscule limb just kind of wiggles about. It doesn't really do anything else. This may need some getting used to.

"Well your arm was caught in the bar. It was able to slow you down a bit, but the force still removed your arm up to your shoulder. Unfortunately, we were not able to locate your arm."

"We had to clone you an arm," Halissy explains. "It will take some time to for it to grow to full size. Other than that, you just needed some metal rods to replace some of your bones."

"Wait, I have metal in me?" I question. "Does that mean that I'm a robot? I am robot Thad."

"You are not a robot, Little Balls," Zinka shoots me down.

"Awe, that's too bad. How long was I out?" I ask still staring at my robot bit.

"Well," Halissy starts out. "You were out for about two weeks."

"Two weeks? God damn."

"Yeah, Leo was only out for a few days and Pangaea was surprisingly okay. She, well, was surprisingly easy to patch up. I had to fight her for it though. You know how she can be. Typical human, too stubborn to use common sense."

"That's racist."

"You were also a stubborn patient. Which is saying a lot considering you were unconscious the whole time," Halissy states.

"Yeah, I've always been a little hard headed," I say, still unable to tear my eyes off my piece of machinery.

"I'll leave you to rest," Halissy says as she gets up to leave. "Just try to relax."

"And I need to go check the coordinates, Little Balls," Zinka says as she makes her way out with Halissy. "And don't get into trouble."

With that last word, she shuts the door and leaves me to my own devices. My eyes still seem fixated on the tiny little arm protruding from my left shoulder. It's an odd feeling, to be missing a piece of yourself and then to have that piece of you replaced by tiny arm.

The door opening takes my attention away from my thoughts as I look to see who is interrupting my thoughts.

"Hey, Little Balls," Pangaea says as she comes in. "About damn time you got your lazy ass up. Did you have a good rest, sleeping beauty?"

I see her eyes go temporarily towards my little arm. She then does her best to avoid looking at it. My arm is gross now. I wonder when it will be fully grown.

"Oh yeah, it was just simply delightful," each syllable drips with sarcasm.

"How are you feeling?" She questions as she takes a seat next to the bed.

"I feel like I was hit by a truck."

"You were hit by a planet, though."

"But on the bright side, it only felt like a truck," I say with a smirk.

"Always the optimist, aren't you?"

"On occasions. On other occasions, life just sucks, and it is on these occasions when being an optimist is just down right stupid."

"I think this may be one of those times then," she says as she looks at the monitors beside me.

"It is, but I have never once claimed to be an intelligent man. At least I keep it entertaining."

"Well you can't argue with that," she concedes before falling into an awkward silence. She just seems to be staring at the ceiling. The silence in the room is too much before she decides to break it.

"You know your hero complex will get you killed one day, right?" She glances back towards me.

"I have no idea what you mean," I reply while crossing my arms behind my head. By crossing my arms, I mean I put my right one behind my head as the left just sort of twitched.

"Just keep telling yourself that, but you know you could have fit both Leo and you under the bar if one of you would have been sat on the other's lap."

"Why didn't I think of that?" I ask more to myself than to anyone.

"Because," she replies. "You don't think straight and your need to save everyone prevents you from actually thinking through your actions."

"Maybe I do need to think things through a bit more."

"Yeah. Yeah, you do." Pangaea says standing up. "Now, lay down and rest, and for fuck's sake, next time, think about your actions for just a little bit longer."

Pangaea makes her way out of the room and the door shuts behind her leaving me to my own thoughts.

Why am I still alive? I'm going to say that I am just really, really lucky.

What the hell was that noise?

There it is again. I look around the room not really being able to find the source of the noise.

The last one causes me to look up to the air vent, that I didn't even notice was there five seconds ago. The vent starts to open as a shadowy figure drops down from it and stands menacingly in the corner of the room. The shadow speaks.

"There is no use in screaming. I have locked the door. Your friends have no way of getting to you."

"Oh shit, hey Elisar. Long time, no see. So, how have you been? I've been great. Just woke up from a two-week coma. Please don't try to kill me," I say in one extremely long breath.

Her response is a gun pointed at me.

"Again, with the gun?" I question.

"You need to die now. This is my last chance. I cannot fail again. I just can't afford to."

"Everyone can afford failure," I say scooching off the table and backing against a wall. "Hell, I'm a broke fucker and I afford it all the time."

She starts walking towards me with the gun pointing at my skull. I look around trying to find a way out of this. There is one door and it is locked. There is also the one tiny detail of it being behind a hostile extraterrestrial with a gun. There is also the vent, but I am in no way near in good enough shape to jump that high.

"I'm so sorry," she says.

"If you are sorry, why don't you just not shoot me?"

"It's the only way. Please forgive me."

She pulls the trigger and time seems to slow down. I try to dodge. Unfortunately, or fortunately, I lose my footing and fall. The laser misses me and hits the back wall. I look around and notice a random piece of scrap metal. Well couldn't hurt to try it again. I grab the piece and chuck it with all my might. Miraculously, the random hunk, of whatever the hell it was, knocks the gun from her hand. This is my chance, so I take it with the only thing I could possibly think of doing. I stand up, rush her, and headbutt her with a loud 'donk'.

Her body collapses to the floor, unconscious.

Tik crashes through the door. He barrels in with his laser gun aimed and ready to fire. "Little Balls! What's going on here."

He looks down at Elisar and then back up at me. He repeats this for what feels like an hour, but it was only like three looks each.

"Is, is she dead?" He asks perplexed.

"No, but she is unconscious."

"Then we must finish her off." He raises the gun towards her head.

I don't know why, but something didn't seem right about that. I can't quite put my finger on it, but it seems like this would be a huge mistake.

"No, wait," I stand between Elisar and Tik's gun.

Pangaea, Zinka, and Leo come running into the room to check the commotion.

"What are you talking about. She's a killer."

"Look," I can't seem to make a logical argument for it. "I don't quite know how to explain this, but I just feel that that would be a mistake."

"She has to die, Little Balls," Leo tries to reason with me.

Zinka chimes in. "Little Balls, she tried to kill you how many times? And you just want to let her live."

"Look, if you are trying to get me to spill a reason then you are wasting your time. I don't have one besides my gut telling me otherwise," I say, not moving a muscle.

"I know you want to try to save everyone, but not everyone can be saved," Zinka says.

"I just can't let you do it. Look, there are bad people in the universe, but there are also good people who are forced to do bad things. People aren't always what they appear, and life isn't always black and white."

"Little Balls," Zinka says letting whatever thought she was going to say simply die on her tongue.

"I say we listen to him," Pangaea speaks up for the first time.

"You can't be serious," Leo says.

"Trust me," Pangaea replies. "I know that sometimes dipshit here tends to react without thinking. I also know that the expression 'the road to hell is paved with good intentions' perfectly describes him and his decisions."

It doesn't seem like she is really helping my case here, but she continues.

"We should still give him the benefit of the doubt here. We all know that he wants to play hero and who can blame him. The man has a good heart. Do you really want to be the reason for breaking that heart?"

She then walks over to me and smooshes my face between her hands before she continues trying to help me by speaking in a baby voice

"I mean just look at this face. You don't want to make this face sad, do you?"

I push her hands away from my face because the whole squeezing face thing kind of hurts.

"Well thanks so much for your help Pangaea," I glare at Pangaea.

Leo jumps into the conversation. "You know, there really can't be that much harm in sparing her."

"Ugh," Zinka says as she tries to rub away a headache. "Fine. Leo, Tik pick her up and secure her to the medical bed. Pangaea, go ask Halissy to come in to check her for injury."

"Yes ma'am," they say oddly in unison.

Tik and Leo leave the room, but Pangaea turns around to address me.

"You," she pushes a finger hard into my chest, "better not make me regret sticking up for you, asshole."

"Aww, aren't you a sweetheart," I smirk.

Pangaea rolls her eyes and exits the room. I look back and notice that Zinka is a little more agitated than normal. She gives me an unusually long glare before leaving. I have no idea what that was about. Tik and Leo come up to me, and Tik speaks first.

"Little Balls, are you sure that you know what you're doing? I mean, this does seem kind of dangerous."

I reply, "Yeah, man. I'm sure. It's just... it's just some of the things she was saying seemed like if she had a choice, she wouldn't do it. I feel like we can help her."

Leo then jumps in, "It is your call. I just hope you're right."

They both leave, just as Halissy and Pangaea come back in.

"Now, Little Balls," Halissy says. "Would you care to explain why Derask's minion is on my table?"

Now how should I explain this to her? I guess the truth is the best possible route here.

"Well, in short, she tried to kill me so I headbutted her. Then I didn't want Tik to kill her because··· my gut says we shouldn't. So, with a little help from Pangaea, I managed to convince the rest of the crew to just roll with it."

"So," Halissy turns to Pangaea, "This is partly your fault."

"Come on," Pangaea says before, yet again, grabbing my face and smooshing it. "Just look at this face."

Halissy gives her a skeptical look before shaking her head and heading over to check Elisar. I push Pangaea's hands away and walk over to the table with Halissy.

"You two be good now," Pangaea says as she leaves the medical bay.

"So, how is she, doc?" I ask as I stand beside the doctor.

"She is just unconscious. She should recover soon."

"So, she'll be fine then?"

"Yup. She will be up soon and trying to kill you again."

"She hasn't tried to kill me that many times. Only twice."

"You do know that that is more than most people get attempted murdered, right?" She sanity-checks me.

"Well yeah, but most people are not me, so shhhhh." I reply. "So, are you having fun on this mission?"

Her response is simply a raised eyebrow.

"Oh, don't give me that look. You just joined the crew right before I got kidnapped, so we haven't gotten a chance to talk."

"What would we talk about?" She's still looking at the unconscious alien.

"Well, has anyone ever told you that you look like a snake?"

"I... I don't know what a snake is."

"Oh, right. Well, it's an animal on Earth."

"That's not much to go on. You know that, right?"

"Oh, right. Just imagine you, but without arms and legs. And a lot smaller. Plus, like eighty percent of people are afraid of you."

"Gee, thanks." She seems mildly offended.

"Oh, shit was that... was that racist? Look, I didn't really mean it like that. I just⋯ oh shit. I am a terrible person. Aren't I?"

"Relax, I know you well enough from the crew's stories. I look forward to getting to know you."

"What slanderous things are they saying about me? Is it that I am a beautiful, amazing, intelligent bastard?"

"Hahaha. You have no idea what slander means do you?"

"Yes," I reply while shifting my eyes to the left and right.

Everyone knows that that is the universal sign of 'I know what I'm talking about'. A voice from the table interrupts my conversation.

"Ugh, where am I?" Elisar says.

The realization that she is bound dawns on her which, in turn, starts to cause her to panic.

"What the fuck? Let me go!" She screams. "Please I need to go. Beason needs me. Please."

CHAPTER 19

Her thrashing turns to a mild struggle and her screams turn into a low sob.

"Now just calm down, Elisar," Halissy's voice is soothing as she tries to calm her down.

I butt in, "Now tell us what you're talking about and who Beason is."

"Beason is my son. Derask took him from me. He said that if I failed him, he...he would kill him."

"He took your child?" Halissy questions.

"Yes. That's why I needed to kill you," She looks pointedly at me.

"Me? What the hell did I do?" I ask.

"Derask feels like your dumb luck could be his downfall," she says between sobs.

Just as she says this, Danny walks through the doorway and steps over the debris of the door Tik destroyed.

"Hey, Thad. I'm glad to see you're up. Did you have a nice two-week nap?" Danny says coming up to me.

"It wasn't a nap, dude. It was a coma." I correct him.

"Ah, same thing. How's it going, doctor?"

"Can't you see we are a little busy here, Danny?" Halissy seems annoyed as she turns back to Elisar.

Danny then notices who is strapped onto the table.

"Hey, Elisar. How's it going?"

"Uhhhh... what?" She questions in a stupor.

"Those straps don't look too comfy. Here, let me help."

Before anyone could do or say anything else, Danny pulls out a knife and somehow manages to cut every strap in a single cut. That is impressive. She doesn't seem to fully register that she is free.

"I... uh...what?" Elisar questions.

I can't believe what just happened, "Dude, what are you doing?"

"I set her free."

"Was that wise?" Halissy questions.

"Yeah. Look, I've seen enough people tied to tables. Just seems like an odd thing to do. Plus, pretty sure it's kind of a dick move."

Elisar slowly sits up on the table. Her eyes move slowly from each three of us, as if waiting for us to attack. Halissy and I are still a little shocked. Danny, on the other hand, is way too trusting and oblivious to care.

"There," Danny breaks the awkward silence. "Isn't that better?"

"Thank you," she acknowledges Danny.

There doesn't appear to be any immediate danger. So, it's time to get back to the previous conversation. Before I can bring it back up though, I hear a strange sound coming from Elisar's pocket.

"What is that?" Halissy asks.

"It's Derask," she admits as she pulls out the all too familiar device.

"Elisar," Derask sneers. "It seems you have failed me, my dear. You know what that means."

Derask walks off screen and comes back a few moments later. Unfortunately, he has a small grey being that he is dragging behind him. The little creature is crying and doing its best to try and get away. Holy shit, that must be Beason.

"Oh god, my baby!" Elisar screams to the screen. "Please don't hurt my baby!"

Derask just laughs his abhorrent laugh.

The son of a bitch then pulls a laser from his belt. I know what is coming. I wish I was wrong, but Derask is extremely predictable.

He puts the gun up to the child's head. The sound of his crying mixes with his mother's. I've gotta do something, but my mind seems to be at a standstill. It is Derask who breaks the palpable silence.

"You know what?" He says as he puts the gun down. "I have a much better idea. Instead of just killing this kid, I have an idea for a fun game. I'm going to give you a chance to rescue the lad."

Zinka takes the bait. "What are you getting at, Derask?"

"I just want to have some fun," he says with a sneer.

"Just tell us what you want already," Danny is impatient.

"Humph," Derask lets out an indignant sigh. "You rude little monkey."

"Wow," I say, "Don't be racist, man."

"But I am incredibly racist towards the human race."

"Well, I guess that is the truer definition of the term racist. Especially considering, we are part of the human race," I'm clearly thinking out loud as I react.

"What did you think I meant?" Derask seems genuinely confused.

"Well, on Earth, ignorant jackasses use the term monkey as an insult towards black people," I explain.

"Well, that's just stupid," Derask seems exasperated.

Even an evil jackass knows that racism is stupid. Derask continues to tell us about his plan.

"You see," he starts. "My hatred for the human race is increasing with each passing day. So, I'm going to put little Beason on a docking ship with Bubba and several of my guards. All you have to do is go on that ship, defeat the guards and Bubba, and rescue the child."

"Is that it?" It sounds too simple, too good to be true.

"No, there's more, monkey. The only three that can go on this little rescue mission are the two stupid monkeys and the one angry monkey."

"So, you only want the humans to come?" Danny asks.

"Yes," Derask says. "There is something almost poetic about the last four humans in the universe on the same ship, where at least one of them will die."

I catch something, "Wait, four? What happened to Landon?"

"Ugh," he grimaces. "That man was the absolute worst. I threw him out on a hostile planet. He is probably dead by now. I'll send the coordinates of where the docking ship will be. You'd better listen to my instructions, or I'll destroy all of you. That's including the docking ship. Safe to say that I don't care if Bubba lives or dies. See you soon. monkeys."

With that, he cuts the transmission and the screen goes to static. Everyone in the room falls into awkward silence. That seems to be happening a lot lately. The silence breaks as Danny speaks up.

"So... what time are we leaving?"

CHAPTER 20

"You can't be serious?" Zinka questions.

After the transmission ends, the entire crew, plus Elisar, gather in the cockpit to discuss the current issue.

Zinka continues. "This is incredibly asinine."

"It's obviously a trap," Leo warns. "He hates you three for some reason. He especially hates you, Little Balls. He will probably kill you as soon as you step on the ship."

"I highly doubt that." Pangaea interrupts. "He is a jackass and he does everything for his own entertainment. This is probably just another game to him, even if it means doing stupid things."

Tik interjects, "Yeah, but Little Balls has stepped on his toes an awful lot. Who's to say that he won't skip the convoluted plan this time and just go right for the throat?"

Danny pipes up, "It's just not his style. I say we go for it."

"I do too," I'm in.

"There is no way I'm letting you three get yourselves killed," Zinka is adamant.

"Look," Elisar speaks up. "I know that none of you have any reason to trust me. I've done a lot of horrible things to a lot of innocent people, but you have to believe me: I did it all for my son. If you were parents, you all would do the same. I don't like asking others for assistance, but if you do this, I will be in your debt."

"You," Zinka points at Elisar. "Have no right to talk. Hell, you have no right to even be here."

"Come on, Zinka, be reasonable," Danny placates.

"Be reasonable? Be reasonable?! She tried to kill Leo. Not to mention, she tried to kill Little Balls twice."

"Well, yeah," I admit. "But I'm still kicking."

My reward is a firm smack to the back of the skull from a green hand. I am definitely going to have a concussion. I may have to ask Dr. Halissy to look at that for me. Although I'm not entirely sure how much she knows about human head injuries.

"We are not doing this," Zinka stands firm. "I won't let my crew get hurt, if I can help it."

Pangaea quietly holds her ground, "Zinka, we are doing this."

Her response is a deadly glare. They both sort of just stare at each other. A lot of staring. I look around the room to see that everyone else is waiting with bated breath.

"Look," Pangaea finally speaks. "Let's face it, this has nothing to do with anything we were originally planning to do, but we have to help, here. He's just a child. If you're worried about these idiots, then don't be. I'll take care of them. I'll make sure they don't get hurt, but you know that this needs to happen. Otherwise, Little Balls will attempt to do it anyway -- you know he will. He is a dumb idiot with a big heart. He also has trouble listening and following directions. The best we can do is to actually make a plan to prevent him from maiming himself."

"Ugh," Zinka groans. "Fine, but we are doing this my way. You three will be careful. Pangaea, you are in charge. You are the only one smart enough to well... to not kill everyone."

Pangaea salutes. "Aye, aye captain."

"Don't you start that, too. You have been hanging out with these two too much," Zinka motions to me and Danny.

"Meet in Docking Port Two in one hour. That is when we will get to the location that Derask said his docking ship will be. You three will take the cruisers to the target."

"Whoa, whoa, we only drove those things once and that was in the simulation. Are we really ready to take them for an actual flight?" I say, rightfully concerned about my piloting skills.

"Actually," Zinka replies. "We all were practicing for the two weeks that you were out. We were able to get up to difficulty level 7 while you were sleeping."

"Great," I sigh. "It's like school all over again. I miss a couple days and when I come back, I have no idea how to fly a space ship. I have tons of homework. Plus, I have a tiny arm."

"How is that like school? And there is no homework," Pangaea points out.

"True, but everything else is just like school."

"Focus, Little Balls," Zinka says in a stern tone. "You just have to pilot the ship to the meeting point. You shouldn't need it to get into a battle yet."

"But what if I want to?"

"You really shouldn't, you idiot," she's right. "We are on course for the ship, so you are all dismissed for the next hour. I will call you when we are there."

"There is a more important thing that needs taken care of first," Elisar interjects. "I'm sorry for waiting this long to tell you, but Derask has bugs and mics in here."

"Wait, what?" Zinka is pissed. "What do you mean bugs and mics?"

"Well, Derask had his puppet, Litethite, place bugs all over the ship. We should find them. To my knowledge, he has seventeen placed on this ship, but I don't know where. I'm so sorry I didn't speak up sooner."

"Oh, for fuck's sake, are you serious?" Zinka asks.

"Unfortunately, yes," Elisar concedes.

"Shit, team," Zinka says. "Everyone spread out and search the ship. We need to find those bugs. So much for relaxing, I guess."

With that, Zinka rushes out of the cockpit with everyone else in tow. Before I can get out however, I feel a hand grab my shoulder. I turn towards the owner of the hand and see Pangaea with nervous expression on her face.

"Hold up, Thaddeus." She's using my real name. Am I in trouble?

"I want to talk to you for a second."

She looks around nervously and bites her lip, trying to figure out how she is going to word whatever the hell she is about to say. I don't think I have ever seen her nervous. This is weird. I don't like it.

She continues. "You...uh, you are into Zinka, aren't you?"

This question confuses me to the point of the blood rushing to my face rapidly. "Wha...what are you talking about? I... tch... I am not into Zinka. That's just so--"

A firm slap to the back of the skull interrupts my denial fueled stuttering. I see that Pangaea has a look of determination on her face. How many hits can a person's skull take?

"Don't be such a coward," She says abruptly.

"Ugh, fine, I'm... I may have a crush on Zinka."

"See," she looks smug. "Was that so hard?"

She says this with a smile, but something about her expression just screams sadness. I can't say with certainty, however, considering her facial features are so hard to read. She is like a book that's written by Landon and is purely nonsensical dribble.

"Well," I say. "What can I do about it?"

"Are you really that stupid?"

"Well... in light of my recent decisions, I'm going to have to say probably."

"You will tell her, and you will tell her now."

"Oh yeah, because that isn't awkward at all. 'Hey, I know we are of different species, but I love you and the fact that you smell of cookies.'"

"I see no problem with that, but maybe word it a little better."

"Aren't we supposed to be looking for things?" I ask her.

"Oh, we have plenty of time. What's he going to listen to, our oh-so-entertaining banter?"

"It feels more like chatter than banter to me."

"Whatever. Just go tell her, asshole."

"What's all this rush for me to get rejected? I thought we were friends."

"We are. That's why I'm making you do this, and it's not definite that she will reject you."

She squishes my face before continuing. "You're a little sweetie."

I push her hands away from my face before replying. "Yup, my massive amount of success when Earth was still around being proof of that. You know, with all the women just lining up around my apartment just to get a date with me."

"Well if they didn't, then they were morons. Being scared is no excuse for cowardice."

"I am pretty sure that is the only excuse for cowardice. That's how being scared works," I smugly reply.

"Shut up. Now go talk to Zinka. Just remember what Leo said during Stuan's funeral. Quit being a bitch. I'll go try to find some of those bug thingies."

Pangaea leaves the cockpit and I am left all alone. Stupid Pangaea and her stupid smart suggestions. Why can't she just let me be miserable? I was content with that. Although content in misery is either oxymoronic or just plain sad. I can't really figure out which. If only I had a dictionary, then I could find out what an oxymoron was.

I leave the cockpit and try to figure out where the hell Zinka went off to. I have no idea where to look. My observational skills require a tad bit of work. I wander into the mess hall and notice Leo looking for bugs. No one else is around. Well she is not here. Seeing Leo in the mess hall brings horrid images of what that prick Litethite did.

I make my way out and start heading towards the armory. She may be there. I peek in the door and notice it is empty. I remember getting my first concussion here. Such wonderfully fond memories.

I start heading down the hall and see a familiar looking door with strange writing on it and a keypad next to it. Well, I do need a little time to clear my head. My finger presses the code and the door opens to reveal a staircase. I begin to ascend the hidden stairs up to the top floor and see the two doors on either side of the hall. I head towards the right one and open it revealing the glass room that looks out to the endless abyss of the galaxy.

I notice a green figure standing in the room looking around it carefully, so absorbed in her current task, she hasn't even noticed my standing there. Part of me was hoping not to find her. That would have been easier and a lot less stressful. The door closing breaks her concentration.

"Hello, Little Balls. Did you happen to find any of the bugs?" she questions while continuing her search.

"Well... no but I'm looking. I'm looking. I... uh... just wanted to talk with you for a second. It's kind of important in a relatively unimportant but slightly important way," I awkwardly blabber as I walk closer to her.

The familiar scent of cookies fills my nostrils the closer I get to her. Cookies are amazing.

"Uh... what?" Is her response.

"Well, hypothetically speaking, what would you say if a talking ape from a planet that no longer exists may, sort of, kind of, have an itty-bitty little crush on you? A crush that makes me, I mean, this ape, go all stupid."

"Uh··· what?"

"You··· uh··· I··· well, you see···"

She just stares at me. She seems to be expecting me to finish my thought eventually. Don't really want to finish this thought but I continue.

"You have a very nice face!!"

Her response is, well, nothing. No facial reaction. No verbal reaction. Hell, she doesn't even look confused, which I thought would be the appropriate response. She is just standing there damn near motionless. I think this was a mistake. I wonder if time travel is possible. If so, it would be very helpful right now.

Her facial expression finally changes. It isn't one of rejection necessarily but more one of sadness. I guess this is going to end badly. Although, that was to be expected.

"Little Balls, I... I really can't."

Well I should have expected this. She continues when she sees my face droop.

"Thaddeus, you are one of my best friends, and I do really care about you, but--"

"Is this one of those 'It's not you, it's me' things that are used as an excuse? Even though we all know that when someone says that it is always the exact opposite."

"No, Little Balls. It's just that Aldinians do not feel the monogamous love that humans do. Our species uses mating merely as a tool for reproductive purposes. The Aldinians never saw reason behind just one partner. Sex is purely a necessity. But you have to understand this isn't your fault. None of this is. It's⋯ it's mine."

"What do you mean?"

"You see I--"

A strange yet familiar beeping noise can be heard. Zinka and I, temporarily forgetting our current conversation, look around for that familiar device.

We search and search but cannot find it anywhere.

Oh, where could that annoying little bit of tech be? I swear I'll destroy this entire ship. An elbow to the ribs distracts me. Nothing distracts like a horridly burning ribcage. I look over and see Zinka pointing to the table. My eyes follow her finger and I see the device sitting on the table in plain sight.

Zinka picks up the message square device and presses the play button on it.

"Hello Zinka, Monkey," Derask says with a smile. "It feels like I just talked to you."

"Blah, blah, blah Hitler," I mock the device. "Monkey this. Unoriginal insult that. Look, you are way too predictable, so just tell us what you want so that we don't have to keep playing this stupid game."

"Aww, someone is a touchy little ape."

"Yeah, you say that like an insult but, I mean, humans did evolve from a common ancestor of apes and we are members of the great ape family so it's not really an insult. Mostly just a statement of fact. You're bad at this."

"Don't think you can try to insult me monk--"

"You have ugly antennae," I childishly interrupt.

"I... uh... what?"

"I said your antennae are ugly."

"Nice try, but--"

"Jerk."

"Stop interrupting me yo--"

"Your eyes are weird."

"Are you done?" He seems exasperated.

"Well, I am for now, but that is liable to change at any moment. I tend to change my mind a lot."

"Ugh," he groans. "Well, I couldn't help but listen to your conversation. Does the little monkey have a crush on a member of a superior race? Even if that particular member is a defect."

"Your face is a defect," I retort. It seems that I wasn't done.

"Zinka, did you release your pheromone to infatuate this little primate?"

I stare questioningly at the jerk on the screen before I look over to Zinka who is looking at the screen with a mix of horror, regret, and maybe a tad bit of hunger, but that is neither here nor there. She immediately turns off the screen before hanging her head low.

"Zinka?" I question softly. "What did he mean, pheromone?"

"The··· Aldinian females have a pheromone sac that they use as either a mating tool or a self-defense mechanism. Whenever you first met me on Earth, I··· I was scared."

My sight loses focus as I take this all in. I'm not really in love. My mind was simply tricked. The sad thing is that I don't even know if this is only temporary or permanent. Will I be cursed to feel like this for the rest of my life, or will I end up getting over it?

Zinka continues. "Little Balls, you have to believe me, I never meant to do this to you. I would never ever want to hurt you."

"How long?" I need to know the truth.

"How long what?"

"How long will this last?"

"I don't know." She momentarily looks down in thought before looking up and continuing. "For Aldinians, it is only temporary. It is merely a tool, so we can procreate. I have no idea how it effects humans though. I hope you can forgive me."

I look at her. Her eyes seem sincere in her apology. I really wish I could be mad at her. I really wish I could hate her. I really wish I could blame her. Unfortunately, I only have myself to blame. All of this is a result of my decisions. I have to take the blame when it's mine to take.

"Look, I don't blame you. I just feel, well, I don't really know how I feel. I just wish I could get back to normal soon."

"Are… are we still friends?"

"Of course, Zinka, of course."

With that last sentence, my head lowers and I feel two arms wrap around me in a friendly hug, and the smell of cookie dough fills my nostrils. My arms find themselves around her in return. The hug is comforting but also damning. My heart, although it knows it's been fooled, still skips a beat when she holds me.

Zinka releases me and looks into my eyes with pure empathy.

"Are you going to be okay?"

"I'll be fine."

"Okay, you wait here. Take some time to think and relax here. I'm going to help the team find the rest of the bugs."

Zinka then finds the bug that was placed in here and destroys it before leaving the room. The door shuts and I am left alone with the never-ending expanse of space to help clear my thoughts.

Yet again solitude is my company. My sadness is temporarily forgotten when a stench reaches my nose. It is a strong rancid smell.

"What the hell is that smell?" I ask no one in particular.

Finally, I realize that the smell is coming from me. When was the last time I showered? Well, I was in a coma for a while. I guess it's time to wash up. The tingling will help me feel better.

Before leaving the room, my eyes take one last look at the massive window that looks out into space. I turn back and leave the room and begin heading towards my own cabin to enjoy a nice relaxing shower.

My room opens, and I walk towards the door on the opposite end of the room. That door slides open and I start to strip naked. The pink liquid starts to run out of the tap. Stepping into it, the tingles come back to my body.

I finish washing my body and step out of the shower. The idea of putting on clothes seems uncomfortable right now. I'm alone. What person hates being naked?

I grab a cigarette from the table and light it. The bed feels comfortable against me and the cig filling my lungs brings upon a sense of peace. Some naked smoking was much needed at this point.

The cigarette burns and gives my mouth a delightful orgasm of the taste buds. The door opens in the middle of my inhale. The sudden intrusion causes a fit of coughs to burst from my lungs. Pangaea comes in the door.

"Hey, Little Balls. Your door was unlocked, so I came in. I just need to⋯"

She trails off as I finish my coughing fit and she just stands there in silence staring at me.

During the coughing, I forgot that I was naked. Now I am just laying on a bed with Pangaea gawking at my naked self. She breaks the awkward silence.

"Are⋯are you a little busy? I mean I could always just come back later."

"Uh. Do you want me to leave or maybe you'd like to cover yourself, so we could talk? I mean, it's your choice."

I pull the blanket over my exposed body.

"There, is that better?" I ask.

"Well, a little."

"So, what did you want to talk about?" I place my one good arm behind my head.

"I heard about Zinka. Are you okay?" She seems concerned.

"Yeah. I'm fine. Wait, how did you hear about that? It literally just happened."

"Meh, I have my ways. You sure you're okay?"

"I will be. It isn't the first time that I've been rejected."

"Okay. I'm around if you need me."

With that she leaves and the door shuts behind her.

CHAPTER 21

All the bugs have been tracked down and destroyed. The entire crew is in Docking Port Two, next to the cruisers. I am completely clothed now. Zinka is nervously pacing back and forth. It gets a little repetitive. Finally, she stops momentarily to speak.

"Alright, listen." She says before continuing her pacing. "We are just outside the docking ship. Bubba is right over there. You three need to make it quick. I have no idea what Derask is planning with this. It would be best to proceed with the utmost caution."

"We will be careful Zinka," Pangaea reassures, putting a comforting hand on her shoulder. "We've got this."

"Listen," Zinka is rattled, "Little Balls. Pangaea. Danny. You three just··· just try to be safe."

We say our goodbyes, and each enter our own ships. I have no idea what exactly I'm looking at. It looks like the simulation, but it feels different to have actual tangible controls sitting in front of me. I wonder how hard flying an actual ship can be. The rest of the crew exits the docking port, so they can avoid the whole vacuum of space thing.

Pangaea is the first one to leave the docking port. Danny is close behind. I, on the other hand, am still trying to remember how the hell you start this thing. Zinka's voice comes over an intercom that I did not know was there. *"Little Balls, the ignition is the button on the far right."*

The transmission ends, and I locate the button that she was referring to. The button that just happens to be twice as large as all the other buttons and is a bright green shade. My finger presses the button and the engine comes to life.

I still sort of remember how to drive this thing. I only hit the walls three times as I leave the docking port. I am an expert.

I see Pangaea and Danny beginning to land on the docking ship. So, I do what any smart and logical individual would do. I gun it. Turns out, going faster is a bad idea considering I forget how to stop. My cruiser rushes towards the docking ship. Now where are the brakes. I finally find the lever to reverse the propulsion and slowly bring the ship to a halt. Unfortunately, I pull it a wee bit too late.

The ship slows but not enough to bring it to a stop. The bottom of the ship smashes against the floor of the landing port. I honestly didn't know that a metallic ship could bounce of another metal surface like that. I finally manage to stop the bouncing and exit the ship. As soon as the door to the landing zone closes, I see Pangaea check a strange device on her wrist.

"The oxygen level is now at a safe level," Pangaea says as she removes her hood.

"Whoa," Danny speaks up. "Where did you get that thing?" He says, pointing to the device on her wrist.

"Zinka gave it to me."

Danny presses, "Why didn't I get one?"

"She thought you would break it."

"Well that's not fair," Danny pouts.

"Well, is she wrong?"

"I guess not. I just like gifts."

Danny and I follow suit and remove our hoods as well. We look around momentarily before the opposite door opens revealing two Aldinians holding weaponry. The first one steps forward before speaking.

"Earthlings," he says in a strange accent. "Mister Bubba is waiting for you in the main chamber. Follow me."

The two turn around and start walking. We are hesitant to follow. Well, two of us are hesitant. Pangaea, on the other hand, gives no fucks, and follows the two damn near on their asses. Danny and I exchange glances before we scurry along after her.

We follow a little way behind the three and I look at the passageway we are walking down. Everything seems dark. The walls and floors are a deep black. The lighting on the ceiling barely gives off a faint glow. The two aliens ushering us deeper in the ship keep a stoic silence among them. The only sound being the soles of our shoes hitting the metallic floor.

We enter the main hall and the door slams shut behind us. I see no Bubba and no Beason. All I see are eight more Aldinians pointing guns at us, as the two leading us go over to join them.

"Uh..." I begin. I am unable to finish my thought.

"Take cover!" Pangaea yells as she pushes me and Danny behind a conveniently placed low wall.

Pangaea takes cover behind another conveniently placed wall on the other side of the hall. "Pull out your weapons," she commands as she draws hers.

The room is filled with a barrage of lasers. The chaos seems never ending as the blasts bounce off the room. None of us have even left the safety of cover. Danny and I did pull out our guns in self-defense, though.

Something seems off. The blasts, though plentiful, do not even come close to where we are hiding. I peer over the barricade and notice they are firing up towards the ceiling and the door where we came in. Some of them are not even trying and are just firing at the ground by their feet.

"Hey, Pangaea!" I shout. "What the hell is going on?"

"I have no idea, but I'm going to figure it out."

Pangaea stands up and moves towards the ten aliens. An expression of fear comes over their faces and they stop firing. I have no clue what it's going on here.

"Hey!" Pangaea gets their attention.

This outburst causes all of them to back up towards the wall. They are ten aliens with guns, and they are terrified of a ninety-pound human. The sight of the quivering extraterrestrials forces Pangaea to take a much softer tone.

"Hey, hey, it's okay," Pangaea says in a soft voice. "But tell us what is going on."

"Okay, look," the one stepping forward explains. "We are prisoners of Derask. He forced us on this ship and told us we could earn our freedom if we stop you."

Danny questions, "Then why didn't you try to kill us?"

"We're not fighters."

Another one says, "We're scientists. He put us on this ship with another one of your kind and a Tauranian child."

"Shit. It's Bubba and Beason," Pangaea says before turning back to the Aldinians. "Where did they go?"

"They barricaded themselves behind that large door there." The Aldinian points behind her.

"Alrighty," Danny says. "You ten, get to the escape pods or whatever. I'll phone Zinka now."

Danny then pulls out his communicator and presses buttons randomly. The ringing of it is loud enough for all to hear. You'd think that they would be silent, considering you never know when you are going to need it. It may be needed in a situation that requires quiet. In other words, no noise. I hear Zinka's voice come over the communicator.

"What is it, Danny?"

"How would you feel if I gave ten Aldinian scientists permission to board our ship?"

"I would say come again?"

He giggles as he childishly interprets her words.

"Danny, what are you up to?"

"Just bear with me, boss lady. We arrived on the ship, like you told us to, and we ran into ten scientists being forced into trying to kill us. I gave them clearance to board the ship."

"Are you insane? Why would you do that, Danny? What the hell were you thinking?"

"Please, boss lady, just trust me. I know what I'm doing."

"Ugh, fine, but tell them that as soon as they get here, they will be spending time in the containment cells till you three return. After that, we will go and address them as a crew and see what exactly their end game is. Is that understood?"

"Aye, aye, captain." Danny then hangs up the communicator and turns towards the scientists before speaking.

"You guys leave. We have a ship right over..." Danny looks around trying to determine what direction the ship is in. He finally gives up and continues. "Just go in the direction your docking port is in. You will see the ship. It's large and metallic and... ship-like. The boss woman says that you have to chill in the prison for a bit until we get this all sorted. Don't worry. You will be safe there, trust me."

"Thank you," one scientist says.

They start to leave. However, one stops and turns around. She addresses us.

"You and your crew must be stupid to try to take on Derask."

I say. "Better to be stupid and fun then smart and boring."

She replies, "I have no idea what that means. Nevertheless, good luck."

She then leaves and the door shuts behind her. We look towards the door where the scientist pointed. Behind that door, Bubba and Beason are hiding. We need to save that child.

Pangaea is the first to act. She presses the button to open the door. The door does absolutely nothing. She tries again and is met with the same result. The third time proves just as fruitless. The fourth time, though, she decides to try something different.

Pangaea raises her gun, pulls the trigger, and blows the keypad to hell. The door opens and reveals a fat, ugly hillbilly sitting in the center of the room. His eyes grow wide as Pangaea pulls her gun and points it right in his face.

"Where's the kid you obese inbred sack of shit?" Pangaea asks.

"What the hell?" Bubba stammers out. "Where are my guards?"

Danny replies casually, "Oh, they left."

"They left?"

"Yeah, they left. We asked if they wanted to leave and they were down with it. So, they left. Now give us the kid before I blast you," he says.

I jump in, "It's over Bubba. Where is the child?" I make a point to keep the gun pointed at his big stupid head.

"Wouldn't you like to know?"

"Yes. Yes, I would. That's why I asked."

Bubba laughs, "You'll never know."

"Dammit Bubba tell me right now or--"

"Or what? You and your two black sidekicks will kick my ass?"

Me, Pangaea, and Danny are stunned into momentary silence. Bubba speaks.

"Wait, I know you," he says pointing towards Danny. "You're that queer that runs the gas station."

"Well that's uncalled for. I know we're enemies, but there is no reason to be rude," Danny chastises.

"It's Adam and Eve, not Adam and Steve, man."

"My name's Danny. Wait, God didn't make Steve? Then who made Steve?"

"Well··· well, God made Steve."

"But you just said he didn't," Danny replies. "Poor Steve."

"God made everyone."

"Then why did you lie to me?"

"Where's the kid at fatty? Tell me or I'll kill you right now," Pangaea says through clenched teeth. I guess she was done listening to that stupidity-inducing banter.

"Alright, fine," he says after a dramatic pause. "Just go look in that bag over there."

"What? Why would I look in the bag?"

"Just do it, you monkey lover."

My response to that racial slur is a death glare. I turn my attention away from the redneck to the bag where he was pointing.

There is nothing remotely interesting or unique about it. I slowly move towards it. My cautiousness is, in large part, due to the fact that I know how Derask is a monster. My feet bring me right in front of the bag. I take one last look around. Pangaea's gun is still pointed at Bubba. Danny is still standing there with his signature grin. I don't think the gravity of the situation has hit him yet.

I reach down and open the bag. I am not prepared for what I see. In the bag is an emaciated small creature. Its ribs are protruding, and its stomach is swollen as if it's starving to death. All its limbs have been removed but I can still see what species it was. This is Beason.

"You son of a bitch." I say. I can't take my eyes away from the disfigured toddler before me.

Before another word could leave my mouth, I see the small being in the bag move.

"Jesus Christ!" I yell. "Pangaea, Beason is still alive! You and Danny need to take him back to the ship now."

Pangaea doesn't hesitate. She runs over and clutches the boy to her chest protectively, then races with him towards her cruiser.

"What about you?" Danny questions me.

"I need to take care of Bubba."

Danny takes my words at face value, and heads towards his cruiser. I look at Bubba, and his response is a smile. This fucker is smiling? He's happy about what he did?

"Why?"

"Why what?" He chuckles. "Why did I join the green freak? Why did I blow up that planet? Or why did I torture that grey thing?"

"Why don't you show remorse?"

"I have nothing to be remorseful for. I did nothing wrong. These aren't people. They don't matter."

At this, I lose it. I throw a punch that connects with his jaw. The force, mixed with the surprise of me throwing a punch, causes him to fall on his ass. Before he can regain his composure, I grip his throat with my good hand. My hand grips tighter as he desperately tries to claw my hand away.

"You know," I say through clenched teeth, "I appreciate life. I've never been hunting or smashed a bug." My hand grips tighter. "I've always felt that life was a precious thing. You, however, don't feel the same. Sometimes the death of one could save the lives of many."

Using my entire body weight, I toss the asshole against the wall. His body hits and then slides down to the floor. He is up in a flash, however. Lowering his shoulder, he tackles me to the ground. We begin grappling. My thumb finds his eyes and pushes in towards his brain. Maybe if I push hard enough, I could explode his eyeballs. That would be neat to see.

I finally get the upper hand and push Bubba off me. Before he gets the chance to get up, I press my foot on his throat.

"Say hi to your God for me."

I raise my foot and bring it down on his throat with all the force that I could muster. His eyes bulge from his head as he begins gasping for air and pawing at his neck. I watch him squirm there for minutes trying to take a breath. His movements start to become sluggish until he finally stops moving.

"Well," I say to myself in the empty ship. "I'll probably be feeling guilty for that later."

I walk towards the docking port where my ship is. My eyes trace the contours of the hall one last time. This ship will be the tomb of one of the last humans. I guess not all life is precious. I guess sometimes death is a necessity. Some beings need to be culled for the preservation of other life.

I board my cruiser and start the engine. It's a little banged up thanks to my landing skills. My cruiser comes to life and I exit the port of the desolate ship. Have fun floating endlessly in space, Bubba. My cruiser comes up towards the mothership, and I hit the request beacon to land. The door slides open and I manage a slightly smoother landing than last time. The keyword there is slightly.

When the docking door closes, and oxygen fills the room through the vents, I see the door to the hall open. Danny comes to greet me.

"Is Halissy with Beason?" I question.

"Yeah, she's working on him. He is pretty messed up, but the doc seems pretty sure that he will be okay."

"And the scientists?"

"Tik and Zinka are questioning them in the containment cell. They seem alright. They are very cooperative. I think it will be fine."

"Well, that's good, I guess. So, did anyone say what the next game plan is?"

"No. Everyone was just a little preoccupied," Danny says as we continue our conversation while leaving the docking port.

"I guess that's understandable."

"Elisar has some amazing news, though." Danny says grinning from ear to ear. "I'll let her tell you. Come on, dude."

I follow Danny through hall. We walk down the metallic hallway towards the medical room. As we get closer to the medical wing, I think about what I did on Derask's ship. I just murdered one of the last few humans left in existence. Though killing him was justified when viewed from a certain perspective, I can't really absolve myself of my actions completely. I'm sure there were other ways to deal with it. I could have brought him in and performed a kind of citizen's arrest. Wait, am I even a citizen of anything? Earth exploded and that was my home. I can't really be a citizen of a place that no longer exists. Wow, I'm a wandering space nomad.

My thoughts are interrupted when we arrive at the medical bay doors. I should learn how to stop getting lost in my thoughts every five seconds. I doubt that will ever happen. The door opens to a sad, yet relieved looking, Elisar as well as a busy Halissy. The child on the bed looks a little better since he got cleaned up and his wounds are dressed.

Halissy speaks up first, "Ah, Little Balls, glad to see you're back. Everyone else came sooner, but I guess you couldn't help but procrastinate coming back, huh?"

I open my mouth to respond but before I could I am caught completely off guard by another surprise hug. The hug count is getting close to the concussion count. Ah, who am I kidding? The count is still nowhere close.

CHAPTER 22

I look down and see Elisar has her arms around me, squeezing. She is squeezing hard. Is she trying to pop me? I don't like being popped. It sounds like it will be painful. This hug is going on for a long time. Should I say something? I think I should say something.

"Uh... it's good to see you too, Elisar," I say as I awkwardly pat her back.

"Thank you," she says through tears. "Thank you so much. Because of you, my baby is still alive."

She squeezes a little harder as she finishes the last sentence. So much squeezing.

"You're welcome. Now, I'm not sure if squeezing someone till they explode is a compliment on your world, but humans don't really like exploding. It hurts us. We find pain bad."

She releases me and scratches the back of her head in embarrassment. "I'm sorry. It's just that... well... I'm just happy to have my little boy back. I already got to thank Pangaea and Danny, but you were taking too long to return."

"That's not all she has to say though," Pangaea walks into the room.

"What do you mean?"

"Well," Elisar says. "Derask took a total of six humans off of your world, not just four."

"What?"

"Well, he kidnapped Pangaea and Danny. He was able to convince Landon and Bubba to willingly join him. However, he also kidnapped two other humans. I was a little too preoccupied to remember this before, and I'm sorry about that."

"Wait, there are more humans out there?" I question with a little disbelief.

"Yeah, man," Danny chimes in. "Isn't that fantastic?"

He leaves and the door shuts behind him, although his cries of joy can still be heard on this side of the metal door.

I wonder why he is so happy. I know it is great news, and I know that Danny is very exuberant, but that still seems a little much, for even him. I will think about it later.

"So where are the humans kept?" I question her.

"That I do not know, but I do know that they are being kept alive."

"Are they safe?" I ask.

"Yet again, I don't know. All I know is that they are alive. He needed them for... his slavery business. He wanted to grab two pairs for the prison. His plans changed when Danny became too much of a handful. So, he sold them to whoever would take them to earn a few credits."

"We will find them," I say as I turn my attention towards the child that is laying on the bed. "You work really fast, Halissy."

"The wounds just needed cleaning to prevent any further damage. All his wounds were cauterized. Whoever did this didn't want him to die, just to suffer."

I still feel no guilt for Bubba. I wonder if I should be concerned by that. Oh well, no time to think about that now. Maybe it will come up later. Halissy breaks me from my chain of thoughts. "I am currently working on cloned limbs for him. They should be ready soon."

Zinka enters and the door closes behind her.

"How is Beason, Halissy?" Her voice is sympathetic.

"Vitals are stable, and the all the sensors are showing his injuries are slowly healing."

"That is fantastic news," Zinka smiles. "Elisar, Halissy, please stay with the patient. Little Balls, you need to come with me, so we can interrogate the Aldinian scientists."

"Alright, I'm coming," I stand up and follow her out of the room.

I follow Zinka to the Aldinian scientists. My mind goes to what Elisar said about the two other humans. Landon is dead and so is Bubba. We may have two more decent humans left. Hell, they don't even have to be necessarily heroes. I will gladly accept normal people.

We stop in front of the clear walls of the containment cell where ten bug people are currently sitting. Though they are technically imprisoned, they still seem genuinely relieved to be off Bubba's ship. I can't really blame them for that. That place smelled like stale beer and chewing tobacco. I don't even know how he got a hold of that stuff.

Zinka presses a button on the wall before speaking. I am going to guess that it's some sort of intercom to talk to whoever is in the cell.

Leo, Tik, and Pangaea come up right behind us.

"Attention, scientists," Zinka says over the intercom. "I have a few questions for you."

"We will answer," one of them says.

"How exactly were you captured?"

"Derask sent his goons in and literally dragged us out of the lab."

"Why you, though? There are thousands of brilliant scientists amongst the Aldinian population."

"He considers us both his biggest threats and most valuable resources," the lone male scientist says. "If you run our profiles, you will find that we are the ten greatest minds on the entire planet. We are capable of either building his empire or destroying it."

Zinka then removes her finger from the intercom button and turns to address the crew that is present.

"So," she asks, "How do you guys feel? Should we see if they want to help us, or should we send them to the prison on Demer?"

"Those are the only options?" Leo questions.

"Yes. It all depends on whether we believe them or not. If we feel like we can trust them, we will offer them an opportunity to join our crew. The ones who accept will be welcomed aboard. The ones who decline will be transported to a sanctuary on Demer where they will be imprisoned to await a trial with the Demerians. Technically, they are war prisoners. This is standard protocol for a large portion of the galaxy."

"I say we trust them," Tik is the first to speak up.

Leo plays devil's advocate, "What if they are lying though? Derask has always been a convoluted villain. This may be part of his plan to infiltrate us."

"I've gotta go with Leo on this one," Pangaea says. "I'm all for helping, but that does seem like something he would do. Would the trial be fair? Also, how horrid are Demerian prisons?"

"The trial would be as fair as it could be in times of war," Zinka explains. "The prison system on Demer is one of the few in the galaxy that is actually compassionate. They treat the prisoners as sentient beings, unlike some who treat them only as if they were parasites."

Zinka looks at me before continuing to talk, "And what do you say, Little Balls? Do you trust them?"

I think carefully over the decision. On one hand, these are the most brilliant minds of their respective race. They could be very helpful in this war effort. On the other hand, this could just be a trap, set up by Derask. He is a bastard like that. I mull over the choice carefully in my head before speaking. "Fuck it," I reply, "I say give them a chance."

"So that means it is two to two," Leo summarizes. "Zinka, what do you think?"

Zinka carefully thinks it over. She turns back to the entrapped scientists before pressing the button to speak to them.

"After consulting my crew," Zinka says, "I am willing to extend an invitation to join our crew to any of you who wish to help us with the war effort. You are free to accept or decline. If you accept, you will be welcomed aboard this vessel. If you decline, then you will be sent to a protective sanctuary on the planet Demer. You will be safe there."

A chorus of grumbling starts in the room. When the grumbling dies down, one of the female scientists steps forward to speak.

"We have discussed it, and Shia and I will accompany you," she says, motioning to the only male of the group. "The others, however, have decided to seek sanctuary. I hope you do not see that as a cowardly move."

"Well," Leo says, stepping forward, "joining a war is a very dangerous activity to engage in. Can't really blame them for wanting to be safe."

The female scientist replies, "No, it is not so much they are leaving the war but, with the Demerian government's blessing, of course, they would like to assist in their efforts to create the faux womb. Derask has spies and bugs everywhere, so we are familiar with your efforts. This may come as a surprise, but most Aldinians feel horribly guilty about the genocide. While we can't erase what happened, we can help in the effort to repopulate your planet."

The last part gets Tik's full attention.

Tik questions, "So, you think you can help my people?"

"Of course," replies the female.

"This is great! I need to speak to the councilor and share this news," Tik says as he runs toward the cockpit.

"Tik, set up a meeting point with a Demerian cruiser so we can teleport the other scientists," Zinka yells towards the fleeting figure of Tik.

Zinka presses the button to open the containment cell, and the group files out of the open cell into the hallway.

Well, this seems like a win to me. We now get the most intelligent minds in the Aldinian race. So, take that, Derask.

Zinka speaks to the Aldinians, "If you will follow me, I will show you to your cabins. You can relax there until we reach the rendezvous point for the Demerian cruiser."

Zinka leads the group down the corridor.

Leo approaches me. "Do you really think that this is a wise move, Little Balls?" He questions.

"I don't think. It just makes everything so confusing… and hard."

"If you say so. I guess I'll trust your judgment on this one," he says with a skeptical tone.

Pangaea joins the conversation, "I'm a little surprised that she chose to let them stay."

I reply, "Why?"

"Well, I thought that with the amount of distrust she has in everything that Derask is involved with, she wouldn't want to take the risk of allowing scientists who are possibly brainwashed on the ship. You remember how against us boarding Bubba's ship she was."

"I can be very persuasive. I am so persuasive that I once convinced a girl to go out with me. It ended badly... but that isn't the point. The point is that I still got that date."

Leo wonders, "Why didn't it go well?"

"Well, it was fine right up to the point where she got in my car."

"What did you do?" Pangaea asks.

"Well, she said that my car was a piece of shit."

"And?"

"And my response was, 'You too'."

"That doesn't make any sense." She is rightfully confused.

"I was nervous. Wasn't really expecting to even get a date."

She rolls her eyes, "I will never be able to understand how you are still single."

"It is a mystery to all," I shrug.

"Fucking idiot," Pangaea says before she leaves down the corridor.

Leo takes a pointed look at me before shaking his head and walking the opposite way. Did I miss an inside joke or something?

I leave the front of the containment cell and head towards Danny's room. I really need to talk to him. I know he is always happy. I also know that the idea that there might be two other humans alive is a very exciting turn of events. However, something about his reaction did seem a little over the top. The dude was not figuratively but literally dancing down the god damn hallway.

I make the trek down the identical hallways towards where I hope Danny is at. I think I've gotten fairly mediocre at navigating the ship. I mean, I kind of know where I'm going. The key words there is kind of.

I finally end up in front of his door and pound on it. I just hope that he is in there. I really hate wandering around looking for people. It's annoying. The door slides open and out pours a cloud of smoke. It appears that Danny was having his own private party in here. I would say that it's celebratory, but he does this constantly, so for all I know, it's just another Tuesday. Wait, is it Tuesday? What day is it? I guess it doesn't even matter anymore.

"Hey, buddy," Danny's clearly stoned out of his mind. "What's up?"

"I just wanted to hang out and talk for a bit man. Can I come in?"

"Sure, man. I was just starting to pack another bowl. Come on in and take some puffs with me, homie."

I follow him inside and the door shuts behind me. I see that Danny's magic weed stash that he got from who knows where is still overstocked. At least he won't be running out any time soon.

Danny takes a seat on his bed and starts to pack the bowl. He passes it to me.

"Guests first, man," he says as he offers the pipe.

"Aren't you a gentleman," I light it and take a toke.

"Manners are always important, man. Always remember that," he advises with a smirk.

I take the standard two puffs before handing the pipe back to Danny. "Look, man." I say. "I just wanted to ask you a couple things."

"Alright, what do you want to know?"

"Well, although I wasn't there for your reaction when you first found out, the reaction you had when you told me was the happiest that I have ever seen you."

He looks at me skeptically for a moment. Well, it's longer than a moment. I'm not sure when the cut off for a moment is, but I'm pretty sure it's well before when he answered me. He finally replies.

"Wait, told you what? Is this about the sliding door thing, because that was a while ago, man? You've got to quit living in the past."

"No, not the sliding door. I'm talking about when you told me about two more humans being alive. Like, don't get me wrong, I'm stoked too, but your reaction seemed a little over the top. Even for you, man."

"Oh yeah, that." He pauses for a moment deep in thought. I have never seen Danny's expression twisted in thought like this before. He then continues. "It's Seth, man."

"You miss him, don't you?" I ask even though I already know the answer.

"Of course. He's my everything. One of the few people who ever really gave a shit about me. I love him." Danny takes his two puffs and then passes the bowl back to me. We go back and forth, a thick silence falling upon the room. I wait until the bowl is dead before I speak up again.

"Do you really think that one of the people will be Seth, Danny?" I ask.

"Look, I'm not an idiot. I know that the chances of it being Seth are slim to none. Hell, the fact that both me and you escaped the Earth being destroyed is a coincidence that is practically insulting to the entire balance of the universe. I just⋯ I just can't give up hope, man."

"True. Hey, maybe you will get stupidly lucky and one of them will be Seth and the other will be a gay Swedish nude model. You could have yourself a good old-fashioned threesome."

Danny laughs, "That's alright. If I wanted to disappoint two people at the same time, then I would just come out of the closet to my parents again."

"That's rough, man."

"Oh wait, they're dead. Hey, I guess there is a bright side to every situation."

"That sounds a little morbid, man."

"Look," he says. "I know everyone says don't speak ill of the dead and whatnot, but I disagree with that. If someone is a bastard in life than they don't deserve immediate forgiveness just because they're dead. If you live like a monster, then you deserve to be remembered as a monster."

"I guess that's true. So, if you don't mind me asking, how did your parents react when you told them you were gay? I didn't meet you till after all that shit went down."

"Well, my parents were typical Evangelicals. Everything in the Bible was to be taken at face value, and never, ever questioned. When I told them, their first step was to send me to one of those gay conversion therapy camps. Once there, all I heard was how horrible I was and shit. They did so much worse, but I would rather not get into all the methods they had for curing my disease."

"Dude, I had no idea."

"It's alright. That is where I met Seth. He was so cute and kind. I fell hard, man. When I got out, I was a legal adult, so I moved out of my parents' and moved in with him. I won the lottery, meeting him. Look, I don't really feel like talking about this anymore. We can talk about this later. I just need to settle my thoughts a bit."

The silence fills the room. I never imagined that happy-go-lucky Danny would has been through all that shit. It's amazing that he is still able to smile his toothy grin. The weed probably helps him out with that.

My eyes drift over to Danny and I notice him just staring up at the ceiling, wearing his goofy trademark grin. I hope Seth is one of them, buddy. You deserve a bit of good news, too.

CHAPTER 23

I leave Danny's room and spend the rest of the time until we reach the rendezvous point alone with my thoughts. I put out the butt of my cigarette and feel my eyes get heavy. A quick nap couldn't hurt. I succumb to my tired state and drift off to my own little dream world.

I look around. My surroundings are a weird little meadow. As usual, something seems off. Although I can make out the ground around me, my surroundings are extremely limited. Past thirty feet in any direction, there's nothing. Nothing lay beyond but a stark white abyss.

"What the shit?" I ask myself aloud.

Of course, the only answer I get is nothingness. That should have been expected. I mean, I am the only one here. It would be a lot more peculiar if I did get an answer.

I am fully aware that this is a dream. Judging, from all my previous dreams, however, this one seems too peaceful. That makes this the most unnerving one that I've had yet.

My eyes wander, as does my mind. I happen to notice something shiny sitting at my feet that I somehow missed before. My body bends down and I grab the round object. It's that weird little globe thing that I won at the space carnival thing.

"What the hell are you doing here?" I question the inanimate object in my hand.

Obviously, I did not receive any answer from the trinket because it's a trinket. This is a dream world though, so all sorts of crazy shit could happen. Wait, if I am aware that I'm dreaming, then maybe I can control it?

Come on, think. A peanut butter and jelly sandwich suddenly appears in my previously unoccupied hand. Yay, a sandwich, but just as importantly, I am lucid dreaming. This is my world now.

My eyes snap open and I see my room on the spaceship. Dammit, I lost my PB&J. Now, I'm just stuck on an intergalactic voyage to save the Milky Way from a douchebag, and I don't even have a sandwich.

"Attention, crew," Zinka's voice comes over the intercom. "We are coming up on the meeting point with the Demerians. Would the Aldinian scientists report to Docking Port Two for teleportation."

The to my room opens, and Pangaea walks in. The unexpected visit causes me to damn near jump out of my skin.

"What the hell? Don't you knock?"

"Oh please," she waves off my questions. "What could you possibly be doing that is so secretive?"

"Well... maybe I was masturbating. Did you ever think about that?"

"Meh, you see one penis, you've seen them all. Oh wait, I did already see your penis."

"Well even with amnesia, I'm glad that you can remember my penis."

"My amnesia is only around memories specific to me. Come on, I knew what a penis was before. Besides, I was trapped in a cell with Danny, and, FYI, his little man is anything but little." She smirks at me.

"I really don't want to hear about my best friend's package."

"Oh relax. Besides, when he was still strapped to the wall in the cell, he would move his hips and make it spin while yelling 'helicopter'."

"Yeah, I can believe that."

"He's a sweetie."

"He is, but why bring that up now?"

"Please. I know that he told you about what they did to me in that cell, and what he did to them in return. Plus, that whole helicopter thing was meant to make me laugh and calm me down when I first woke up. Sadly, it actually worked."

"Yeah, he is something else. I just hope he doesn't get his hopes up too high."

She already knows, "Are you talking about Seth?"

"How did you know?" I question.

"We talked about things in that prison. I just ended up putting two and two together."

"Why wasn't I able to do that? I knew Seth existed. Hell, I ate dinner with the two of them."

"Look, you aren't exactly known for your ability to think through situations and come to appropriate conclusions."

"Well, what am I known for then?"

"Your ability to almost die but somehow make it through," she responds with a shrug.

"Yeah. That sounds about right."

"It's not all bad, though, because at least you're a smooshy-face." She smooshes my face again.

I push her hands off my face. If she keeps doing that, it's going to start to bruise.

"Why do you squeeze my face? Is it really necessary?"

"Everything I do is necessary, Little Balls."

"Everything?"

"Everything."

"Good to know," I reply. "Now why did you come in here?"

Her mood suddenly shifts to nervous. Did... did I push a button that I didn't know about? Why am I always so damn terrible with women?

"I just wanted to give you this back," she s reaches into her pocket, fumbling for something. She pulls out the odd trinket from the festival.

"Here, this is yours," she says, holding the sphere out to me.

"But I gave it to you. You know, that whole reminder thing and all that."

"Well, I don't need it. Although, I don't know who I am, I do know why."

"I am... more confused than I usually am."

"Do you remember when we crashed after leaving Elisar's ship?"

"Well, I remember crashing, and then I remember waking up from a two-week nap."

"Let's just say that Halissy found some very interesting things when she was patching me up."

"Are you pregnant?" I question.

"No, I'm not preggo."

"Am... am I pregnant?"

"I sure as hell hope not," she replies with a chuckle.

"Well? What did she find then?"

"I'm... a robot."

"Like a computer or something?" I question. "Do you have Minesweeper?"

"No, not like a computer. I think the term she used was cyborg."

"Well, what's the difference?"

"Apparently, robots are all man-made. Whereas cyborgs start out as organic beings with cybernetics added to them. According to what Halissy found, my cybernetics where implanted a year before Danny was even abducted. God only knows how long I have been in space."

The room is enveloped in silence as it seems like she is waiting for a response. My brain starts trying to figure out an appropriate comment.

"Neat," is all I can come up with.

"What do you mean, neat?"

"What do you mean, what do I mean?"

"Well, I'm not human."

"How aren't you?" I question.

"My body is full of a shit-ton of robotics. I'm a freak."

"Pangaea, I want you to look at something," I say.

I remove my left arm from my suit. The little mini nub finally makes its way out of the fabric. It has grown to about the size of a pencil. It's slowly getting bigger. I continue.

"Pangaea look at my tiny appendage." I wave the hand at her. "Now, I may not be one of those smart types, but I'm fairly certain that this is not normal."

"So, what you're saying is that I'm not a freak?"

"Well, no more than anyone else on this ship. Hell, even the ship itself is a freak. I mean, who names a space vessel Gravity Bong?"

"Uhm, you did."

"You're god damn right. Do you know why? I did it because I'm a freak."

She chuckles lightly as her face takes a much softer expression. "Thank you." She replies.

"Oh, and you can still keep the globe. Regardless, you are still human and still should have a reminder of your past. Besides, I made you a promise that we would at least try to recover your memories. If there's one thing I'm good at, it's making attempts."

I am then smothered in a hug. "I can't thank you enough, Thad," she whispers before she lets go.

Pangaea stands up and heads towards the door. She stops at the frame and turns around before speaking to me. "I'll see you later, Little Balls. Try not to die while I'm gone."

"No promises, but I will attempt to continuing living," I reply with a grin.

She shakes her head and leaves as the door closes behind her. I am just learning all kinds of stuff... today? I don't know the time frame anymore. I light a smoke to relax. Is there any better taste than a cig after a nap, or, in this case, a second post-nap cigarette?

I puff the cigarette away, then head to the docking port. I don't really know if any of the other eight scientists are still here or not. Oh well, probably won't see them much anymore, anyway. Before I get there, I turn towards the medical ward to check in on how Elisar is doing.

The med bay doors open, and I see Elisar staring at an unconscious Beason. She tenderly strokes his cheek as the steady beeps of the medical machines creates a background noise in the room.

"Hey, Elisar," I slowly approach her. "How's it going? Stupid question, I know, but I really don't know how else to start this conversation. I have no idea how to handle this situation."

"Hey, Little Balls. I⋯ am⋯ better now. Beason is stable. According to Halissy, he is not out of the woods yet. Even though it pains me to see him like this, the fact that he is alive is a gift in and of itself."

"Well, Halissy knows her stuff. She kept me alive. She will keep everything running smoothly."

An extremely uncomfortable silence takes over the medical bay. It is very hard to try and make a conversation with someone who tried to kill you a couple times. Ages seem to pass before she finally breaks the silence of the room.

"Why?"

"Why what?"

"Why did you risk your life to save my son? You don't know him, and you certainly have no reason to do me any favors."

"I have no reason to do any of the things that I do. That is part of the reason why I am so, so delightful."

"For your efforts, I think I know how to make it up to you," she continues closely watching her slumbering child.

"How's that?"

"Well, I know of your efforts to build an army to go against Derask. I also know of your failure to garner any support besides that of the Demerians."

"Ah, nothing I love more than being reminded of my failures," I reply with a small hint of sarcasm. Don't want to be too much of a dick.

"Well, what if I told you that I know of a race that will definitely help you?"

"Really? Who?"

"Mine," she replies. "I meant to tell you before, but I am actually the daughter of the Godking."

"What's a Godking?"

"Essentially, the ruler of my planet. A Godking is a democratically elected ruler, and Beason is his grandson."

"Damn. Derask does not know when to pick his battles, does he?"

"When my father, Grakken, finds out what he did to his precious grandbaby, he will want blood."

"Well, I'll talk to Zinka about going to Tauran, then. We can use all the help that we can get."

"Trust me, Grakken will help."

"Okay, I need to go. I'm going to see if I can talk to the scientists for a bit."

"I'll be here. I don't want to leave till my baby wakes up. Thanks again, though, Little Balls."

Is it weird that I'm getting used to that now? I hate my friends. Always making that sexual innuendo at my expense.

I leave the medical bay and head towards where the scientists are. The docking port opens, and it reveals that the other eight are gone. Dr. Shia and the female scientist are still here, however.

"Hey, scientist peoples," I say when I get nearer. "How's it going?"

"Hello, odd hairy creature," Shia says.

The lady thought his comment was rude or something and she decided to reward him the same way everyone around here seems to reward me. Concussions for everyone.

"Shia!" She scolds him. "Don't be rude to the human. He saved us, in case you forgot."

"His kind also kept us in bondage," Shia coldly reminds her.

He seems a little racist. She turns towards me with an apologetic look on her face.

"I am sorry about Dr. Shia. He is a little sore, and, unfortunately, he decides to blame the whole for the sins of the one," she says that last part while glaring at Shia before she turns back and continues. "I am Yekk."

"I'm Thaddeus, but most people just call me Little Balls."

"Is that because you have small genitalia?"

Great, even an alien knows that there is a secondary meaning to that.

"No, no. Zinka just thinks that she's funny by giving me a nickname that implies a sexual deficiency of some sort. She's a dick," I reply awkwardly.

"So, your genitals are not microscopic?" Shia asks in a rather snarky tone.

"They are average."

"Average for humans, or average counting all species?" He asks again.

"I··· I don't know. I have no clue how big other species' balls are. I never really thought about checking in on that. Do you know?"

"...No," he admits after a small moment of hesitation.

"So, you don't know everything," I'm a smug bastard, too.

"Fuck you," he replies coldly before leaving down the corridor.

I think I made him mad. I am good at pissing people off without even trying. Maybe that's my superpower. I really need a better superpower. Why couldn't I be able to see through walls, or fly, or some shit?

"Well, it is a delight to make your acquaintance, Little Balls, but I should probably go check on Shia to make sure that he isn't breaking anything."

"You too, Yekk. Talk to you later."

We head our separate ways. I don't really have a destination. Or do I? What do I have to do? Oh yeah, I need to go tell Zinka what Elisar told me about. Sometimes I forget that there is this whole war thing going on. How do I forget that? I really need to stay focused. I should try smoking less weed··· or more weed. One or the other, I guess.

The cockpit opens, revealing Zinka pressing buttons on the computer navigation thing.

"Hey Zinka," I say, coming up behind her. "So, I have news."

"Good news or bad news?" She questions without looking away from the machine.

"Well, I'm pretty sure it's good. Although, I guess that perspective is entirely subjective."

"Alright, what is it?"

"I was just talking to Elisar, and it turns out she is the daughter of the God-king. Which means that Beason is his grandchild. She says that after he hears about what Derask has done, he will also want to murder him. So, we may have another fleet to help us take down the Colossus."

"That's great news!" She spins around to face me. "Our chances would easily double with the support of the Tauranian army."

"Out of curiosity, how good are our chances if they do decide to help?"

"About 14%."

"That's it?"

"Well, it was at about 7% before."

"Woo, we are unstoppable," I say sarcastically.

"Aww, is poor Little Balls scared?"

"I am never scared⋯ except when something terrifying happens."

I take a seat as Zinka goes back to pushing buttons on the computer. "I'll punch in coordinates for Tauran now. We should arrive there in no time."

I pause to look around the cockpit. My attention is drawn to the various pieces of alien tech that are blinking and beeping and whatnot. A question pops into my head as I'm staring around.

"Hey, Zinka, can I ask you something?"

"Why, so that when I answer, you can zone out and pretend that it helps you understand better? Even though I know you just have a small attention span?"

"You can't prove me wrong about that. You don't know me."

She rolls her eyes at me before she speaks again. "Go ahead and ask your question, Little Balls. I also promise that I will try to put it simply."

"Well, how are we able to travel so much faster across the galaxy than the speed of light? It doesn't make much sense."

"Are you familiar with the idea of wormholes?"

"Yes," Pangaea says as she walks into the room. "Wormholes are kind of like a fold in space. They could be theoretically used to travel through space. Able to cover vast distances in a shorter amount of time."

"Exactly," Zinka replies.

I say, "That is exactly what I was going to say if someone didn't interrupt me."

Zinka continues, "Well, this ship has a piece of tech called the multi-core drive. It can create temporary wormholes to travel through space. It has its limits, though, and requires a cool down period before it can do it again. That is why we cannot simply appear right next to our destination. Plus, the calculations have to be meticulously plotted."

"Aren't wormholes unstable and dangerous? I mean, don't they run the risk of exposing us to dangerous matter, as well as affecting the gravity of nearby celestial bodies?" Pangaea questions.

"That is why the calculations have to be perfect."

"Sounds like witchcraft to me," I reply.

Pangaea speaks up, "Meh, I guess that is Clarke's third law in real life."

"Who is Clarke and why is he so special that he gets laws?" I question.

"He was a writer," Pangaea replies. "He created laws that became essentially common tropes for the sci-fi genre. His third law states that any technology that is so advanced is indistinguishable from magic."

"So, he is a witch? If that is his third law than what are his other two?"

"The first states that when a distinguished but elderly scientist states that something is possible, he is most certainly right. When he states that something is impossible, he is probably wrong. The second is that the only way of discovering the limits of the possible is to venture a little way past them into the impossible."

"I could come up with better laws," I say.

"Shut up, Little Balls," Zinka says to me. "Pangaea is right. I think. Now the coordinates are set for planet Tauran. When we get there, we will meet with the God-king. After that, we still have one more chance to grow our army before we attack."

"What stop is that?" I question.

"Planet 739," Zinka replies.

"What is Planet 739?" Pangaea wonders.

"And why is it not special enough to get its own name?" I ask.

"Planet 739 is a planet run by mercenaries," Zinka answers. "The planet was just a desolate rock before the outlaws settled there."

"So, we are going to try and get the help of criminals?" Pangaea asks skeptically. "Isn't that a little dangerous."

"Yes," she replies honestly. "But Planet 739 also has the only being that Derask is afraid of on it."

"He is afraid of someone? Who is this guy?" I ask.

"Her name is Preet, the queen of the mercenaries. She is a being of immense power. She is the last of her race. She has something that no other being in this galaxy has."

"What's that?" Pangaea inquires.

"She is a shape-shifter. She has an evolutionary trait that allows her to alter her atoms to appear in any form. Her natural state is that of a semi-visible gas globe."

"Hard to believe Derask is afraid of someone," I say.

"Well, he knows her strengths far outweigh his own. If she gave two fucks about power, she could probably rally an army to take over the galaxy."

"You think we will be ready?" Pangaea asks.

"No, but we don't have a choice. This is all the help that we can get."

It is getting closer. Before I kill Derask, though, I'm going to have to remember to find out where the other humans are. Danny needs that, and I need Danny happy. A sad Danny is something that is just so unnatural that it should not exist.

I look out the cockpit at the emptiness of space. We are coming Derask. We are coming to kill you and your stupid face.

CHAPTER 24

The ride to Tauran is remarkably uneventful. I am guessing this is because the witchcraft of Clarke and his laws. We fly to just outside the gravitational pull of the planet. Zinka starts pressing buttons on the communicator to pull up visual communication to the Tauran flight control people.

Elisar comes into the room, because, let's face it, this will go a lot smoother if she is present. She is the daughter of the leader after all. The monitor comes to life and I see another face of the stereotypical Greys.

"Attention ship," the alien on the screen starts, "You need to leave this airspace now or you will be shot···"

It is at this moment that he sees Elisar standing in the background. His jaw drops in an almost cartoonish fashion. Kind of funny to see.

"Your Highness," he whispers, "You're finally back! This is amazing news. Your father will be ecstatic to know this."

"We need an emergency medical transport. Lord Beason is severely hurt and in need of medical equipment that we do not have on the ship. We also need a council with my father immediately. It is of the utmost importance."

"Yes, of course. You are cleared for landing, and I will get a hold of him and the medical staff immediately. Please proceed to the palace."

"Thank you," She replies in a sweet voice before ending the transmission. "I'll type in the coordinates for the landing zone at the palace."

Elisar types in the coordinates, and we begin our descent down to the planet's surface. As we approach the surface, we see a lush green planet that seems to be teeming with life. There are strange creatures everywhere.

Creatures that look like jellyfish fly through the sky. A herd of unicorns with six legs and the faces of grumpy old men graze in the field. It reminds me of a bad acid trip I had once.

Our ship slowly and carefully lands on the pad of what I assume is the palace. Zinka gets on the intercom.

"Attention crew. We have landed on the surface. The landing party will consist of myself, Elisar, Halissy and Little Balls. Tik, you are in charge while we are on the surface. Halissy, please prepare Beason for patient transport. Thank you." She turns off the intercom.

The three of us walk towards the exit of the ship and leave the Gravity Bong with Halissy trailing shortly behind. We are greeted by several short grey beings, similar to Elisar. Several of them hurry towards Halissy and Beason and guide them off. I'm assuming that they are going to their hospital. The one that is left steps forward. He is dressed in elaborate clothes and fancy accessories. This must be the God-king.

"My daughter has returned," he excitedly says before he slaps her face.

Wait, why did he slap her face? That just seems a bit excessive. She then proceeds to slap his face in return.

"Father," Elisar says. "This is Little Balls. He is responsible for saving Beason and freeing me."

"Hello, sir⋯" That was all that left my mouth before an open palm slap connected with my fragile, delicate face.

"I cannot thank you enough my good man. I am Grakken, ruler of this world."

"Why did you just slap my face?" I question.

"What do you mean?" The Godking is confused.

"Why did you hit me with your hand in the face?"

"Oh, I understand. You are foreign. I'm so sorry. That is just the affectionate greeting of the Tauranians."

"Oh, I get it," I say, before winding my arm back and slapping him with as much force as I can muster.

Now, I may have hit him a little harder than what was necessary. I do get pissed when people slap me, though. Punches, I am fine with, but slaps just infuriate me for no reason.

Grakken simply stands there in a state of shock for a bit. Maybe I crossed the line here. I really need to find some information on proper extraterrestrial manners.

He suddenly bursts out laughing, breaking the extremely uncomfortable silence. "Wonderful, simply wonderful. Come, follow me. I believe we have some very important business to discuss."

We follow Grakken into the large palace. Even though the outside looks extravagant, the inside is simple and plain. It is the polar opposite of what the councilors on Demer live in.

We stroll down clean white hallways. There are no decorations or knick-knacks adorning the walls. It is all just a soothing and calming environment. We come up to an ordinary door which opens up to a large domed room that still feels ordinary.

Grakken takes a seat at a rounded table and the three of us follow suit.

"Now, Elisar," he begins. "Where did you go and what happened to you and Beason?"

"Well father, we··· we were kidnapped by Derask. He threatened Beason's life if I did not do as he asked. He··· he made me do horrible things. I have much blood on my hands because of him."

Grakken holds a stoic expression on his face. It seems that he is completely absorbed in Elisar's tale. She continues.

"This continued until he sent me on a mission to kill Little Balls, here. On the second attempt, he managed to detain me, and they found out why I was doing it. Little Balls and two other members of the crew then risked their own lives to save Beason's."

Grakken sits there, thinking. God only knows what's going on through his head. I have no possible way of understanding how he feels or what he is going through. Zinka is the one who breaks the silence.

"Excuse me, sir. I know that this may be a bad time, but we were hoping that you would be able to assist us in taking Derask down."

The God-king stands up and wanders over to the window. He stares out blankly. I take this moment to gaze around the room. Yep, it's still remarkably ordinary. Just plain white walls connecting to plain white floor. Windows adorn the one wall and that's about it.

This is going on longer than what is necessary. Seriously, when is he going to just say something? At this point, it is no longer building tension. It's just really annoying. I wonder if I have time to take a nap.

Grakken finally speaks, "You saved my family, so it is the least I can do. Derask must be stopped. He is a threat to the entire galaxy. We will lend you the aid that you need."

"Thank you, your majesty," Zinka replies graciously. "With your help, our chances of overthrowing Derask have greatly increased."

"To 14%!" I exclaim excitedly.

"Little Balls, shhhh," Zinka whispers.

"We will gather our forces. Let us discuss your plan," Grakken wisely requests.

"Sure, we have a plan. Kind of," I reply before Zinka can put it more eloquently.

"Elaborate?"

"We use space ships to blow up his space ship. It's simple."

He looks at me skeptically and raises his eyebrow muscle, considering Tauranians don't have eyebrows. Huh, humans are the only species that have eyebrows that I've run into so far. Yet, every species has the same reaction when I talk to them.

He finally speaks, "That is your plan?"

Zinka answers for me, "No, there is more to it than that. I'll send the mission dossier to you when we get back to the ship."

"Excellent," Grakken seems placated. "Now, I want to check on my grandson."

We follow the God-king toward what I am guessing is the medical bay or hospital. The trek goes through more blank white hallways. I guess they don't really put much thought into decorations on Tauran. That's respectable.

We come across two large doors with odd writing written above them. I assume that it says hospital or some synonym. The doors creak open, revealing a sterile and clean room. Halissy and the Tauranian doctors are at the far end of the room, huddled around Beason.

"How is he, doctors?" Grakken asks the bustling doctors.

The first one speaks up. "He is stable. He should wake soon, sir."

"Excellent." Grakken walks right up to the glass, which is probably some decontamination thing, and places his hand on the side. "Don't worry, young one. We will make the one who is responsible for this pay," Grakken promises the slumbering toddler.

He turns and heads out of the room with the rest of us in tow. We end up back in what I assume is the main throne room of the massive palace, as the God-king sits in a humble throne. He looks to be considering something for a moment, then lifts his head before talking to me.

"Excuse me, Mister Little Balls."

"What's up?"

"You aren't the first human this planet has seen."

"What do you mean?" I question.

"Well, before you arrived, we received a visit from a rather··· odd individual. I believe he said his name was President Landon."

"What the hell?" I ask disbelievingly.

"I thought he was dead?" Zinka questions.

"He left just as your ship was docking. I have no idea how he managed to land without the docking authority catching him."

"Well, what did he do?" Zinka asks.

"Nothing we can understand -- he started shaking people's appendages and saying how happy he was to be in a place called China. He did not appear to be entirely coherent."

"Is that all?" I ask.

"He also started handing out these notices to each being he met."

Grakken pulls out a square. It wasn't just any square though. It was a flyer which read:

Make the

Universe

Less Like Crap

Again

Landon for

President of Everywhere

"Wait a minute?" I stop to think. "Does he know we are in space or not? There are some major continuity issues here."

"Should we be worried about this?" Zinka asks.

"Honestly⋯" I start. "Probably. We weren't worried about him being president when he ran. Everyone just thought it was a joke. However, due to how our election system is run, he got elected by pandering to essentially the worst of Americans."

"We can deal with that later. We have more pressing matters to attend to first."

Grakken speaks up. "If I may interrupt, this is a time for celebration. You are all cordially invited to a party that's to be held in your honor. We may yet be able to garner the support of the other two planets in this solar system that have life."

"Will there be music?" I question.

"The finest Tauranian musicians will be here," he affirms.

"And food? What about the food?"

"There will be edibles from gor fruit to the meat of the halk beast."

"What's a halk beast?"

"You may have seen them on your arrival. They are the six-legged animals that were roaming the clearing."

"We are going to eat a grandpa horse?"

"If that is what you call it, then yes."

"What about alcohol? It's not a party until you have something that will kill brain cells."

"There will be the finest Tauranian wine, of course," he says, smiling.

The thought of what happened in the bar on Demer comes to mind. "Will I be able to drink it without dying?" I ask.

"Tauranian wine is safe to be consumed by all races."

My focus turns towards Zinka as it is, ultimately, her decision. She is the captain, after all. Even if she says no, I may still be able to convince her.

Zinka seems to ponder this for a moment. Is she thinking about eating a grandpa horse? Is she wondering how it will taste? My guess is it will taste like the combination of a horse and an elderly man.

"Alright," she says. "We will boost our chances if we can get aid from two more armies. God-king, it will be our great pleasure to attend."

The short grey skinned alien beams at this answer. Then he slaps Zinka's face. She, in turn, gives him a slap of his own. She seems more accepting of the slapping than I do. After the slap fest, she radios to the rest of the crew.

"Attention crew, we are going to have a slightly extended stay on planet Tauran. All crew are to attend a gala in our honor. Each crew member should find a diplomat suit in their closet. Formal dress is mandatory."

She then kills the radio and turns towards me.

"Let's go, Little Balls. We have a party to go to."

Grakken speaks up. "This is wonderful. I will contact the Apazians and the Oxites. I'll arrange the party to be held in two hours."

He quickly bolts out of the room in an excited manner. I've never seen someone move their little legs that fast before. Zinka begins to walk towards the exit and I follow behind.

"Zinka, why the hell do we have diplomat clothes?" I question as we step outside.

"Diplomacy is a vital tool in war, Little Balls."

"Will these clothes fit?"

"Yes. The ship makes clothes tailored to each of its crew. It got your measurements, race, and gender when you first stepped foot inside," she replies.

"Why does it need to know my race and gender?"

"It makes formal wear based on your species and subculture. The data showed that you were Human, American, and male, and determined what formal wear is common to you."

"Hmmm." It kind of makes sense, I guess. You need to be able to make allies. Wait, does that mean the ship knows what I look like naked?

The docking port opens to let us enter. Halissy saunters in shortly after. The rest of the crew is standing there, confused. They don't seem to understand why we are going to a party in the middle of an important mission.

It is Leonidas who speaks up first. "Why are we attending this party?"

"We may be able to get more aid. I never considered the Apazians or Oxites before, but with the Tauranians on our side, we may be able to convince them to help us."

"So, party time?" Pangaea questions.

"Yes, party time."

"Taco bash!" Danny yells before bolting towards his cabin.

The rest of the crew files out of the room, each waiting to kill time before the party. I feel it is a good idea to visit my closet, to make sure the ship got the formal attire right. I don't want to look silly.

Heading into my room, I make a beeline for my closet. Opening it reveals a black tuxedo hanging up in there. How have I not noticed that before? Seems like something that would stick out like a sore thumb. Where did that expression come from? Oh well.

Upon closer inspection, I see the standard black coat, a black vest, a black undershirt, black pants, and black shoes. According to the ship, formal attire means making everything the color of a funeral. My eyes then spot a black bow tie.

"How the hell do you tie one of these?" I question to myself while holding the piece of fabric.

I am a man of average intelligence. This should be a cinch. I survived how many things that should have killed me. Tying a tie should be the easiest thing that I will ever do in space.

CHAPTER 25

As it turns out, the bow tie was invented by someone who hates necks and wants to see them get strangled. The piece of cloth was contorting into every shape except the one shape that it's supposed to be in. My hands fumble with it again, and it still refuses to do what I want it to do. Why does it hate me?

I move my hands around trying to make a shape out of it. When finished, it looks like a crumbled mess. A mess that loves to poke my delicate throat. It feels like I'm being choked by someone with weak muscles. I've been spending the better two hours just trying to tie this son of a bitch.

The sound of a knock takes my attention away this great battle of life and death. Danny comes in without waiting for an answer from me.

"Hey, man. You ready to go?" He looks at my clothes and sees that the bow tie isn't quite working out. He continues. "Need a little help?"

"If you could, that would be nice. This damn thing is trying to kill me. I hate it."

Danny comes over and, in a flash, he unties the tangled mess that I'd made and ties it the proper way. I didn't know that he knew how to do that.

"There, much better," he says, clearly satisfied with his work.

I look over at Danny and see he is dressed like me, the only real difference being that his undershirt is white.

"How do you know how to do that?" I'm still impressed by his bow-tying precision.

"No idea, but it doesn't matter. You ready to go? Everyone else is waiting in the port."

"Yeah. Only took me two hours to get dressed, but I've got this."

This will be my first space party. Part of me is still a little surprised to be on an alien world. Life is just full of surprises. Entering the docking port, I see the rest of the crew in their formal clothes.

Leonidas has a simple black shirt on. His race may not be all that formal. Tik is wearing a bright orange onesie, covered in little baubles. As for the Aldinians, Shia wears what looks like a dark purple trench coat, while the girls have on what looks like military formalwear on Earth. Halissy is wearing a kilt. It's even plaid. Lastly, Pangaea has on a long black dress and is hating every second of it. I pin my left sleeve up to cover up my tiny arm.

"Glad to see everyone's clothes fit," Zinka examines the crew. "Just remember to be on your best behavior. The Tauranians are allies, and I would like to keep it that way."

We exit the Gravity Bong and head towards the palace. Ships are parked all around it. No idea when they all got here, but the party seems to be going off already.

Opening the door to the palace, we are greeted by music that is the bastard child of dubstep and polka. I see two different alien species which I am assuming are the Apazians and the Oxites. Don't know which is which, but I'll figure it out eventually. One of them appears to be purple blobs with two fly eyes on their face. The second race are big, woolly, and muscular creatures, which remind me of a Wookie. Hair covers their faces and the only feature that can be see are horns sticking out from each side of their face.

Looking around, all three races are mingling. Zinka heads towards Grakken. With him, there is one blob guy and one hairy guy. They may be the leaders of their respective races. I feel a tug at the back of my tuxedo and get pulled in a direction. Looking at the source, it is Danny who is pulling me.

"Come on, dude," he says eagerly. "Let's go get drunk."

I shrug and follow him. We make our way to the open bar and grab two drinks. I down the glass in one gulp. It tastes pretty good actually. The fact it is delicious makes it easier to take a second⋯ and a third⋯ and a fourth. After that, I may have lost count. It's not my fault that it's delicious.

The world starts to get a little fuzzy. The ground doesn't want to stay still. The damn thing just keeps wiggling all over the place. They should really get a scientist to look at that. Can't be too good for a planet to wiggle. The aliens around me seem to be wiggling around with the world. Everybody should see the same scientist for that. It's an epidemic.

"Hey Danny?" I question. "Why is everyone and everything moving?"

"The real question is, why are there three of you?"

My eyes try to focus as I see a green blur moving towards me. Damn green blurs, always coming to get me. The blur gets closer and closer until I can make out the distorted appearance of Zinka. When her face becomes a little clearer, I could see the disappointment in it. What did I do now?

"We're literally moments into the party, and you two are already drunk?" She's rightfully disappointed in us.

"Well," Danny starts. "It's free drinks. If we don't drink them then some assholes will just come in and drink all of them."

"You two are those assholes. You drank nearly all of the drinks."

"Exactly," I reply. "We had to do it before someone else had a chance to be the asshole. We are preemptively being the assholes."

"Don't do anything stupid. The Apazian leader, Commander Xert, is coming over soon. He wants to talk to you, to get a feel for the crew."

Just as she says this, I notice a large brown blur moving towards me. I guess the Apazians are the hairy ones. The large hairy blur moves next to me and begins to speak.

"So, you are the illustrious Little Balls that I've heard so much about," he says in a deep booming voice.

"I have no idea what illustrious means, but it's good to meet you, man," I raise my hand for a handshake.

He stares at my extended appendage as if unsure about it.

"I find the stories I've heard about you unreliable after meeting you," he's brutally honest.

"Uhhhh⋯ thanks? I guess," the insult goes right over my head.

The Apazian turns towards Zinka. "I will consider your proposal. For now, I'll enjoy the party."

The large hairy creature leaves and Zinka seems disappointed at the meeting. She should be used to the crushing reality of life. Hell, I'm used to it. I've been used to it. Not sure what that says about me. "Well, that could've gone better," she says in an exasperated tone.

"My bad," I say, feeling partially responsible.

"It's fine, he's difficult. Just⋯ just be sure to have a good time, and don't do anything stupid, Little Balls."

Zinka leaves. I look around for Danny and notice that I can't see him anywhere. Where the hell did he get to? My eyes scan the room, looking for the stoned man. A noise brings attention to a man eating all the food at the buffet table. He is eating a piece of halk beast and I can't help but fight back my gag reflex. The old man face just makes it seem icky. I make my way over to the hungry dude.

"Enjoying the food, man?" I question when I get to Danny, because of course it's Danny.

"It is delicious," he replies before stuffing more into his face hole. "Do you want some?"

"Nah, I'll pass on the old man meat."

I feel a finger poking my shoulder and I turn around. When I do, I see Pangaea looking up at me. "Are you two idiots drunk already?"

"Or is it more likely that the rest of the world is drunk, and we are sober?" Danny pipes up between bites.

"You guys are so stupid," she says, looking me up and down. "Hmmm, you clean up okay, Little Balls."

"What can I say? I am a beautiful piece of man flesh."

"Get a room!" Danny jokes, still shoving food into his face. "No, seriously. Get a room, because that means more food for me."

"Idiot," Pangaea deadpans.

Danny pays no mind to the comment and continues to destroy the buffet. No idea how a man that skinny can eat that much. Fairly certain he has eaten more than his body weight by now.

The music in the air changes to a slower pace. Still seems like dubstep and polka, but it is a much slower melody this time around. Pangaea looks up at the speakers before turning to me. "Come on. Let's dance." She puts her drink down.

"Uh… what?"

"Confusion later, dancing now," she pulls me onto the dance floor.

"But I have no idea how to dance."

"You don't need to. It's dancing. It's not like it's rocket science."

"But I don't know rocket science either."

"So, I said it wasn't rocket science."

"Yes, but that means that I have nothing to go on. I'd like to have a reference point," I blabber.

"Lighten up, drunk," she says when we get to the floor. "Here, just put your arms… uh, arm around me."

I do as she says, and mostly just try to not embarrass myself. My right arm goes around her waist.

She continues. "Now just move your body to the rhythm. Just like this."

She starts to move her hips back and forth. I just try to move with her, letting her take the lead. My drunken movements are clumsy and uncoordinated. Her movements are much more eloquent and smoother.

"There. That's not so hard," she states.

"Says you," I reply. "This is requiring more effort to stay focused than anything I've ever done."

"Oh, you're fine, you big baby."

The music continues, and I slowly become more confident about the situation, but you know what they say: Pride comes before the fall. This happens in a literal sense. My right foot gets caught on my left foot. Which results in me falling backwards.

I fall directly on my ass.

Pangaea laughs her ass off at my misery. I need better friends.

"You are so graceful, Little Balls," she says, still laughing. "Now come on, get your ass up."

This is the second time my clumsy nature has caused me pain in this adventure. I pick myself up and dust off the tuxedo.

"Don't worry. I'm alright. It's fine to just laugh at me instead of helping," I reply in a sarcastic tone.

"Look, Little Balls," she says, "Sometimes you have to help yourself. Just remember, when you absolutely need help, I'll be there."

"Thanks. You're just so sweet."

"No problem and thank you for the dance. We'll have to do it again sometime." She pats my cheek and takes her leave.

Well, that was interesting. My attention returns to the open bar. More drinks are always a good idea. At least, until it's not. After reaching the table with the drinks, I down one or twelve more. These are so good. I don't want to know what it's made of though. There's a good chance that would ruin this beverage for me.

The world gets more and more fuzzy as I drink more. Maybe if I drink even more, the world will settle down. It seems like a good plan. I look around the room to see what the rest of the crew is up to. Danny is still eating everything in sight. Zinka is still hanging out with the ambassadors. Leo seems to be cracking up with some Oxites. It's good to see him laughing. Halissy is talking to the Tauranian doctor from before. Yekk is near Danny, using odd instruments to poke at the food. Tik is gone. No idea where he went. Lastly, Shia is skulking in the corner. I move towards Danny to inquire about Tik.

"Hey Danny. Have you seen where Tik went?"

"Yeah man. I saw him take a blob person to another room. I think that they might be doing the horizontal tango. Not one hundred percent sure, though."

"Whatever makes him happy," I don't really want to imagine that.

Danny continues. "He's getting the blob, man. He's getting the blob."

I down my drink to try and drown that image out of my mind. I already need therapy. There is no need to add even more therapy to that.

Danny seems to have gone back to his gluttony, so I decide to go join Leo. I want to see what is so funny. Everyone could use a laugh.

Wandering over to Leo, the laughing can be heard louder and louder. Before I can get there however, my eyelids become heavy and black out drunkenness takes effect and the world goes away.

CHAPTER 26

My eyes open as I feel a sharp pain in my sides.

"Ow, what the hell?!" I clutch at my ribs.

Pangaea is grinning down at me. She looks rather smug, for someone who is hurting someone else.

"Wake up, lush. We have to go to planet Oxe."

"Why are we going there?" I ask as the hangover punches me in the head.

"The Apazians have already agreed to help us. We have to meet with the leaders of Oxe, though. They want a private discussion with us."

"Well, it's good that we have the Apazians' support," I groggily stand up.

I start heading back to the Gravity Bong. Pangaea is following me, and Elisar is walking right beside me. How long has she been there? I really need to start being more observant. I could, however, just do the exact opposite of that and hope for the best. That seems like the most logical choice, or at least the laziest.

"You're coming with us?" I question.

"I'm going to shoot Derask in the skull."

"Part of me thought that you would be staying here."

"Beason is being kept in a drug-induced coma while his injuries heal," she explains. "He is in the best possible care. I need to make sure Derask doesn't do anything like this to any other family."

"So, shoot him in the head?"

"Indeed. I'm going to shoot him right in the head."

"Seems like a rational reaction," who am I to judge?

We enter the ship and I head toward the cockpit, because surely Zinka will be there, typing away. When I get to the cockpit, though, I see Yekk is at the controls.

"Yekk? I didn't know that you knew how to fly one of these."

"Please, I'm an Aldinian. We learn to fly these when we are larvae."

"When I was a larva, I played toy cars. I made them go zoom because that's how a car sounds."

She looks at me and smiles. She shakes her head before returning her focus back on the controls.

"No offense, Little Balls, but I don't think that you should ever be allowed to fly this ship. Or any ship, for that matter."

"None taken. Honestly, I have to agree with that."

The ship begins to rise and shoots out of the atmosphere of Tauran. Considering planet Oxe is in the same solar system, it should be a short trip. Only five minutes pass before Yekk breaks the silence.

"Coming up on Oxe. Getting ready to land at the received coordinates."

The Gravity Bong lands softly on the planet's surface. When it is settled, the entire crew exits the ship. Zinka takes the lead, as she knows where to go. Little blob dudes line the path that we follow. Every one of them is armed to the teeth. I don't think they trust us.

Our surroundings are a desert-like landscape. A massive reptile creature lays upon a rock in the distance. It looks like a dragon. This planet has a motherfucking dragon and that is amazing. I wonder if I could ride that dragon. In the distance, I see purple blobs yelling and holding signs at a statue. There are also identical purple blobs shouting at the first group of blobs. What's that about? I'll figure it out later.

We follow Zinka as the blobs stare at us. Coming up in front of us is an odd spherical building. Upon entering, the building looks like a hoarder's nest. Random junk is scattered in piles over the place. This leader is a slob.

A giant archway looms at the end of the hall. The architecture would be very impressive, if not for the mess. On the other side of the arch, a large circular table sits in the center, where a blob man sits.

"Ah, there you are," he says. "Enter and let us discuss this matter further."

The crew each takes a seat at the table and we all turn our focus on the blob man.

He continues. "For those of I did not meet at the party, I am the leader of the mighty Oxites, Scott."

"Scott?" I question.

"Yes. In our language it means, Brave One."

"Your name is Scott?" I reiterate.

"Yes. Why? Is there something wrong with the name Scott?"

"No, I was just expecting something a little more alien, like Bribbleborp or something."

"You're just making up words," he dismisses before turning the conversation. "So, what is your plan for taking out Derask?"

"Simple," Zinka pipes up. "Combine forces for a full out assault on the Colossus."

"And you think this will work?" The blob man questions.

Pangaea replies, "Worth a shot."

"Hmm, it doesn't appear very thought out."

"Relax," I say. "We've got this. Thinking does nothing but get in the way."

"Please, Scott," Tik jumps in. "We have the aid of the Demerians, the Apazians, and the Tauranians. After this, we are headed to Planet 739 to get the aid of mercenaries. Your army would greatly improve our chances."

"You are going to seek help from criminals?" He questions.

"That is how desperate we are, sir," Zinka replies. "We need everyone to pitch in for this one. Taking down the Colossus will not be easy. We are going to need a lot of ships, and a lot of fire power. But one thing is clear: we have to stop Derask."

"Well, since you already have the support of the Apazians and the Tauranians, my hands are tied on this one. It is essential that we keep on good terms, and if they believe in your cause, then I suppose I must, too. We will join your cause. Send the mission dossier to me at your earliest convenience."

This is vastly improving. Bet we're at 22% success rate or better, now.

"Hey Scott?' I question. "What's the deal with the yelling people outside?"

"Well, one side is protesting to keep a statue that the government decided to take down later. The other side is counter-protesting. They are in favor of taking it down."

"Why all this hoopla about a statue?" Tik questions.

"Well over a century ago, this planet was much different: one ethnicity was kept in bondage as slaves. After a bloody civil war, the anti-slavery side won. This part of the world was part of the pro-slavery side. Decades after the conflict ended, they erected statues to commemorate their heritage."

"Ethnicity? I don't want this to be misconstrued as racism, but you all look the same."

"How many color wavelengths does your species eyes detect?"

"Uhhhh…" I don't know the answer, but Pangaea saves my stupid ass.

"Three. Humans see in three color wavelengths."

"Ah, you see, the Oxites see in twelve color wavelengths. That means we can see colors that you can't even imagine."

"What do they look like?" I question.

"You… you can't describe colors. Anyway, to your eyes we look the same but, in our eyes, we appear different."

"Why is the one side so keen on saving the statues?" Danny questions.

"Well, two reasons. One, they are too stupid to understand that you don't have to be proud of all your heritage. Two, it's racism under the guise of historicism. That means that they are racist, but they are too cowardly to come out and say it."

"Well, that was enlightening," Zinka says after an appropriate pause. "Thank you for your support, Scott. We greatly appreciate it."

Zinka stands and we all follow suit. She shakes Scott's hand and makes an exit out of the room. Yet again, the entire crew just mimics her actions. Leaving the palace, the shouts at the statue are still going full strength. The armed guards lining the path still stare us down.

The ship opens, and we board. I guess now we get to go to a planet with residents of a questionable reputation. It can't be all bad though. We may be able to convince them to, you know, not kill us on the spot. For all I know, Preet may not be all that bad. She may be a very reasonable queen of mercenaries⋯We are so dead.

Elisar breaks off and goes towards her quarters. Yekk heads towards the cockpit. I don't know where I should go. I just stop in place and try to figure out where to head from here. Ten minutes pass and I find myself still in the same spot.

After a while, I find myself being pulled along by Danny.

"Hey, Danny. Where are we going?"

"Tik and I are getting high, and you are coming."

"Okay. Sounds good, but why such a rush?"

"Well, there is a small chance we may die on the next planet. It's not a huge chance. Honestly, I'd say we have like a 99% chance of living, but there is that small chance that we'll die. I don't want to die without another smoke."

"I'm surprised, Danny. I didn't know you needed a reason to smoke."

"Well, I really don't, but I figured I should probably just make one up this time. Just for a bit of unneeded exposition and unnecessary emotional attachment to a substance that only provides me with joy. Mostly, so people can overemphasize my hobby into a dependency so that people can bitch about it."

"Yeah⋯ you lost me, bro. Let's just get baked."

Danny drags me to his cabin. Tik is already packing a bowl. He is dexterous with those long meaty claw finger things.

"Ah," Tik speaks up as he sees us enter the room. "I see you have found Little Balls. Shall we start your amazing Earth custom now?"

Danny replies, "Yeah, man. Let's light up."

We all take our places in the stoner circle. With three of us, it is more of a triangle. That doesn't seem to have the same ring to it, however. Whoever heard of a stoner triangle? That's just stupid.

With the bowl packed, Tik begins to light up and inhale. The bowl dwindles as it makes its way around the triangle. Now that I think of it, a triangle just sounds stupid when you say you pass it around it. Maybe that is why it is called the circle even though it is never actually a circle.

The bowl dies and everyone involved is blazed out of their minds.

"I've enjoyed our time together!" Tik yells.

The yelling causes me to flinch. Dammit, I thought I was used to this by now. Unfortunately, I am not. It hurts, but Tik is still a damn good guy.

"We have enjoyed this too, man," Danny replies calmly. Clearly, he is used to it.

"If only this feeling could last forever!"

"That may not be the smartest thing," I reply. "You have to be sober sometimes."

Danny replies, "Blasphemy."

"Well, you're a special exemption. Your brain functions just as well with it."

CHAPTER 27

I decide to take advantage of the flight time to Planet 739 by getting a few winks. I still have no concept of time, but that shouldn't stop me from sleeping when I want. I wonder what nightmare visions will come to my unconscious mind this time. My eyes close.

The world around me seems dark momentarily until it starts to take shape around me. It appears I am in a house, a very poorly decorated house.

"What the hell?" I question.

A disembodied laugh rings out from all directions.

"What the hell is that laughing?"

More laughing fills my ears. It's not a malicious or evil laugh. It's more of a laugh like someone is forcing it. It's like someone is trying to portray something as funny even though nothing of any comedic value has happened. A voice calls to me from the kitchen.

"Are you home dear?" I recognize Pangaea's voice.

She walks into the living room where I am, and she looks⋯ odd. Her clothes are like something out of a 1950's TV show. It looks a lot more disjointed, considering she still has her tattoos and shaved head.

"I'm glad you're home, honey. How was work?"

Wait, honey? Work? What is going on here? I might have to just play along to see where this goes. Plus, what else am I going to do?

"Uh, work was fine, I guess··· dear."

I look down and see that for some reason I am wearing a three-piece suit. Why am I wearing a three-piece suit? I don't even own a suit.

"Now, don't forget, we are hosting a cook-out for the neighbors in ten minutes."

"Why?"

That damn laughing.

"Because we have to be good neighbors, of course."

Did she just giggle? I never imagined her as a giggler. Something seems off about the world, but I can't put my finger on it.

She continues. "Now go get dressed in your casual slacks and get ready to be the grill master you claim to be."

What was funny there? It's like I'm in some bizarre world that requires fake laughs to trick people into thinking that something entertaining is happening. What could that mean th··· oh shit, I'm in a sitcom. Well, it's clear that I am dreaming. Let's see what happens next, though.

"Uh, honey?" I question. "Where do I keep my slacks?"

"Oh, come on Thaddeus." Did she just call me Thaddeus? "They are up in the bedroom, silly."

"Right··· and our bedroom is where?"

"Oh Thaddeus, you always were the funny one. Now, off you go. Get dressed. Our neighbors will be here soon," she says as she walks off.

Okay, I'll just go upstairs. That seems like a good place to look for the bedroom. The hallway seems like something decorated from a hand-me-down store. Everything seems odd and peculiar. Ancient novelties adorn the walls.

I head towards the end of the hall where a random door is situated. If I had to make a guess, I would say that is the bedroom. It seems likely, considering it is the only door on the second floor. Why is the hallway so long, if there is only one door? Oh well. There's no use questioning things in a dream. I hope it's a dream. If this is reality, then··· well, it wouldn't be any weirder than what was happening before.

I open the door and see an old school bedroom. The first thing that catches my attention is the fact that there are two twin beds in the main bedroom. Why are there two beds?

My hand grips the dresser drawer and I pull it open revealing a set of silk pajamas. Now, I know that this is not what she meant when she told me to put on casual clothes, but who in this world could resist silk pajamas? This is my dream, dammit. I will do as I please because I'm an adult and I'm capable of making my own choices in life.

I take off the monkey suit that I am currently wearing and don the silk pajamas. The idea of wearing them tricks my brain into thinking that I do have on the silkiness. The brain is such a powerful thing.

Now that I am dressed appropriately, or inappropriately depending on your view point, I make my way down towards the backyard where I hear noise and commotion. Guess the party started.

The door outside opens to reveal an odd sight. Gathered in the yard, I see all the people that I've met in space. All the men are wearing creased pants and sweater vests, while the women are dressed in poofy dress-things. I never thought this was possible, but I feel a little under-dressed in my silk pajamas.

"Hey, honey," Pangaea says, making her way over to me. "Now, come and mingle before you start up the grill."

She seems unfazed by the fact that I'm adorned in sleepwear. At least I am incapable of making any social faux pas in this dream. I should get naked. Just to see what would happen.

I walk up to Leo in his fancy vest. He is not wearing pants, probably because pants won't fit onto his bug-like thorax. He doesn't wear pants and it is socially acceptable, but when I do it everyone's like 'put on some clothes' or 'that's not appropriate church behavior'. Everyone is so prudish.

"Why hello, Thaddeus," Leo says to me. Why is everyone calling me Thaddeus? "How are you this evening?"

"Well, I'll let you know as soon as I know."

Oh good. The laughing is back. I missed it so. I will destroy that disembodied laugh.

Leo laughs right after the other laugh ends. "You are just too much."

"Yeah, I'm too much of a lot of things."

That laugh will drive me insane.

"So," Leo starts again. "How was the office?"

"Uh⋯ very⋯ office-y."

It is very polite of him to wait until after the prerecorded laughing finishes each time before he starts speaks. It also seems a little awkward, having to wait for twenty seconds before he replies.

"Well, thanks for the invite, neighbor. I'm going to talk to Derask. Hey, let me know when you got those burgers done."

Leo then walks away. Did he say Derask? Derask is here? Oh my nonexistent God. I have got to sneak a peek at him sometime before I wake up. Whilst lost in my thoughts of Derask dressed like a stuffy dude from the 1950's, I feel someone placing something in my hands. I look down and see chunks of cow flesh on a plate. I look up to see who handed me the plate, and Pangaea is standing there, smiling. She sure is smiley in my dreams. It's not a bad smile, mind you, but it just seems so out of place from her usual expression. She's never been very emotive.

"Here you go," she says, while the smile never leaves her face. "Time to get to work, mister. We have hungry guests waiting for your world-famous burgers, honey."

"Uh⋯ yes⋯ cooking. I can definitely do that," I bluff my way into making her think that I can cook.

I take the plate over to the grill and try to think of how the hell I am going to turn it on. Common sense dictates that I should press every button and turn every dial on the contraption until something happens. The grill finally sputters to life.

The fire rages as I throw the hunks of meat on the grill. The meat starts to sizzle, as I try to figure what the hell I'm supposed to do now. Is anything else required for me to cook it, or do I just wait for the fire to do its thing? I'm going to go with the latter. Mostly, because that one requires less work.

I zone out, and the burgers remind me that I'm required to do other things, because fire starts to burn, and by burn, I mean that they are on fire.

"Ahhh, fire!" I yell, backing away from the inferno.

Pangaea, either sensing my duress or just noticing the large fire that's in front of my face, comes in with a fire extinguisher. With the flame out and the food covered in large amounts of white stuff, Pangaea turns towards me with a winsome expression adorning her face.

"Oh yeah, you really are the grill master, aren't you?"

"Hey," I reply. "I was under the impression that you liked them well done."

That damn laugh. I nearly forgot it existed. I really need to find out how to turn that off. It may have been a little charming for the first twenty seconds, but now it is just unnecessary and grating.

"Sure honey," She says with a giggle. "It's okay. I'll cook. You just go and have fun at the party."

"I can do that."

"I know, sweetie, I know, but you've worked hard, and you need to relax." She pushes me away from the grill and toward the crowd.

I am on a mission to see Derask in old time clothes. It is one hundred percent necessary to laugh my ass off at dream Derask's expense.

I walk through the crowd, trying to find the familiar evil face. My eyes come across the object of my search and it is even greater than any of my wildest dreams. The dreadful face is nullified a bit by the fact that his torso is covered in a polo shirt, and his legs are adorned with creased khakis. The image is made even better by the fact that he is smoking on an old school corn cob pipe.

Now normally, I would avoid talking to this asshole at all costs, but I have a mighty urge to see how he talks.

"Hey, Derask," I say moving closer to him. "How's it going?"

"Why, howdy there, neighbor. Working hard or hardly working?"

That line is older than me. I don't know any person who still uses that, and if I ever met anyone who did, I would immediately stop conversing with that person. I do not need that type of terrible influence in my life.

"Well, that's all I wanted," I say as I slowly step away from him. "I'll talk to you later, dude."

"Dude?"

But I didn't really pay much attention to his last question. I need to leave before I bust a gut. I turn to leave and catch my foot on uneven Earth. The result being me finding myself quickly coming to a face to face meeting between me and the ground. Right before my skull collided my eyes snapped open and I found myself lying in my bed on the ship.

That dream was so worth it.

CHAPTER 28

"Attention Crew, we are preparing for descent onto Planet 739," Zinka's voice comes over the intercom. "I request that Pangaea, Leonidas, Little Balls, and Danny assist me on the landing team. Tik and Elisar, please oversee protecting the scientists and Dr. Halissy, as well as the ship. If you need any assistance, radio the landing party. Now, landing party meet me at Docking Port Two for exploration."

The intercom cuts off. Is she expecting some trouble? Oh well, no use worrying about that now. I'm sure Preet is a very lovely and delightful individual, or, at least, I hope so. I really don't want to have come this far only to die on some strange planet.

I head towards Docking Port Two to meet the landing crew. The hallway there seems longer than usual. I guess that's because I don't know what to expect. I mean, I didn't really know what to expect from the other planets, either, but this one seems different. Don't really know why, but it seems a lot more dangerous to go to a planet of criminals. Maybe I'm just being too obtuse.

The door to the docking port opens, revealing the rest of the team. Why am I always the last one to get here? Why is everyone so fast? Am I just slow and lazy? That seems like it could very well be the case.

"Okay crew," Zinka addresses. "This planet is highly dangerous. Everyone grab a weapon, but make sure you don't pull it out unless you absolutely have to."

She then motions towards the gun rack and we all grab one and a holster belt. I feel like a cowboy, a space cowboy. Suddenly that song makes sense.

Zinka continues. "Make sure you watch your back and watch your teammates' backs. We are going down with five, and I want to return with five. Is that understood?"

A chorus of yeahs and nods is her answer.

"Great. Now let's go."

We follow Zinka out of the ship. The sight that greets us is a desert landscape. Little towns dot the surface of the horizon. One of the towns stands in front of us, with its buildings sitting low. Buildings may be a strong word. They all appear to be made of random space junk. Bits of metal ships and scraps make up the walls and the roofs. All of them appear raggedy and decrepit. It seems that this was by design, however. Someone built it shitty on purpose, like a symbolic aesthetic to show what type of world this is. It could also be that I'm over-thinking this.

Zinka begins to walk forward, so we all follow. Her head is held high as we start to pass different forms of alien life that call this world home. She and Pangaea both take the lead with a positive, confident demeanor. Leo, though not appearing scared, doesn't appear confident either. His facial expression is more of a neutral glare. Danny is just blissfully unaware of what is happening. I, on the other hand, have no idea what my face is, but if I had to guess I would say that, from an outside perspective, I am the biggest wimp in this group.

We weave our way through the streets of the rundown town. Zinka then spots the building that she is looking for and makes a beeline for it. The building is no more special than the rest in this town, but I assume that is where Preet is.

We enter the facility and see a huge set of stairs heading underground. As we begin descending the stairs, I notice the complete lack of guards. On every other planet, the leader was surrounded by soldiers that are armed to the teeth. Preet, however, has no one here to protect her.

At the bottom of the stairs, a giant door looms ahead of us. Zinka pushes it open without a moment of hesitation. A giant square room opens up before us. There is no furniture in the room, except a table with a few chairs around it. Torches line the walls of it, illuminating the room with a faint orange glow. A voice interrupts my thoughts.

"Ah, visitors. Do come in and please shut the door behind you," the feminine voice echoes in the room.

Leo closes the door, as I look around for the source of the voice. A being then begins to move out of the shadows. It is a cloud of barely visible gas. In the center of the gas cloud there appears to be a glowing orb that emits a blue light. The gaseous cloud speaks again. "I am Preet. Do you require my assistance?"

"Preet," Zinka speaks up. "We ask for your aid in taking down Derask."

"Derask?" Preet questions. "That is going to be a very pricey job. At least three billion credits."

Zinka pulls out Derask's credit chip and uses a computer to transfer the credits to the mercenary.

Preet laughs, "Is that Derask's credit chip? I love it. Making him pay for his own death. That is just so morbid that it's delightful."

She turns towards me. I think she turns towards me. It is hard to tell where someone is looking when they don't have a face. She moves towards me, however, which reinforces the fact that she did turn to look at me. When she is right in front of me, she speaks.

"A human? Am I correct?"

"Uh··· yeah."

"Glorious," she replies with glee. "It has been so long since I first saw one of you. I had great times visiting your primitive little planet."

"You visited Earth?" I question.

"Indeed. It was a little more than two thousand of your Earth's rotations ago. I shifted into some white lady in the Middle East and I did some magic tricks."

"Wait, you did magic tricks?" I ask.

"Yes. It was fun for a bit, but they nailed me to some wood and threw me in a cave, so I left."

"Wait, were you Jesus?"

"It appears so. I even read the book your people wrote about me. I'm not going to lie, I am a little offended that they changed my gender. Like it really mattered. To be perfectly honest, my species doesn't even have genders. I just always prefer a female form."

"I didn't know Jesus was a girl. Hell, I didn't even know he, I mean she was real."

"May I try something now?"

"Sure, go ahead." I don't see how agreeing with an alien's request could backfire.

She raises what appears to be a tentacle made of a semitransparent gas and touches it to my head. This gives me a massive headache, as if someone is repeatedly hitting my skull with one of those over-sized dildos. The pain subsides and the figure in front of me has changed.

Preet has used her transforming skill to change into the form of a human female. Preet's skin is now pale, her face dotted with a light dusting of freckles. Her eyes are a piercing blue, which matches nicely to her short, blue hair. Her body has changed to an hourglass figure that is slightly larger than what the societal definition of beauty would dictate is attractive. To hell with that, though.

"Holy shit. You transformed into that mall girl," I exclaim.

"Mall girl?" Danny questions.

"Yeah. This one girl I saw at the mall before, but I was way too much of a wuss to actually talk to her and tell her I thought she was cute."

Preet speaks up. "It's been awhile since I was a human. I figured I needed to update my human form."

"Did you just probe my brain?"

"Pretty much," she replies looking at her new form. "You said okay when I asked, though. You should ask some follow up questions before agreeing next time. Consider this an important life lesson."

"That··· is a very good point." I concede.

Preet turns towards Zinka to talk about the situation. "Now, what is the plan?"

"Well, I'll send you the coordinates for the attack. I know where

Derask's ship is. It hasn't really moved for a while. We will be working with the Demerians and the Tauranians in our plan to take him down. We also have the support of the Apazians and the Oxites."

"Splendid," she turns toward one of the chairs at the table.

She has a seat and appears to be thinking hard about something. She continues, "I'll wait for your beacon."

She motions for us to leave, so we decide to go ahead and take her up on that. The trek up the stairs feels slightly less heavy. I guess that meeting went as well as we could have hoped. No one died, which is a win in and of itself. Maybe I should raise the bar on what I consider a win, though.

As the air hits us upon us leaving the odd building, we hear a deep voice yell in our direction.

"What the hell do you guys think you're doing!" the voice shouts.

We turn our attention to a massive creature. The being stands at about nine feet in height. His four large arms are excessively ripped. Other than that, he reminds me of a cyclops from the old myths. His head is smooth, and face only consists of a mouth and a singular eye. Rough, scaly skin covers his body. He continues.

"You aren't welcome here."

"We were just leaving, big guy," I reply nervously, backing away from the beast.

Pangaea raises her gun, "Get out of the way you prick."

"Aren't you just an adorable little thing. Might want to put the toy down before you get hurt." The large creature looms over Pangaea as if trying to intimidate her. I don't think that that is even possible.

"You want to try to make me put it down?" She replies in a calm, yet menacing, voice.

"Enough!" Zinka shouts stepping in between the two. "Out of the way, asshole. You say we don't belong here, but if you hadn't stopped us, we would already be gone."

The large being glares and starts to reach for his gun. I guess I was a little too optimistic when I said none of us died. Damn my jinxing mouth. Pangaea's finger is hovering over her trigger, while Zinka's hand slowly begins to reach for hers.

"Groddie," I hear Preet's calm voice come from behind us. "What are you doing?"

The alien stops immediately, and an expression of pure terror comes across his face. Preet continues.

"Don't tell me that you were making trouble for our new clients."

"N-no, of course not, your highness," he stutters.

Preet comes out of the shadows of the building while still in her human form. She speaks up. "Good, because, as you know, I demand that all customers be treated with respect, right?"

"Of-of course, ma'am."

"Good. Now leave."

As soon as those words left her mouth, Groddie was gone. At least, I assume his name was Groddie, or that is just some alien insult that I don't understand.

Preet speaks. "You five have a good trip. Don't keep me waiting too long, now. I tend to get very impatient."

She retreats into her hovel and leaves us alone. I glance around, and all the beings back up.

I take a step forward, and all of them in that direction step back. Hmmm, I am going to try something. I take a step back and they go forward. I take one forward and they go back. I then decide to do this for about five minutes.

"Little Balls!" Zinka yells and she smacks my skull. "Quit terrifying the criminals."

"I was just having a little fun."

"Back. On. The. Ship. Now!"

My response is an incoherent grumble. One that not even I could understand, even though I'm the one who made it. I walk back to the ship with the rest of the crew.

The landing team boards the ship again. Everything here seems like it always was, so I guess nothing happened.

"Say it again you stupid son of a bitch!" Elisar yells, echoing down the hall.

Hmmm, spoke too soon. I tend to do that. Yet, it never seems to backfire on me. We run toward the sound of the shout. It sounds like it came from the science lab. When the door opens, the scene is peculiar.

Inside, we see Elisar trying to choke Shia. Tik appears to be trying to hold the girl back from killing the man. Yekk is trying to pry Shia from the Tauranian's grasp. Halissy, on the other hand, is just kind of chilling in the corner with her arms crossed. She has an expression of indifference on her face.

"Halissy?" Leo says walking up to her. "What happened?"

"Well," she starts. "Long story short, Dr. Shia made Elisar upset, so she's trying to kill him."

Halissy seems very indifferent to the chaos happening around her.

"And the longer version?" Leo questions.

"I'll let one of them explain everything," she points to the two who are caught in the scuffle.

Zinka decides to step in "Everyone, enough!"

Her shouting causes everyone to stop the shenanigans and look toward the small green lady. The pause gives Shia the perfect chance to exit the grasp.

"Someone care to explain to me what happened?"

Shia rubs his throat to try and bring relief to his aching esophagus. He tries to speak through his raspy voice. "I was just minding my own business when this psychopath tried to kill me. Leave it to a Tauranian to be so brutish."

Elisar is quick to reply, "Look, I don't give two shits about your racism, but what you said about Beason is unforgivable."

"What did he say?" Zinka asks.

Just thinking about it enrages Elisar to the point of where she is unable to form words. Shia looks embarrassed and ashamed. Finally, it is Yekk that answers.

"He said that the little grey skinned bastard got what he deserved and if he dies then that will just be one less Grey to infest the world."

"What the actual fuck?" Danny questions, clearly taken aback by the blatant racism.

"What I said was true," Shia responds, trying to defend his stupidity.

"And you were just watching?" Zinka questions Halissy.

She simply shrugs before responding. "I figured either he would die, or she would tire herself out. I could revive him if I acted quick enough. Asphyxiation isn't that big of a deal. If it was the latter, I'd just put her on an I.V. drip, so she stays hydrated. No big deal."

"No big deal!" Shia shouts. "She tried to kill me!"

"Yeah, but she didn't. Look, you're still alive," she replies calmly.

Zinka rolls her eyes and turns back towards the bickering duo. "Shia, if I were you, I'd watch my mouth. Elisar is one of the best assassins in the galaxy. It may just be better for you if you just kept quiet."

"What the hell?!" he shouts. "She almost kills me, and you idiots are blaming me?"

"You were the one who spewed racist comments about her son, asshole." Pangaea pipes up. "You're just lucky Tik is a better person than I am. I would have just let her go."

"I… I can't believe this," Shia stammers. "I nearly get murdered, and yet I'm the bad guy."

Leo replies. "Yes, plus it's extremely hard to feel bad for a racist."

"Exactly." I say. "It's like if you see a news story about a man getting killed. At first, you're like, that sucks. Later, it's revealed that he was a Nazi or a grand wizard of the KKK and you no longer feel bad."

Shia gives me a dead eyed stare. "I have no idea what a grand wizard is or what a KKK is," he says.

"Well the KKK is, essentially, just a bunch of terrible human beings. The Grand Wizard thing is just what they call the leader. It's a horribly distorted game of D&D with the robes and the fantasy names. Except instead of playing a fun game, they burn the symbol of the religion they belong to and they hate everyone who isn't like them."

"That doesn't make any sense."

"Well neither do any of the things that they believe or do. Speaking of D&D, I could really go for a game. Too bad I'm a terrible dungeon master."

Danny offers, "I'm not bad. If we can get our hands on some dice, we may be able to play a game of it."

"What is D&D?" Leo questions.

This time it is Pangaea who explain, "It's a tabletop RPG game.

Essentially you make a character and join in an interactive adventure with dragons and orcs and dwarves and--"

"Alright," I interrupt. "Someone's a little nerdy."

"You started it. Shut up."

"Everyone shut up!" Zinka yells. "You," she says pointing towards Shia. "Watch yourself; and you," she turns her attention towards Elisar. "If he doesn't keep his mouth shut, just hide the evidence."

Zinka heads toward the cockpit. Elisar glares at Shia, then retires in the direction of her cabin. This seems to be going very well. I'm glad we are all get along.

Shia just mumbles under his breath and leaves. Yekk turns toward the rest of the crew that remains and speaks.

"Look. I am very sorry about Shia. His actions were inexcusable, and I assure you I will try to keep him in line."

"I wouldn't worry about it too much," Tik reassures. "I'm pretty sure Elisar can handle herself. Besides, you can't hold yourself responsible for his actions."

"Would you believe me if I said that he's not all bad?" She turns to tinker with something on the table. "He created the cure for one of the most devastating diseases that the Aldinian people have ever seen."

"Hard to imagine a guy like that doing anything nice," I reply as I come up next to her at the table.

"It's true, but simply because he has done some good work, it doesn't absolve him of all the bad. I've been trying to eradicate the indoctrination that he's had since I've met him."

"How is he indoctrinated?" Pangaea asks, joining the conversation.

"Well, believe it or not, we once had a leader worse than Derask. Although Derask's focus is power, this man's focus was race. He would stand upon the podium spouting nonsense of Aldinians being the superior race. Shia's father was his second in command. He spent his larvae years constantly being told about how low other beings were. The brunt of the hatred was focused on the Tauranians. I see good in him, but good can't be seen behind a cloud of hatred."

I wonder, "Do you think that you could ever be able to help him?"

"I don't know, but I hope I can, before it's too late."

I nod and leave the conversation at that. I make my way out and head towards my room. On the plus side, we have somehow managed to gather three armies to help us. We originally set out for three, so I guess we are at par. Hooray for meeting expectations.

The door to my room opens. I grab my pack of smokes and light one up. The cigarette fills my lungs and makes me temporarily happy. I wonder what I'm going to do on the day that I run out of smokes. Maybe I'll be dead by then. Here's hoping.

Zinka's voice comes over the intercom. "Attention crew. I request that everyone meet in the cockpit for the mission briefing. I have informed our alliance of the plan and I need all of you to be aware of the roles that you will be expected to play."

The loud speaker cuts out. Well, I guess it's time to listen to the plan that I will probably end up ignoring. There is nothing wrong with winging it in lieu of an actual plan. I leave my room and head towards the cockpit.

CHAPTER 29

The entire crew is amassed in the cockpit. Stoic faces stare on, anticipating orders for the siege on Derask's death vessel. Zinka is the last one to arrive in the room, and all eyes fall on her. She makes her way to the center and throws a cautious eye across everyone in the room.

"As you know, we are preparing for our assault on the Colossus," Zinka begins. "Taking out that ship is our primary objective, but we also need to kill Derask, here and now. Therefore, we are going to have two separate attack teams. The outside team will work on taking out his defensive squadron. The inside team will try and take out Derask and destroy the ship from the inside. The inside squad will consist of three separate teams."

"The first team will consist of Demerian soldiers. They will be led by Tik. Second team will be the mercenaries. They will be led by Little Balls. Finally, the third team will be Tauranian stealth killers. They will be led by Elisar."

"So, I am going into a dangerous situation with a bunch of criminals to watch my back?" I question.

"Trust me, Little Balls. If I thought they were going to kill you, I wouldn't have put you in charge of them. Preet assures me that you will be safe. They fear her." She replies calmly. "Leonidas, you, Danny, me and Pangaea will be heading the outside attack with the pilots of all the alliance. While Halissy, Yekk and Shia will stay on the ship. Their knowledge and Halissy's medical expertise are far too valuable to be put in danger."

I raise my hand to ask a question.

"You don't have to raise your hand," Zinka points out, "Just state your question."

"How large are each of the inside teams?"

"Each team will consist of the leader and nine other crew members."

Tik raises his hand.

"Tik, like I just told Little Balls, you don't have to raise your hand."

"The cruisers are a little small to fit ten people."

"They are boarding the ship with three transporters," Zinka says.

I raise my hand again.

"For fuck's sake, Little Balls just spit it out."

"How are we getting into the Colossus?"

"They have no shield, and we managed to steal the code to open the docking port. Once the landing party is close enough, all you have to do is type in the code and the doors will open."

Danny raises his hand. She lets out a long sigh.

"Yes, Danny. What is it?"

"Will there be snacks afterwards?"

"Yes, Danny there will be snacks," she reassures.

"Yay!" Danny shouts with his child like enthusiasm.

"Any other questions?" Zinka asks as she looks around the room. "Alright. ETA for the rendezvous point is in one hour. I'll call you all to your battle stations when we get closer to it. I will send out the mission dossier for all the details. Crew dismissed."

The crew of the Gravity Bong files out of the briefing room. What the hell am I going to do for an hour? As if reading my mind, Danny pulls me aside.

"Hey, dude," he says with his signature goofy grin. "Tik, Pangaea and I are going to my room to get stoned, and you are coming with us."

Without giving me a moment to answer, he pulls me towards his room. The door of his room closes behind us and we take a seat in a circle on his floor. The stacks upon stacks of weed still line all the walls around us.

Danny works on packing the bowl. Part of me is wondering if getting high before a deadly mission is a good idea. The doubts I have, though, vanish as I am passed the bowl. I take a sharp inhale and the smokes enters my body.

The bowl gets passed around the circle, and the plant turns to ashes in the pipe.

Out of nowhere, we are all squeezed into a massive hug by Tik. No one fights it this time. We all just enjoy the embrace. Well, Danny always enjoys it, but that is just how he is.

"Can you believe what we are about to do?" Danny questions when we are all released from the death grip.

"I know, man," I reply. "Going to take down an evil alien overlord. It's like something out of a movie."

"What?" Danny asks confused. "I was actually talking about flying space ships stoned but that too, I guess."

Pangaea replies. "That is still like fifty minutes away. I'm sure we will be sober by then."

"You will be sober by then, my dear." He laughs, "I, on the other hand, plan on smoking another right before we leave."

"Is that smart?" I question.

"Meh, who cares? I'm going to do it anyway because I love it. If you deny what you enjoy in life, then you might as well be dead."

I think it over for a moment, and I guess he has a point. I am just too high to know what I'm thinking. It could go either way.

"Hey, Danny?" Pangaea interrupts my thoughts. "What are you going to do when you run out of pot?"

"Impossible."

"How is it impossible?"

"Because magic, duh." He replies as if it is obvious.

"You guys are my best friends!" Tik screams out of nowhere.

"Yay, I have a friend," I say.

Pangaea replies, "Aww, our little Thaddeus has a friend. They grow up so fast."

She then proceeds to squish my face like she appears to like to do. I shove her hands away from me and reply.

"We both know that I'm in your top four humans that still exist."

"There are only four people left. You know that, right? Or maybe six." She replies after doing a double take at Danny.

"Well then, I'm in your top six."

"You're an idiot."

"A delightful idiot."

"Shut up."

The atmosphere takes on a silent tone. Well, it's as silent as it can be with Danny humming a song. It's not an awkward silence, though. It is just··· comfortable. We are all just relaxing.

Eventually, the drowsy effect of weed takes its toll on both Tik and Pangaea. Both of whom are sleeping soundly. Tik is sleeping sprawled across Danny's lap. Pangaea appears to be sleeping in a V-shape. Her legs are being supported by my side and her upper body is leaning against the bed. Danny is still just happy, and I am starting to sober up.

"Do you think I'm jumping the gun a bit?" Danny asks out of nowhere.

"Jumping the gun on what?"

"Seth."

As soon as he says his name, my heart jumps in my throat a bit. I don't know what I should do in this situation. Do I keep his hopes up or try to be realistic, so he doesn't get hurt? I look over at him as he is patiently waiting for my answer.

"Danny, look," I say honestly, "I don't really have an answer. Do you think he is still out there?"

"Yes, yes I do."

"Then all I can say is don't lose hope, and just remember that no matter what, I'll be here for you."

He appears to think about my statement for a few moments. He then speaks. "Thanks, dude. That··· that means a lot to me."

An air of heavy emotion falls over the room.

"How did you and Seth meet?" I wonder, hoping to bring back a happy memory of him.

"Well," he begins. "Do you remember that I told you I met him at that stupid gay conversion camp?"

"Yeah."

"Yeah. I'd just turned seventeen. My parents found out that I was gay. They were not too happy about that."

"Why did you agree to go?" I question.

"Well, if people tell you that you are broken enough times, eventually you are going to believe them. I was so down on myself. I truly thought that there was something wrong with me."

He pauses for a moment to dwell on that. Maybe this wasn't the best idea. Didn't want to make him upset. Danny continues.

"Anyway, when I got there, my self-esteem was at zero. That's when I saw him. He was beautiful. Me thinking that just made me feel even worse about myself. I was originally planning on just ignoring him. That plan failed. After what seemed like a dozen therapy sessions of more people telling me how broken I am, he came up to me."

This thought brings a smile on his face. Now this is the desired effect. He goes on with his story.

"After so many conversations, I just started falling harder and harder for him. He was gorgeous, but his personality was even more amazing. We started going out, and the rest you know. He helped me get out of my funk. He helped me realize that I'm no more broken than anyone else."

Silence overtakes the room again. Only this time, Danny is thinking all of the happy thoughts of Seth. Good. Hopefully, that will keep him well for a bit. After a while, Danny decides to keep the seriousness of the conversation going.

"Who do you think was the first person to see an egg come out of a chicken and think, 'Yup, I'm gonna eat that son of a bitch'?"

The only thing that I can do is look at Danny in confusion. I have been friends with this man for a while and yet he still manages to surprise me.

"I··· I don't know."

"Do you think it was a sexual thing?" He questions.

"I still don't know."

"I think it was a weird sex thing. The same dude probably also decided to suck the milk out of a cow's nipple."

"I thought they were called teats on cows?"

"I believe those words are interchangeable. Like I could call my nipples teats."

"Why are we talking about nipples?" I reply.

"The better question is why we have waited so long to talk about nipples?"

"That isn't a question most people ask."

"Well, they should. We all have teats. Most mammals have teats." He shrugs.

"Most? I thought all mammals had teats."

"No, the platypus doesn't have teats. They do have milk patches on their skin though. Those beautiful duck beaver bastards."

"Duck beavers?" I question but I can't help but think of my drug induced hallucination.

"Yeah. They look like a beaver had sex with a duck. Of course, that wouldn't happen."

"Is it because the duck dick is shaped like a corkscrew?" I ask.

"It's also weird that they fall off."

"Yeah, just imagine if your dick fell off each year. I like always having my penis."

"I like to make mine into a helicopter," Danny says.

"I know. I heard about your phallic shenanigans from Pangaea."

"Sometimes you just need to have a little fun with it."

I pause for a moment.

"How did we get on the subject of dicks?" I ask.

"Well, it started with chicken."

"Oddly enough, this isn't the first time we got high and started talking about your genitals."

"And it won't be the last. We have many years of smoking pot and talking about my baby cannon and ammo bags."

"This is a high-quality conversation," I state.

"This is the type of intelligent dialogue that the people always crave. Give the people what they want."

"What people?"

"The people." He simply replies.

'Attention, crew,' Zinka's voice comes over the intercom. 'We are ten minutes away from the meeting point. All crew members meet in Docking Port Two and get ready for battle.'

Zinka's voice cuts out. The message wakes up the other two and we all stand to go to the port. I guess we will see how all of this plays out. Hopefully, we won't die. I still enjoy living. At least for now I do. Maybe later I will get sick of it, but for now I am still trying to figure shit out.

CHAPTER 30

We all meet in the docking port, and see that the three infiltration teams are there, as well. Screens on the walls display the exterior teams and their leaders. The Demerians, Oxites, Apazians, Tauranians, and the mercenaries are all wearing intent, determined expressions. They seem way more prepared for this than me. My eyes lock momentarily with Groddie's. His response is a simple guttural growl. I don't think he likes me. Hooray.

"Groddie," Preet floats in behind him in her original gaseous form.

He immediately freezes. Thank god he fears her. Preet turns toward me. It is very hard to tell, considering she has no face. This is remedied by her morphing into her previous human form.

"Well, well, well," she says as she walks towards me. "Since our meeting, I've heard all about how much you have pissed Derask off in your time in space. I have got to say that I am impressed."

"Impressed?"

"Yeah, of course. Not many people possess the ability to get under his skin like that. He really wants you dead."

"Uh··· thanks? I guess."

"Trust me, being on his bad side isn't a bad thing. He thrives on people being afraid of him. It makes him more confident. When he is pissed, he is much more likely to make mistakes. Your skill of annoying him may just be his downfall."

"Well, I feel special now. I am just the greatest annoyance in all of the galaxy."

She runs her finger down my chest when she gets in front of me. Must be some weird alien way of greeting people.

"I could make you feel special." She says with a wink.

Is she hitting on me?

"Uhhhh?" This being the only response that I could think of.

"I'll be straight with you. I have never fucked a human male and I want to change that."

Okay, I guess she was hitting on me.

"Uhhhh." Is my smooth response.

"Just think about it."

Pangaea interrupts, "Can we please just focus on the task at hand, and worry about getting off afterward?"

She pauses for a moment and glances at Pangaea before replying. "Of course. I just get a little excited."

Preet walks off past Groddie and into the crowd. Yay, sex, weird, weird alien sex. I'm going to blame porn for making this feel okay to me.

That allows me to momentarily forget about the fact that I'm going on a mission where I will likely die while being surrounded by dangerous criminals. Maybe the fact that their boss wants to do the horizontal tango with me will help keep me safe. It may give them an incentive to not kill me. A man can hope at least.

"Landing party leaders," Zinka addresses. "Get into your ships and prepare to board the Colossus. I have installed the coordinates of Derask's throne room into these." She passes each of us an odd metal bracelet.

"He will most likely be there to watch what he assumes will be his victory. This will also let you communicate with the other landing team. You need to corner him in his throne room, so you will have to enter through three different docking ports. The rest of you get on your cruisers. It is time to start our assault on Derask. Dismissed."

The crew departs the meeting and I head towards the transport with my party. The entire walk to the ship, I get dirty looks from Groddie. I don't think he likes me. Oh, please non-existent god, please let his fear of Preet prevent him from trying to kill me. I really don't want to die today. Existing is the only thing that I'm at least mediocre at. I can't lose that.

The hatch opens on my ship and Groddie stands behind the controls. That is probably for the best.

"Our docking port is on the far side," Groddie says, staring at the coordinates. "We will have to travel around. Hopefully your dumb ass won't do anything to kill us before we get there."

"I'll try," I shrug.

"Stupid monkey."

"Racist."

His response is a vicious death glare. Why does everybody either glare at me or roll their eyes at me. Well that's not true. I also get smacked and face smooshed. I don't want Groddie to smoosh my face. That seems like it would be unpleasant for all parties involved.

We come towards, what I assume is, the Colossus. Its immense size looms menacingly in the distance. Small cruiser ships dot around the enormity of it. They seem ready to fight. I look out from the cockpit and see ships from the Demerians, Tauranians, Apazians, Oxites, and the mercenaries around us. The other two ships of the landing party fly on each side of our ship.

The silence of the impending battle looms heavy over the alliance. It was inevitable that Danny was the one to break the silence over the ships radio comms.

"It looks like a giant metal boob."

"What?" I question.

"Yeah, it's definitely a giant metal boob. Just look at it. It's spherical and has that random little nub on the front of it."

Zinka interrupts. "Danny this comm is for important mission information. It's not the place for your inane observations."

"Now, hold on a second," I back him up. "Danny has a point."

"What are you talking about, Little Balls?" Zinka replies.

"Well, just look at it. We are going to fight a giant metal tit."

"Titty fight!" Danny shouts into the intercom.

"It's the great Titty Wars," I joke.

"Oh, please god, just stop it." Zinka replies.

"I think I saw a porn flick called Titty Wars."

"I never expected you to be interested in a porn called Titty Wars, Danny." I am slightly confused.

"Well the sex scenes weren't my jam, but it had a very immersive plot."

"You watched a porno for the plot?"

"Yeah. How else was I going to figure out if Princess Boobies was going to make it out of the kink dungeon on Planet Dildo?"

"Good point," I relent.

"Can we please just focus on the impending space battle?" Pangaea questions annoyed by our tangential conversation. "It's just like the simulation all over again. Except this time, people could actually die."

"Yes, please just focus. I know that is hard for you two, but you need to try. Little Balls, don't make me regret putting you in charge of one of the landing teams," Zinka busts my chops. "Enemy forces are coming into range. Attack on my signal."

Zinka pauses and silence once again takes hold. Time appears to be going at a much slower pace. All eyes look ahead at the enemy forces and the futility of it gnaws at the back of my skull. We are outnumbered ten to one. I think. Zinka's voice comes over all our communicators.

"Attack!"

With that shout, all our forces charge ahead. Lasers blasts erupt all around us. Chaos ensues. Explosions take up all my peripheral and I can no longer tell which ships are friendly and which are foes.

Groddie seems to know where the entrance point is as he expertly dodges all the enemy vessels. His face is contorted into one of concentration. The Colossus becomes larger as we slowly gain distance on it. The massive ship grows to the point where it takes up my entire field of vision. An overwhelming sense of insignificance washes over me and brings my own fragile ego down a couple more notches.

The ship makes a sharp turn and a small access point comes into focus. I guess it's time to do something. The gun feels heavy in my hand as I ponder the implications of what we are about to do. Bubba was the first being that I've killed. Can I really bring myself to do it again? Obviously, he deserved it but are all these Aldinians just as guilty as him, or are they just mislead?

An explosion right next to us brings me out of my thoughts and a familiar voice comes on the com.

"You know, Little Balls," Pangaea speaks up. "I am getting really sick of saving your sorry ass all the goddamn time."

"Aww, Pangaea has a soft spot for me. I feel so special."

"Head in the game, asshole. Head in the game."

The comm goes dead as she continues her assault. I have avoided death a lot since I've been in space. I am extremely lucky. I wonder how long that luck will continue? My guess, it will continue forever. I can never die, and my hubris will never come back to haunt me. There is never any character, whether they be fictional or factual, that has ever been taken down by over confidence.

Our ship enters the docking point. Groddie, the other eight, and I exit the ship with our guns cocked and ready.

"This is Thad of the Mercenary team," I say into the communicator. "We have landed aboard the Colossus and are making our way towards the central throne room."

"This is Elisar of Tauranian team. We are preparing to descend into the Colossus."

"This is Tik of Demerian team. We got cut off by Aldinian fighters. We must try and lose them. We will radio when we have landed."

"Copy that. Stay safe Demerians," I say into it before raising my gun in defense of the anticipated gun fight.

"The throne room is over this way," Groddie says, checking the coordinates.

I go the way that he pointed. If I'm the leader shouldn't I have the coordinates? Instead, I'm just going the way that he is pointing. Who is the real leader here? Oh well, I guess there is no use thinking about useless shit.

The team heads down the corridor which is oddly devoid of all life. Common sense would dictate that we would have come across some resistance by this point. Instead, the only thing greeting us is a long silver hallway amongst even more silver halls. Common sense would also dictate that the Aldinians went a little overboard with all this chrome. I have no need to see my own reflection. Seeing my ugly face reflecting off every single surface puts me off the whole rebellion thing. This is no time to focus on my own appearance insecurities.

"Make a left up here," I hear Groddie yell behind me.

I listen and head towards the left. I am immediately greeted with laser blast flying beside my skull and singeing off a small amount of my hair. Aldinian troops greet us.

By some miraculous amount of luck, cover fire walls line the corridor. Why are these here? I have no time to think about this as more blasts come towards me. I dive behind one of the walls as the rest of the team does the same.

I pop out of cover to fire back at the opposition. Unfortunately, they outnumber us ten to one again. I am not good with math. There are like thirty of them to our ten, though.

One of my blasts manages to hit the skull of one of Derask's goons. His body falls to the floor. My lack of conscious repercussions implies that was either necessary or I am slowly becoming jaded towards the violence.

A mercenary yells in pain beside me.

He is a random amorphous blob from some race that I never learned the name of. He looks slightly different from the Oxites. Though, he does look similar. His corpse falls, and green blood begins to pool out of his wound. It spills out on the floor around me. I have no time to focus on this death, as I need to concentrate on not getting killed during this siege.

More of their soldiers fall, as well as three more of ours. When the fire stops, thirty Aldinians lay dead and six of us remain.

"Good job," Groddie says as he turns towards me. "I guess you aren't entirely useless after all. Just mostly useless."

"Aren't you just a sweetheart?"

He replies with his guttural growl before responding.

"We have to continue down this path and then make a right at the fork."

He loves me. Everybody thinks I'm just so delightful, except, of course, Derask. He hates me. I have no idea why? Maybe if we got some lunch one day and just talked it out. It's a shame I have to kill him though. Maybe I'll just get some lunch when all this is over. The fact that I haven't heard from Tik by now worries me. I pull out my communicator.

"This is Thad. Tik, Elisar requesting status update."

"Elisar reporting in. Making progress towards the throne room."

I wait for Tik's response, but it never comes.

"Tik, status update now."

Silence is the only thing that greets me.

"Thaddeus," Groddie says breaking the silence. "The Demerian ship's beacon is gone. It never made it inside the ship."

"Bullshit!" I yell. "Tik is one of the most capable soldiers that I've ever met. He wouldn't go out like that."

I turn my attention back towards the communicator.

"Dammit, Tik, answer me."

Stone silence as my hope dissipates at Tik's survival becomes more lost in the dark void of space. I feel a hand gently land on and then prominently squeeze my shoulder. I turn to see Groddie give me the only sympathetic look that I've ever seen on his face.

"That is the cost of war." He says in a voice softer than what I anticipated. "Friends will die, but it is only when you give up that their death becomes immaterial. We must push forward. Our cause is noble, and Tik knew that."

I nod in response and head down the corridor. Though I don't know which soldier shot him down, I do know that his blood is on Derask's hands. Earth, Goron, Stuan, and now Tik, all of which are directly attributable to him. He will pay for with his own blood.

"This is Elisar. We are pinned down."

"Do you need support?"

"No, we've got it covered. Just focus on taking down Derask and we will join you when we take down this squadron. Elisar out."

"Keep me updated, Elisar," I say before turning away from the communicator.

With guns raised and minds focused, we push forward towards the throne room. The rest of the trip is uneventful. Soon, we make it to a large black door with a giant gold D above it. I'm going to assume the D stands for Derask, though I can think of other names that start with D and are more fitting.

"The throne room is on the other side of this door," Groddie says pointing to the dark entrance.

"Alright we move on three···One···Two···Three."

I then kick the door open, and we enter a large domed room. There are screens all around it showing the battle raging right outside. There is a single chair sitting in the center with a solitary being occupying it.

"Hello, monkey," he says with smirk.

CHAPTER 31

"Derask? Is⋯ is that you?" I question in disbelief.

"Yes, monkey, it is I, the fearsome Derask. You are stammering due to fear and the profundity of my almighty glory."

"Well no, it's not that, it's--"

"That I am the living embodiment of evil and power. Yes, yes I agree."

"No, it's just that⋯ you're really, really short."

The three-foot-high creature takes offense to my comment and he stands up in rage. The veins are popping out of his little face due to the anger.

"Fool. I am the average height for Aldinians," he replies in a huff.

"Well, no. No, you're not. Literally every other Aldinian that we have met was taller."

"I am not short. They were just freakishly tall."

"All of them?" I ask.

"Yes, all of them!" He shouts with rage.

"Do you not know what average means?"

"Silence!" He shouts with rage.

Derask presses a button on the arm rest of his chair. An energy dome surrounds us. The dome manifests so fast that the other five of my team can't get inside with me and the short green prick.

Groddie pounds on the outside of the dome trying to break through, but to no avail. The only result is, I imagine, sore hands on his part.

"Groddie," I shout to the cyclops dude. "It's alright. I'll be fine. I want you and the rest of the team to double back and assist Elisar."

"Fine, but don't die."

"I didn't know you cared."

"I don't, but Preet wants you kept alive, and she is not one that you should disappoint," He replies before leading the crew to help the Tauranian assassin.

"D··· did he just say Preet?" Derask stammers.

"Oh, is someone afraid of Preet?" I mock the small being.

"Shut up, monkey!"

"You should really think of another insult. This whole monkey thing is losing its effect. It's stale. For someone who claims to be so smart, you sure have a very limited imagination."

His face shifts to one of intense hatred and anger. Well, more than before. He just keeps getting madder. Maybe if he keeps getting angry, he will just explode.

"You dare mock me? You are an inferior creature. You should be in awe of my very presence."

"I'm in awe of how incredibly short you are. You looked a lot taller on the video chats."

"I'll will not let a lower life form talk down to me like that."

"I know you are, but what am I."

"What?"

"What?"

"Oh yeah, I have to pull my gun." I raise the gun and point it towards the being.

"You really are stupid, aren't you?" He asks with a smirk on his face.

"Yes, but that is neither here nor there."

"I am coated in a rare mineral that deflects laser blasts. If you shoot me, I will not be harmed," he smirks as if he is just so clever.

"Why not give that to your crew, so they, you know, don't die?"

"Stupid monkey. Do you have any idea how expensive this stuff is? I would go bankrupt."

"Yeah, we kind of already did that for you."

"What?"

"Yeah, we took your credits and spent the last little bit on mercenaries. You are now officially broke," I inform him.

"Why, you little⋯"

"Where are the other two earthlings you abducted from Earth?" I question as an image of Seth passes through my mind.

"What are you on about?"

"I heard you had two more Earthlings on here. Where are they?"

"You really are an idiot," he replies with a chuckle.

"Yet again, neither here nor there. Answer me now, dammit."

"There are no other beings from your planet. I purposefully fed false information to Elisar in case she would betray me. Which she did."

"Why would you do that?" I question.

"To crush your hopes. A major component of a battle is mental."

"Why, you son of a bitch!" I shout as I raise my gun once again.

"Laser proof mineral. I am always one step ahead of any of your little plans. You can't beat me."

"Then there is one thing that you didn't plan on."

"And what is that monkey?"

"I always wing it and I don't make plans!" I shout.

"Wha⋯ hmmph." he begins before he is interrupted by my gun, which was thrown from my hand, hitting him square in the face. "Ah, my face."

Before I could realize that it is a bad idea, I rush him and proceed to kick him in the throat.

He lets out a pained grunt when I connect with his esophagus.

The force of the impact causes him to fly into his own barrier and bounce off. In my haste, I forgot one important rule of kicking. That rule is to never do it. It hurts both parties involved. The floor reminds me of this fact as it encounters my elbow.

"Ow, ow, ow. Right on the funny bone," I cringe as I hold my damaged joint. "This is the worst thing in the world."

In my pain, I momentarily forget about the short creature I am fighting. When I remember to look up, I see him reaching for his gun. With the speed of a fat, old dog and the grace of a one-legged cheetah, I still manage to get to his weapon first. To get him away and give myself some room, I shoulder check the little bug man.

I laugh with triumph, "I've got your gun."

"Give me back my gun, monkey!" He jumps towards his pistol.

I hold it up high just out of his reach. He repeats the process of jumping for it. This obviously fails. That doesn't deter him from trying again and again. This goes on for ten minutes. Literally ten minutes of him jumping. The first minute or two, it was funny, but now it's just sad. Finally, boredom causes me to resort to the only conceivable way of ending this, a kick to the balls.

Never matters how big or, in this case, how big one thinks he is, a strong kick to the groin will bring any male to their knees in pain.

"This isn't how this fight is supposed to go," he gasps. "It is supposed to be an epic fight between two worthy adversaries in a battle for the soul of the universe."

"You didn't count on me being terrible at fighting then," I gloat as I raise the gun.

"Laser. Proof. Mineral. You idiot." He grunts as he rises to his feet.

"Oh yeah," I say, looking at the gun, then back at the Emperor.

Well, it worked once.

The sound of the gun bouncing off his head echoes in the room.

"Stop doing that, dammit," he bites out through grit teeth.

"Well, I kind of ran out of guns to throw at you."

He picks himself up and glares and me menacingly. "I see I'll have to deal with you with a lot less eloquence than I normally use."

Without a moment's hesitation, the little guy lunges at me and locks his jaw around my arm.

"Get off! Get off!" I shout as I run around the dome, Derask firmly attached. "Your little teeth hurt so much."

I go to the wall of the dome and smash the bug man repeatedly against it. Each smack against the wall seems to only make his teeth clench harder. Finally, with one last good smash, his jaw loosens, and he falls to the floor before quickly standing back up.

"You bit me!" I shout. "Who the hell bites someone?!"

"I told you, less eloquence."

"Yeah, but I was expecting fat momma jokes or something about her having a scandalous reputation but not biting. You're a weird little creep."

"I always find a way to win, monkey," Derask says as we begin to circle around each other in the sealed dome.

"Again, with the monkey shit. Come up with a new insult, asshole."

"You're an asshole," the Emperor fires back.

"Seriously, are we back in middle school? That is no different than the I'm rubber, you're glue schtick. Insult me right, or don't do it at all."

"I am not adhesive!"

"What?" I should've expected him to take my words literally, since he wouldn't know an old Earth idiom.

"I am going to show you what happens when you mess with me," he gloats. The small man lunges at me. He brings his fist out and it connects with my genitalia. The force of the blow knocks the wind out of me and causes me to fall to my knees. I look up and see him drop his pants. This fight has gotten weird.

His dick extends and wraps around my throat. Shit, forgot they could grow and grab shit with their dick. It tightens around my throat and cuts off my air passage. I can feel his heartbeat pumping against my neck. This has definitely gotten weird..

My eyes raise to the level of his face, and it has a look of pure hatred and joy on it. Please don't let him finish, if you know what I mean. My death seems imminent, and it appears that this is how I'll die. I'm going to die with an alien cock wrapped around my throat. Couldn't really say that I saw this coming.

My mind races as I try to figure out how to escape this situation. Out of instinct, my good arm raises and grabs the base of it. All my strength goes towards my arm as it pulls at the appendage. I feel the tendons rip and the tissue come apart. Blood spurts out of it.

"Aaaahhhhh!" He shouts when I remove the disgusting appendage from my person. His dick loosens up and drops to the ground. My lungs take in all the air that they can possibly inhale. I raise my head and see him writhing in pain.

His dick grows and regenerates as his screaming stops. He brings his pants back up. Thank god for that. Looking back down at the removed penis, I see it flop around like a fish out of water. It should not still be moving. That is a little unnerving.

The sound of a gun cocking causes me to look up. Derask has his laser pointed directly at my face. Never fun to stare down the barrel of a gun. I know because I have done it a few times now.

"Any last words, monkey?" He stands ready to fire.

"You looked taller in a sweater vest," I rasp from my damaged throat.

"What?" He starts to get pissed but rethinks it. "You know what, I am tired of playing this game. It is time to bring it to an end. Prepare to die."

A feminine voice comes from behind me.

"Why hello, Derask. It's so pleasant to see you again."

Derask's eyes go wide with fear as he stumbles backwards a tad. I look over my shoulder and see Preet prancing toward the dome. Her form is that of a strange reptilian creature that I do not recognize. I know it's her voice, as does Derask.

"What··· what do you want? Why are you here? I have held up my end of our agreement." His back hits the wall. He drops his gun out of fear.

He could have killed me by now. Fear makes people stupid. It's the same with aliens.

"Yes, I know." She says, getting closer to the dome.

"What does he mean agreement?" I question her.

"Derask and I came to a truce about a century ago. I stay out of his business and he stays out of mine."

"Yes," Derask affirms, "And I have kept my side of the bargain. Now why aren't you keeping yours?"

She turns back towards the little green man and gives him a smirk that would frighten the most hardened criminal. Well, maybe; it frightened me, at least. That could be because her reptilian form has rows upon rows of jagged teeth.

"Yes, yes you did, but things change. Beings change. I have changed. I no longer wish to do business with you, and I've decided to help this young man kill you painfully."

The fear in his eyes increases at this declaration. His limbs all tremble a bit. Tensing out of fear, I suppose. Even the dismembered penis on the ground convulses. In all honesty, that part is slightly disgusting, and it may be a bit of nightmare fuel.

"Well··· let's see you try. I am in an impenetrable dome. If you let me escape, however, then I'll··· I'll let this monkey live."

Again, with the monkey. At this point he is just beating a dead horse. Is that expression relevant for this situation? Fuck it. I'm still going to use it.

Preet simply smiles again, her sharp reptilian fangs gleaming.

"You really think this can stop me?" She runs a finger along the edge of the dome. "I am one hundred percent sure that I can get through this."

"What makes you so damn sure?!" Derask screams.

"Well," She starts. "This dome appears to be made of Perulianite. Is that correct?"

"Yes, and···?" he questions.

It is clear that he doesn't understand the significance of her observation. Which is the exact opposite of me. I understand completely. No, no I don't. I lied.

"You see Derask, Perulianite is a flexible and strong material. It is so malleable because, though it's solid, its molecules can freely move as if it's water. The fact that its molecules aren't as close as other solid materials means that there are slight gaps between them, and that means···"

She evaporates and appears on the same side of the dome as us. This action causes Derask to let out a whimper which would have been adorable if not for the fact that he is evil and whatnot. She continues her speech when she is fully formed.

"If someone has the ability to alter their own molecules, like a shapeshifter, then they can use that ability to pass through it."

Preet slowly moves towards the frightened little guy. The panic in his eyes is clear, as if he is nothing more than a cornered rat.

"Now, Derask, give me one reason why I shouldn't kill you and I may just let you live. However, you'd better make it a damn good reason," she commands.

"We worked together for how long? We were partners, for a time."

"We were partners for a decade, right before our little arrangement. Do you know how brief a decade is when you're an immortal being? It is essentially no more than the blink of an eye."

"I'm not dying like this!" Derask shouts before pressing the button to get rid of the dome.

Derask hits another button that opens a trap door underneath him. He disappears into the floor.

"Where the hell is he going?" I ask looking at the where the trap door was.

"He went to his escape pod," Preet replies coolly.

"We have to catch him. He has to die."

"And he will die, but right now we need to focus on destroying the Colossus. That is the primary goal. This station is the entire source of his power. Even if he doesn't die, destroying this dump would significantly decrease his influence and essentially just make him another poor deranged bastard in the universe."

Though my need to see him die is strong, her words are true. This station needs to be destroyed, and it must be destroyed now.

"Hold on. I'm going to tell Elisar and the rest of the team to evacuate. I don't want them to be caught up in the blast."

I pull my communicator up to talk to her.

"Attention Elisar," I start. "Derask has escaped, but we are preparing to destroy the Colossus. Retreat immediately."

"Oh, come on," she jovially replies. "I was having fun. These guys are just terrible. I could do this for hours."

"Elisar, that's an order. Did Groddie and the mercs find you?"

"Yeah, they're here. Just kind of chilling. They aren't really needed."

"Retreat now, Elisar."

"Ugh, fine, but I'm not happy about this. Elisar out."

The communication dies, and I am greeted with silence. I see a random metal bar lying on the ground. I know what to do here so I grab the bar with my only arm. My mind goes back to Pangaea on Elisar's ship.

"Alright, let's hit some shit," I charge towards the control panel. I use all the force I can muster to try and destroy it. Hitting it with every ounce of motivation in me, the structure begins to crumble before me.

"Uh, Little Balls," Preet tries discreetly to interrupt.

However, I am too focused on my work. The metal bar begins to leave my hand sore and raw.

"Little Balls."

Sparks start to fly as I feel like I am making immense progress on destroying the ship.

"Little Balls!" Preet's final shout breaks me from my focus.

"Oh god, I'm deaf," I hold my ears in pain. "What is it Preet?"

"What are you doing?"

"Destroying the control panel so the ship will explode."

"First off, that isn't the control panel. That's a fridge."

"Oh."

That is my only response as I look down at the damaged machine. It is a fridge. All the food and drink spilling out of it is a clear indication of that. Why is there a fridge in the cockpit? I take one more look at it before continuing to talk to Preet.

"That is definitely a fridge. I meant to do that, though."

"Uh-huh."

"I did. I was making sure to destroy Derask's provisions to weaken his resolve," I reply defensively.

"I'm not disagreeing with you."

"Good," I reply. "Because it's true. All I know is that people get upset when there is no food."

"Sure," She's a good sport. "And second, why don't you just press the self-destruct button?"

"What? It has a self-destruct button? Why?"

"I don't know. Don't ask me."

She grabs my shirt sleeve and drags me to the button that for some reason exists. The button is massive and blinking. She releases her grip on me when we get in front of it.

"Here," She points to it. "This is what we have to press."

CHAPTER 32

After pressing the button, with all the heroism that task entails, everything starts to spark. The walls are sparking. Bits of the floor are sparking. I even swear that I see the sparks sparking.

I follow Preet down the halls towards her ship. Loud sirens buzz all around us and the ship shakes and rattles to the point where I think it's going to fall to pieces beneath our feet.

"My ship is right down this hall. I buzzed all fleet members to retreat so we can avoid the blast. The explosion should take out the remaining Aldinian forces," Preet explains.

"How do you know he didn't tell them to evacuate?"

"Because he doesn't care enough about their lives. I know Derask, and I know his types of plans. I guarantee he told them to stay close to the ship to prevent to many people boarding it. Just trust me, they will all die. Hell, we might even die."

"Hmmm, good to know."

The docking port that she came into looms ahead after we round a left turn.

"Don't worry. I will do everything I can to keep you alive. I still want to have a first time with a human male," she says with a wink.

"I, uh⋯ uhm. Yeah. I uh," I reply smoothly. "Wait, you keep saying human male. Have you ever had sex with a human female?"

"A couple times. When I visited Earth as Jesus, I met a prostitute named Mary."

"No shit?"

"Yeah, it's true. I don't know where your people got that whole bread is my body and wine is my blood thing. It's eerie when you think about it. In reality, it was just a nice, innocent interspecies lesbian smashing. Your race is weird and took it to a weird place, though."

"Yeah, we really are."

"Just try and stay close to me, though. I still want that chance to get with you."

"Well··· I··· uh··· uhm···"

"No reason to be nervous. I'll be very gentle. That is if you want me to," she replies coolly with a wink.

I always did have a way with women. By have a way I mean they do not generally like me.

"Well··· I··· Uhm," I reply even more smoothly.

"Would it help if I wasn't a lizard?" She changes from the lizard alien to her human form.

"Well," I reply. "I guess it is better than having a T-Rex hitting on me."

"See, I can be very accommodating."

"Well, the problem is I've never done, well, that before," I stammer, embarrassed.

This is a weird time and place to have this conversation. Running through a crumbling space station doesn't seem to be an ideal place to really have any conversation.

"Aww, you're a virgin?"

"Yes, laugh it up. I'm a 25-year-old virgin. Let's all laugh at the loser."

"It's nothing to worry about. I never had sex with a human man either. We could have fun trying to work it out. Now, let's finish this conversation when we aren't running for our lives."

"Oh yeah. We might die."

"You forgot?"

I reply with a shrug.

We enter the docking port and she physically drags me towards her ship. She throws me in the cockpit and enters shortly after that.

The engine kicks to life, making the ship rise off the ground. An explosion ignites on a distant side of the Colossus. Preet guns it out of the port, and the fireball soon appears, chasing our ship.

"Oh, fuck! Explosions!" I shout. "Get us away from deaths by fire!"

"Oh, relax," She's cool as a cucumber.

My attention goes back towards the inferno that's on our ass. It appears to be getting closer by the second. My bowels are close to evacuating. I see the flames engulf the Aldinian ships that weren't even aware of the impending danger. The fire kisses the ass end of Preet's ship. My focus goes towards her and she… she is smiling? Why is she so damn happy? We are close to death.

"Preet, why are you smiling?"

"I'm having a great time."

I respond with a raised eyebrow, so she elaborates.

"When you don't age, the biggest rush you can have is almost dying. The only possible way I can die is by outside sources. There is no natural death for me."

Realization dawns on me. "The ship can go faster can't it?"

"Of course."

"Then why aren't we going faster?"

"Where's the fun in that?" She replies with a giddy smile.

"Preet, this may be a rush for you, but I am part of a species that does age. Death is scary. So, for the love of every single deity that the universe has ever manifested, please go faster."

She rolls her eyes but complies with my request. She punches it up a notch and the ship easily outruns the hot death wave that scared the crap out of me momentarily.

"Damn, you are just no fun." She is clearly unhappy with the change of plans.

My eyes turn back towards the raging fireball that was once the most feared ship in the galaxy. Derask may not be dead, but we have hurt his power. His army is dead, and his most powerful weapon is just bits of debris now.

The flames extinguish quickly once the explosion reached its max distance.

"We are meeting on the nearby planet of Xios. It is uninhabited and is the rendezvous point if the mission ends successfully," she says as she steers the ship in the desired direction.

"What do you mean if?"

"Meh, you're not exactly the most gifted or most dependable being. Your reputation is spreading quite quickly through the galaxy for being a failure that somehow manages to get lucky."

"Yay, I'm famous. Wait, why did no one tell me of the whole meeting on Xios thing?"

"They did," she replies. "They sent out advanced mission dossiers to everyone. You replied all and laughed for four pages about the word dossier. Apparently, you thought that it meant butt."

"That sounds like something I would do, but I don't remember it. Was I high?"

"Yes, you explained that in the fourth page."

"Must have been the last time I smoked with Danny. I should really pay more attention to things that are around me··· or not."

Preet lands on Xios and I see the remaining soldiers from all the squads. I also see the entire Gravity Bong crew. Well, almost the entire crew. I remember Tik's face and his crazy hugs. He was a valuable crewman and, even more importantly, a friend. Rest in peace, friend, rest in peace.

When the ship touches down on the ground, we are greeted joyously by all who survived. Pangaea is the first to greet me by giving me a death hug. Why is someone so small so strong? She releases.

"Little Balls, it's good to see that you didn't get your dumb ass killed. Not going to lie, I am a little surprised."

"We both know you would have cried if I died," I say with a smirk.

"You can't prove that. I deny all your accusations. Hell, I should cry that you're alive. That means that I owe Leo twenty credits."

"Would you swear on a Bible?"

"Unlike Danny, I'm not devout, so that isn't going to make a difference. Just remember though, if you die, I will bring you back just to murder you."

"Why do people keep telling me that? That is very hurtful, you know."

"Whatever. I'm just happy you're not dead yet," she says.

"It wasn't from a lack of trying. Derask bit me."

"He bit you?"

"Yeah. Oh, and it turns out that he is only three feet tall," I finish with a chuckle.

"No way!" Pangaea says.

"Yup. He was adorable except for the whole trying to kill me thing."

Zinka and Danny come up next both wrapping me in a simultaneous hug. Why is everyone so huggy? Zinka still smells like cookies though. I wonder how long that will last. Everyone loves cookies. Although, I would like it to end soon.

"Did you know he was short, Zinka?" Pangaea questions.

"He who?"

"Derask."

"Well, yeah. He has what you humans call a Napoleon complex," Zinka replies.

I look towards Danny and remember what Derask said about Seth. I have to tell him.

"Hey, Danny?"

"What's up, man?"

"I found out about Seth. It turns out… it turns out that Derask made it up. It was just another one of his mind games. I'm… I'm really sorry, man. I know how much you were hoping."

Danny responds with a reaction that I did not expect. He responds with a smile.

"It's okay, man. Well, as okay as it can get. Part of me knew it was stupid to hope, but the closure does bring me some comfort."

His face drops slightly into a face that I've never seen on Danny. His face is one of sadness, regret, and depression. It is a heartbreaking sight. This is Danny. He is supposed to be happy. He is supposed to be energetic. He is supposed to be, I don't know, Danny. I pull him into a friendly comforting embrace because it is the only thing that I can think to do.

"Danny," I attempt to comfort him. "I know this is hard for you, and not just about Seth. I know how close you were to Tik. Hell, we all were. But the one thing that no one can take away from us is all the memories he gave us, and all the memories that Seth gave you. Everyone we lost on this journey gave their lives for the betterment of the entire Milky Way."

"I don't want to lose anyone else," he says as we let go. "I don't have many friends left."

"Just like I told you before, I will always be here, man. Even if I have to drag my half dead corpse back from the afterlife. I will always try to be here."

"Thanks, man. I appreciate it."

"Don't be so mopey, Danny," Elisar says as she comes up to us. "Just look at this."

Elisar raises her wrist thing up and on the screen appears words that I cannot read. Danny looks at it for a moment. He then looks at it for another moment. Looking up at Elisar briefly, his mouth opens but then closes again.

"Uh," Danny starts. "I don't know what that says."

"Oops. I should have known that you can't read Aldinian. These are receipts showing the names of two Earthlings sold into enslavement by Derask."

"Wait," I reply. "He told me that he intentionally fed you wrong information."

"He's a liar. He lies. He lies about lying. That's what he does. I don't know the reason behind this lie, but it says here that he sold two members of your planet. He also has their Earth names. There is a Miss Sarah Hernandez and a Mister Seth Foxworth."

"Holy fuck. Seth. Seth's alive. I··· I can't believe it. Seriously, what are the odds that he grabbed three people from the same town? It seems highly unlikely," Danny says before turning towards me. "Dude, we have to find him. Please man, I··· I need this."

Looking at his pleading expression, the realization dawned that it would be impossible to tell that face no.

"Well, Zinka is the captain, but I don't think that she would be opposed to it."

"No, I'm not," Zinka confirms.

"See. She's not opposed," I reply.

"No, you idiot. I mean, I'm not the captain," she replies.

"Wait, you aren't the captain? Then why the hell have I been listening to you all this time?"

"Listening?" She raises her eyebrow muscle.

"Pretending to listen, fine," I roll my eyes.

"And I was captain, but you are now," she says.

"Are you high?"

"Nope. I received a message from planet Aldin. I am being appointed to the advisory council for the new Emperor. You, as second in command, get to captain this ship which will now be an official Aldinian military ship."

"I don't know how to fly. Also, official Aldinian military ship? Does that mean that I have to listen to the Emperor?"

"You don't need to know how to fly," she states. "You have two more Aldinians on board. We are taught how to fly at a very young age. If I were you, I'd trust Yekk. As far as the official military ship goes, it is more or less just a title. You will be able to pursue whatever you feel is important."

I look at the ship on the horizon, and then look at Danny's face. "Well, looks like we have a rescue mission coming up."

"Thanks, man," Danny says pulling me into another hug. "I just hope we can find him before he gets hurt."

Danny wanders off into the crowd. I hope he is okay. That dude is an amazing human being, and I love that man like a brother, and as his brother, I will murder anyone who hurts him. Right now, namely: Derask.

The rest of the crew comes to greet me after Danny leaves. Leo, Yekk, Shia, and Halissy come up to me, each one giving me a hug upon seeing me. Hell, even Shia gives me an awkward hug. I guess I am just a very huggable person. Hooray for physical contact.

"You did it, Little Balls," Leo says with a smile.

That is the first smile that I've seen on his face since Stuan's death. I feel like I must apologize for failing though. The dude was counting on me, and I let him down and dropped the ball on this one. I set my hand on his shoulder. This seems like a comforting move.

"Look, Leo," I start. "I'm sorry I couldn't take Derask down."

"It is alright. We will have another chance. His empire has fallen, and he has no influence over the Aldinians anymore."

"It's true," Zinka replies. "The new emperor has already taken power."

"How do we know they aren't just another Derask?" I question.

"Because I know her. Her name is Biole and she is a being of integrity and compassion. Aldinians will flourish under her rule. If she wasn't, then I wouldn't have accepted the advisory role."

"How do they already know about this though? It literally just happened."

"I informed them of what we were planning to do when we were still on Earth. They had the utmost faith in our endeavor. Right before I landed, I told them of our success," she replies.

"Why? I mean we aren't exactly the most skilled soldiers."

"I have no idea, but they still had faith. Don't try to take that away from us. We may not be capable, but we are at least very optimistic."

I take a moment to gaze up at the wreckage that is visible in the sky. How is it visible in the sky? It is outside of the atmosphere and the light from the sun coming in should block the view. Fuck it. I'm done caring. The Colossus is nothing but pieces of destroyed rubble. Nothing but bits of wreckage of the previous powerhouse. Derask may still be alive, but we will find him. His death will be celebrated throughout the galaxy.

A white square catches my attention when I look back over the horizon. I wander over to the mysterious object in question. It is a paper flyer. The words written on it make my jaw drop. How could I fail to recall that we still had another problem to deal with? Why can't anything be easy? The flyer reads:

Vote Landon

President of Everywhere

So very Presidential

Most Presidential President in History of Presidents

PS

Everyone Gets a Gun

Unless you don't Like Guns

Then No One Gets a Gun
Please Vote for Me

Thank you for reading Thad Saves the Galaxy. If you enjoyed the book, please leave a review on Amazon. Independent publishers like us need all the help we can get from our community. It only takes a minute and makes a huge difference. We really appreciate it!

C.T. Fleck is working hard on the next book in the series. Want to know when it is ready and get a free advanced review copy? Sign up for our newsletter here:
https://www.chandrapress.com/newsletter-page/.

— The Chandra Press Team

BONUS CONTENT – RIJEL 12: THE RISE OF NEW AUSTRALIA

CHAPTER 1: INTERGALACTIC PENAL COLONY

The President of the Assembly, an aged and respected Sudonji named Frilic, suddenly stood up and cleared his throat. The murmuring inside the gigantic hall swelled into that kind of roar that comes as a result of hundreds of people making discreet and not so discreet comments to the neighbors seated next to them.

Pig-like, rotund, and gruff just like most full-grown Sudonji, Frilic's throat-clearing was like a snarling, snorting, gurgling growl, but even this had little effect on the mass of beings crowded inside the convention hall. It was a gigantic building, spanning a quarter mile square, located near the supreme government building in the planetary capital of Suidonj. The interior was a cavernous facility made of stone walls, stone floor, and a remarkably high ceiling. It was lit only by lamps and chandeliers suspended from the vast wood-beamed ceiling above. Sudonji didn't really need or even like bright lights. Their extremely sensitive snouts directed their movements more than their eyesight; their floppy ears carried out the rest. But their buildings and rooms were extremely large. Large beings as they were, they liked having lots of space to move around.

There would still be a few moments of tense murmuring within the crowd before he'd be able to regain control. Frilic could already tell this would take a while. It usually did. So, he stood and waited patiently for the tumult to subside. No use in trying to regain order—that would be like interrupting ancient earth pigs at a feeding trough, back in more barbaric times when swine were bred for slaughter. But on Suidonj, the evolutionary process that led from tiny rodents to wild boars and then on to pigs continued to advance that life form into a bipedal sophisticated being, which grew to dominate other species on its planet. Sudonji learned to stand, to walk, to communicate, and to develop higher technologies over the millennia.

Frilic was the duly-elected leader of this year's meeting, honoring a tradition that had gone back over seventy galactic years, the equivalent of three hundred one earth years. The Interplanetary Convention had been held every galactic year since the Peace Treaty of Slartigia, which ended the war between planets Zorgolong and Enosh. This first convention was conducted by the very wise and gentle Slartigian planet elders and was held to establish terms for peace between those two bitter long-time rivals. After that, the event was moved annually from one planet to another, to promote fairness and balance in decision-making. Tradition held that the host planet would choose its own President for the annual convention. This particular galactic year, comprising four point three earth years, the convention was held on planet Sudonj.

Frilic gripped and lifted his gavel, but the murmuring still rose. No one heeded his gesture – determined gavel-grabbing somehow didn't seem to draw their attention. He even thought for a moment about raising his hoof to calm them. Sudonji had hoof-like claws that could grip much like a human's thumb and fingers. The difference was that their grip was incredibly strong, as were their bodies.

The audience was made up of ministers and delegations from all six planets of the Interplanetary Authority, as well as their colonies and their satellites. This throng of advanced beings dealt with issues affecting free and open trade, as well as threats to the health and welfare of the galaxy's billions of citizens. Today, the proposal being presented to the thousand-odd life forms in attendance was very nearly as controversial as it was ingenious: the creation of an

Intergalactic Penal Colony for violent criminals.

It all started with a proposal that originated from the Earth delegation regarding prison over-crowding and the "practical treatment of inmates." Murmuring had begun just a few minutes before, after Frilic had announced that debate would soon begin on the measure. Behind him a giant screen, the size of a soccer field, was activated and switched from its usual static image of the Interplanetary Authority logo, to an electronic banner which read: NEW AUSTRALIA PLANETARY PRISON. Then it began scrolling down and detailing in Galactic exactly what the proposal included. On smaller computer screens located inside each planet delegation box, the same information was being conveyed in that species' native language as well. However, most of the creatures in the audience were highly educated, preferring to read and speak in Galactic. As the audience read along, the murmuring rose higher and higher as more details were revealed.

What the Earthmen suggested was to develop a global penal colony on a barren planet located inside a distant star system. As the Earthmen explained it, the twelfth planet in the Rijel system already had a small mining operation, located far below the surface. What they desperately needed was labor, and below the forbidding planet surface, it would be easy to support a population of forced labor with the planet's already available supply of subterranean aquifers. Less than a mile below the surface it was quite easy to dig wells inside the planet's infinite cavern system, they claimed.

The commercial mine could simply be purchased, it was further proposed. The current staff and administration of the mine could be retained, and all the Interplanetary Authority needed to do was create a prison to supply the mine with workers. Existing labor there could continue to be employed as supervisors and foremen. "The whole thing will come together quite easily," they boldly professed. That's when the derisive comments began to fly, then grow in intensity.

"*Sss-simple!*" scoffed one of the members of the Zorgolongian delegation, causing the others in his section to emit hissing snickers. It was just like everything else proposed by those slippery Earthmen, and therein lay the irony: almost nothing about Earthers and their so-called "ethics" or basic "logic" was in any way simple.

The underlying issue lay in Earth's long-standing reputation for deception and ulterior motives when it came to intergalactic politics. They always seemed to be justifying their policies or actions by claiming it was necessary for the greater good; oblivious to how it might negatively affect other planets or the natural order of things. Other delegations could readily assume those crafty devils were trying to devise some scheme to either rid their own planet of a problem, or perhaps to make a lot of money. Then again, it might be a combination of both. It was always like that with those shifty Earthmen. Their "logic" as they called it, always seemed to rationalize away most anything resembling morality or common sense much like a fresh coat of paint being used to cover up rusted metal.

As the famously wise Slartigian planet elder Sektar once put it, "They aspire to greatness which they cannot truly achieve, so they espouse noble ideals which are quite beyond their capacity." Another way of putting it might have been that Earthers, "humans" as they called themselves, were compelled to accomplish more than their natural abilities could accommodate. So, they would typically embellish, boast, and exaggerate. They would very often portray an image of what something could be, rather than what it would become. They would make unrealistic projections, then decry and chastise the failure of those involved in its implementation. The human way of developing and managing an operation was typically to set goals which were technically unachievable, then blame everyone but the planners themselves for not reaching them.

Certainly, all planets had the occasional violent criminal who was beyond reform. But most had a more black and white view of the treatment of antisocial behavior. On Enosh for instance, they followed a very simple code when it came to errant acts. These cat-like creatures believed that an offender should have the capability of repeating the offense removed from their person, so they could continue their contribution to the greater good of society without being able to commit the same offence. A rapist? Castrated, no questions asked. A thief? Severed paw or paws, depending on what was stolen. A liar or blasphemer? Tongue removed. All Enoshi grew up knowing the consequences of their actions, so it was also known that if an adult committed the act, it could only mean they'd made the choice to violate the law and deserved punishment.

The difference with humans was that they could lie – and do so quite skillfully. That was what made them so confusing to other beings in the galaxy. Just what were they up to this time? An intergalactic penal colony where the galaxy's violent criminals could be disposed of? The different species in attendance hastily weighed in with their opinions.

"That is immoral," stated the Slartigians. "If Earth needs to house and reform its criminal element, then they should do so with better prison systems and larger facilities which might reeducate their inmates and reintroduce them into peaceful, law-abiding society."

By way of comparison, the short and lizard-like Zorgolongians assumed that the Earthmen were merely looking to capitalize on the untapped potential of the twelfth planet's mineral resources by using "free labor." Of course, they should have thought of it themselves, frankly, but it was far too late now, and that frustrated them more than anything else. Hence, the sarcastic sniggering and sniping barbs being hurled from their section of the convention hall. "Don't be naïve, my friend," remarked the Zorg delegation leader, "I'm sure they know exactly what they're doing."

As for the diminutive rodent-like Schpleefti delegation, they simply sat in confusion. For them it was difficult to understand the concept of institutionalizing the processing of criminals. Polyamorous by nature, this rodent-like species functioned on the sheer whim of emotional inspiration, for the most part. Violent criminals were merely banished from their communities. Nevertheless, they thought the Earthmen's proposal was a refreshing idea. What's more, they wanted to make sure they got an even cut of the profits. A global mining operation, like the Earthmen were suggesting? That could be quite lucrative, and the leaders within their delegation fully realized the implications.

Such was the hullabaloo over the Earth delegation's proposal, that Frilic needed to just stand there and let everyone argue from their delegate boxes until all had spoken their minds. It always worked out better that way, letting the delegates fight it out for hours on end, occasionally summarizing points repeatedly made until everyone had heard all angles and every side of the issue. It was important that delegations understood potential consequences of Interplanetary Authority policy, and that they avoid rushing into hasty acts or decisions which might adversely affect one another in the future. That's partly why these conventions were only held every galactic year, because the debate sessions could last for hours, sometimes days.

Yet, Frilic could let this debate last for only so long before he had to step in and get back in control of things. That was also his job as president. Eventually, it would become time to vote; to pass this measure would require only a simple majority. Four delegation votes and the Earthmen would have their prison, plus the full cooperation and financial backing of the Interplanetary Authority. There were only six planets, so the likelihood of requiring a deciding vote from Frilic was minimal at best.

Debate raged on of course, but those sly Earthmen knew exactly how to sell it. As the Earth delegation minister put it, "Prisoners will only be sent there to serve their sentences, work hard to achieve production goals, in exchange for housing and food. Hard work and the removal of opportunities for criminal behavior will give errant beings the best chance for reform. They can be returned to their societies renewed, cured of their criminal urges once and for all." It wasn't long before that bold statement drew a reaction as well.

"Typical Earthmen," scoffed the Zorgolongian minister, standing up from his delegation box, "always exaggerating things." This drew an indignant snort from Convention President Frilic; nevertheless, he chose not to interrupt. The delegation leader continued, "Cured once and for all? My good Earthman, that's preposterous-sss! The reason they're criminals in the first place is that they cannot control their urges! Do you think we're idiots-sss?"

But the Earth delegation minister, one Robert Gunton from the province of North America, was unflappable. He rebutted, "My dear fellow, I hasten to point out that the natural deterrent to further criminal behavior shall be the planet itself. You must understand that.

No one will want to be sentenced there, and absolutely no one would wish to be sent back there either." The Earth minister glanced at his Zorgolongian counterpart to see if he had any further comments, but the little fellow—at least for the moment—did not. Thus, he continued, "They shall repay their debt to society for committing crimes, return home, and live out the rest of their lives on their home planets as good citizens." That's all the minister from Earth was proposing and this served to quell any further interruptions for a while. He knew he held all the cards and what he started hearing from other delegates only served to support this belief.

"My fellow delegates," remarked the minister from the Schpleefti delegation, "let's not miss out on this wondrous opportunity. If the Interplanetary Authority does not approve of this scheme, then we must consider what might happen next. Earth will simply develop the mine on Rijel 12 by herself and cut us out of the deal completely." This made sense, even to the brooding, warrior-like Enoshi who due to their imposing size always seemed to garner cautious respect from other species at these gatherings – even if they weren't particularly bright.

What's more, he was quite right, the furry little creature from far away Schpleefti. Earth would make a veritable fortune and hold a virtual monopoly on mineral distribution throughout the galaxy. Minister Gunton from Earth sensed it was time to close the sale.

The Earth minister's message, once it was his turn to speak again, was simply this: "If all planets participate this, my friends, will become a global operation with the funding to build Rijel 12's mining network into an economic success. And do it rather quickly according to our projections." He then feigned a bit of well-timed humility in order to suck them in further. But it really wasn't necessary; it went without saying.

"Of course, Earth could do this all by herself, but the Rijel system is many light years away from us. Several planets, as you may note, are closer. Much closer."

The Sudonji and Zorgolongian delegations immediately reacted to that obvious fact. So much nearer to the Rijel star system, they could easily reach Rijel 12 and develop it. But alas, it was Earth's idea and they'd be wiser to participate in the new plan. Earth, as everyone knew, had all the best technology for deep shaft mining.

Only the wise and sedate Slartigians held fast to their argument against this shameful idea of forcing prisoners into what they deemed to be slave labor for the sake of profit. Their contention was that it would only lead to abuse and oppression over time. Nevertheless, when Frilic held the final vote on the measure it was approved five to one. And with that, the intergalactic penal colony of New Australia was created.

Chapter 2: Life on Rijel 12

Over the years, the penal colony expanded. Certainly, in the early days it was slow going. The planet's surface was impossibly forbidding. Nevertheless, within a half century, the population grew and grew, from a couple hundred to over a hundred thousand. The different planets in the galaxy, even cultures which were hesitant about it at first, found they could send convicted felons of all kinds. Murderers, rapists, thieves, political agitators, and other social undesirables could be delivered to this facility and thereby rid their home planets of the dangers they posed. But it didn't take long for things to degenerate into something far more sinister.

At first the sentences were reasonable, spanning three to twenty years, with only extremely violent offenders sentenced there for life. The planet itself was completely barren and devoid of any flora and fauna, covered on the surface by global deserts, volcanic mountains, and extremely forbidding temperatures during the day. At night, temperatures often plunged into the teens, but during the day it could reach one hundred fifty degrees Fahrenheit. It was certainly unrealistic to live on the surface, but far underground, the planet had massive caverns that extended for miles and miles in every direction.

On Rijel 12, there was just enough atmosphere to provide

breathable oxygen for most creatures, but the Interplanetary Authority chose to expand the already existing system for manufacturing purer oxygen for the caverns, so that workers could maintain better stamina. The planet's oxygen was too thin and could lead to light-headedness and fatigue during prolonged exposure. Therefore, the mining operation was sealed off from the surface and the oxygen production system could be added onto in phases. Blowers moved manufactured air around the caverns and tunnels to keep workers healthier and more alert.

The Rijel 12 planet interior had hundreds of underground glaciers located miles below the rocky barren surface, protected from the incredibly hot daytime sun. Subterranean aquifers closer to the surface provided water to the new inhabitants, but it had to be filtered. The original miners, years before, didn't actually drink the water from the aquifers. They imported purified water from nearby planets, and it was very expensive to do so. However, scientists believed the water on Rijel 12 could be made safe for prisoners to drink. Earth advisors devised an elaborate filtration system that extracted water into great reservoirs then filtered it into drinking water at hundreds of stations throughout the mining network.

Technically it was fine, but not surprisingly, those human engineers designed a system that needed to be maintained at a hefty cost, a cost that less ethical prison operators didn't prefer to continue paying as time went on. Systems deteriorated over time and needed repair. Mine operators looked the other way, and gradually prisoners suffered from consuming bad drinking water.

They had no choice. Besides, these same prison managers were making money for their employers. Profitability was being reviewed constantly, and no one felt inclined to speak out about the deteriorating conditions for prisoners. Better water could be imported for the guards and operation managers, so why worry about those hapless prisoners being slowly poisoned below? More prisoners arrived all the time to replace the ill and dying. It didn't really matter to those cynical, over-worked, profit-driven mining operators, always under pressure from their superiors to achieve lofty goals.

In only a few earth years, the prison complex was constructed a mile below the treacherous surface, and then expanded over the decades to where it housed thousands of prisoners. Earth ships arrived regularly, and construction workers in the early years worked feverishly to create more barracks below ground.

New facilities were built to house the ever-expanding prison labor supply. When a new cavern was opened up, these laborers would build a prefabricated barracks and live in it while they built the infrastructure around it. The air system would be connected to new parts of the mine, and new water filtration systems would be installed then tapped into underground aquifers. When each new section was complete, the construction teams would leave; the barracks they lived in would then be occupied by new prisoners sent there to work the newly opened section. For years it went on like that, ever-expanding the mining network as more and more convicts arrived.

However, these barracks would soon become overcrowded as more prisoners were sent to work there, and over the years they became dilapidated. As the decades passed, prisoners eventually resorted to carving out homes inside caves.

Additional mineral deposits were discovered. Veins of gemstones were found too. It seemed the opportunities for wealth being extracted from Rijel 12 were boundless; this only served to fuel the machine. Mine expansion required additional labor, and every planet was soon being urged to keep sending more convicted criminals. It became all too easy for abuses to occur. New prisoners being brought in meant even more barracks and even more supplies. Expanding the mines required more equipment, which led to more expenses and even more aggressive production goals. This would have been the case for any rapidly growing labor-intensive industry. But in the case of New Australia Planetary Prison, the difference was that labor was free.

Things eventually got overlooked, neglected, or downright ignored. Greed replaced compassion or even any semblance of justice, and everyone gave in just a little, if not completely. The greater good became nothing more than the motivation of greater profit, and from the top down, no one wanted to admit it. When existing veins of minerals were expanded and dug out further, even more workers were needed to fill the workload, as well as replace the dying and ruined laborers below. New Australia Planetary Prison became a death sentence to most all prisoners sent there, and within fifty earth years, few expected to return.

"So, how long you boys in for?" asked a rather portly guard assigned to oversee prisoners being led into the dusty hold of a large ship orbiting the Earth's moon. Francois had spent three weeks inside a stinking pit, a lunar prison ward designed to temporarily house a thousand men awaiting transportation to Rijel 12. However, the weeks of waiting as well as the ongoing flow of convicts into the facility had led to overcrowding of epic proportions. There were easily ten times that many crammed inside. Beds stacked six high required ladders to reach the top bunk and were arranged in rows so narrow even a submariner would find them cramped. Sewage backup and sickness from poor food made the untenable situation impossible to stand, yet they had no alternative. That's why arrival of the prison transport felt like a godsend.

The size of the ship dwarfed even tall buildings, and it was outfitted with advanced warp drive technology, which enabled it to travel at twenty times the speed of light via the creation of a warp bubble in space that allowed the craft to ride the wave to its intended destination. This theoretical phenomenon had been proposed centuries before back on Earth by a bright young scientist from Mexico City.

With a target programmed into the ship's computer, the now-perfected mechanism simply propelled it across the warp bubble, allowing passengers to move through time and experience very little in the way of aging. The ship could not be steered, didn't have to be maneuvered or even controlled for that matter. Using the warp drive, the ship simply appeared in its desired location months later with the onboard computer having calculated the entire journey and executed it systematically.

For security reasons, prisoners were placed in lidded compartments where they'd be put to sleep until the time of arrival. The mines needed healthy strong bodies, and the limited staff on board could not be tasked with supervising them during the months they'd spend in space. That was far too dangerous.

"Three years," replied one of the prisoners, and in response the guard snickered. "Three years, huh? Well, that's not so bad I guess. You can make it three years I'm sure." Then he chuckled cryptically. Others within the crowd of prisoners weren't so tactful.

"Oh, don't bet on it, pal," remarked an older fellow among the mass of men being herded into the ship's hold. "You might make it through," quipped the burly man. "Might not. Hard to say. But don't go fooling yourself about no getting home to your momma. Ain't nobody coming back to get you when you're done with your stint." The guard shot an icy glare toward the fellow, then shook his head. Yes, he'd heard the same things, and yes, he'd experienced similar realities during his last three junkets to Rijel 12. For only half the ship's hold was filled with prisoner compartments. The rest was full of supplies, food for the prison staff mainly. And the entire hold was destined to be refilled with tons and tons of extracted mineral ore, such as platinum, nickel, copper, or iron.

Even the prisoner compartments themselves, those not covered up under mountains of raw material during the return voyage, would be occupied largely by the crew. He himself would occupy one of them for the long flight back to Earth, only to reload more doomed souls for the next trip across the galaxy. New Australia Planetary Prison and its thriving mining operation had by now expanded into a diabolically efficient, decades-old, going concern.

Prisoner processing and assignment to work details were handled below the surface. Rijel 12's original mining operation was established on the site of a canyon formed from the collapse of an ancient cavern. A surface facility was built next to it; the canyon was eventually converted into a loading bay for supply ships. It used a landing pad lift which elevated to the surface to receive arriving spacecraft. Once landed, the elevator descended several hundred feet to be processed. Then a retractable roof closed over the canyon to seal it off from the forbidding elements of Rijel 12.

New prisoners would be unloaded and assigned to some part of the mines that required more workers, randomly at first, then gradually based on species. There were always new job openings, and there were always more prisoner ships landing. When transport ships were emptied of prisoners, the other side of the bay would open, and vehicles would haul in loads of mineral ore to be loaded onto the craft. Upon completion, the retractable roof would open, the elevator platform would ascend back to the surface, and the craft could take off once again.

By the fiftieth Earth year of operation, there was a freighter landing every few weeks, and usually there was another in orbit around Rijel 12 waiting to land and offload new prisoners. Pilots and crew were never allowed to leave their ships, and most didn't wish to. This was a prison after all, and security was air-tight at all times. But what did these pilots and crew see when they landed? It was enough to send the message back to their home planets that this was a truly hellish place. They didn't need to see what was going on below. Construction workers finishing their projects could shed even more light on the realities of New Australia Planetary Prison, but even they didn't care about inmates in a prison. They just wanted to leave Rijel 12 and get back home as quickly as possible.

With all the financial backing of the Interplanetary Authority, those enterprising Earthmen were brutally efficient in devising a prison system that continued to feed the mining operation, and production goal-setting became increasingly aggressive as the years passed. Government officials began to see dollar signs. Profitability increased, and the operation was a success within only a few galactic years. Everyone was thrilled with the results.

Well, most everyone was, anyway. Prisoners in the early years were immediately pressed into service working in the mines until they completed their sentences, and just like the Earthmen had promised, these prisoners who'd paid their debt to society were able to crawl or limp onto freighters and eventually returned to their home planets. They'd be aged and broken down by then, but at least they could finally go home. Go home and die at a very young age and in terribly poor health, that is. It was hard to feel sorry for them. After all, most had certainly deserved to be sent there. Law-abiding citizens could rationalize it that way. But it was nevertheless shameful, treating other intelligent beings in such a manner. And it was a reflection on the societies themselves who allowed it to go on like that.

Then it got even worse. Eventually the planets stopped going back to get their prisoners. It became an embarrassment really, seeing a released prisoner all haggard and crippled, withered and squinting from daylight which they hadn't seen in many years. They'd return to their home planets almost unrecognizable to their loved ones.

The Slartigians were the first of the six planets to stop sending prisoners to New Australia Planetary Prison, protesting that conditions there would have to improve before they'd resume. After nine earth years, they ceased transports of criminals entirely, but they left thousands behind to finish out their miserable lives and chose to forget about the whole nasty experiment.

Enosh threatened to do the same, but eventually relented. Enoshi were very strong and capable of bearing up to the rigors of the workload. Plus, the Enosh government couldn't bear to miss out on their share of the profits from the mine. The other planets, by way of comparison, kept right on going. They began seeing it the way Earthmen portrayed it from the very start.

"Violent criminals and repeat offenders need to be removed from a society for the greater good of their communities, and once they've repaid their debt, only then may they return to their home planets," is how the Earth delegation put it each galactic year at the Convention. Yet this commitment to "reforming" criminals gradually faded into a distant memory when governments felt the backlash of social revulsion over the results of even a three-year sentence. Frankly it was the lure of incredible wealth and the expansion of their planetary economies that caused them to temper their protests. Soon they stopped protesting completely.

Most grew to look at it the same way as the Earthmen. At the conventions, the Earth delegation would delight in reporting production numbers and exaggerate the vast improvement in social order: "We're shipping out mineral ore, and shipping in our criminals and ne'er-do-wells to work the mines. It's still a win-win."

Crime didn't stop, nor did crime rates fall. Beings still murdered, stole, raped, or conspired against the government. Yet it didn't matter. It only fed the machine. The justice systems didn't have to worry about prisoner reform. Murder another being on your planet, and you got sent away for life. It made perfect sense at first. But eventually even first-time offenders were being dragged onto transport vessels headed for Rijel 12 to serve "minor sentences." Within fifty Earth years, even they would never return. No one went back to get them.

Initially, much like any poorly thought-out social experiment, the stated intent turned out to be unachievable. From the start, the promise was to respect the concept of a set prison sentence and to return the convict to society upon its completion. Greed got in the way of that. But, so did the fear of political repercussions at home when freed prisoners returned and spoke of the conditions at New Australia Planetary Prison. Earth and Zorgolong were the first two planets to stop returning their prisoners. Schpleefti never did in the first place. In their world, a Schpleefti who'd severely broken the law was banished from their community. For them it was just plain common sense. Threaten the peace and tranquility of society, and you lose the privilege of living within it.

The Enoshi followed suit. Given time, they began to see how it fit in with the philosophy of their culture. Removing the capability of repeating the crime by severing a paw, castrating, or removing a tongue meant that the example was set for all those tempted to duplicate the act. But this was even easier. Just send them away to Rijel 12 and the problem was solved.

For Slartigian prisoners it was different though. Most couldn't handle the conditions in New Australia and perished within a few years. However, not all of them died. Their innate intelligence and wisdom became highly valuable to other prisoners and some lived on to serve vital roles in prison society. Besides, Slartifigians had much longer life-spans than humans. This became very important later on, for the sake of the other inmates' survival.

The hard life of mining killed off thousands of prisoners every year, and there was no predictable pattern to it. Stronger prisoners died in the mines just as easily as weaker prisoners. Determination to survive, or resentment at having been sent to this subterranean hell, could certainly sustain a being for a while, but accidents were quite common. Death could come easily, and at most any time. Prison administrators didn't care. They didn't have to. In another few weeks, there'd be a ship arriving with more prisoners anyway. Life deteriorated into a matter of brutal survival for the desperate beings on Rijel 12.

After half an Earth century of dumping unfortunate prisoners on the planet, the place had become a death sentence, and everyone knew it. Inmates would tell newly arrived prisoners, and even prison officials communicated the same message. As one infamously cruel guard used to put it to arriving convicts as they were processed in the receiving bay, "You have been sent here to die, and that is likely what you'll do. Accept it, and your miserable existence here may end peacefully. Who knows? You may die tomorrow. We don't know, and we don't care. Work and you eat. Eat and you live. That's all you need to know for now."

And yet fifty Earth years after its creation, even when faced with such an impossible existence, amazingly, some beings learned how to survive. They adapted, and they overcame by creating a society of their own. Leaders arose, structure developed, and the situation stabilized, partly driven by necessity and partly due to the sheer determination of intelligent creatures seeking to exist, no matter what the circumstances. They figured out ways to live on.

CHAPTER 3: CRYSTAL DISCOVERY

"Nebelung? Hey, Nebelung! Break is over, brother. We must get back to work now." yelled one of the other prisoners. In a daze, Golan Nebelung snapped out of his temporary solace. He had been dreaming of his wife and little ones back home, and in the twenty minutes it had taken for equipment to be moved in for his crew to continue work on the new tunnel, he'd fallen into a deep sleep.

Exhaustion was a foregone conclusion, as he'd come to learn. Covered in fur from head to toe, he, just like his fellow Enoshi, didn't need nor wear any form of clothing, and in the cool, damp confines of the mine, his thick gray coat was perpetually soggy and speckled with dust.

His workmates were all Enoshi in this section of the mine and suffered the same deprivations. It did no good to try and clean their fur. Every last one of them stayed filthy every hour of the day, until their colors and stripes were all but indiscernible. It proved virtually impossible to tell one breed from another, which was vitally important in their culture. Breed denoted status. But then again, status was yet another of the many luxuries abandoned or forgotten once they set foot inside the mines of Rijel 12.

"You take the front, Nebelung!" shouted another one of his

crewmates. "We'll work in behind you. That delay has set us back a bit, and we still have to make quota if we're to be fed today, brother." That perked him right up. Nothing was more important than fulfilling their load requirements by the end of their work shift. To fail meant going hungry. Going hungry meant a long night curled up in his cave trying to sleep through hunger pangs.

It had gone on like that for weeks, months, years. Golan didn't know just how long he'd been down here. The same was true for most anyone on his crew. And it would go on for as long as he could muster the wherewithal to get up from his pallet and go back to work. Only death would deliver him from this nightmare. Dreaming of home was about all he had to cling to, and even those pleasant memories of his family back on Enosh were already beginning to fade.

"Right," muttered Golan instinctively. "It's my turn, I know," he then added with a yawn. There was no use arguing and for that matter why would he? His team of miners took turns at the more dangerous duties they faced, including burrowing into a freshly dug tunnel and hoping against hope there'd be no cave-in. If that happened, they could suffocate under tons and tons of rocks and berm, and the lead worker? He faced the worst of the danger. Rescuing crew members was something Golan had experienced before, and it didn't always work out very well for the victims.

"Had yourself a little nap, did you?" joked his neighbor on the work line. The big Enoshi, a member of the Angora clan and quite large for his breed, patted Golan on the shoulder with a monstrous paw. His once-beautiful white coat had been stained and matted with so many years of grime that his color was a matching shade of gray compared to Golan's once shimmering hide. Now practically no one from back home could have told the difference between them.

"Yes, brother," replied Golan with a grunt as he bent to pick up his tool set – a long pick which would have required both hands if he'd been a human, along with a bucket and trowel the size of a spade. "I was dreaming of home. Trying to remember my wife's face and eyes again. It's getting harder and harder to recall her beautiful face and the smell of her fur. Every day it gets a little fuzzier," smirked Golan with a defeated sadness in his tone. "I miss her so much."

"We all miss our loved ones back home, brother," remarked the hulking Enoshi. "Like it or not, the sooner you try and forget her, the better. I'm sorry to say it, I really am. You know as well as I, there's no chance of seeing them again. No one's getting out of here. We must accept it. Have to get our job done and if we do we get food. Fond memories of home are useless to us. Understand?"

Golan knew his crew mate was correct. This had become reality for the doomed souls in his section of the mine. As far as he knew no one was being released anywhere in the infinite networks of tunnels and shafts. The dead were discarded and replaced. New workers fell right into line with the living. Day after miserable day, week after miserable week. Never a day off, or even the faintest hope of getting off this rock one day. After many years, inmates realized no one was ever coming back to get them once they got sent to New Australia Planetary Prison.

Governments spun lies about it publicly. In news conferences they denied a cover-up. Otherwise they ignored it or claimed they had no knowledge of what had happened to prisoners who'd finished their sentences. When family members inquired as to the fate of their incarcerated loved ones they got nowhere. No information was forthcoming. Moreover, there was no record-keeping at NAPP after a while either. Files on prisoners were created in the early days, of course, but then in later years, these files were simply "misplaced."

Families of inmates never fully grasped this. Rijel 12 was simply too far away to have to pay a freighter to transport home one, five, or even twenty convicts and NAPP was not in the business of tracking down a prisoner once they'd been sent into the mines. Meanwhile, prison wardens and their managers were making quite a good living for themselves under the table. There were port fees, docking fees, and loading fees. Ships landed to offload supplies, then took on as much ore and raw gemstones as they could. Neither the ship captains nor the warden bore any concern for fulfilling promises made by other planets regarding completed sentences.

But then something happened that made conditions even worse. A new discovery deep within the mines of Rijel 12 caused quite a stir. Discovery of large veins of perovskite on Rijel 12 occurred in the thirty-fifth Earth year of operation. At that time copper, lead, and zinc could already be mined in abundance and refined into silver to make silver wire, a commodity in high demand.

Perovskite could be mined from Rijel 12 in great abundance. Quartz was also discovered, and when crystals the size of an office building were found within the planet's depths, it was merely a matter of burrowing down and extracting them. This required many hours of labor for the already hard-pressed inmates because they had to dig around the massive crystals with hand tools to finally free the giant crystals for extraction. This eventually meant that space craft could be powered by crystals mined from Rijel 12.

Immense power could be drawn from these crystals, enough to get ships across vast reaches of space. The key was piezoelectricity. Certain crystals could become electrically polarized when the crystal was subjected to mechanical pressure, thereby generating voltage. Compression and stretching generated voltages of opposite polarity. The piezoelectric effect merely needed to be amplified and then channeled along silver wire, preferably, to create a vast amount of energy. Rijel 12 had all these raw materials in one convenient place.

Once scientists announced that the crystals could now be used to power generational spacecraft, the stock markets went wild and demand for the crystals skyrocketed. Now ships the size of cities could explore and colonize the universe. Suddenly Rijel 12 had a brand-new income source. And the new warden, an unscrupulous Zorgolongian named Gaah, began to see how he could become extremely wealthy. The only problem was figuring out how to most effectively capitalize on this incredible opportunity.

"Good day Warden," said a young assistant to the general staff and effectively the warden's lackey. His job as scullion was to see to the warden's basic needs and comfort, as well as relay messages from him to other prison staffers. Most importantly, he had to screen calls from overly stressed operators trying to elevate issues and complaints to the front office. "And how did we sleep sir? Are we refreshed and ready to tackle the day?" asked the assistant timidly. Warden Gaah hissed in response.

Now for a Zorgolongian, hissing could mean most anything – from joyful acknowledgment to dismissive sarcasm. It depended upon the intonation and the circumstances. In this case it was the latter.

"Not really," sighed Gaah. He'd gone back to his quarters the night before worried about production goals and had endured a fitful sleep thinking about his plight. This new opportunity, mining perovskite crystals for generation ships now being designed by all six planets in the coalition, meant trillions in profit, if he could only convert portions of his operation to their extraction. It also meant redirecting the work efforts of thousands upon thousands of convicts below. It was a daunting task, and one quite worthy of keeping him up late. He'd hardly slept a wink. "But we'll rise to the occasion my young friend. That we will do, whatever it requires of us," continued the pot-bellied little warden.

Zorgolongians were prized for their ruthlessness when managing things, especially other intelligent beings unfortunate enough to be in their charge. Merciless, they were. Well known for it too. Gaah sat in his high back chair and paused for a few moments to tap on the glass of a small terrarium located on his desk. Inside, small creatures, unevolved rodents imported from his home planet Zorgolong, cowered in fear seeing what was to them a giant lizard glaring at them from outside their container. Soon, one of them would be the beast's breakfast.

"Give me the reports, please," quipped the warden, and the young scullion quickly produced an electronic notepad from on top of his little desk in the outside reception area. "Let's hear the good news, if there is any," Gaah added smugly. "How are we doing getting those loathsome devils to stay on task?" he asked coldly. "Do we need to transfer more convicts to the new sector?" His assistant hesitated to tell him the latest. It wasn't all bad, but it certainly wasn't likely to please his cold-hearted commander.

Lately there hadn't been much to celebrate in terms of production successes. Freeing giant crystals and transporting them to the surface had proved to be phenomenally difficult. Highly profitable once accomplished, sure, and when a freighter had loaded them up for transport? When that was finished, it meant a huge payday. Plenty to keep him employed and able to present his superiors with glad tidings whenever they saw money transferred into their operating accounts. But those successes were long in coming, and in between would be endless messages and inquiries from management about what progress was being made.

The problem, it seemed, was the prisoners themselves. He could work them to death, and true, he often did. Yet the challenge was in supervising their efforts in the many hundreds of locations surrounding those gigantic crystals during extraction. Managing that process had been the most difficult task he'd yet faced in his long, rather shady career. "Well you see sir," replied the scullion. "It seems the prisoners in that sector··· well, the crew leaders I mean··· they've been making demands." The young assistant braced himself for an angry response.

Warden Gaah was a Zorgolongian with a past full of piracy, who had taken over after the third prison warden had retired. By that time, the realities of New Australia Planetary Prison were accepted at face value. They were only there to make money for the Interplanetary Authority, and as long as production goals were met or exceeded, there was plenty of *lucre* available for Gaah and his managers to enrich themselves. He got rich quickly. So did his cronies. Warden Gaah also instituted new reforms which changed the way things were done on Rijel 12. For as far as Gaah was concerned, the whole concept of work performance could be managed by the control of food.

Guards were difficult to recruit from other planetary systems, especially as the years went by, so the quality of beings willing to work there had declined markedly. But it also became a wonderful place to go disappear for a while if a being needed a fresh start: if he was running from the law, business associates with a score to settle, an angry spouse, or family obligations. Gaah seized upon this to recruit guards who would carry out his orders without question – or be sent back home to face justice. It was an approach that worked well in fostering loyalty among his staff.

These new guards, recruited by Gaah or by his administrators, rapidly replaced the original staff, and their function eventually became distributing food and achieving production quotas. To do so, they learned to manage their sections of the prison by delegating work detail to the prisoners themselves—then allocating food based on performance.

That was how Gaah envisioned it, much like in the way pirate ships operated in his youth. Work and you eat. Mutiny and you die. The system worked quite well that way, and guards became nothing more than well-armed proprietors for the food depots. Meanwhile, these depots became fortified underground military outposts.

Then a remarkable thing happened. A social structure developed among the prison population where crews established themselves to protect the flow of supplies, making sure everyone got to eat as well as providing protection to its membership from other crews. Some crews developed more quickly than others and benefited from stronger leadership, so over time prison officials found they could refer more and more of the supervision duties to crew leadership. Crews gradually took over almost everything involving prisoner management. They would train and manage their own work shift supervisors, order materials, tools, and supplies. Guards developed into mere go-betweens, commanding sections of the ever-expanding mining network, and dealing with crew leaders exclusively.

Though requiring filtration, water was plentiful. Slartigian prisoners were excellent engineers and because they often lived very long lives, many crews prized them. However, food was not, so the planet imported most all its food stuffs, sending supplies down into the mines to be provided to well-performing teams meeting their quotas. Enforcing discipline was otherwise relatively simple: work hard and your teammates ate well. Thus, crew chieftains were incentivized to keep their crews on task. Amazingly this system worked quite well, and death or disease from malnutrition began to stabilize or even decline. At least for a while, anyway.

"Demands?   Is that what you're telling me, scullion? Preposterous-sss!" blurted the warden with yet another hiss. "They have the temerity to make demands ⋯ on us-sss?" He flew into a rage at this unwelcome news, even if he shouldn't have been so surprised. His method of organization – his strategy of letting crews control their own work details – had led indirectly to this conundrum. Nevertheless, he couldn't comprehend what he was hearing. Prisoner laborers banding together and sending their elected leader to try and negotiate terms of servitude? Given his pirate background such a notion was absurd. It simply would not be tolerated. Gaah reacted immediately.

"Shut down everything in their sector! Shut off the lights – shut off their electricity! Cut off all food rations! Let them starve in the dark, the bastards. Then we'll wait ⋯ wait until they submit."

The nervous young scullion nodded in obedience, though indicating a measure of hesitancy in his eyes. After all, he knew Warden Gaah had spent nearly an hour on a video conference call with his superiors the evening before. They'd been reviewing his production numbers and asking difficult questions. The kind of difficult questions upper management always asks of middle managers, really. They did it because they could – and because it was going to be their own necks on the chopping block when it came time to face shareholders. The minion was only concerned that a shutdown of one sector of the mine might lead to further delays in reaching their production requirements for the quarter. What's more, the demands reported from the guard station several miles below? They were actually quite reasonable. Regardless, the warden was adamant.

"Tell them! Tell those cowardly guards down there. Call the power plant and tell them too. You hear me? We'll put a stop to this right now!"

Unfortunately, Warden Gaah in his hubris was underestimating the determination of his adversaries – the very prisoners he sought to control with his vast resources and "limitless" power. If only he'd known what was truly going on in the infinite caverns and tunnels of Rijel 12.

The evolution of crews into hierarchical communities, based on specialties and exhibited service to the crew, had led to prisoners identifying themselves with their new crew identity rather than with their previous lives. As prisoners, they gained a level of respect for each other: in spite of whatever they'd done to get sent to prison, they had indeed endured this hellish place together. That was something they all shared in common.

But even with this amazing effort to find a way to survive the un–

survivable and create a meaningful existence, the beings of New Australia Planetary Prison still faced the failings of character and ethics that inevitably accompanied the evils of absolute power. The last straw occurred when prisoners would meet quotas, only to find supplies being held back by corrupt guards who cruelly demanded higher yields in order to further their careers. Many post commanders did that, and when they felt they could get away with it, they'd try and starve prisoners into submission. Warden Gaah had never been informed of that handy little piece of information.

Prisoners would naturally be compelled to step up production, boosting the numbers of those unethical guards engaging in this practice. But prisoners would often die from malnutrition as a result. It required so many calories to work a full shift. Malnutrition led to exhaustion. Exhaustion led to illness. Illness led to death.

Air and water systems needed maintenance, tools needed repair, and food quality was often quite lacking even when plentiful. Sanitation was downright abhorrent. Risking disaster, the crew leaders began finding ways to organize and call a strike to damage production. It did little, except for repeatedly proving the immorality of prison administration. Warden Gaah made things far worse whenever prisoners decided enough was enough and went on strike to demand better living or working conditions.

In order to quickly bust strikes he would suspend food deliveries in order to starve the malcontents. Warden Gaah simply cut off all food distribution to that sector, including electricity to the fans, lighting, and water filtration systems. Days later, work would inevitably resume. A hasty meeting would be called with striking crew leaders and a settlement would be reached. But little would change, and a few more prisoners would die from malnutrition each time it was attempted. Nevertheless, crew leaders had to at least try and force change. Their very position as leader of the crew demanded it. Failure to defy the guards could be construed as complicity, and crew leaders could and did get deposed on occasion.

Malnutrition wasn't the only major problem. There was a lack of medical supplies for injured or ill workers. Not being able to secure these supplies could lead to resentment toward crew leadership.

After all, the crew leader had promised strong leadership, safety, and had taken responsibility for their well-being. Crew leaders often argued during these negotiations that the warden should consider the potential threat of losing this crew leaders and subsequently lose control of the entire prison if there were to be a wide-scale riot. Crew leaders really were the key to maintaining order. There were over one hundred thousand prisoners in those mines now, and only about thirty-five thousand guards. In their view, Warden Gaah needed their help in preventing a rebellion.

"That's far enough, Leptailurus. Stop where you are. We can smell you from where you're standing," sneered the Zorgolongian commander. In a clearing, there was a no-man's land out front of a blockhouse occupied by armed guards with automatic weapons trained on the Enoshi chieftain's torso. The large feline had approached, illuminated by spotlights run off reserve batteries during the blackout imposed by the warden. He stopped and stood still; paws outstretched to show he was unarmed. He raised his voice until it echoed throughout the cavern.

"You know what we want! We've asked and asked. You've agreed that our demands are acceptable, Commander. Now we must have them! We need medicine! Antibiotics especially. You know what will happen if we don't get them. My brothers who will continue to die. And if they rise up, my friend, it might be a new chieftain you'll be dealing with next time. One far less reasonable I'm sure. If you can't help us, then let us present our demands to the warden so he might understand our situation."

The Zorgolongian post commander had no doubt that was a plausible threat. If Leptailurus returned to his brother Enoshi empty-handed, he'd likely be assassinated, and the next day there'd be a brand-new leader presenting demands. The strike would continue, and production deadlines would be missed. There was little choice but to give in and provide the hulking beast with a crate full of medical supplies, including enrofloxacin for respiratory, skin, and urinary tract infections. Those were common ailments for Enoshi working in the mines.

The post commander thought long and hard about the potential consequences, then he directed several of his comrades to carry out a large box containing the drugs. Syringes, vials of medicine, and bottle of pills were included. This scene was repeated throughout the mines of Rijel 12 on numerous occasions as of late. The warden rarely heard of these secret arrangements. The less he knew, the better. Leptailurus quietly walked over and picked up the massive crate, returning to his crew with their much-needed medicine. The strike ended an hour later and the prisoners in his section returned to work without any further delay.

No, Gaah never knew what was going on way down in the mines. For example, he didn't know what kept provoking the strikes. He never found out how deliveries of antibiotics might be withheld in order to force prisoners to achieve higher output. Given that he was the only one who could control the food supply, electricity, and, the guards themselves, he didn't need to worry himself with the workaday issues down in the mines. He simply couldn't conceive of the prisoners rioting. How could they expect to succeed? Food depots were armed fortresses. Prisoners possessed little more than mining tools. They'd stand no chance against modern weapons. And attacking a guard station? Well, that was suicide.

He didn't know that negotiations were ongoing below the surface. Once they were concluded, peace would temporarily be restored in that section of the mine, and production would return to acceptable levels. For a while. Each strike would lead to some mild concessions or promises of reform, but nothing would be done to deal with the actual issues.

"Brothers!" bellowed Leptailurus triumphantly. "They agreed! I got the antibiotics we demanded." The large crate he was gripping with his paws was unwieldy and difficult to carry through the tunnel leading to his crew's cave network. Their housing facility had collapsed years ago. Now, parts of it had been pulled off the original structure to fashion walls and doorways for makeshift homes hewn from the rock. A crowd formed as several more crew members emerged from their caves, some of them too weak to stand. Some limped toward their brave leader with the aid of a friend.

"You did it! All hail our brave chieftain!" cried one of them with a triumphant growl. Soon others chimed in. "Great work," yelled another. "We sure needed this." And that was quite correct. Enrofloxacin was more valuable than a bag full of diamonds right now, and Leptailurus had been wise in calling the strike to try and obtain it. Only problem was, they couldn't have held out for even one more day before his brothers would start dying from starvation. The difference was, and the guards would have had no way of knowing this, Leptailurus had an ace in the hole.

Years before, the crew had taken in two injured and exhausted Slartigians. They were in no way capable of handling the rigors of working in a mine. Their bodies dried out quickly from the dust. Their health had declined to the point of withering away like rose petals on a hot asphalt street. But some clever Enoshi working alongside of them had taken an opportunity to spirit them away from the worksites and nurse them back to health. With their immense life-spans, those same two Slartigians had not only recovered, but had gone on to serve the next three chieftains.

Now they worked for Leptailurus, and what little they could harvest from a secret farm, located nearly a mile further down the tunnel, was barely enough to sustain their fellow crew members during this latest work stoppage. This top-secret farm had been concealed from the warden's guards since long before Lepatilurus had become chieftain. Without this they could never have survived a work stoppage.

By stockpiling task lighting left over from construction teams, sifting through food rations and droppings for seedlings, and using filtered water from a nearby aquifer, the Slarts had managed to develop a hydroponic farming operation. They grew vegetables and citrus fruits which supplemented the crew members' diets. What's more, the they had meticulously calculated the precise caloric requirements of the crew down to the last minute when the strike would have to end. Leptailurus had barely made their deadline, even if those selfish guards had no inkling just how close he'd come to capitulating.

"Have some food, Chief!" yelled yet another among the brethren as they formed up into work details. Some were munching on dried spinach leaves trying to fortify themselves for a long day of digging. They'd have to scramble to make their quota, then they could dine on prison rations and replenish themselves. "You really came through for us this time," added the dust-covered Enoshi with matted fur. He smiled, revealing dark green flecks lodged in his fangs. In response, Leptailurus grabbed a piece of spinach and bit into it with a grin. Crisis averted. He was still in charge, for now.

Long term, it was known that a successful hydroponic farm network, one which could be connected globally to all other crews, was the key to surviving a planetwide general strike. A farm network capable of feeding the entire population of miners for some reasonable period of time to gain an advantage over their heartless jailers was needed. With this in place, greater concessions could be achieved.

But that dream, shared by crew leaders as well as the Slartigian scientists and engineers, was taking too long. They still had to rely on their captors for food and medicine, and there was little they could do about corrupt individuals raising production quotas in isolated sections of the mine. The guards would behave for a while, but eventually they'd slip back into their old habits.

Over time it became apparent to the prisoners of New Australia: open rebellion was the only answer. Even the cautious Schpleeftii were compelled to admit it. The naturally warlike Zorgolongians, Sudonji, Enoshi, and humans downright demanded it. The only thing left to do was organize. Planet-wide. Come together as one. It was time for action.

CHAPTER 4: OPEN REBELLION

Riots are an ugly thing. Prison riots especially. They aren't organized. A singular act sparks an explosion of violence and then things escalate. Destruction, bloodshed, and tragedy follow. But rebellions can take many forms. An armed rebellion usually centers around a charismatic leader who steps forward to state very eloquently what everyone else is already thinking. People rally around that leader to go out and fight the forces of oppression. Rebellions need that: a catalyst to organize and direct their anger. That's all the prisoners on Rijel 12 needed, and one day such a creature came forward. His name was Architeuthis.

Early in the harsh days of New Australia Planetary Prison, a Slartigian named Architeuthis was sentenced to permanent banishment. His crime back on Slartigia was not known. That was often the way it was with prisoners from that planet. Their culture was built around the maintenance of one's image, and embarrassment or humiliation were the only strong emotions for a Slartigian which might elicit a detectable reaction. Architeuthis came to work in the mines and struggled to survive just like everyone else did, laboring away for many years. No one asked questions about his past.

Life on Slartigia was an advanced form of what Earthmen might describe as a feudal society. From top to bottom, all "Slarts," as beings from other planets referred to them, had a role which they must serve in society, and they were expected to be satisfied with their station in life, regardless of what it was. Every farmer was expected to be happy with his function as a farmer. Every mother, father, craftsman, builder, manager, driver, pilot, bureaucrat, doctor, or college professor knew what their role was and accepted it. Early in life, a Slart was identified as having an aptitude for either higher education or apprenticeship to a trade, and they were brought up in that trade or educated to run or manage things according to this early evaluation. Slarts simply could not lie, guess, or exaggerate. They countered with sober evaluations of what they estimated was the truth and said only what they deemed to be irrefutable fact.

Though a Human might speculate, theorize, claim, postulate, accuse, or outright lie, a Slart had neither the ability nor the inclination to do so. They were squid-like in appearance, and their head was conical-shaped, with eight little tentacles extending from around the base of their face. These little appendages performed no known major functions but would flutter comically when a Slart spoke. Their speech was soothing and musical, much like the sound of an oboe or a baritone saxophone. Their lifespan was twice that of most species including humans. They had two long tentacles which formed from what humans would call shoulders. These tentacles were quite adept at grabbing and manipulating objects of any kind, and their grip was quite strong. A Slart stood erect on a set of eight shorter tentacles which served as feet and enabled him to scurry about. Compared to most humans they were shorter, averaging five feet tall.

Architeuthis, by way of comparison, was a giant by Slart standards, towering over six feet in height. Nevertheless, he struggled just like everyone else to live in the hellish mines of New Australia Planetary Prison those first few Earth years, and there was little else that might distinguish him from any other prisoner, except for his size.

Well, that and the fact that he spoke out. He spoke out often, too, and in early times when other beings were becoming demoralized or being abused by guards, Architeuthis was often the only voice of reason. Guards appreciated his cool head and prisoners respected his wisdom. He had an aura about him. Incredibly wise and honest, he could explain things in a way that everyone, regardless of their mentality or their underlying intelligence, understood his advice or counsel. He didn't convince or persuade, he patiently simplified things in a way that all could understand, making clear what the correct course of action should be.

Architeuthis believed that all intelligent beings, deep within their souls, knew the true path they should follow which would benefit both themselves and the society around them. All beings desired balance. They only feared taking the right steps toward achieving it. It was fear that was stopping them: fear of failure, fear of losing face, or fear of humiliation. He believed that fear led to a lack of confidence. And the lack of confidence was the root of every conflict between intelligent beings.

Architeuthis was instrumental in persuading other Slarts to aid in the development of prison society. This effort was vital to the welfare of those realizing they'd been sentenced to die on Rijel 12. Architeuthis inspired prisoners of all species to persevere despite the immense hardship they faced. Most Slartigian inmates were humiliated at having been sent to New Australia Planetary Prison. Many had resigned themselves to dying of starvation and disease. They gave up, and since suicide was not acceptable in their culture, most would remain in a depressed state, slogging through their daily work detail, hoping for death. Inviting it and longing for it even.

Architeuthis explained to them how their devotion to the betterment of the beings around them, and their aid in supporting other prisoners' survival, would heal their "radula," meaning their tongue, but it was a Slartigian metaphor for one's ego. This would eventually return to them their sense of dignity. Best of all, it would free their hearts to love one another and themselves once again. Slarts incarcerated in Rijel 12 slowly began to accept his wisdom, and when they applied their intellect to matters of repair, maintenance, sanitation, farming, and medical care, the woeful state of affairs on Rijel 12 began to stabilize. Architeuthis' legend soon grew.

He became a sort of spiritual leader for the struggling beings on

Rijel 12. And though he was not a member of any particular crew, the crew concept was inspired by him. The Schpleeftkorkii were his main protectors, but he professed no allegiance to them. This crew, which was a hodge-podge of several species including humans, Schpleeftiis, Enoshi, Zorgolongians, and some Sudonji, had been one of the first formed at New Australia Planetary Prison, and had absorbed other crews over the years.

But when the corruption of the guards proved to be a threat to survival, Architeuthis again spoke out. Up until then, his philosophy had been for his fellow prisoners to accept the fact that their home planets had discarded them. Now, they must embrace their new life and identity as a member of their associated crew. Their crew would care for them, benefit from their labor, protect them, and see to their needs.

"All of us must work together to achieve production goals and earn our food rations, so we might survive and flourish. Your crew is your family now. And they will protect you while you serve them ⋯ for the rest of your lives," Architeuthis explained. His philosophy was communicated throughout the growing convict population, giving beings of all species some form of hope. Yet the prisoners were reaching their breaking point, and Architeuthis recognized this. The policies of the new warden, Gaah, had led to new levels of suffering.

The discovery of quartz and perovskite meant wide-scale tunneling throughout the planet's interior, and the creation of giant shafts for moving these humungous crystals. In so doing, the entire planet was slowly being connected. Crews, once isolated, were now able to communicate with each other. This meant the spread of information was much wider, and communication meant sharing of ideas. Everyone was talking about it. A rebellion was now possible to coordinate planet-wide. The planet's spiritual leader Architeuthis needed only to say the word.

After another series of embargos on medicine were reported through the new network, Architeuthis had finally had enough. He knew it was time to speak out against the regime of Warden Gaah. What he actually said was something quite unusual for a Slartigian. A Slart didn't say things like that in normal circumstances. But these were far from normal circumstances, and when Architeuthis spoke these words to a gathering of prisoners at a meeting held deep inside the caverns of Rijel 12, it set in motion a series of events that Warden Gaah could not have foreseen.

In his baritone voice, Architeuthis addressed an assembly of leaders from the farthest reaches of the planet. It had been planned a month in advance, and carefully concealed from the prying eyes and ears of guards and post commanders in such a way that only a handful knew of it. These chieftains had snuck through the infinite network of tunnels and caverns to a top-secret location. The meeting was conducted within the borders of the Schpleeftkorkii territory.

The event had been kept necessarily hush-hush during the planning process, with emissaries relaying the message from one mining sector to the next. All participants had been sworn to secrecy, upon pain of death. They were only allowed to bring a bodyguard troop of up to five trusted members from their home territory. No weapons were permitted. Attendance required them to leave old rivalries and historic resentments at the door. Everyone invited heeded the call. Only Architeuthis could draw such solemn dedication from otherwise violent individuals.

"Beings of New Australia," began Architeuthis in a soothing voice. "It is time to rise up and face evil, for evil is facing us." The reaction in the crowd of chieftains and their loyal cohorts was to be expected. They fell silent as a church when hearing a Slart speak that way. Most had never seen him in person; however, they all respected his reputation.

"It is an evil which is facing down upon us," continued the tall figure, "oppressing us and threatening societies that we have struggled and strived to create in this, our new home… far from our original planets. The enemy is stronger than us, has more technology than us, and controls our very livelihood. But there is one thing our enemy has never been able to take from us, not the whole time we've been here. The enemy cannot and never will take away our spirit."

Eyes moistened, even among those crew leaders who'd risen up from among the ranks to become undisputed chief. Strong, brave Sudonji. Quick, nimble Schpleeftii. Clever, ruthless Zorgolongians.

Smart, fierce humans. Ferocious, warrior-like Enoshi. All of them. Heartrates rose. Murmurs and even a few shouts emitted from the audience. Hardened beings who'd survived years of deprivation were standing with mouths agape, hanging on the very words Architeuthis spoke – wanting him to say those things they'd longed to hear. This was the day, and this was the moment they'd all been waiting for. But would he really say it? Would he call upon them to make *war*?

After a calming sigh which fluttered his facial tentacles, Architeuthis went on to satisfy their yearnings for inspiration and provide the impetus to organize their efforts. Didn't take long to get what they came for.

"And so, we will challenge this evil which threatens us, and we will overcome it. We will use the resources of our minds and the cooperation and skills of the over one hundred thousand of our brethren struggling to survive throughout New Australia. We will declare war on our oppressors. Yes, there will be bloodshed. But we will succeed, and we will survive, like we always have. And when we have achieved our freedom, we will once again see the Rijel sun shining upon the surface of this very planet, this world which now belongs to us."

At the moment he concluded his speech, Architeuthis bowed his conical head and closed his enormous eyes as if in prayer. The crowd erupted. They cheered wildly, all those crew leaders and their bodyguards who'd risked detection traveling across the globe for this clandestine meeting. Soon a chant arose among them which became the nickname for the revolt, and eventually the new moniker for the beings of Rijel 12. For upon hearing their leader refer to their home as "New Australia" instead of Rijel 12, they became wildly inspired. They boldly screamed "NEW AUSTRALIA," repeatedly and with several different accents, until it gradually started sounding like something else.

The chanting and screaming continued for several minutes, until the audience kept hearing something run together that sounded like "Nah-sty" or "Nah-stees". It was an historic moment. One, or perhaps a few, eventually started shouting "NAUSTIES! NAUSTIES! NAUSTIES!" And within a few moments, the whole chamber was screaming their new title.

From that point on the name stuck. From then on, the revolt and the rebels on Rijel 12 became known to each other by that name. From that day forward, they were prisoners no longer. They were now "Nausties". The Naustie Rebellion had begun.

Mobilization for the uprising took nearly a year to put together. This was not a prison escape. This was an armed rebellion against vastly superior technology. Prison security troops, which numbered only about thirty-five thousand, carried electrical impulse cannons, or EIC's. These weapons were hand-held, much like an old Earth machine pistol or Thompson submachine gun. They used an electrical charge from a crystal powered generator and could fire a .30 caliber projectile into targets at rates of five thousand feet per second, without using gunpowder. The target of an EIC would often become mortally wounded by the impact, devastated internally by shrapnel, because the projectile was designed to disintegrate upon striking organic tissue.

EIC's were automatic weapons which fired up to three hundred rounds per minute. They could be sprayed at a crowd of protesters or a wave of attacking troops, rendering appalling casualties in a matter of seconds. Larger fifty caliber versions were installed in kill slots on the outside walls of every guard outpost, and they could mow down beings of any species that came within range.

Guard outposts were formidable, constructed of steel, and safely secured along major access tunnels throughout the planet. One was attached to every food depot. Each outpost was garrisoned with at least 300 guards and located next to elevator shafts or output collection sites, where prisoners would bring in their daily production to earn rations.

Slart mechanics, repairmen, farmers, scientists, engineers, and physicians embedded in all the crews now began nominating the best and brightest among their kind to come together and become a planning team for the revolt. A headquarters was established and protected by the Schpleefti crew, so that the planning team could go live and work directly with Architeuthis in devising the initial planet-wide attack. This group of geniuses assembled immediately and began assessing what the Nausties had to work with in terms of developing battle solutions for enemy defenses. Despite the challenges, within a few weeks they had many working theories.

"Let us begin," intoned Architeuthis. That was his usual way of beginning sessions with his staff. They were Slarts, most of them, mixed with a Sudonji, a Zorg, an Enoshi bodyguard or two, and a couple of Humans. These beings were not necessarily part of the think tank itself but would occasionally be called upon for input. Mainly, they were there as military escorts for the Slarts who'd been volunteered from their home crews.

One Schpleefti was in attendance as well, occasionally eyeing his Zorgolongian counterpart across the room whenever he thought Architeuthis wasn't looking. Their two factions had a rivalrous past that went back several decades, due to their homelands neighboring each other. Didn't help matters much knowing that Zorgs during olden times used to hunt rodents, but no conflict was to be tolerated this day – not when there was serious business to be discussed.

This was the thirty-third consecutive day of meetings, oftentimes stretching for ten hours at a clip. Architeuthis would broach a topic, present a challenge that had to be considered, and then wisely fall silent while his brilliant planners hashed it out and argued, at least by Slart standards, over their proposals. Their subtle style and patient dispositions, even when disagreeing with one another, were quite amusing to their escorts; yet after days and days of this, it was more likely to lull them to sleep. Probably would have, if it weren't for the vital issues being raised. Chances were just as good that Architeuthis might call upon one of them to weigh in with their opinions.

They knew things. Architeuthis needed this knowledge, and so did those brainy Slarts. They had abilities – every species did – which exceeded those of Slartigians. Strength, endurance, agility, plus years and years of bottled up resentment. Loads of it. When it was their turn to address the planning session, their commitment was both assumed and expected. The Great Leader, as he was now being referred to, had to count on every last one of them.

"We left off yesterday discussing our initial assault phase," continued Architeuthis, calmly. "Coordination of this is crucial, as we agreed, and it has been established that we need lightning-quick attacks which will subdue at least a handful of the outposts within a short period of time, lest the enemy alert the entire network and stage a counterattack. Shall we begin?" He then as always grew quiet, encouraging his panel of advisors to respond.

One of the planners spoke up immediately, a Slart named Cyathus. His crew was made up primarily of Sudonji who were known for their durability and strength. Diggers and burrowers by nature, they developed into fabulous tunnelers. The elder Cyathus already had a brilliant idea in mind and was anxious to provide details on it to the others.

"If I may, Great Leader, I'd like to start by proposing we consider a prolonged period of tunneling leading up to the day of the assault. A clandestine operation is what I envision, intended to surprise the enemy and limit casualties during our frontal attacks. This would hasten the capture of outposts if successful." Architeuthis nodded and gestured with a long tentacle for him to elaborate.

"What I envision is sending units up under the outposts as well as through the roofs ⋯ dropping through ceilings and emerging from floors. Our brethren from among the Enoshi, assuming the breach is large enough of course, can then crawl through and provide our hosts with a nasty surprise. This could happen during the frontal assault, when the guards are otherwise occupied fending off the main attack."

Architeuthis was intrigued. If he was hearing him correctly, this would mean any frontal assault would thereby become a mere diversion. If successful, it might also imply that those troops committed to the main attack would not have to suffer heavy casualties. Simply keep the occupants of the outposts busy long enough for shock troops to break in and slaughter their opponents, right about the time the enemy were sensing victory. It sounded magnificent.

"Outstanding," proclaimed Architeuthis. "I like your thinking, Cyathus. Please go on. We've got a possible solution to one of our problems, would everyone agree?" Consensus was, for once, almost immediate. The other Slarts nodded politely in agreement. Reactions from the Enoshi, humans, Sudonji, Zorgolongian, and Schpleefti were far more pronounced, however.

"Yes." snorted the Sudonji proudly. He went by the name Scrofa.
"My crew could pull this off quite easily, given enough time. Quietly
too. Those bastards won't even know we're there until it's too late!"
He shot a glance over to his Enoshi counterparts and grinned widely.
"If the tunnels can be dug big enough and wide enough, perhaps even
an Eno could squeeze through. If not, we can always get Zorgs to do
it. That is, if they don't mind killing their own kind."

The lone Zorg in attendance shot a look of profound annoyance
toward Scrofa. Then he smiled and gave out a "Hmmmph." If called
upon, he knew his crew of cutthroats would have no qualms about
murdering every last one of the guards they faced. Years of
oppression had affected them just as much as any other being living
under the heel of Warden Gaah. No matter what species they found
inside, death would come swiftly once they broke through – no
question about it. "You can count on us, pinky," retorted the defiant
Zorgolongian ….

What happened in the meetings was never discussed outside of
the meetings, not with anyone. Battle strategy for the upcoming
attack had to be kept top secret until everything else was in place
otherwise the entire enterprise could be compromised. Secrecy was
an absolute priority and attendees were sworn to keep their mouths
shut, even with their crews. The beings of New Australia knew
something was going on but had no idea what was being discussed or
when they might be called upon to act. It was frustrating, and the
members of the meeting knew it, but it simply had to be this way.

There were pressing matters that had to be addressed: for one
thing, infrastructure. To conduct a large-scale military operation, the
Naustie Army would need ways to move supplies and information
quickly. Global tunneling meant they could set up a communication
network with runners relaying messages throughout to organize
coordinated attacks. It took months for Sudonji diggers to improve it,
but when the network of tunnels was eventually connected, Zorg
runners were soon sprinting in relay teams, keeping all the crews
updated on progress and deadlines. Zorgolongians were quite well-
suited to that function. Spectacular runners, they could cover a mile

or two of open ground much faster than a human.

The planning team also knew they needed scouts to work with the Sudonji and Zorgs, shielding them from detection. For that task, the Schpleeftii, or Spleefs as they were nicknamed, made perfect candidates. Spleefs had sensitive snouts which could sniff out gases, salt, sulfur, and body odors quicker than any other being. Next, the Slart planning team ordered the crafting of carbide lamps.

Calcium carbide would need to be acquired from the guards for this. Longer term, it could be manufactured by heating coke and lime into making acetylene, but there were already large stocks of it for cutting torches used in the mines. In the short term, they'd have to stockpile their own carbide lamps to create lighting for the communication tunnels. Stockpiling them was an easy solution for supplying the tunnels with lighting; however, the planners knew they'd need a lot more. Once Warden Gaah shut down electricity in the mines, which he would, they'd be in complete darkness, and those lamps would be their only means of light.

The biggest issue was food. The planning team meticulously calculated just how many calories a warrior would burn during a prolonged attack on a guard station. Next, they calculated just how long the whole planet could survive once the revolt began and the network of food depots was shut down by Warden Gaah. A carefully devised a time table for this, down to the very last hour when their fellow convicts would begin to starve, was developed.

"Five days, Great Leader," said one of the more mathematically-inclined Slarts on the team. They all were excellent at math, really, but Dofleini was exceptionally gifted. It was now the one-hundred and ninety-eighth consecutive day of meetings, and he'd determined they'd have precisely five Earth days to capture at least thirty food depots before the entire planet would run out of food.

"Five days?" asked Architeuthis. The two Enoshi growled apprehensively. Scrofa the Sudonji snorted nervously. The Zorgolongian hissed. It had been nearly seven Earth months, and the target date for the initial assault was fast-approaching.

The topic of discussion on this particular day was consequential effects following the initiation of hostilities. Architeuthis felt it was important that they consider all conceivable outcomes. "Failure is not an option" was a Human saying, and typical of their reputation for hubris. Slarts didn't think like that. Failure was a very real option and had to be planned for as a possible outcome. If not, there'd be no contingency in place for it.

Architeuthis had no doubt Dofleini was correct. However, he had to fulfill his role as facilitator: engage his staff in discussion, foster debate, get everyone involved in picking apart every idea, proposal, or factual observation, take all the time necessary to address any relevant factors. The stakes were the highest they could be, lives were on the line. For every mistaken assumption, hundreds if not thousands of lives might be lost. What's more, the rebellion could fail quite easily if his staff were not precise in every aspect of their determinations. Therefore, Architeuthis put a question to the floor, "Are you absolutely certain five days is all we have?"

"Yes, Great Leader," Dofleini responded solemnly. "We have five days, no more no less, according to my calculations based on our projected food supply as of the date we're planning to attack. We have to be in control of thirty food depots within five days and be able to distribute their contents globally before that period ends. I've run the numbers repeatedly the figures are correct."

Architeuthis did not argue. The other members at the meeting table certainly pressed Dofleini for details, as well as the sources of his information and their reliability, but few doubted his accuracy. The elder mathematician, pushing one-hundred and thirty in Earth years, patiently answered them.

"To calculate this, I took into consideration the amounts of food stored in a typical depot. They receive a shipment every seven earth days via a massive elevator system. Each day, the freight elevator will send up ore output in the same shaft. Guards travel in the same manner, but they only refresh their staff every Earth week when food shipments arrive. Each depot has a one-month reserve, just as a precaution in case of cave-ins or mechanical breakdown. But to control prisoners, the guards give out daily rations only, as we all know, and those distributions are based on production from the previous twenty-four-hour period. You see, the system was originally designed by Earthmen, so they tended to observe Earth-like time tables in its creation." Dofleini continued as the others patiently listened.

"Subsequently, food rations are calculated precisely to feed a specific number of beings of every species with enough calories to sustain them for twenty-four hours. Based on statistics I've compiled from crews as to their membership and numbers of each species, I was able to work backward and project how much food would be stored in each depot and how many depots we need to capture to make this operation a success. As I said, we only have a limited amount of time to achieve this goal and distribute food throughout our network."

Architeuthis was impressed as always, but he wouldn't be doing his job if he didn't make sure they'd thought of everything that could go wrong. He decided to play devil's advocate and spark further debate.

"Very well then," he stated, now addressing everyone. "And how can we ensure this works out properly, my friends? Assuming we capture thirty depots of course – which we must. I hasten to point out we can only estimate the amount of food we'll capture. Might be more. Might be less. What if we're wrong?" Dofleini's fellow planners were quick with ideas.

"The best option, I believe, is to step up production for at least six months to earn ration bonuses and stockpile food," suggested Sepiolida. He knew such an idea would not be well-received but decided to mention it anyway. "It will be difficult, but it will buy time for our hydroponic farmers to increase crop yields deep inside the mines."

This was a potential solution. The problem was in convincing already hard-pressed crew leaders to place such a heavy burden on their membership. They agreed on it though, eventually, and Zorg runners were subsequently sent out to relay directives throughout the global network. It was one of many issues decided upon that day, only to be followed by other ingenious solutions in the days and weeks following. Information was pouring into headquarters all the time, and edicts were being sent to outlying sectors regularly.

The only major item left to accomplish was for an initial battle plan to be devised and implemented. That was something Architeuthis knew he needed help with. Slarts couldn't do it. He most certainly couldn't do it himself. For this he needed a strategic mastermind, a general.

In front of each food depot was a receiving area for bringing in production output on electric dump trucks which were the size of a house. This was the only approach to a food depot, so attacking en masse across this killing ground could very well be disastrous. Because of this, the planning council proposed that a more thoughtful approach would be necessary to reduce casualties until warriors could get close enough to employ spears or javelins, which human prisoners were already designing and crafting back in their homelands.

This became their specialty. Earthmen, with their more dexterous fingers and hand/eye coordination, had superior ability for craftsmanship in designing weapons for close order combat, so many of the stronger but less agile Earthers, as they were often called, became blacksmiths for the Naustie Army.

Naturally, Enoshi arose as the most fearsome and fearless warriors. They were larger for one thing, standing an average of six and a half feet tall; whereas human males averaged about five feet ten. Plus Enos, as they were sometimes called, were highly skilled at hand-to-hand combat. Thus, it was they who initially became military commanders and trainers for the assault forces.

Yet surprisingly enough, Earthers proved to be the next best fighters, and quickly dispelled any myths others might have held about their ferocity. Earthers could dish it out and they most certainly could take it, as everyone soon discovered. Enoshi drill sergeants were delighted with how fast they learned, and how ruthless Earthers were in physical combat. They weren't just brave; they were downright cruel. But they were also smart ⋯

"By the gods!" exclaimed the giant, a burly sergeant named Chase Burmilla. He'd just witnessed something he thought he'd never see in nine lifetimes. A Human had bested his clan's champion in a grappling match. A big pit had been dug after a long night of training, and two champions chosen from each crew had jumped in to battle it out. No weapons; the combatants had to fight hand to hand, and as the dust settled a clear winner had just been determined.

Ecstatic cheering arose from the crowd gathered around. It was almost deafening. It was like seeing a thirty-point underdog in an old Earth college football game pull off a stunning upset of some highly favored opponent. Yet, this hardly looked like an upset, thought the fearsome feline. It looked more like an ambush.

"By the gods," he observed once again, shaking his head. Sgt. Burmilla was directing a series of war games with a human prison crew which occupied a neighboring cavern. Many years before, mining sections had been organized according to species, to prevent conflict and further enable standardized labor practices. Now, most crews within the prison's network, with the exception of the Schpleeftkorkii of course, were made up exclusively of either Sudonji or humans – Enoshi or Schpleeftii. There were also eleven crews made up primarily of Zorgolongians.

"Don't say I didn't warn ya' Sergeant. 'Cause I did, diddun I?" laughed the beefy Irishman standing next to him. 'Ole Daniel there ⋯ he's a beast. Hell, I wouldn't a' wanted to go up against that monster o' yours either, but that Danny Craft ⋯ he sure took down that big cat." He then screamed, "Good on ya' Boy-o!" as he joined in with the celebrations and jeers from the exhausted convicts watching the match.

The Earther now speaking to Sergeant Burmilla was also a soldier of sorts. His name was Edward McGrath, and, in his past, he'd murdered a man back in the tiny region of Ireland, now part of the Province of Western Europe. His current role in the "Whyos" was primarily enforcer. But now, given the newly established Naustie Army was about to be initiating hostilities, his function had changed.

Tough as a coffin nail, Eddie McGrath was put in charge of training his troops to be fearless when faced with certain death, and to acquire the necessary skills to achieve victory in combat. That's what tonight's wargames session was all about. Burmilla was flabbergasted. What's more he was quite humbled.

"Yes, he did!" roared the beast. "I mean, I would have thought that – well – I would have imagined – I mean, by crumb, this was not what I expected." Eddie McGrath slapped him on the back, causing a cloud of dust to rise off the beast's dingy white fur.

"Yep. And you wouldn't take the odds I offered ya'. Wouldn't take the bet. Too bad. I woulda cleaned up tonight." laughed Eddie. Sergeant Burmilla was still getting over the shock of seeing an Earther practically dismantle one of his strongest warriors.

"It was amazing," Burmilla said stroking his dirt encrusted beard. "For every move, there was a counter-move. For every punch or swipe of my champion's paw there was a block, a kick, or a jab. Your Earthman, you say he is called Dahn-yahl?" To this McGrath nodded as Burmilla continued. "Wasn't much more than half his size. Yet he moved quickly. Seemed to me he observed our champion's moves and devised defenses for them while he fought. What's more, he used his opponent's own force of motion against him. Incredible. Practically threw our guy into the wall whenever he lunged at him."

To this McGrath chuckled even more. Truth was Daniel Craft had weaved and bobbed and dodged so well that the Enoshi was repeatedly off balance during the contest. Threw him over his shoulders. Blocked punches. Sent the monstrous creature sprawling.

"More than once, Boy-o. Tossed your big fella' at least a couple o' times by my count." Then McGrath sighed and collected himself. There was no point rubbing it in. Years and years of surviving in this God-forsaken hellhole had transformed him. He still talked like an Irish mobster, yet he was by now a changed man.

"But why quibble, eh? Let's get the boys together and have 'em call it a night, eh? Maybe in a few days, you know – maybe we can do some more trainin'. Whaddya say to that? I'll bring a different crew with me next time. Let you 'n yer crew show 'em how to be better fighters. That be alright, *a chara*?" Sergeant Burmilla was more than happy to oblige. Today had changed everything he'd ever thought about Earthers and their abilities.

"Certainly, brother. You do that, yes. Bring more. We'll get them ready for battle. And let me say this, my friend," he then added, turning to face the former gangster, "When it comes time for us to charge the enemy, I'd be honored to have you and your Earthmen protecting us with your javelins and charging alongside of us into the fray." Burmilla held out a humungous paw for Eddie to grasp, which he did in the Enoshi style, by grasping the forearm above the wrist.

"Bang on, Boy-o!" exclaimed Eddie McGrath. He knew full well how serious of a compliment this was. Enoshi didn't do that sort of thing unless they sincerely and truly meant what they were saying.

The truth was, Earthers possessed better instincts during a fight, they used their minds and their bodies, and over time Slart planners took notice. Soon, they began choosing Earthers over Enos to become officers, and once they did, some very fresh and creative ideas emerged from newly-selected Earther captains and lieutenants. Enoshi were indeed very brave and fearless, but humans were crafty and deceptive. Members of the planning council were amazed at their innate ability to complicate matters for a defender and create an isolated advantage or window of opportunity that might only exist for a few minutes yet yield a chance for overall victory. Thus, when it came time to select a supreme commander, it was not an Enoshi. It was a human.

In fact, it was Archibald Hicks of the Templar Knights who was eventually promoted to General of the Army. Bald and razor-shaved from head to toe, Hicks had tattoos up the sides of his neck, as well as his arms and legs. He, like most prisoners, had abandoned clothing by now, and merely wore a loin cloth. The Knights were Caucasian humans from various parts of Earth, and one of the most feared crews on New Australia. Hicks also displayed an eight-inch Templar cross tattooed on the back of his shaved head, from the nape of his neck all the way up to the top of his cranium. At his first major strategy planning meeting with the council, he explained his ideas for assaulting a fortified guard station. When he showed up at headquarters the members of the council were both shocked and amazed at his audacity, right along with his terrifying appearance.

"Welcome everyone," stated Architeuthis pleasantly. The Great Leader then gestured with one of his tentacles toward an imposing-looking figure standing at the entrance to the secret cave where the council had been meeting daily for a year. He was beckoning for the man to come join them.

"My friends, after careful consideration, it is with great pleasure that I present to you our new General of the Army, Archibald Hicks.

Please join me in welcoming him." As Architeuthis said the words, Hicks walked in like he owned the place, followed by his second in command, a slender but wiry human with noticeably fewer tattoos on his body. There was no doubting who was in charge now. Hicks acted as though choosing him to lead the army was a forgone conclusion.

General Hicks leaned forward over the planning table and glared for a moment, nodding subtly toward the other Slarts seated at the slab of polished stone which had become their conference table. Then he said in a gravelly, emotionless voice, "Alright, gentlemen, let's get started." He established authority easily with both his confidence and his stature. The room grew quiet as the new supreme commander began presenting his plans. Even Architeuthis settled in to let the man speak.

"I'll get right to the point," continued the General. He had little patience for formalities. Heads nodded. "My men and I have come up with a multi-step process for eliminating those damn blockhouses we're goin' up against next month. With your permission, I'm now going to detail exactly what we're gonna do."

He then looked around the room at the other members in attendance. Two Enoshi. Another human. A Sudonji. A Spleef and a Zorg. He didn't know these creatures, and it made him pause for a moment. "Are we uh – is this a secured room?" he asked with a raised eyebrow. Architeuthis acknowledged his concerns by nodding, then gestured with his tentacle for the scary-looking fellow to proceed. Hicks snorted, then launched right in with his presentation.

"Very well then, first we draw out the commander of the enemy garrison and assassinate him. Simple as that: cut him down right where he stands. You follow?" Several heads nodded, more eyes blinking with apprehension. Clearly, Architeuthis had picked someone who was not inclined to mince words when it came to the subject of killing.

"Food deliveries and changing of guard staffs occur every seven earth days, as I'm sure you all know by now. The plan is to catch them off balance during one of their personnel changes. Kill as many as possible while they're moving in and out of the station. That's how we create chaos. And, gentlemen, in this engagement, chaos is our friend," Architeuthis nodded. Yes, that's exactly why the Great Leader wanted a human formulating battle tactics in the first place. This was the sort of thing they excelled at. Archibald Hicks was only getting started.

"Now the guards that survive this initial attack will flee inside the station if they can and lock down the place, thinking they can fend off the assault. Meanwhile, our Zorg friends will do the job of convincing them it really is a frontal attack. That's what they'll expect. But it's not." General Hicks then cleared his throat, still glaring at the creatures watching him. He was blunt, but most liked that he didn't take long to get to the point. Hicks then reached around and pulled out a three-foot-long, two-foot-wide diagram of a food depot. Those seated at the table slid back on their stools to give him room.

The diagram, which displayed arrows and directions of attack, had been drawn onto an actual cutaway picture of a food depot and its accompanying guard station barracks. It had been part of a blueprint at one time. How he'd acquired it was anyone's guess. It was probably lost somewhere years before by work crews constructing one of the depots, left behind once the project was complete and later discovered by miners. Hicks's adjutant had affixed the diagram to a large metal plate, and it included an overhead, as well as profile view of one of the facilities. These depots had been constructed in exactly the same way in factories back on Earth, then shipped in components to Rijel 12 to be assembled. Therefore, the Nausties could use the same attack plan on every food depot on the planet.

"Zorgs are quick and small," continued General Hicks. "We'll use them as light infantry to draw fire from the guards while our heavy infantry moves up – protected by boulders and transport vehicles is what I'm planning on. Now, these boulders I'm speaking of will be discreetly placed, and transports will be parked in a random fashion so as to create narrow kill zones. Meanwhile, our heavy infantry will move from protective cover to protective cover while taking fire, slowly working their way toward the guard station. Casualties will be high, but this is necessary while we get our infantry close enough to fire salvos of javelins and eliminate guard positions."

Of course, the meticulous Slarts were not terribly impressed with the battle plan so far, but they nodded politely anyway as Hicks stopped, gave a big long humorous glance over at his handsome assistant, then looked back at his audience with an icy cold look on his face. He spoke again.

"But it's only a feint." All the emotion drained from his face. At that, he turned back to the diagram. It was lying on the large stone conference table, so everyone could see what he was pointing to. Hicks gestured with his hands as he described the rest. "You see, gentlemen, by drawing fire from the guards posted in those kill slots, we'll be able to burst through the floor of the station and come right up between their legs and right up their asses."

He grinned while he gestured in an underhand motion with his thumb. Then he reached over the top of the diagram and pointed downward, saying "Our Sudonji will also drill through the ceiling of the tunnel. Break in through the roof. By the time those guards realize they're being crushed like a grape, our infantry will be able to cut through the gate of the depot with acetylene torches and eliminate the entire garrison."

All eyes immediately shifted to Architeuthis. This was precisely the idea devised months before by the planning council. And yet Hicks had arrived at the same conclusion, on his own. *How? Those discussions had been kept top secret.* There was no way the General could have heard about them, not from the council anyway. He was presenting the same concept, as though it were fresh from his mind. The Slarts who'd come up with it a year earlier started to react, however Architeuthis raised a tentacle cautioning them to remain silent. By now, he was far more interested in what the human would say next. It turned out that he was not alone.

Hicks continued. The plan would require a thousand soldiers for each food depot, with teams of Sudonji drilling and tunneling carefully above the roofs of each structure and below the floors simultaneously without being detected in the hours leading up to the attacks. The tunneling would need to be completed before the actual assault could begin. Finally, each attack would commence once the shift change was happening. This would require coordination on a global scale, but that is what the tunnel networks were for. It was a brilliant plan. And it proved once and for all that given a little bit of freedom to think up solutions, those Earth men were nearly as bright as the Slarts themselves.

Architeuthis chuckled, causing his facial tentacles to flutter. "Excellent. Go on General," he said calmly, deciding against revealing that his staff had thought up the same thing months ago. General Hicks nodded impassively and proceeded with his presentation.

"Casualties in the diversionary assault will be heavy," he stated coldly. "But, those Sudonji tunneling in will face a mauling when they break through the floor and the ceiling." Hicks was very blunt about that part; nevertheless, the Slarts liked the new General's boldness, nodding toward each other, as well as toward Architeuthis.

"General Hicks, we appreciate your thoroughness," said Architeuthis. "Your ingenuity and cunning have served you well in this endeavor, and we are grateful for your efforts. We also thank you, Perry, for assisting in the presentation." Perry was the name of Hicks' right-hand man.

The General's adjutant smiled proudly. He wasn't looking for kudos that day. He was only there to make his partner look smart. But Perry wasn't just an assistant: Perry was also the man's devoted companion, and actually the brains in that power couple. Emboldened, Perry politely asked if he could add something to the meeting, and to everyone's amazement the rough-edged general suddenly became quite apologetic when he realized he'd skipped over something terribly important: smoke bombs.

"Oh yes, I almost forgot," snickered the grizzled warrior, "My partner here has something more to add. Something that'll make things a little easier on us." Perry snickered and winked subtly at Hicks, then composed himself hastily as he spoke.

"Thanks, General. We've determined that smoke bombs can be made, to use as a screen to disguise our movements within the guard station as we try to climb through the holes. To break inside the roof and floor of the guard station, our Sudonji friends will use acetylene cutting torches. The noise outside should be sufficient to keep the guards distracted on one end of the station, while they cut through the steel. Once through the hole they can hurl smoke bombs inside, and confuse the occupants for long enough to climb in." Perry smirked humbly at his audience, appreciating how vastly intelligent they were.

"Now I'm no scientist, but anyone with a working knowledge of chemistry knows potassium nitrate and brown sugar is about all you need: three quarts of potassium nitrate and two quarts of raw sugar, to be exact." The Slarts blinked patiently. They understood what he was talking about, but not exactly how he intended to use such a compound. What Perry proposed was to boil the mixture in a cast iron vessel until liquefied, then pour it into metal boxes lined with aluminum foil wrappers, which came out of the food ration packets. Before the mixture had set, a fuse could be embedded in it. Before tossing the bomb inside, it could be lit with acetylene torches to ignite the smoke. What's more, barium salt could be added to the mixture, so that the smoke would have a green color and be more terrifying to the trapped defenders.

Perry enjoyed his moment in the spotlight, talking through his clever idea, concluding with, "Our Sudonji tunnelers, supported by lightning quick Zorgs, can then climb through ceilings and floors to get safely inside, before attacking and eliminating the last of the guards."

Casualties would be heavy, but this attack plan was innovative and had a good chance of success, if all went to plan. What's more, if conducted in several parts of the mining network, against several different guard stations simultaneously, there'd be no time to send a relief force to quell the uprising – not before the Nausties would have captured enough food to supply the rebellion for a full week if things turned out well. They'd also have a very large cache of captured weapons for their assault on Warden Gaah's headquarters.

"Very impressive," said Architeuthis. He sat forward on his stool and addressed the Human. "But General, if I may, how do you propose we get all the way up to the main terminal to attack and overwhelm the security forces protecting it?" General Hicks smiled. Clearly, he had done his homework. He again cleared his throat.

"Well sir, that's where it gets really interesting." He gestured toward the table that the Slarts were sitting around and pulled out a grease pencil that would usually be used for drawing a target for a power drill or cutting torch.

"With your permission, gentlemen?" he asked. The Slarts moved back from the table while the half-naked man leaned over to begin drawing a rough sketch of the planet's inner network of shafts and tunnels. As he wheezed and murmured to himself, the tattooed fellow meticulously created a detailed picture from rote memory. It took several moments for him to draw it, while the Slarts fluttered their facial tentacles, fascinated with the General's thoroughness.

What Hicks had remarkably memorized over the years, was a blueprint diagram of the elevator network and maintenance ladders used in case of a breakdown. This was because the same diagram was posted on the inside wall of the guard commander substation near the Templar Knights' section of the mine. When entering guard stations to negotiate better conditions for his men, Hicks had learned how ore and crystals were being shipped from the planet's depths, as well as what happened to them afterward. Now, he was showing the Slarts just how his troops could get back to the surface, along with what they'd find when they got there. Hicks spoke in a low voice, while he drew a cutaway view of this elaborate system.

"Long ago, these freight elevators were constructed in deep shafts drilled into the planet. We've all figured that's what they did, anyway. But what I learned is they connect to one main tunnel system that spreads around the planet like a giant city grid. Up there, massive dump trucks ferry the materials back to the loading bay here, where the main terminal is located." He drew a large oval to indicate the bay. "We can ascend several of these shafts simultaneously, using emergency ladders attached to the walls, if necessary. Better that we capture a working elevator or two, but from this tunnel we'll form a bridgehead to supply the final assault on the main terminal."

Architeuthis was impressed. "Yes, I see." he exclaimed. He remembered vaguely, from years before when he was brought to the planet, how the transport ship had descended below the surface several hundred feet to a distribution center where he was off-loaded with the other prisoners. This must be what Hicks was referring to. He asked politely, "General, how do you propose we fight the security forces defending the terminal and the transport tunnel?"

Hicks looked right at him and grinned. Once again, he was not about to mince words. "Bloody carnage, sir. We'll use weapons we've captured off dead guards to fight them, but I'm expecting ten- if not twenty-thousand dead and wounded by the time we're through with this operation. I'm sorry, but that's what it looks like."

The other Slarts from the planning committee gasped and murmured to each other in their native Slartigia, mixed with some Galactic. It didn't matter. Hicks could understand them just fine.

"I know, I know gentlemen," he said in a raised voice which quieted the cacophony. "It's a tall order, but we've thought this through and it's the only way. We've got explosive charges we've used for years to blast open cavities and cut away rock to free crystals. We'll get in eventually. They can't stop us forever. The sacrifice will be great, I'm not pretending otherwise. But, if we want to win this war, it is required." He did not break eye contact with the group while he replaced the cap on his grease pencil. Perry, standing nearby, crossed his arms and stared at the Slarts right along with his partner.

The gravity of the situation was finally hitting Architeuthis and sank in, lodging deep in his soul. Was he really willing to sacrifice so much? Could he order such an attack and endure the devastating loss of life that was bound to occur? General Hicks was fully prepared to go forward. Clearly, he was willing to risk the lives of his crew members, his lover Perry, and for that matter even his own. *These humans··· these Earthers··· do they really have no fear*? he thought. Was it brilliant and likely to work? Or was Hicks just brash and foolhardy, like Earthmen were often said to be? Architeuthis was convinced it was the former not the latter.

The leader of the rebellion looked around the room and saw the sad, emotion-filled eyes of his fellow Slarts. He looked back at the determined face of General Hicks, and the confident expression of his partner Perry. The Sudonji would fight. The Zorgs and Spleefs would fight. The Enos? They'd rush into battle headlong with the fearlessness of jungle cats. All Nausties would sacrifice everything they had to support their brethren in this epic battle.

Architeuthis thought for a moment. He needed to decide right now. What's more, only he could make the decision to send thousands of fellow Nausties to their deaths. Only he could take responsibility for this, come what may. With a deep sigh, Architeuthis calmly said, "General Hicks ⋯ you may proceed. Inform the planning committee of all your supply and manpower needs as well as your timetables. Communicate with no one outside of this room about what we've discussed tonight. We will convene again in thirty Earth days."

Chapter 5: The Naustie Revolt

Maintaining the utmost in secrecy, General Hicks of the new Naustie Planetary Command established battle groups throughout the planet in order to coordinate attacks on key guard posts. As was agreed, Sudonji did the tunneling, and work crews carefully moved large boulders or vehicles into place in a tactical grid pattern in front of their objectives. After that, they went right back to work and awaited word on when to mobilize.

As the time for the assault approached, unit commanders were told of the plan: on the day of attack, a unit of Zorgs was to assassinate the captain of the guard as they conducted their shift change and new guards were arriving from the surface. The goal was to kill as many of these miserable cretins as possible, while only a few of their comrades were still inside manning their guns.

The Zorgs would use deadly slingshots, with which they'd demonstrated proficiency during training. Their weapons were simple devices, thick rubber tubes around a metal brace which locked over the wrist and fired a stone projectile the size of a golf ball. At thirty yards they were fairly accurate and were deadly if they hit the head of a victim. Even closer in, these "slingers" hardly ever missed. Earthers were better at using javelins, so they were to move up and occupy forward positions and attempt to impale as many guards as possible after the Zorgs knocked off the commander.

Yet, despite the presentation to the planning commission months earlier, Hicks and his partner Perry had decided to attack only three guard posts for the initial assault. These first three guard posts selected were located nearest to elevator shafts leading up to the main terminal. General Hicks calculated that by securing these simultaneously all remaining guard posts would be abandoned planet-wide, once Warden Gaah believed his stronghold was threatened. With the objective secure, they could assemble assault troops for the ascent. The entire offensive could then be directed on the main terminal. It was ambitious, to say the least, and a hard sell. Hicks had to convince Architeuthis and the others to sign off on it.

"Good day Gentlemen," began General Hicks. This was the last full meeting of the council before the big day. Everyone in attendance, from the Great Leader on down, was exhausted from months of planning and issuing deadlines to already-overworked crew leaders, farmers, blacksmiths, and soldiers, training for battle. The general was to give them a run-down of his objectives for the attack, which would be commencing within a few days.

"I'm adding a few more wrinkles," he admitted. As usual, he got right to the point without wasting time on formalities. "With your permission, I'd like to focus our efforts on these three food depots that I believe will yield the best results." As he said this, he pointed to a detailed diagram that Perry had drawn for him on a piece of prefab taken off a collapsed housing facility. For the past seven Earth years, it had been used to wall up the entrance to his and Archibald's cave back in the Templar Knights' homeland. Today, it was serving as a drawing board.

By now, Architeuthis knew that Hicks always came prepared, always had an answer for their objections. The Great Leader had chosen this general for good reason, and there was no doubt the man appreciated that he had the authority to carry out his duties however he saw fit. He wasn't stubborn – just supremely confident in his own judgment. That's what made him difficult to disagree with.

"Having determined the enemy's vulnerabilities, I've selected three strongholds to attack simultaneously. These three outposts are located next to main elevator shafts and what's more, are closer to the surface. We'll hit these first and use them as a bridgehead. Things should fall into place rather quickly after that." He then paused to allow for the inevitable reaction and debate to follow. Hicks, too, had learned something about his counterparts on the council. They liked details and they were diametrically opposed to bold assumptions.

"Three?" retorted Cyathus. "But General, three outposts won't provide us enough food to sustain ourselves. The offensive, that is. According to our calculations, this will never suffice. We need many times that number. Otherwise, within a week we'll start running out of supplies." As usual, Hicks and his partner Perry had anticipated their questions and were ready to respond. Perry had a way with the Slarts, due to his patience, so the grizzled General typically let him field their initial questions. Afterward, he'd summarize what Perry said, speaking directly to Architeuthis. This formula had worked repeatedly in extinguishing prolonged debate.

"We're aware of that, Cyathus." Perry stated respectfully, without waiting for Hicks to attempt a response. They'd been together so many years they knew each other's cues, just like an old married couple. "But there are greater issues here to deal with. Let's look at the bigger picture, shall we?" Hicks raised up, stood back from the table, and let his adjutant wear them down for a while.

"We know what these folks are like." continued Perry. "They're thugs, and to beat them we have to take them out, one by one, as rapidly as possible. It's not simply about just the food depots, either. I mean the guards themselves. We need to capture the entire service tunnel network within days. On the first day, preferably. Cut them off. Cut off any potential counterattack. Do that, and we can mop up the remaining depots in short order. With no central command, and finding themselves isolated miles below the surface, they'll be easy to handle." After that, General Hicks was quick on the draw to close the deal. He turned to a wide-eyed Architeuthis and gave his summary with typical bluntness.

"You see, it's better to go for the jugular instead of trying to secure numerous food depots in hopes of consolidating our forces for a prolonged engagement. That won't do shit for us when it comes to dealing with that bastard Gaah. It'll never work, and we all know better. But let me tell you, what'll most certainly happen if we fart around too long is organized retaliation. Within weeks, if not days, those guards up there'll invade our caverns and kill everyone who resists. I can guarantee you that." He then paused as he turned to the council members. "That's how it is, gentlemen. Like it or not. The only way to win out is to go all out. We only get one chance to pull this off. And we'll never get a better one than right now, when we have the element of surprise."

Architeuthis fluttered his facial tentacles, as did the other Slarts sitting around the conference table. Most were taken aback. This was not what they'd anticipated at all. A gradual, systematic elimination of enemy strongholds was what they'd thought the plan was, with the primary objective being to capture supplies and sustain the offensive. Accomplishing that, they'd hold all the cards. Then they could make their move on Gaah's headquarters with their full army and win the war.

Hicks was already way past that, and it was obvious. He wanted to aim right for the very heart of his opponent and overwhelm him while he was off-balance, before he could organize, before he could consolidate. The idea had merit.

The only problem was how dangerous this could be if the attack fizzled out only a few days into the campaign. *And what of this so-called service tunnel?* Architeuthis wondered. No one had ever seen it. Didn't know what they'd find there, even if they made it all the way up. It could turn into an ambush.

Nevertheless, Architeuthis was out of his element when it came to military tactics. Hicks knew what he was doing. *Or perhaps he is a madman*, speculated the large Slart. That, too, had to be considered. Architeuthis sighed and thought for a moment, raising his tentacle to placate his outraged planning staff. It was his decision now. Not theirs. But what should he do?

If he overruled his general, he'd be setting back the clock on an operation that was ready to move forward within a day or two. He could shut this down right now and in so doing save thousands of lives.

But what if he was wrong? What if this was their one big chance to go for the jugular? He weighed the alternatives as best he could, but he had to decide.

He only knew what he'd always known. Humans were ruthless, and his enemy was the same if not worse. Hicks had the advantage in terms of numbers, there was no question of that. He also had the element of surprise, as the general had so eloquently put it. Besides that, his troops were totally committed. Committed to achieving their freedom and inspired to make sacrifices. What's more, if Hicks was right and thousands of Nausties made it into that service tunnel, what could stop them? Who could stop them? With no time to organize, would prison security forces even stand a chance?

Architeuthis stood. This he never did during meetings. And when he raised himself up, he stood eye-to-eye with his glowering, fiercely-determined commander – the one he'd bet all his fortunes on to deliver his fellow Nausties from tyranny. He fluttered his facial tentacles and spoke directly to the man, to convey his answer and let there be no doubt he'd approved the general's audacious plan. He'd take full responsibility, come what may. History would record it as such, regardless of the outcome.

"Very well, General," the Great Leader said. "I approve. Proceed." He then placed a dusty tentacle on Hicks' shoulder before adding one more thing. "And may the gods protect us in all our brave endeavors."

Thus, using Earth time measurements, the worldwide attack was slated to occur at 05:00, two days later. Architeuthis and his Slart planners sent out the message to the rest of the planet's crew leaders, ordering Zorg runners to spread the news. When the big day came, all of New Australia braced itself for the Great Naustie Revolt. They were about to go to war.

The planning, training, and preparation paid off, for as luck would have it, all three stations fell within a few hours. It wasn't even a fair fight. By burning sulfur combined with potassium nitrate, Slart scientists had developed a corrosive incendiary they called Vitriol. They contained the substance inside clay vessels which were hurled against fortified guard positions. As planned, Zorg slingers took out the post commanders at each station with a single salvo of stones, then hurled these sulfur bombs at kill slots located on the outside. The burning liquid corroded and burned the eyes and flesh of the surprised defenders.

Earthers who had trained at the javelin then stood up from behind boulders and fired salvos of throwing spears, while heavy infantry units made up mostly of Enoshi warriors moved up behind mobile steel blocking shields attached to a wheeled chassis. In the final phase of the outer assault, Earthers using acetylene cutting torches sliced through the security gates and made it into the stations to exterminate the last of the guards.

Eventually, the defenders were demoralized and fighting desperately for their lives. In the case of one guard station, they were reduced to huddling terrified in the center, tending to their wounded, only to find their floor being cut away, and the ceiling being sliced open by Sudonji diggers. The smoke bombs Perry had designed were tossed through the openings and in the confusion, light infantry hopped through and butchered several guards with daggers fashioned from hand tools. When Enoshi warriors finally burst in through the sliced-open security gates, it was all over. In close combat, Enos could easily overwhelm the most formidable fighters quite easily. Most of these meagerly-trained prison guards didn't stand a chance.

Zorg runners circulated news of the victories using the communication tunnel created for them months earlier. And when word got out, troops assigned to the second phase of the attack amassed at all three locations for the long climb to the surface. The easy part had been accomplished. Now came the hard part.

Architeuthis, upon hearing of these tactical successes, heaved a deep, resonating, almost burbling sound, like Slarts commonly did when acknowledging something joyful. He then sat down with a relieved sigh, collapsing and curling his legs into a sort of bed, as Slartigians often did when at rest. It had all happened so fast, and as reports got back to the Great Leader of the victories, he so completely wanted to share in the jubilation of the other Slarts and staff members at headquarters. Unfortunately, there was still too much weighing heavily on his mind.

"Great Leader! We are winning." the Zorg messenger exclaimed. He was breathless from excitement, combined with the exertion from his run. Information had been relayed all the way down to Naustie headquarters deep below the surface; ten different Zorgs had been involved in the process. Skeeesh, as he was called, was the last runner charged with delivering the message. Architeuthis could only nod feebly in acknowledgment. All that ran through his three hearts was an icy feeling of dread.

"Yes, that is wonderful news, Skeeesh, thank you," was about all he could muster. His enormous head was adrift in a sea of worries. The poor young Zorgolongian, sentenced to this penal colony for aggravated assault five long years before, couldn't imagine what was afflicting the Great Leader so.

"Architeuthis? Are you alright?" he asked timidly, still wheezing trying to catch his breath. The large Slart calmly gestured with a big tentacle that he was fine. "Yes, I'm okay. Go on, Private. Give me the news. I'll be alright," he said. The youthful Zorg was only too happy to oblige.

"Well, Great Goddess of the sss-Sea!" he proclaimed. That was a common expression among Zorgolongians, who believed life on their planet had been created at the bottom of the ocean by divine beings which separated fish from amphibian – from whence all Zorgs had evolved. "Warden Gaah has sounded a general alarm and shut down the elevators," he went on to say. "He has cut off his guard stations, abandoning them to fight to the death!"

The rest of the news was outstanding, however. One, then two, then three depots, one by one, had fallen like dominoes to the Naustie Army. The ecstatic Zorgolongian hissed with excitement, flicking his reptilian tongue. "Yes-sss, all three depots in a matter of a few hours. The guards are now trapped below with us. Gaah has cut them off!" It was just as predicted. The heartless Warden had left his hapless security forces to battle it out on their own. Shut off the elevators. Pull back into a defensible position. Make it harder to get to him.

Architeuthis had prepared for that, yes, but these early reports were not completely accurate. Messengers arrived later and clarified: one elevator that had been captured was able to send up a unit of

Enoshi and human shock troops, armed with captured EIC's taken off the dead bodies of the guards. This unit had made it to the service tunnel several miles above, right before Gaah's staff had gone into lockdown. It turned out the evil Warden's only plan for defense was to hole up in his fortified headquarters and let his guards below fight it out until the whole planet below starved to death.

Now to be fair, Gaah had every reason to assume such a strategy would succeed. The depots below the planet surface had only enough food to supply the rebelling prisoners for one month. Moreover, they'd have to capture all of these depots and defeat the garrisons, just to get to it. Even if they could accomplish this, the rebels were doomed to failure, and once they began to starve, thought Gaah, they'd fear disaster. Then they'd surely surrender. Besides, even if they didn't they'd wither away eventually. Just like any pirate captain, Gaah merely planned on bringing in thousands more prisoners once the mutiny fizzled out. In a few months, he'd be right back in business.

This did not concern Architeuthis, because General Hicks' plan already took that into account. Hicks had assumed that Gaah would shut off power to the elevators as a security measure. In desperation, any trapped commander would encircle himself with his best troops and just let the enemy come to him. But Gaah didn't yet consider himself to be trapped; that was the difference. He had underestimated his opponents and presumed he could defeat them by starving them into submission, just like he'd always done. Sadly – for Gaah anyway – he was dead wrong.

True, General Hicks didn't know which of the three food depots would fall the easiest, so he had a thousand Enoshi shock troops in reserve, at the ready, at each location, to try and board freight elevators before power was cut off. It would be a twenty-minute ride to the surface in those gigantic cargo lifts. If all three captured elevators worked, that would make things easier, but if none of the elevators worked or didn't carry the warriors all the way to the surface, then the next few days would be very rough going for the rebels.

Luckily, however, one elevator was still serviceable all the way to the surface before Gaah shut off power to it. While the other two food depots were being secured by the rebels, a thousand brave Enos scrambled into the first captured freight elevator, along with a platoon of Earther fire teams accompanying them. Each fire team used captured weapons from dead prison guards and set up barricades to protect themselves for when the elevator door opened at the service tunnel above.

"Prepare yourselves, brothers," growled Sergeant Burmilla. It was his unit now packed into the lone elevator which had been captured intact and still operable. "It's a long ride, we've been told. You Earthers up there ⋯ get ready with your weapons. When that gate opens, unleash hell, you hear me?" This command elicited more than a few determined grunts from the mass of sweating, anxious soldiers crowded in around him. They'd waited weeks for this day – and had been held back from the initial assault. Now, they were spoiling for a fight.

Not sure what they'd find when it opened – an ambush or a lone sentry, the Earthers at the front prepared for a deadly battle. The elevator hummed, whined, and groaned, then lifted the comparatively light load of grime- and dust-covered bodies for twenty terrifying minutes as it ascended from the bloody scene below. Packed in shoulder to shoulder, it was going to be an agonizingly long journey. Would the elevator complete its ascent? Or would it stop somewhere along the way, and leave them with another thousand feet to have to climb using service ladders? No one knew for sure.

"Well, you heard him, private," remarked Corporal Martinez. "When those doors open – the gate I mean – we'll blast them all to hell. Everyone we see – no matter who they are. You know that, right?" He was standing next to Hans Offmier, a German and former chef from the Earth province of Central Europe. Offmier had poisoned his unfaithful girlfriend and been convicted of murder. Now, he was intensely focused on the wall of the shaft in front of them. As long as he could see the car was moving, he knew things were going to work out fine. Still he struggled with the wait.

"And don't you worry about this here elevator. If we get stopped, we can climb out and go up that ladder over there," Martinez said, indicating with a subtle head gesture. He was still gripping his EIC and feeling around the buttons trying to remember all their functions: blast, scatter, etc. It reminded him of better times, when he was a cop back in New Los Angeles ··· before the shooting, before the trial, before he'd been stripped of his badge and sentenced to this awful place. He was soon interrupted by the platoon's resident cynic, Private Drummond.

"Yeah, just be sure if that happens you hold on real tight," he drawled. "Probably don't wanna mess up and let go. Long fall to the bottom if that happens, you know? Give you time to think about things before you splatter, eh Hans?" The burly Nebraskan then chuckled derisively. Corporal Martinez turned his head to glare at him, but it was too crowded to make eye contact. Instead he hissed at him to be quiet. This was no time for wry humor.

"Don't listen to that asshole. You stick with me, Private," Martinez assured the nervous German. "Focus on the mission. We gotta clear out that service tunnel in every direction." Private Offmier nodded as his eyes continued blinking from the dust inside the compartment. *Bitte beweg dich schneller!* he thought, *if only this damn elevator would move more quickly!* He continued to watch the wall of the elevator shaft as the massive lift crept ever so slowly upward.

Thankfully for the heavily armed Enoshi and Earthers holding carbide lamps in case of a power shutdown, the elevator completed the ascent. Then, to their relief, the doors opened and only about a hundred Zorgolongian security troops were awaiting its arrival. Only this was no ambush. The poor guards were still expecting an empty elevator to open up for them to ride down and suppress the rebellion. Remarkably, their Lieutenant had called the elevator right about the time the Enoshi and their Earther allies had boarded it, so the entire band of Zorgs were anticipating an empty chamber. Most hadn't even activated their weapons yet.

As the lift crept over the edge of the service tunnel floor, Earthers holding EIC's and manning larger EIC machine guns on tripods opened fire, decimating the surprised security force, and scattering those not immediately killed. That's when the massacre began.

"No quarter!" cried Sergeant Burmilla. "No prisoners!" he then roared. Corporal Martinez, by way of comparison, was blunter. "Kill 'em all boys!" he yelled, as they rushed out into the tunnel, stepping on dead Zorgs as they did so. It was, as General Hicks predicted, bloody carnage.

As the last of the prison response team fell or tried to flee in terror, Enoshi warriors went wild and rushed forward to slaughter them, as well as more than five hundred mining engineers, truck haulers, and unarmed personnel working in the tunnel. These terrified civilians employed by the mine had been working in relative safety for years, never expecting anything quite like this. Their screams and cries for help filled the tunnel for miles in every direction, as bloodthirsty killers chased them down to butcher them mercilessly.

"Get that one!" yelled Martinez. He was screaming at Private Drummond to shoot down a fleeing Zorg who'd panicked and dropped his EIC before sprinting away. Drummond was quick to comply. "Hell yeah!" he called out, as he aimed his weapon and fired. He paused for a brief moment, only to set it on spray. The Zorg was nearly cut in half. "Got him, Corporal!" he responded with a hearty laugh. And with that, the platoon of Earthers moved into a tight formation and began trotting forward in a mass of combined firepower. They advanced as one, shooting anything that moved.

So many years of oppression and humiliation came to an end for these brave warriors. Left on the doorstep of an eternal hell by their home planets – abandoned to serve out the rest of their lives in near-darkness – occasionally starved into submission – abused and over-worked by heartless prison guards. Enraged Enoshi and their Earther allies became overcome with bloodlust. They killed anyone they saw, maimed and mutilated everyone they could catch. Soon an orgy of violence was engulfing the service tunnel in both directions, as Earther Nausties blasted round after round from captured EIC's until they ran out of ammunition. Then, they picked up unused weapons from dead security troops and started all over again. Everyone was an enemy. Everyone was a target. There would be no prisoners taken today, and as Sergeant Burmilla commanded, no quarter given. Those who tried to surrender were shot or bludgeoned to death. Those who tried to escape were heartlessly mowed down.

"You can run but you'll die tired!" screamed a human from the

Earth province of North America. A Texan, he'd been dreaming of this moment almost every night for nearly a year. "You like that?" he yelled tauntingly. "How about that?" he then added, as he clipped off twenty more rounds into the face of a surrendering Sudonji tunnel driver. The poor fellow's head spattered like a crushed watermelon.

The slaughter continued for hours, until the main terminal was only a mile or so away. Victory was within their grasp. Yet, they would need reinforcements to try and tackle Gaah's headquarters. Inside the terminal on the planet surface, located under a large tinted glass dome the size of a small city, was a military base that housed thousands of security troops and personnel from several different planets. This was their goal, and it would be one tough nut to crack.

But General Hicks had prepared for this. Below the service tunnel, nearly a mile underground, Schpleefti light infantry were already scrambling up service ladders inside the two deactivated elevator shafts. Spleefs were rodent-like beings that had evolved from rats and mice on their home planet, to eventually become the dominant species. Yet, they were just as brave as they were cunning, standing about four-and-a-half feet tall on average. They were fast and nimble, able to scramble using claw-like hands with strong fingers, perfect for the task. Possessing daggers, their job was to burst into the massive tunnel through maintenance hatches, using explosive charges if necessary. Then, they were to fan out to slaughter anyone and everyone they could find. If possible, their orders were to reactivate the elevators and send up Enoshi, Sudonji, and Earther reinforcements.

Zorg units followed, and their task was to reinforce any bridgehead established by the Spleefs. Not quite as nimble at climbing, Zorgs were nevertheless bigger and more powerful. They were far crueler and more cold-blooded in combat, too, so if the Spleefs faltered or scattered in the face of enemy fire, their Zorg allies were quite capable of sustaining the attack until help arrived.

Eventually, word got back to Warden Gaah that prisoners had broken out and were threatening the main terminal bay with a small force of infantry. Still not fully grasping the seriousness of the threat, Gaah merely ordered electricity shut off to the mine. Planet-wide, the convicts below found themselves in total darkness, and had to rely on carbide lamps to move about. However, that left another major problem to contend with: how to capture all the remaining well-defended food depots, in the dark, and feed those tens of thousands of Nausties below.

Architeuthis and his planners had prepared for this as well, actually. Springing into action on the day of the attack, Earthers, Sudonji, and Zorgs commandeered captured mining vehicles and transport trucks, while Spleefs hurried to collect the hydroponically farmed crops, then raced through miles of mining tunnels to distribute food. Abandoned guard stations and food depots were also assumed to be available once the guard stations below were vacated. That's what Hicks had predicted would happen, once Nausties made it into the service tunnel, yet now, trapped inside, were thousands of terrified guards, left behind to fight it out on their own. It seemed the Nausties would have to conquer each one.

Architeuthis and his planners didn't panic, though. They merely hoped, now that the first three depots had fallen, the same tactical plan could be used over and over again to secure these remaining strongholds. It would be at the expense of thousands more killed or wounded yes, but eventually, they could be taken. Hicks and his staff went right to work mobilizing units for assaults on the remaining depots, and within hours, he had battle plans for the next fifty.

"Well, gentlemen," began Hicks at his next meeting with Architeuthis and his team. As his army was busy mopping up in the service tunnel up near the surface, he had made one last trip down to headquarters to meet with his superior. Things were coming together, and he was brimming with confidence. He entered the secret cave as though he were a conquering hero.

"The good news is, it's gonna be a lot easier hittin' these 'ole guard stations in the dark." Then he grinned. Perry chuckled darkly. If Slarts were capable of laughing derisively they would have as well. Instead, they merely nodded and fluttered their facial tentacles. "We're gonna take 'em out one by one though," Hicks continued. He proceeded to detail for them his strategy for accomplishing this.

But then an amazing thing happened. Guards at the remaining food depots actually began surrendering. Sure enough, after a day or so, seeing the futility of their situation, and cut off from any communication with headquarters, guard posts began negotiating terms for surrender. When large forces of Nausties appeared outside, most simply gave up and tossed out their weapons.

General Hicks ordered all their lives to be spared, of course – they'd be vital sources of information later in the war. Thus within a few days, the Nausties had secured nearly the entire planet's interior. Soon they were massing inside the service tunnel itself. The tide was turning; however, this was still going to be a desperate battle.